In The Valley of Nineveh

BOOK ONE

L. Steven Rencher

Frayer & Williams Publishing
P.O. Box 16
Florida, New York 10921

ISBN: 978-0-9763464-6-3

Visit the author's website at LStevenRencher.com

*This series is dedicated to the woman
whose love and support encouraged me to
write when at times I felt like quitting.
My darling wife, Joanne.*

PROLOUGE

Almost nobody speaks of the disappearances anymore. Though it seemed like a decade had passed, it was only three-and-a-half years ago. That is when roughly one-third of the world's population inexplicably vanished leaving no traces except for the clothes they were wearing at the time. It was without question the single most astonishing event in human history. Later, after months of grieving by incalculable numbers of people from every corner of the globe, its extraordinary magnitude had thankfully faded in the minds of everyone to become nothing more than a tragic footnote in history.

It was, in fact, a knee-jerk survival reaction of cognitive dissonance from the desperate hordes who clamored to make sense of it all. And with no logical explanation in the offing, they latched onto the most reasonable possibilities offered up by the media, the apologists and the so-called "experts in their field" who peered out from their lofty confines to expound on bizarrely plausible theories.

With the disappearances came the anguish of Vacant Womb Syndrome; the newly adopted clinical term used to signify expectant mothers whose fetuses had suddenly vanished. This was followed by the discovery that millions of couples around the world were unable to conceive. Approximately one out of two-hundred men and women had been stricken sterile by some unknown agent, so they speculated. A battery of tests for the exact cause proved inconclusive. Worst still, there were no children under the age of eight (or thereabouts) anywhere on the earth. They were gone—taken by whatever mysterious force was responsible for the disappearances.

The global economy, having lost an inconceivable percentage of its workforce, was sent into a tailspin. With so much money, lives and careers at stake, it became easier to simply relegate the past events to the fantastical, and thereby acknowledge the countless missing. And then, with all credulity, fully erase their existence from memory.

Nearly all concluded, better that, than to accept what happened as the harbinger of something even more profound. Its evidence was characterized by an almost insensible amnesia; one that allowed them to carry on effortlessly without skipping a beat.

Months prior to the disappearances, a micro-meteor shower, unprecedented in span, pelted the earth's upper atmosphere. Depending on the hemisphere at dusk and early dawn, they could be seen on a clear night as millions of falling stars. It would last for several hours; beautiful to behold and yet, possessed with an eerie foreboding that inclined some to want to run and hide. The meteor shower was followed by an increase in paranormal phenomenon, supernatural manifestations and numerous sightings in the sky.

Witnesses spoke of glowing disks darting along mountain ranges; silent, hovering orbs, and multiple points of light holding a fixed formation and streaking across the sky at unheard-of speeds. To the skeptics, what was most alarming was that the sightings weren't occurring in the usual places. Not the rural, backwater, one-diner-and-a-gas-station towns in the center of nowhere, but over New York City, Berlin, Bangkok, Sydney and other major metropolitan areas all over the globe.

News networks had been inundated with every manner of video. Though many turned out to be easily explained, it did evidence the anxiety and excitement that gripped the nations. Only after extensive authenticating were the most compelling broadcast over the air. Not as the light, sardonic fair generally saved for the end of the broadcast, but finally bestowed the respect of credibility and televised as teasers, and lead news stories.

One was even touted as the smoking gun evidence, the Holy Grail of UFO investigation; that of an otherworldly looking craft hanging motionless in the late afternoon sky. Not blurry and out of focus as was so often the case, but with the sharp, defined edges, visible apertures and shimmering skin of an object that contradicted every known principle of aerodynamics and propulsion. So good in fact was the video that, had it not been shot by a local news crew, it would have been scoffed by researchers as just another clever, computer generated hoax.

It was during that period, with nerves already heightened by fear, that astronomers, monitoring the Sun's normal eleven-year rotation reversal cycle, were observing the increase in sunspot activity. They began correlating them to the atmospheric changes occurring globally, and in particular, on the northern and southern lights that are the aurora—nature's own magnificent light show.

Dancing columns of light of various hues, and normally reserved for the southern and northernmost inhabitants of the globe, now stretched an unheard-of distance from both poles as far directionally as the equator. On a clear night, people from diverse locales, unfamiliar with the sight, would come out and stare up in awe at the glorious spectral display. The sky would come alive as a billowing blanket of flickering luminescence.

Meanwhile, back on terra firma, the resultant geomagnetic storms were wreaking havoc with satellite communications worldwide. In all, the sum of celestial and atmospheric events drew rational speculation to what many believed an obvious conclusion—that nearly a third of the earth's population had somehow been abducted by visitors from another planet. In the absence of a logical explanation, the general consensus became the overwhelming favorite. Even in the absence of hard scientific and empirical evidence.

What began as a theory had morphed into fact. Country heads of state were extolling the visitations as Earth's historic and bold initiation into the cosmic community of civilizations. Venerated scientists declared this to be the start of a new epoch; a turning point in the evolution of man—our very first contact with a race of beings not from this earth.

While the remaining population, caught between grief and exhilaration waxed philosophically, adjusting or completely revising their belief systems to include our new neighbors in the heavens, an ominous threat was brewing deep beneath the earth's crust. Within days it revealed itself in the form of a magnitude 12.7 earthquake that shook the planet to its very core.

California, for years the focus of doomsayers who trumpeted their predictions of "the big one" someday striking, were vindicated in their obsession. The state was finally devastated, losing half of its land mass to the Pacific Ocean. The rupture traveled at lightning speed up the San Andreas Fault ending at the massive Cascadia subduction zone off the northwest Americas.

The abruptly shifting plates gènerated a mega-tsunami that swept over the archipelago of Pacific islands in a torrent of death and destruction. It left the islands of Hawaii a scoured formation of rocks on the ocean surface. That same tsunami smashed into Japan and the Philippines with the force of a titanic deluge. Days later, two more magnitude 9.7 and 11.2 quakes fractured the earth, this time ripping through Alaska and leveling Japan.

The tremors continued for several days after, some reaching as high as magnitude eight. The worst of them triggered volcanic eruptions of Indonesia's Mount Merapi and the massive Yellowstone caldera in Wyoming. The ejecta of flaming rock from the eruptions were launched into the atmosphere. It all then fell to earth in a veritable rain of fire that ignited vegetation ablaze around the globe. The accompanying smoke and ash cloud blanketed two-thirds of the globe, casting the daytime sun in a scarlet haze and dramatically altering weather patterns.

The earth's climate, already the subject of heated debates regarding humans' impact, had experienced its most extreme weather effects to date. Areas that normally saw their rainy season had experienced drought for the first time. Dry places which had barely seen rainfall saw baseball sized hailstones hit the ground like large rocks. Relief efforts began almost immediately after the onslaught had ceased. The world's resources were stretched perilously thin; the humanitarian effort, exacting a toll of life and limb that only added to the untold suffering.

Though no system could accurately measure the loss of life, the estimates ranged from 50 to 80 million people had perished in what was termed, "a global cataclysm of historic proportions."

After two years of arduous resurrecting and rebuilding, the world's paralyzed economies began to show glimmers of recovery. In the quake epicenters and flood zones, new construction had already begun. Grain imports helped to supplement needy countries food supplies. In those metropolitan areas which sustained modest damage, people went to their places of employment, shopped and enjoyed life as usual, unaffected by the calamity occurring in the rest of the world.

New York City was one of several major eastern cities in the United States that suffered comparatively minimal damage. Within days of the last tremor, the Army Corp of Engineers went to work repairing the infrastructure. The network of interstate arteries was unclogged enabling commerce to flow again. Meanwhile, government intervention restored the pulse to the nation's financial heart—Wall Street.

Two-hundred-and-thirty miles from there, the seat of government at 1600 Pennsylvania Avenue continued to function, unabated by new catastrophes which only served to strengthen its resolve. The country was at a state of war; not with a malevolent fundamentalist regime or some despotic potentate with a Napoleonic complex, but with the earth itself.

Economic recovery came by way of a war-industrial-machine not seen since World War II. Money was poured into manufacturers of heavy earthmoving equipment, the auto and airline industries, businesses, and startup companies that addressed the nation's reconstruction needs.

With able-bodied workers in short supply, jobs were plentiful and wages more than double the norm. Soon, unemployment was at record lows. The nation was once again thriving, despite the grave circumstances that lead to its growing prosperity. Materialism became the panacea for wounds of the heart and mind. People were happy and starting to forget the past.

Presently, all attention is focused on the Middle East and Asia. The carefully orchestrated peace negotiations between Israel and the Islamic State has resulted in a temporary treaty. Both sides agreed to relocate the sacred Dome of the Rock from its long-held site on the Temple Mount, and rebuild the third temple of Jerusalem in its place. But the treaty was short-lived due to the forced stoppage of animal sacrifices. Tensions erupted between the two factions leading to a resumption of Jewish persecution; the conflict bringing both sides perilously close to war.

North Korea is rattling its saber at South Korea, prompting a buildup of troops on both sides along the demilitarized zone. Fighting has broken out between India and Pakistan over the rightful claim to Kashmir as the world watches and worries over which country will press the nuclear button first. Meanwhile, with the United States economy currently in the rebuilding phase, China has eclipsed all other nations to become the world's leading superpower.

The failing European Union and its leadership continue to spearhead a global initiative to fold holdout nations into the newly formed Federation of States, led by its charismatic and recently appointed president, Baldo Jović. And amidst rising familial discontent, Belgian scientists, in an effort to jumpstart population growth, finally succeeded in cloning the world's first two developing human embryos, to which they've impiously given the names—Adam and Eve.

In the United States, it's an election year and moral decay is widespread. A generation of teenagers operates without boundaries or respect for those in authority, including their parents. The few Christian churches still operating are under severe persecution by the government and private sectors. Most have been boarded up or taken over by merchants.

Monetary notes are no longer used as legal tender. Instead, a person can either use a bank card for all transactions, or submit to the growing trend of folks who chose to keep all their vital information on a VERIF-i microchip implanted in the back of the right hand. With a simple pass under a scanner, the host's net worth, medical data and bank account balance are available for viewing in a matter of seconds.

For the past month, astronomers around the world have been closely monitoring the planet Mars and the strange phenomenon occurring on its surface. A brilliant light, flickering at sporadic intervals, had been spotted emanating from an indiscernible point on a ridge of the Valles Marineris Canyon. Its source had yet to be determined, fueling speculation that its unknown origins might herald another wave of extraterrestrial visitations.

Not since the cataclysm had so much attention been focused on the perils that lay just beyond Earth's atmosphere. And, thanks to the ongoing Spaceguard survey, 82 percent of a particular peril, near-earth asteroids (NEAs) one mile across and larger had been detected. Their trajectories were tracked and the closest, though none posing an eminent threat, were placed on a watch list.

But presently, with all the earth's telescopes trained on Mars, locating the remaining eighteen percent of NEAs would have to wait. Little did anyone know that among that eighteen percent, a colossal rock, two-and-a half-miles in diameter, would collide with a neighboring asteroid, have its trajectory altered, and set on a portentous track through the cosmos.

In its path was the planet Earth.

DAY ONE

Chapter 1

"The subpoena's going out today.—No.—I agree...he wouldn't cooperate. He left us no choice.—Yes.—Yes.—Well, I believe he'd make the perfect character witness...honest beyond reproach. The client describes him as a pretty straight shooter. That makes his testimony critical. It could only bolster our case and shifts the burden of proof squarely on the defense."

Trent Hayes sat comfortably behind the wheel of his new Cadillac Escalade. Its roomy interior provided just the right leg and headroom for his six-foot, three-inch frame. He was captive and listening between moments of reverie to his wife, Nora. Sitting next to him and talking into her cell phone, she continued to explain to her boss pertinent details of an upcoming trial.

An attorney for the Wall Street law firm, Beckett, Cranston & Little, she was a veritable dynamo when it came to her work—meticulous about the details, and tireless in her pursuit of victory for their clients. That's what Trent always admired about her, and was as equally critical of. Especially during times of disagreement when all he wanted to do was discuss the matter without it turning into a contest of wits. Hearing her, though, spit out legal terms with the ease and self-assured parlance of a tenured law professor was impressive, nonetheless.

He had the opportunity to see her in action once while in the city on business. The trial was a grueling one, stretching into several weeks and monopolizing her time, both in and outside of the office. He slipped into the courtroom that afternoon and quietly ducked into a seat. The case involved a construction worker who lost his right arm when a crane fell on top of him while on a jobsite. Nora was in the middle of cross-examining the site foreman. She was trying to disprove his claims of ignorance regarding unsafe work conditions when the evidence said otherwise.

She paced between her desk and the judge's bench, while at the same time, darting glances over at the jury with each refute of the foreman's claims. It was a skillful maneuver that drew all eyes to her as though she were a priceless jewel. She was impeccably attired, attractive and statuesque looking in a navy-blue suit against caramel brown skin. All the while she inflected her words with just enough of a suggestion to make his testimony doubtful in the minds of the jury.

She worked the floor as if the courtroom were her stage and the jury her audience; and used her attributes to their fullest so that winning became the curtain call after a four-act performance. They won their suit two days later with a 2.5-million-dollar judgment.

It's no wonder I can't win an argument with her, Trent thought to himself. *My case is flawed...my strategies are too weak, and she knows it. The minute I slip-up, she's all over it like a pit bull. Too bad I didn't get a law degree along with the marriage license.*

Trent kept his eyes fixed on the road ahead and tried not to let the half mile of new construction to his right distract him. He wished he'd gotten on the construction bandwagon two-and-a-half years ago, right around the start of the building boom. That's when every other person it seemed owned a contracting company of some sort.

After the cataclysm, a virtual sea of survivors, destitute, beaten down and haggard migrated east looking to start over. Some got rich—and some lost everything when supply started to outstrip demand. Consequently, every few miles there was a new residential development, or small office building either underway, nearing completion, or left unfinished and abandoned.

Outside, the sky above them never looked bluer. It was a gorgeous mid-July day, comfortably warm and dry, and with the smell of freshness hanging in the air. *Perfect for playing hooky from the office,* Trent thought. That's when he pictured the slow, uniquely black woman's twist of Nora's neck toward him, and the contorted look of incredulity on her face at the mere suggestion of it.

Traffic was remarkably light for a Monday morning. Normally it would be teeming with commuters in the thick of rush hour. On this day, the flow seemed peculiarly sedate causing Trent to wonder if it might've been a holiday. All the same, it made for a pleasant drive.

With any luck, we could reach Wall Street in less than an hour. Enough time, he thought, to flesh out some of the grating issues bedeviling their marriage.

Trent's restaurant was doing well. Opened just over two years ago, he beat the odds—a profitable, four-star eatery succeeding where others had failed. His expert management might have been key, but it was the cuisine that kept people coming back; a combination of Caribbean and southern soul that catered to an underserved market of newly arrived middleclass blacks to the mid-Hudson valley.

They left behind the astronomical dollar figures that priced them out of the New York City real estate market, for the greener and wide-open pastures of life in the country. And for a while, it was paradise. Trent, leaving his job as Vice President of a hedge fund, cashing in his company stock, and then fulfilling his lifelong dream to be a chef and restaurateur.

He enrolled in culinary school, completed a 30-week accelerated program, and left with a certificate of achievement. After tapping into their retirement savings, investment portfolio, and hitting up a few well-heeled friends and family for a loan, he bought out a floundering restaurant. He then renovated it and changed its name to "The Caribe Grill." He broke even in six months.

After a year-and-a-half, he fully expected Nora to stop working—except she didn't want to. She was too busy fulfilling her own dream, that of being made partner at her law firm. As a consequence, she often worked late hours.

When she did make it home, she always managed to bring much of her work with her. A box here, a portfolio there, a FedEx delivery on weekends, long business trips and conference calls—she was driven, and there was no steering her off course.

Their dual incomes may have allowed them to live lavishly, but now Trent wanted his wife back. *There's no reason for us both to be missing-in-action.* For all of his reasoning, in the back of his mind, he knew it wasn't fair to her.

If anything, he felt he owed it to her. After what he had put her through, he believed that allowing her this was the least he could do. Besides, being a lawyer was all she ever wanted. He encouraged her to pursue it back when they were both struggling college students. Even more so after graduation and when she went onto law school.

Back then, their schedules were tight and the money, even tighter, but the promise of prosperity loomed just within their grasp. It kept them exhilarated as if on a runner's high, and made the weariness of hardships bearable until they reached the finish line together.

Afterwards, they married. She even found time between light court cases to have a baby, and then two more once their income permitted it. Despite the overwhelming devastation of years earlier; the incalculable loss of life and property; broken families and a nearly bankrupt economy that crippled the nation for months on end, nobody could tell them that the American dream still wasn't alive and well.

Now twenty-four years into their marriage, he felt it time they both reevaluate their unspoken work and home-life arrangement. There was much to talk about, if only she would get off the phone. He turned and gave her a look that said as much, hoping she would read it in his face, but she never bit.

They were a few miles from the George Washington Bridge which led into Manhattan Island, and from there, another twenty or so minutes from Wall Street. He was about to switch on the radio when his cell phone rang through the car speakers.

"Hello?"

"Hey, Daddy, it's Jennifer."

"What is it, honey?"

"I don't think Justin was in his room last night. I don't know how he got a key, but I heard him come in through the back door this morning after you and Mommy left. I think he's been out all night again. Now he's upstairs locked in his room with the music blasting...and he won't turn it down. You need to talk to him, 'cause he's not listening to me."

Jennifer was their oldest, a bright young woman with her mother's knack for thoroughness. She had just completed four years at Penn State and was home basking in the freedom of no-more-school-work before embarking on her job search.

Back only two days after a week spent at Myrtle Beach partying with her Gamma Kappa Theta sorority sisters, she was still feeling the ill-effects of late nights, lecherous boys and much too much alcohol. Her little brother only added to her lingering hangover.

"Is he still in his room?" Trent could hear the pounding blare and slurred rant of some techo-rap fusion song playing in the background. He wondered if Justin, who was grounded for sneaking out the house just two weeks ago, could really be brazen enough to do the exact same thing again.

"Yes, Daddy," she said angrily, and approaching the shut door of his room.

"Put him on the phone."

"I'd be happy to if I could get him to open the door. Justin...Justin!" she yelled while pounding on the door. "It's Daddy on the phone. He wants to talk to you. Open up, fool!"

Trent, expecting to hear a lie that might send his already borderline blood pressure into the red zone, took a deep breath, activated the car's cruise control and waited. He gave Nora a quick look to see if she heard any of the commotion going on at home. She had already cupped a hand over one ear while her other ear became one with the cell phone allowing the dialogue to continue without a glitch.

Annoyed by her seeming disinterest, he turned his attention back to the roadway and waited. He listened with increasing frustration as almost a minute passed, dominated by steady pounding, banging and shouting. A blast of music followed, likely from the bedroom door opening; next, a further exchange of insults, and then a *ka-thump* sound as if the cordless hand been hurled in anger and landed on the floor.

"Yeah, Dad," Justin said in a lazy voice that took too long to answer and seemed to lack any regard for the person on the other end.

"Were you home last night?"

"Huh?"

"I said were you home last night?"

"What?"

"Maybe if you turn down your music, you might hear me."

Trent heard the receiver drop a second time followed by a sudden stoppage of the irritating background noise. "Okay, is that better?" Justin said with a heavy dose of sarcasm.

"I want to know if you were home last night. Jennifer said she heard you come in this morning after we left. Is that true?"

✳✳✳

"No! Jennifer doesn't know what she's talking about. She's an idiot. I was home all night...in my room, sleeping," Justin said, switching from impudent to feigned outrage over the accusation. He lounged fully clothed on his bed. One leg was bent at the knee with his sneaker sole resting flat on a tousled comforter that lay more on the floor than on the bed. A videogame controller was in his left hand.

His bedroom, with clothes flung all over, had the ransacked appearance of a freshly committed burglary. It was also a high-tech treasure trove complete with smart pad, a smart phone, and the latest game console. A flat screen television hung on the wall and paused on a video game scene of chainsaw wielding, blood splattered carnage.

Four months shy of his 17th birthday, he thought the nearness of it should allow him the freedom to come and go with limited restrictions. His friends were all on a lengthy leash that seemed to be getting longer with each test of its limits. He, therefore, saw no reason why he should not be accorded the same amount of latitude. He repeatedly pushed the envelope hard until either Trent or Nora pushed back, which was not very often.

"So you're saying she's lying...that she didn't catch you entering the house this morning?"

"Well, not exactly. I did run down the street to a friend's house early this morning to borrow a videogame. I came straight home afterwards, though."

"What friend is this?"

"It doesn't matter, Dad. You never met him. I'm telling the truth...really."

"We took away your key...remember? How'd you get in without a key?"

"I didn't need a key. I never locked the door. Is there anything else you wanna know?"

"You're supposed to be grounded. That means you can't go anywhere...not even to your friend's house down the street. I'm dropping your mom off at her job and then stopping at the fish market. I should be home in a couple of hours. I expect you to be home when I get there. Do you understand?"

"Yeah, what's not to understand? I'm your prisoner and you're the jailer...so what else is new? It's the same old stupid rule. Just like all the other stupid rules around here."

***

"Let me talk to Jennifer," Trent said, restraining a yell to spare Nora any embarrassment with the senior partners.

He barely got her name out before, "Hey, Jennifer...pick up the phone!" Justin yelled out. "Warden Hayes would like to speak to you."

Seconds later speaking from his home office phone, "Yes," Jennifer said, sounding at the point of exasperation.

"You call me if he leaves the house again. I'll deal with him when I get home."

"And when exactly will that be?"

"Well, we're almost at your mom's job, and then I've got one more stop to make. I should be back in about two or three hours after I drop her off."

"Not soon enough for me." And with that, Jennifer abruptly hung up.

A goodbye would've been nice, thought Trent after realizing, seconds into his wait, that there was nobody on the other end. The image of Jennifer terminating their conversation with the ease applied to a stranger, much less her own father, troubled him. His children were becoming more impertinent in their dealings with Nora and him.

Jennifer had grown demanding, and it seemed, had little patience for either of them. Rachel, the youngest at 15 years old, and the most sensitive of the three, was also the most controlling. A bit boy crazy, as well, she was not afraid to throw a mild fit when denied a request.

Their biggest challenge, though, was with Justin. He was not a rambunctious teenage boy by current standards, just headstrong and suffering from the typical displays of rebellious fervor that beset his peers.

Trent always knew that theirs was no idyllic family portrait; the five of them going in five different directions as the day demands. But now it seemed especially glaring when compared to the uncomplicated household he once envisioned. Their lives had become a clutter of work, engagements, and separate activities; of weakening family ties, offset by compensatory gizmo's, gadgets and toys when a day's precious hours did not allow much time for anything else.

Trent wanted to use this drive to the city to talk things over. *I wonder how much different our children might've turned out if just one of us had chosen family over career*, he thought just as Nora was wrapping up her phone call.

"Were you just talking to Justin?" she asked while taking a moment to quickly thumb through her phone's inbox. "Is everything alright?"

"I suppose so. Jennifer called to say she thought he may not have been in his room last night. She heard him come in after we left. He told me he just ran to a friend's house this morning and came right back. I'm not sure that I believe him."

"Isn't he supposed to be grounded? Why risk sneaking out and getting into more trouble," Nora said, sliding the phone into her satchel.

"Justin never did respond well to threats. He sees them more as a challenge. That doesn't leave us many disciplinary options, does it?"

"Maybe we can ask Jennifer to help out. She's home now, and all done with school. She can keep an eye on both him and Rachel, just the way she used to when they were younger," Nora said.

"First of all, Jennifer could use some disciplining herself. She's wilder now than she was before she left for college. Secondly, Justin will never listen to her...not with only four years separating them in age. What he needs isn't going to come from his big sister."

"Then what do you suggest we do?"

Apprehensive, Trent kept his head pointed straight and darted a corner-eyed glance her way. "I'm glad you asked," he said.

Nora blew a weary sounding breath from her lips. "You're not going to bring that up again, are you?" she asked.

"Well why shouldn't I. This is important...this is our family we're talking about here. Our kids are out of control and it's partly, if not entirely, our doing. How can you not see that one of us needs to be home for them?"

"How can *you* not see that our kids aren't exactly kids anymore? And another thing...it really galls me when you say, 'us', when you actually mean, *me*. You want *me* to stay home with them. Let's say I did quit my job and did just what you asked. What exactly would I do? Jennifer's an adult and Justin's going to be a high school senior this year...half the time they won't even be home."

"You're forgetting Rachel. We still have some control over her. It's not too late to make a difference in how she grows up."

"Are you sure of that? She's not some impressionable little darling. She was a pampered child who, thanks to you, now thinks she's a diva. She's spoiled—"

"All three of them are spoiled," Trent said, interrupting her. "That's where we both went wrong with them. It wasn't just me."

"Well, even so...I should spend my days at home doing what? Cleaning...shopping...watching soaps while I wait for you to come home from your satisfying day at the restaurant? That's not my idea of fulfillment."

"I understand, but we have to do something. We have to try and undo some of what we've done...for their sakes."

"Yes...but what you're asking me to do isn't fair. I've come too far...worked too hard and invested too much to throw it all away like that. You, on the other hand, can sell the restaurant tomorrow. And it's not like we need the extra income. You know I earn enough to support us."

"If anyone is going to be supporting us, it'll be me," Trent said.

Visibly riled by the comment, Nora turned to face him. "And there lies the problem," she said sharply. "Your pride won't allow you to be supported by your wife."

"That's not it."

"Well, what is it then if it's not that?"

"I have no problem with you supporting us. There's just no reason for you to have to. The net income from the restaurant is almost twice your salary. It wouldn't make sense to sell. In fact, we can work the restaurant together...you and me, as partners."

"Don't you mean silent partner?"

"Well, I do know more about the business than you do. But you'd still have all the rights and privileges of a full partner."

"Only in principle. In practical terms, I won't, and you know that. Plus, you say, 'rights and privileges' like it's part of some contractual agreement we'd have. I'm your wife, and a fifty percent owner in the business, which means...I'm already a partner. But as far as I'm concerned, the restaurant is yours. It's your baby...not mine. I know you're just as committed to *it*, as I am to my career. Besides, we both know you would never tolerate me being an active partner in it...never."

Trent could not argue with that point. He knew there would be fireworks the minute she tried to assert herself in the restaurant's operation. Even the most innocuous of suggestions by her would prompt him to want to have her escorted off the premises—if it were only that simple. As usual, Nora found his weakest point, sharpened her facts, and used them to chop him down like a common tree.

Exhausted of words and feeling defeated, he switched on the car's radio to fill the cabin with something other than the gloating he imagined given off by her.

✳✳✳

Nora, likewise, was feeling not too talkative and a bit angry. He had ruined what started out as a pleasant drive by again raising an incendiary topic. At the heart of her anger was a sense of indignation that he would place the onus of such a decision on her shoulders. There was also a degree of guilt that in spite of her hard-line position, that he may very well be right. The children just might have benefited from having a full-time mother at home.

Nora's pursuit of the brass ring was not weighted by economic circumstances but by uncompromising self-interest; of unmitigated over achieving; a win-at-all-costs approach, and a near obsessive compulsive zeal to please her corporate lawyer dad and make partner, just as he did. She and Trent had become the consummate power couple; renown in the annals of boardrooms and financial journals as bonafide successes in their fields.

Thanks to her father's influence, their circle of acquaintances included some of the luminaries of the Wall Street elite; the legal strategists, the power brokers, investment bankers, politicians and anyone with considerable clout. And she loved being counted among them, even if only in an ancillary role. To relinquish her current lifestyle, she thought, for that of a common homemaker was worse than a step down. She likened it more to a death sentence. But the flipside was that she loved her children and recognized the developmental consequences of having an absentee mother.

✳✳✳

On the radio, the news anchor was interviewing a campaign strategist regarding the upcoming presidential election and his thoughts on the Mars phenomenon. The incumbent President Daniel Schaefer was facing a strong challenge from his chief rival and globalization proponent, Senator Thomas Bartlett.

Attitudes regarding the matter had changed appreciably after the cataclysm, forcing many nations to lean heavily on each other. Rescue, Recovery and Rebuild had become the new catchphrase among community organizers, heads of state, and a host of decimated countries. Among the entertainment industry, close to one billion dollars in aid was raised through benefit concerts. Among the avarice, the RRR acronym was used to turn a quick profit on the fronts of T-shirts, caps and the like.

Borders were opening up and barriers coming down, thanks in large part to the charismatic leader of the globalization movement, President Baldo Jović. He would entreat his listeners with a referendum of solidarity and preparedness. In light of his argument, and fearful of an impending Martian threat, it made the possible forfeiture of a nation's sovereignty, less of a concern among the populous. Even in the minds of an increasing cross-section of Americans.

Trent had no opinion one way or the other. He believed both sides made a good case, but never gave it any serious thought as he split his attention between the road ahead and the picturesque view just to his right.

The New York City skyline was always a breathtaking sight to behold. Its tall and majestic buildings glistened from a layer of dew that had yet to be burned off by the morning sun. On this day, it all looked especially magnificent sitting against an Azure blue sky. The vista moved gracefully behind the cables of the George Washington Bridge as his SUV crossed over onto Manhattan Island. On their approach to an adjoining highway, traffic had thickened, but not to the point of crawling. Even as they turned off onto another highway of newly laid blacktop and cascading traffic lights meant to keep the procession from resembling NASCAR. They encountered few if any snarls, and still they had not said a word to each other.

Along the street, the usual hustle and bustle persisted, seemingly unperturbed by the events dominating the world stage. The city, for all its vulnerability, came out of the cataclysm virtually unscathed. Except for a dusting of volcanic ash that settled into and atop unreachable places, there were no other visible signs of a recent disaster.

There was not a single fractured facade, collapsed structure or roadway to jog memories into earnest reflection. The vendors prepared their curbside stands for the day. The delivery trucks belched out pollutants. Yellow cabs darted in and out of lanes with temerity, looking to gain the slightest advantage in the race to Wall Street. Trent hoped, as with every drive into the city that his brand new Escalade would make it there and back home without a scratch.

The 108 story World Trade Center, the gleaming centerpiece of lower Manhattan, stood like a sentry near the footprints of where the original Twin Towers once graced. Its monolithic scale resembled a polished silver needle pointing straight to the clouds. Trent craned his neck upwards for a hasty glimpse and marvel of its height as he passed, and only minutes away from dropping off Nora who seemed none too impressed.

***

After a few turns and a tight squeeze past a double-parked car, he pulled up in front of a much less sublime office tower that was Nora's place of work. She grabbed her satchel and threw its strap over her shoulder, then pulled down the visor for a quick once-over in the mirror.

"Okay...bye," she said in a deliberate tone meant to convey her mild annoyance. Nevertheless, she directed a furtive glance at him wishing she had been less so, given the circumstances. "I don't think I'll be working late tonight, but if so, I'll call you."

"Alright," Trent said, coolly returning her annoyance. He regretted it almost immediately and gave her a corner-eyed look that wished for a warmer goodbye between them. She opened the door and stepped out, looking back at him briefly enough to catch his eyes express what pride would not allow either of them to utter. Trent stayed his attention on her, leaning forward slightly as their distance widened and the crowd increased. There it remained until she became lost in the surge of working people that proceeded into the building's lobby.

Chapter 2

John Coltrane's saxophone was keeping Trent company for the hour and a half drive home; that and the salty smell of six live lobsters which lay in a crate in the cargo area of his Escalade. Though he would've preferred the air conditioner on such a warm day, he purposely kept the windows open. He wanted to keep the cabin ventilated so that the fishy scent wouldn't settle into the leather upholstery.

Lobster had always been an expensive treat, but since the cataclysm, the price had more than doubled to the point where only the well salaried could afford it. Since few of his regular patrons were in that position, he decided to make it affordable for everyone. It would come in the form of a lobster bisque appetizer on tonight's menu. He had just crossed the George Washington Bridge and was making his way down a two-lane expressway. He kept a frequent eye on the speedometer, wary of the state police who were a scourge along that strip. They liked to hide behind the bends in the road in wait for a lead foot to zoom past. At that hour, traffic was always lighter heading away from the city than going toward it. Still, there were just enough cars on the road to keep him from easing his acceleration too far beyond the posted limit.

Trent relaxed in his seat, rested his head back, turned up Coltrane and fell in line behind another car. There he planned to stay until the next turnoff when, at that instant, he was suddenly jarred out of his tranquility by a thunderous explosion.

Nerves rattled, he momentarily lost control along with other cars on the road, but quickly recovered. Several other drivers chose to pull over onto the shoulder, likely to collect themselves. Fear rushed through Trent as he continued down the highway, avoiding two cars that had stalled, either from the explosion or through driver fright. He switched on the car radio but heard nothing but static. He then frantically scanned through the tuning dial only to discover the same blank reception on every station. That's when he suspected something awful had happened. He was about to pull over and call home when a loud rumble was heard, rolling up in volume like a distant thunderstorm getting closer. Suddenly, the Escalade began to bounce wildly. He grabbed the wheel with both hands in order to keep the car from spinning out of control.

Just ahead, he watched in horror as an overpass, heavily traversed with cars and people, began to crumble before his eyes. It came crashing down on top of a minivan that could not get through the underpass in time. Two other drivers directly in front of him struggled to maintain control of their cars. They finally lost it and crashed into each other, stopping within closing feet of his own car. Trent made a sharp maneuver to avoid them, but skidded off the road nose first into a ravine. His airbag deployed with an explosive burst that pinned him to his seat sending bits of broken material falling through the spaces.

His Escalade, totally wrecked and resting at a forty-degree angle, continued to shake and rock as if the ground were moving beneath it. Seconds later the rumbling ceased. Trent undid his seatbelt and tried to get out through the side door, but it wouldn't budge. He leaned over and tried the passenger door, but that wouldn't budge either. Car alarms were sounding from every possible direction, as were the sounds of people moaning in agony and screaming out begs for help.

Trent was about to crawl out the driver's window when the shell of his Escalade was rocked once again, this time by something decidedly more powerful. His SUV lurched up like a fish on a hook and flipped completely over onto its roof. Trent lay trembling in a contorted mass on what had been the ceiling; too frightened to move a muscle. He was surrounded by assorted items that had fallen from various compartments and instantly blown about the cabin.

One arm was pinned behind him, and one of his legs, bent at the knee. His calf was right-angled upwards and resting awkwardly against the upturned seat. A wind like nothing he had ever experienced was roaring past him and through every open window of his cabin. It became impossible to draw a breath. He put a hand over his nose and took in short breaths while wincing in agony as all manner of debris pummeled him from both sides.

Outside the window directly facing him, he saw nothing but a thick blanket of weeds and tall grass, gale blown and lying flat against the soil. Unable to move just yet, he feebly raised his head against the onslaught and looked toward the rear window. The glass was surprisingly still intact and acting as a break against the full brunt of the wind. It was likely the only thing keeping him from suffocating. It also provided, given the embankment the vehicle rested on, a small, unobstructed view of outside. To his shock, Trent noticed that the daylight was totally gone and replaced by a windblown blackness. It rushed into the cabin, enveloping him like a rampaging flood. And there it tried to steal the last bit of breathable air he had left.

Chapter 3

The solid oak conference table was massive in size, practically as sturdy as the tree it came from and polished to a mirror finish. Large enough to accommodate a twelve-member board meeting, it resided in one of three conference rooms on the two leased floors that the firm called their own. Although it was too large for its intended purpose that morning, it and the sheer lavishness of the décor, did serve to make a statement—that the firm had a successful track record of winning large settlements for its clients. Nora sat at the table scribbling notes for a probable trial in between her second-chair, and her legal assistant.

Directly across from them were the other litigant's attorneys and a court reporter. Nora's client was being cross-examined by the opposing attorney. He was attempting to determine the veracity of his injury claim and how well it might translate before a jury if it ever got that far. Though her client appeared nervous, there was no need to be, thought Nora as she believed his to be an open and shut case. After all, it's not every day that a person is burned over thirty percent of their body after a newly installed sprinkler system failed to activate during a fire.

The multiple skin grafts and the compression garment he wore to minimize the scaring spoke louder than any statement he could possibly give. The almost certainty of a victory allowed her to briefly multi-task her thoughts onto an image of Trent and the chilly way in which they parted that morning. She decided to call him the minute there was a break for lunch. And maybe discuss calmly how to best reach a compromise regarding the children.

Outside, the sun had inched its way over the roof of a neighboring skyscraper to shine brightly through the large, picture window of their 33rd floor conference room. It reflected a glare off the table and right onto the face of one of the attorneys. Nora requested a break in the proceedings and immediately asked her assistant to go over to the window and draw the shade. During the wait, the opposing attorneys conferred privately, no doubt comparing the plaintiff's statement to what was already on record.

Nora, detecting a hint of settlement in their body language, lifted up the corner of her notepad and on a clean sheet, wrote in small letters, "thumbs up." She secretly showed it to her second-chair who wisely remained poker-faced. Her assistant returned, and was just about to sit when at that moment, a thunderous explosion; comparable to only one other thing in lower Manhattan history, startled a terrified gasp out of everyone in the room.

"What on earth was that?" Nora asked, instantly flashing back to 9-11 and the horrific events of that day.

"I don't know," one of the attorneys said, standing to his feet. "Do you think it could've been a terrorist attack?"

Nora's assistant ran to the window. "I don't see anything...just a lot of people standing and looking every which way, probably wondering the same thing we are," she said, then climbing up onto the sill to get a better view of the sidewalk. Another attorney went to the window to see for himself, while Nora's second-chair went out into the hall to see if anyone knew anything.

"Look...I don't know what's happening, but I think we need to get out of here," the second attorney said. The court reporter, her hands noticeably trembling, looked at both of them for a cue as to whether to pack up her stenotype or not. Seconds later, a voice came over the public address system.

Good morning, ladies and gentleman, this is chief of building security. Apparently there's been an explosion somewhere in the vicinity. As of now, we are unable to determine its exact location, or what caused it. But whatever it was, it seems to have knocked out all television and radio signals. We're trying to contact the city's Office of Emergency Management, but as you can imagine, the phone lines are quite busy. So right now, we have no information to give you. I would ask that everyone remain calm. There's no fire. The building has not been structurally compromised. We're going to evacuate anyway...just as a precaution. When the alarm sounds, let's follow our usual fire drill procedure. And please...let's do so in an orderly manner. Thank you for your cooperation.

"What procedure is he talking about? We haven't had a fire drill in almost two years. All I know is I'm not walking down thirty-three flights of stairs," the assistant said.

"Looks like we'll have to adjourn until a later date," the attorney said, looking at Nora between collecting his things.

"We may not have to," Nora said, believing his rush to leave to be more than coincidental. "If it turns out to be nothing serious, we could meet back here after lunch. My client's been waiting long enough. I'd rather not delay this any longer than we have to...if it's okay with you."

"Ms. Hayes, you may be anxious to move this thing along, but my client is in no hurry. The smart thing to do, considering the situation here, is to postpone it. I'm sure even your client would agree."

Nora looked over at him, only to see him looking uneasily back at her and vigorously nodding in agreement with the attorney's suggestion. "Alright, we'll adjourn for the day. I'll have my assistant call your—" Nora screamed suddenly when, at that instant, a tremor, occurring like a jolt from out of the blue, staggered everyone standing in the conference room. She and two others fell to the floor.

Voicing sounds of absolute fright, they tried to pick themselves up or crawl underneath the conference table for shelter. The room appeared to stretch and bend into a distorted tableau. Cabinets toppled over, sending brick-heavy law books flying off shelves.

Pictures jumped off walls that now looked all cracked and mottled like sun-baked clay. The smoked glass that once set apart room from room, shattered in sonorous twangs that seemed never ending. Light fixtures fell from ceiling cavities, causing their florescent rods to pop in a series of rapid-fire detonations. Cries of panic from men and women alike were heard from the outside hall. Nora staggered to her feet only to fall again.

The entire building seemed to shake and sway from side to side. Some people were running for the nearest stairwell while others cowered beneath the sturdiest object they could find. A hand reached out from beneath the conference table, grabbed Nora by the arm and began pulling her under, just as the shaking seemed to be subsiding. Anxious seconds passed where only ceaseless whimpers were heard, unbroken by movement or a single word.

Satisfied that the floor under foot had finally settled, they began to crawl out from their hiding places. Soon after that, they felt the building begin to lean abruptly as if it were being pushed. Outright panic ensued as visions of the Twin Towers collapse stirred a mad dash for the stairwell. The buildings concealed innards cried out in horrific sounds of stressed steel and wood. The entire room leaned further and further until suddenly, they heard a climactic crash.

Nora was still trying to push her way out the conference room to the stairwell. With chaos erupting all around her, she looked in the direction of the crash and saw that the large picture window had completely shattered. A gale force wind rushed in like a wanton intruder, creating a veritable blizzard of paper, glass and solid projectiles that battered people at will. But the most frightening sight lay just past the window where the daytime sky resembled that of midnight.

Chapter 4

The twenty-year-old subdivision sat on a bucolic expanse of rolling countryside in the heart of the mid-Hudson Valley. Richly dotted with billowing oaks, maples and lush evergreen trees, its rural charm was offset by rows of stately McMansions; the oversized relics of conspicuous consumption that bespoke all the excesses of the pre-cataclysm upper-middle class. Nestled comfortably on finely manicured lawns, their sheer size looked strangely out of place amidst the quaint homes and sprawling farms that lay just outside of its main gate.

The serene environs created a seemly mix of country living and suburban opulence. The ideal balance for the dozens of New York City transplants that happily called Wellington Estates their home. But behind the brick and stone veneers, the grand entryways and the bold capstones that sit like lookouts atop huge arched window panes, resided a façade of a different kind. Behind the walls of tempered glass lived shattered families, forever estranged from their vanished loved ones and surviving like existential castoffs; of certain wives who found healing in online pharmaceuticals, and certain husbands who found love in the arms of someone else; of diverse young people who, with only New Hollywood as their mentor, believed it cutting edge to blur the lines between decency and debauchery. Just the sort of influences Trent and Nora thought they had left behind when they moved into their four-bedroom home along a quiet cul-de-sac twelve years ago.

The sunlight danced on the surface of their pool where Rachel, in a scanty swimsuit, lounged deck side on a chaise. A cell phone was in one hand and a loosely held Tootsie-Roll Pop in the other.

"What time are you coming over?—Well, how should I know?—Okay...whatever! She told me she might be here between one and two this afternoon. But what do you care? She ain't think'n about you.—So? I'm the one inviting you. You're not supposed to be asking me about some other girl.—Save it...I don't want to hear it. Are you coming over...yes or no?—Yeah, it's cool. My mom is at work, and my dad is probably gonna be at the restaurant all day," Rachel said, then sucking her teeth in disgust after glancing up to see Jennifer step out onto the deck and wearing a swimsuit.

"I've got to go now. My nosey sister is here. The less she knows about this, the better. So I'll see you at one...right?—Okay, bye."

"C'mon, I'll race you to the end of the pool," Jennifer said, grabbing Rachel by the hand and playfully tugging her toward the water.

"I don't feel like it right now."

"Well if not now...when? I thought you wanted to swim. What are you dressed like that for if you don't plan to get wet?"

"I do plan to get wet...just not right now. Don't you have someplace to go today?"

"Nope...I'll be home all day today. Oh, I'm sorry. That doesn't mess up your plans, does it?"

"I don't know what plans you're talking about," Rachel said, rolling the Tootsie-Roll Pop around in her mouth after each response.

"I'm talking about your pool party this afternoon. That's right...Mom and Dad already gave me the heads-up. They said you're not to have pool parties when they're not home."

"Why not? You had parties all the time, and they didn't know about half the stuff that was going on. Why can't I?"

"I don't know. I guess they don't like your friends. And I'm pretty sure they wouldn't like that swimsuit you're wearing. You know it's too small, but you wear it anyway...you little tease."

"Look, stay out of my life...alright? This doesn't even concern you. Why'd you have to come back home anyway? Why couldn't you just stay in school? Things were so much nicer when you weren't around," Rachel said, then chomping down and gnawing on the Tootsie-Roll center until only a cleaned white stick was left. "Why can't you be more like Justin and leave me alone? He couldn't care less what I do, as long as I stay out of his way."

"Yeah, that sounds like real brotherly love. I'll bet you two had a good'ole time while I was gone. Well guess what, the party's over. The sheriff's back in town so you better get—" Both Jennifer and Rachel jumped suddenly as a loud but distant explosion was heard that momentarily shocked them into silence.

"What was that?" Rachel asked, having sprung straight up to a seated position. She was looking directly at Jennifer who seemed equally as puzzled.

"I don't know. Maybe a plane crashed or something," she answered nervously, and then hurried inside the house, followed closely by Rachel. She stopped in front of the television just as Justin came running down the stairs.

"Did you guys hear that...what the hell was it?" he asked, stepping into the kitchen to join them.

"I'm not sure, but it sounded like a plane crashed," Jennifer said, switching on the set, but seeing nothing but an empty blue screen. She tried several stations, but got nothing. "What's going on? There's no picture on any of the channels. Rachel, go see if you can get anything on the radio."

"What radio?"

"I don't know...any radio. Try the one in Dad's office. Hurry up," she said, growing more uneasy by the second.

Rachel was about to go when suddenly, the ground dropped right out from under her. She fell to the kitchen floor, hitting the back of her head on the terra-cotta tiles. The entire house began to heave and buck. It rumbled and shook so violently that Jennifer believed the roof were seconds away from caving in on them. She ran screaming as she frantically looked for a place to hide, finally diving under the kitchen table where she laid face down with her arms covering her head.

Justin had fallen off balance against the kitchen wall and then sideways until his back was wedged into the room's corner. There he collapsed into a squat, his knees bent and arms wrapped and trembling around them. He peered over the top, wide-eyed and looking more frightened than he had ever been in his life. Window panes throughout the main floor cracked and shattered like discarded puzzle pieces. The television, which before showed only a blue screen had now gone totally black. It hopped along the counter and right off the edge, smashing into pieces on the floor. Cabinet doors flung open, spitting out dishes, glasses and the like. It all came crashing down around them in a frightening scene as if their home were under siege by some enraged poltergeist.

Rachel crawled on the floor in search of cover from the raining assault. The sharp edges of the cracked tiles cut into her hands and knees for every inch she gained. And then, just as abruptly as the quake started—it stopped. They remained for a minute in their respective places, silent, shivering, and expectant in the stillness.

"Is it over?" Justin asked, his eyes glistening a teary crimson from the corner of the room.

Jennifer, her hands trembling, looked up from beneath the table. "It seems like it might be," she answered. "Rachel, are you okay? Rachel!" she called out again. "Answer me!"

Rachel, looking shell-shocked and still wearing only a swimsuit sat kneeling amidst the shattered remains of their kitchen. "Yes...I heard you," she replied softly.

"Are you okay?"

"I'm not sure. My head hurts, and I think I cut my hand."

Jennifer crawled out from under the table and went over to help. "Let me see your hand," she asked. After steadying her own hand, she turned Rachel's over to see blood from a small gash pooling in the center. There were several scrapes on the heel of both hands, and also her knees. "You have a bump on the back of your head," she said, rubbing her hand across it. She grabbed a nearby dish towel and wrapped it around Rachel's hand. "The cut doesn't look serious. I didn't see any glass in it. Just make a fist to keep pressure on it and it should stop bleeding."

"Look at the house, Jen...it's ruined. What are we gonna do? Everything is ruined," Rachel said with a rising whimper in her voice that bordered on hysterical. "And what about Mom and Dad...are they alright?"

"I sure hope so," Jennifer said before turning her attention to the other side of the room. "Justin! Are you okay over there?"

"Do I look like I'm okay? I was so scared I practically pee'd on myself," he said, brushing the dust from his arms and face as he stood to his feet. "Did we just have an earthquake?"

"I don't know. It doesn't seem possible, but it sure felt like one."

Just as Jennifer said that, a loud crash was heard at the front of the house, followed by a barrage of smaller impacts all slamming into the house and sounding like thousands of baseballs being thrown at once. A ferocious, hurricane category wind suddenly blasted though whatever traces of window glass were left. It entered the house like an explosive burst, finishing off whatever hadn't already been completely destroyed. Anything not nailed down was instantly turned into a lethal weapon.

The force of it sent them screaming as they ran for the nearest place to hide from the rampaging wind. They found it in a closet-sized pantry. Once inside, it required their combined weight, just to push the door shut. They fell back, exhausted against the shelves. Outside the door, the wind roared and pounded on it like a living thing trying to force its way in.

Chapter 5

The ripples of incomprehensible cries were unnerving in their rhythm. Awash in a resonance of shouts and moans, they echoed as parts in a chorus of unseen pain and suffering. Trent rested on the sounds for a moment while his mind slowly recovered from the shock it was in. Though he had not moved a muscle yet, he was looking straight ahead at the floor and seats of his SUV and wondering what time it was. Clarity finally struck, reorienting him with his current predicament.

He was on his back and covered in debris that had blown in from outside. "I must've passed out," he said aloud, and to confirm for himself that he was not dreaming. He wiggled out from under his blanket of earth, and then out through the nearest window. Looking around, he discovered much to his horror, that the scene outside was worse than any dream.

The sky was the color of doom, an ashen gray with sweeping billows like rain clouds—only darker and more threatening. Trent looked at his watch, hoping that several hours had passed between the time he had fallen unconscious and now. It showed only ten past twelve. *It can't be midnight. It's gotta be afternoon,* Trent thought with a bewildered look up toward the sky. *Otherwise, it would be darker out*. To his reckoning, roughly forty-five minutes passed from the moment he first heard the explosion.

He turned and looked at his flipped over Escalade, its skin battered and bruised, nose bashed in, bottom up in the air and lying woefully in a ditch. He briefly recalled his upset on discovering a small scratch on the door only a week after driving it off the dealer's lot. Now it all seemed shamefully inconsequential as he turned and began to make his way up the embankment. Once at the top, he looked around in disbelief, shaking his head in utter denial while a need to weep panged his emotions. He instantly dropped to his knees, overcome by the magnitude of what he saw.

There, a massive pileup of cars either crushed or turned over, lay debris covered and tangled up in a jumble of steel and rubber. A scattered few had thick smoke pouring out from beneath their hoods, or had ignited into a blazing inferno. The rabid flames set off other cars whose leaking gas tanks provided the trail that led back to them like a fuse to a stick of dynamite. The occupants of one car, who apparently were too injured to free themselves, screamed and flailed for help. The hot flames, too intense for any rescue, licked at their necks, ultimately engulfing them in fire. Trent could only watch in horror as the regrettable image seared itself onto his mind's eye.

Meanwhile, amidst a wave of catastrophic suffering, there was not a single first responder anywhere to be seen; no sirens cutting through the anguish with the hopeful blare that signaled help was on the way; no dutiful police or fireman tending to the wounded; no National Guard troops swooping down in copters to airlift out the sick and dying; only teams of rescuers doing what, for some, seemed to come quite naturally.

From end to end, the stunned and dazed meandered through the crumpled wreckage like Nazi prison camp survivors. The strong weaved through the twists and turns to aid the trapped and helpless. The fumes wafting over were difficult to ignore; a smoky cloud of gasoline, burning rubber, and the unsettling smell of charred meat.

They combined to assail Trent's nose and throat, and make breathing a task that his stomach found hard to cope with.

They couldn't actually have done it...could they? Did those extremist fools actually manage to get a nuke into the country and detonate it, wondered Trent. He cautiously entered into the bedlam in hopes of getting an answer.

The sights and sounds were even more horrific up close, but strangely, not as jarring to his composure as he feared it might be. He maneuvered through the disaster, unshaken by the bloodshed, and mindful of himself and where he was in relation to everything. He saw a small group gathered just up ahead and started toward them. The closer he got, the more he began to feel his dread rising, and with it, his priorities coming into clearer focus. It was then that the myriad possibilities began to coalesce into a chilling scenario and a heightened urgency to know for sure.

"Nora," he uttered fearfully as a warm panic sweat began to rush over him. That—and the instant detachment from every other thought that was not her and the kids. He stopped, pulled out his cell phone and speed-dialed her number before noticing, soon after, that his phone had no bars. That meant the network was most likely down. If there was an attack, he was certain that New York City would have been at the center of it.

How far did it reach? he wondered as he slid the phone back into his pocket. Although he thought it unlikely that a single blast would have a wide enough radius to reach his upstate home, he still wanted some assurances to that fact. Jennifer, Rachel and Justin were there waiting and, granted there was any news of what had happened, no doubt wondering if he and their mom were okay.

Nora's fate, though, was running roughshod through his imagination. The thought of her suffering filled him with worry the longer he dwelled on it. He decided to hold his emotions together until he knew for certain. His thoughts turned circumspect and narrowed onto the faces of his family as he approached the small gathering.

They stood in a loose huddle, five men and one woman, near a disabled commuter bus. Each seemed unwilling to step outside of their circle of safety to lend hands in the rescue efforts. The men were debating whether to stay and wait for resources to arrive, or leave and take their chances on foot.

Without waiting for an opening, "Does anybody have a clue as to what happened?" Trent, abruptly butting in, asked.

"We're all asking the same question, mister," one of them said. "Nobody seems to know for sure. The only thing that makes sense is a nuclear bomb. The question is...who did it? The Muslims, the communists, the Russians, the Chinese...heck, it may even have been domestic...some U.S. born nutcase with an ax to grind. So many people hate us these days, it could've been anyone."

"Have you heard anything at all about New York City? My wife is there. I need to know if she's okay."

"Nobody knows. I've got family there myself, so I know what you're going through. Our cell phones are useless, and you can't get a radio signal or anything. We're pretty much in the dark. That's why I say we wait here until the National Guard arrives."

"But what if they're busy and they're not able to get to us right away," another said, clearly reiterating his point in an insistent tone. "We're looking at a terrible tragedy here. But this is nothing compared to what New York City must look like right now. That's if they *did* get hit. We may not see any help for days."

Not exactly the comforting words Trent was hoping to hear. He pushed his hands down into his pockets to quell an onset of fret he felt rising up. The doubts that came with them were even harder to subdue.

Frustrated, he studied the faces of others nearby to see if any of them appeared better informed. He spotted an elderly couple sitting in their car, frightened but apparently unhurt. He started toward them when, without warning, their vehicle suddenly exploded. It was struck by something fiery from the sky. Whatever it was, punched through the roof and set the entire compartment ablaze. The concussive blast sent Trent reeling back in shock. More explosions began to ring out, one after another at random intervals to sound like a strafing salvo of artillery shells.

The screams were heard seconds later, coming from all around and seeming to rush in every direction. A good-sized rock suddenly slammed into the pavement and only inches from Trent's feet. It was charred black and smoking as if it had just been spit from a furnace. That's when Trent looked up to see the sky lit by countless balls of fire raining down through the gray haze and torching anything flammable.

Trent ran back toward the disabled commuter bus, hoping en route that he would not get struck by a flaming chunk of rock. He closed to within a few feet and was about to duck under it for cover when its door suddenly swung open. The driver sat behind the wheel, signaling to him with a hurry-up pump of his arm to get onboard. Trent bolted up the stairs, just as the door slammed shut behind him. He bent over, gripping his knees, head down and gulping in air. Meanwhile, falling rocks of various sizes slammed into the roof and side of the bus; pelting it with dents and maddening thuds that reverberated through the coach like a terrorizing rain.

Outside, trees that lined the roadway were catching rocks in their foliage and going up in flames. Sadly, those people who sought protection at their bases suffered the same fate, and were burned alive. Most of the fifteen or so passengers on the bus turned away from the windows, unable to bear the ghastly scenes any longer. The remaining few stared out at it with a petrified gaze, unable to tear themselves away.

"Thank you," Trent said to the driver. "If you hadn't opened that door when you did, I'd probably be dead."

"That's okay. I'm just glad I saw you," he said, then turning for a moment to look out his driver's side window. "Is this not the craziest thing you've ever seen? It's like the end of the world or something."

"I know. I've never seen anything like it, either. I've never been so scared."

"Yeah...well, I've got a bus full of people here who feel the same way...including me. I got a friend from Colorado who moved here right after the cataclysm. The way he would describe the scene back then is similar to what I'm seeing outside."

"Have you heard any news at all?"

"I'm only getting snippets off my HAM radio. Yeah, I know...it's old-school, but it works, and it's cheaper than a cell phone. I got a few good buddies out there...we sort'a look out for each other. We've been trying to talk, but it's hard to get through. There's too much interference on all the channels. And what little I do hear isn't easy to make out."

"What have you heard?"

"Well...like I said, I can't be certain, 'cause it wasn't very clear. I'm also trying to keep my imagination from filling in the blanks. But when you look outside...how can you not get creative."

"What is it, man...please! I've got family out there."

The bus driver's voice switched from glib to earnest. "Well...it sounded like, well...like they said something really big fell out of the sky over New Jersey."

"Like what...a plane or something?"

"It was fuzzy after that...too much interference. But I don't think a plane could've done all of this...even if it had a nuke on board. Besides, they'd need a lot more than one bomb to cause all this," he said, turning to look out his window again. "These folks on the bus are thinking it was probably one of them UFO's that must've crashed...y'know, like at Roswell. But I think it was something else."

"What?"

"I think it was an asteroid...a big rock, y'know...like the one that killed the dinosaurs. What else but an asteroid could do this much damage."

Trent, listening intently as the driver pontificated, looked in his eyes. He was searching for any hint of lunacy to impugn him with, but found none. He then looked over at the nightmare occurring right outside the window and thought, *What if he's right? Hollywood certainly did their share of convincing the world of the possibility.* Still, he found it difficult, even in the face of so much death, to wrap his mind fully around it.

He wanted to believe there was a more earthly explanation; some other type of natural disaster like the ones that plagued the earth during the cataclysm. Back then, those caught in the middle of it must have surely thought the world was about to spin off its axis. And even after the worst of it had passed, the conventional wisdom was that civilization, given all the perils that threatened it, may not last through the millennia. A frightening prediction that, in retrospect, made the asteroid theory sound more plausible by the second.

Trent sat down in the nearest seat and nervously waited out the barrage. His worries repeatedly shifted from Nora, to the children and back again in a tug-of-war-like battle to seize his hopefulness. Besetting him were provocative imagery of where they might be right now, what they must be doing, and how they must have panicked when the sky started to fall. But he stopped short, after feeling a melancholy heaviness begin to take hold, of picturing them gone. Meanwhile, the steady drumming of rocks against the outside of the bus was beginning to slow.

"It looks like its stopping. I might be able to get some more news over the radio," the bus driver said as he started fiddling with the dials.

"I can't wait for that," Trent said.

"Why not...don't you want to find out what's happening out there?"

"Yeah, I do...but I don't have time. I've got to get home."

"Me, too," a woman passenger sitting across from him said. "But there doesn't seem to be any way out. How do you plan to get home?"

"I'm not sure. All I know is I can't wait for the police, or the National Guard to come to the rescue. I think they've got their hands full right now. So I'll walk if I have to."

"Where do you live?" she asked.

"In Ellisville over near the country club. It's about two miles from Newton Lake. Are you familiar with that area?"

"A little bit. I know where Newton Lake is. My husband and I, we used to take our kids there, that is before they...well...you know."

"Mister, Ellisville's at least fifty miles from here. Are you seriously planning on walking that distance?" asked the bus driver, looking at Trent as if he were witnessing a mental breakdown.

"What choice have I got? I can't stay here...I've got to get home to my family. I'm prepared to take my chances. Besides, it's better than sitting here and waiting for help to arrive that may not come for days."

"Alright, mister...I think you're making a mistake, but it's your life. Good luck," the driver said, then opening the door to the let him out.

"Wait a minute, you said Ellisville, right?" asked a male passenger a few seats down. "I'm going with you. I live in the next town over from you. I should've been home hours ago. My wife is there all by herself...probably worried sick about me." Two other passengers voiced their desire to join them and stood in preparation to leave.

"Are you coming with us, miss?" Trent asked the woman sitting across from him. She looked at him and his party, and then out the window at the scorched roadway.

"I'm going to stay. It's not safe out there. What if the rocks come down again? What would we do? I think it's better to wait. They know people are here. They're not going to just leave us. They've got to send help." Trent couldn't blame her for being afraid. Staying probably made the most sense under the circumstances.

He gave her a cursory nod of acknowledgement and then, stepped off the bus along with the other three in his group. They paused momentarily in the doorway and looked out onto the devastated landscape of gray and black ash. There were others walking among the ruins who, like them, had apparently reached a similar decision and began their own pilgrimage to parts unknown. Trent and his group looked at each other with an affirming sigh of agreement. Then, joining the flow of people heading north, they set out on the smoldering, rocky layer that had become the new terrain.

Chapter 6

A steady flood of frightened and harried people poured out the four stairwell doors leading into the lobby. Nora came rushing out of one of them, high-heels in hand and nearly breathless. She followed the stream of fleeing employees over broken chunks of the once exquisite granite that minutes before, had covered almost every square foot of the floor and walls.

The race down the stairwell from her 33rd floor office was a nightmarish descent. Unnerving sounds and constant tremors would rattle through the bowels of the building like a deathly warning. There, a crush of bodies had packed into a much too narrow passageway, creating a gauntlet of shoves, jutting limbs and unsure footing where one misstep could have resulted in death by trampling. On each completed landing, the specter of the grim reaper loomed; conjuring fears that at any minute a Twin-Towers-like implosion would seal their fates and entomb them in a field of rubble.

When she finally did burst out from the stairwell, it was as if someone had turned the oxygen back on. She slowed, in her torrid rush for the exit, just briefly enough to slip the pumps she carried back on her feet. She did so in two halting strides in lieu of a full stop so as not to lose pace with the others.

Building security stood at several points, moving them along in a swift procession that oddly resembled the running of the bulls in Pamplona, Spain. They herded them out through what had earlier been an entire wall of glass, now laid to waste and leading out onto the sidewalk. Along the way, shattered glass covered the floor inside, crackling underfoot like a crystalline carpet. Outside, directly in front of the building, lonesome vehicles of every type rested bumper to bumper along a pockmarked stretch of road. The pavement apparently rose and fell suddenly, only to end as a gaping trench that swallowed whole cars nose first.

The violent wind had abated, but the sky was abnormally dark and belied the actual time of the day. Once Nora reached the outside, she was met by a seemingly endless mob that poured out into the street from adjacent buildings. Some were sobbing, some screaming, but all appeared equally as frightened and anxious as she was. They were all inexplicably running in one direction through a milieu of devastation that berated sanity and swept them up in a frantic torrent of escape. Narrow jets of super-heated steam vented up through jagged fissures along the ground; its lethal nature evidenced only by the severely scolded victims laying wayside and writhing in agony.

The countless fleeing sloshed through inches of water gushing up from the century old cast-iron pipes that crisscross the city's underground, and that routinely rupture, even under the most benign conditions. A mild tremor suddenly shook the ground under them causing many to stumble as they ran, and even some to faint, if not collapse dead. It triggered homogeneous shrieks from the mob that echoed up through the cavern of empty office towers to become a toneless, unceasing hum in the ear.

Meanwhile, sheets of window glass, that had not already shattered, peeled wobbly from the sides of buildings in huge angular plates that came crashing down on unsuspecting survivors. Nora pushed herself forward, screaming between hyperventilated breaths as she ran, and wearing shoes that even under normal conditions her feet might have rejected after a few blocks walk.

A loud crash was heard behind her causing some to look back toward the sound. Several more crashes were heard in quick succession and sounding from all directions. People suddenly began dropping one by one all around her, accompanied by a thumping crunch and chilling screams that made death seem all but imminent. She stumbled over a body that collapsed in front of her. Upon regaining her balance, she happened to look up to see the sky all aglow from what appeared to be balls of fire hurtling to the ground.

The rocks pummeled everything. Some chunks disintegrated on contact, spraying those nearest the impact with stone fragments that bit into their flesh like shrapnel. Nora ran for her life, too panic stricken even to scream. She spotted a mass of people running toward a nearby subway entrance and hurried to catch up to them, completely ignoring the two people fleeing only feet away from her who fell hard to the ground; struck down in mid-stride by random chunks of falling rock.

She was almost halfway down the subway steps when she encountered a wall of bodies, all pressing forward in a desperate push to reach the lower platform. She slowed to avoid them, but was suddenly thrust forward by an unyielding deluge of people at her back. Most of them were still caught at street level and faced the full brunt of the onslaught. Nora found herself caught in the center of it, safe from the falling rocks, but not from the weight of a crushing mob whose only aim was self-preservation.

Unable to move or even raise her arms, she begged for mercy in labored breaths that fought to push back against the increasing pressure on her chest. Her ears were ringing with the voices of others also caught in the mob's inescapable grip and crying out in pitiful moans. Their pleas for release joined with the thunderous crashes aboveground to create a symphony of terror that drove many to scream with madness.

Nora's eyes began to flutter uncontrollably. Her head nodded forward like a ragdoll's, loosening the tears that had welled up. With freedom, they streamed down each cheek in a fearful prelude to the pernicious tingle she felt creeping through her limbs, and the airiness that sought to commandeer her thoughts. Though she tried not to succumb to deaths knell, she had little fight left in her to resist it. She closed her eyes and wept on the images of Trent, Jennifer, Justin and Rachel so that theirs would be the last faces she saw.

Seconds later, her eyes began to open ever so slowly as she felt the weight lift from her chest. Her lungs involuntarily expanded in a fully drawn inhale. She soon found herself moving forward in unison with the crowd, just as the life blood was returning to legs. Her head was regaining clarity with each new breath. Before long, she was standing on the packed lobby floor of the subway station, still surrounded by the same body of people. They hurriedly filed, without the bedlam that dogged them earlier, through the four narrow turnstiles that were the apparent source of the bottleneck, and which nearly cost her her life.

She rushed through one of the stiles when her turn came, and then followed the others down the platform in search of an unoccupied spot to rest at. Once found, she dropped to a seated position on the wet floor, indifferent to the water soaking through the skirt of her business suit and the slight spread of her legs that suggested she left her modesty back at the office. She was just glad to be alive and out of the storm which still pounded overhead like a rain of artillery shells. Every blast reverberated through the quake damaged tunnel to further rattle nerves already striped raw.

The lights repeatedly fluctuated from bright to dim, and back, finally dimming to a permanent state, symptomatic of damage to the power grid. Nora stared blankly out across the tunnel at the other subway platform opposite them. There, a few hundred survivors sat in a weary slump of momentary relief that surely mirrored her own platform—communally crammed and bound together by a shared experience they doubtless would sooner forget than relive. Secure in the subway, her relief quickly gave way to concern and a new careworn expression that grieved for the sake of Trent and the children. *They have to be alive,* she declared to herself. *They just have to be.*

Chapter 7

The dismal silence inside the pantry where Jennifer holed up with Justin and Rachel was matched only by the quiet she was hearing just beyond its door. She sat in the pitch blackness, traumatized and barely uttering a sound as thoughts ran wild with speculation concerning the fates of her mom and dad. The windstorm had ended a short while ago, at least ten or fifteen minutes to her estimation. But she was neither curious nor willing to peek outside at the additional devastation she was certain awaited them.

"This is silly. I'm opening the door," Justin said, heard but unseen in the blackness.

"No, wait," Rachel blurted out. "Jennifer, make him wait," she insisted.

"Wait for what...there's nothing happening out there. We've been sitting here in the dark for long enough. I can't take much more of this. I gotta see what it looks like out there." Jennifer, knowing it would have been pointless to try to dissuade him, kept her silence. If anything, she welcomed his courage hoping that it might jumpstart her own. She felt him stumble to his feet and move toward the door, nearly tripping over her folded legs as he groped for the knob.

A narrow slip of dim light entered into the pantry on his opening the door. Where normally he would have yanked it in a foolish display of machismo, he forsook that in favor of a slow, steady pull with trepidation as he peered out the expanding gap. Jennifer rose and stood behind him in the now fully opened doorway. It yielded just enough light to reveal Rachel, darkly lit and cowering in a secluded corner behind them. She seemed comfortable hidden away there and out of sight, that is until Jennifer and Justin stepped out the pantry. She immediately jumped to her feet, ran up close behind them, and clutched her sister's arm.

They stood just off the kitchen entrance, mouths agape and painfully gazing out at the dusky hue that had overtaken the space. The anemic light had reduced the edges of everything into a fuzzy gray.

"What happened to the sun," Justin asked. "I don't think I've ever seen it this dark in the daytime. Not even when there's a storm coming does it get this dark."

Jennifer looked around, momentarily dumbstruck by the catastrophic state of their home. The bright sun that had greeted her this morning, and that was with them up until an hour ago, appeared to truly be gone. What little light there was only accentuated the widespread damage.

The high-priced furniture that used to sit so proudly in the adjoining rooms, and that her parents were always anxious to show off at dinner parties, was in ruins. Their prized original signed artwork, the decorative pottery, the exquisite African carvings, porcelain statues and every other tangible item that defined home from memory to present, had been torn from its usual place and thrown throughout the house like worthless jetsam.

Leafy soil, rocks, tree limbs and assorted debris from outside had been blown indoors by the fearsome windstorm. It also laid down a coat of coarse, agrarian sediment onto just about everything.

"I don't know what's more upsetting, the sun being gone, or that our home is in a shambles," Jennifer said tearily. She then wiped her hand in a disbelieving sweep along a layer of grit to reveal a swath of granite countertop hidden just beneath it. Afterwards, she reached for the light switch, if only to confirm for herself that the power was truly out, which it was.

"What are we gonna do, Jen? The house is wrecked, and Mom and Dad aren't here. What if there's another earthquake...what do we do?" Rachel asked in a frantic voice. "We're not even supposed to have earthquakes here, right? Not in New York...we don't get earthquakes, right? Or hurricanes either...right?" All the while, she looked at Jennifer with weepy eyes that pleaded for an atypically comforting response from her. "Am I right, Jen?"

At that moment, Jennifer wanted to lay bare her own emotions, the fear, the anxiety, the tension, all bound up and sitting in the pit of her stomach like so much angst. But she could not bring herself to unhinge as freely as Rachel. Just seeing her standing there, bruised, dusty, and still in her swimsuit was pitiable enough. There was an inherent vulnerability, expressed in perceptible quivers from head to toe that, for the moment, ousted her impudence and arguable maturity. It triggered a protective impulse in Jennifer to reach out and wrap her in a consoling embrace. And she would have done so if it were not such an uncharacteristic reflex.

Her bashfulness notwithstanding, she settled for a tender, reassuring hand on Rachel's shoulder. There was little she could say of comfort that would not be paled by the visceral toll of nature's fury, and the havoc already inflicted on them. "You're right, Rachel. That's how it's supposed to be...or how it used to be, I guess. Look, things just aren't as predictable as they once were. I'm not one-hundred percent certain about anything anymore...ever since the cataclysm. But I honestly never expected anything like this."

"So that means we might die, doesn't it?" Her fright filled question was overheard by Justin who was in a nearby room going through their damaged belongings.

"Yeah, tell us what you think, college girl...are we gonna die?" he asked, kicking up the debris as he reentered the kitchen.

Jennifer, somewhat puzzled by the timing of his sarcasm, was thrown by their unexpected candor. In her gladness to have survived, she shortsightedly believed that their greatest threat was behind them. But one more look around caused her to ponder a new question as she deliberately weighed the possibility of their dying; letting the matter hang unanswered for a moment, in spite of her better judgment telling her to refute it immediately for Rachel's benefit.

Justin, on the other hand, not one to mince his words, seized on the opening in his typical insensitive fashion. "Here's how I see it, little sis," he said, turning a fallen chair upright so that the back faced them. He then straddled the seat with his arms crossed and resting along the top. "We're in a pretty messed up situation right now. I'm afraid another quake could bring this whole house down on our heads."

On hearing that, Rachel turned and looked fearfully over at Jennifer, who then turned and directed an incredulous stare onto Justin.

"Stop talking like that. Can't you see how scared she is?"

"Hey, I'm scared, too, but it doesn't take a college degree to see that two-plus-two equal's danger, the longer we stay here. The next question ought to be, what do we do now?"

Though she found agreement with him detestable given the time-honored nature of their sibling warfare, it did serve to validate her increasing concerns regarding their welfare from that point forward. She was about to concur with him when the three of them were suddenly aware of the distinct sound of voices mingling with the dust in the air. Though faintly heard, it was definitely conversation, and it was coming from outside their house.

Justin was the first to jump up and run to investigate. Jennifer, who was averse to the grim textures outside the window, was not in any particular hurry to venture out into it. Or to discover the degree to which her neighbors' homes had been ravaged by the quake and subsequent windstorm. Nevertheless, she followed cautiously behind, along with Rachel who was still clinging to her as if their past skirmishes had never happened.

Since they were both still in their swimsuits, Jennifer searched the floor until she spotted their large dining tablecloth poking out from beneath the debris. She yanked it out, accompanied by a dusty spray of aggregate, and draped it over her and Rachel's shoulders. They then proceeded outside.

Just as she had feared, her senses were accosted by a nightmarish scape of gloom and random devastation; of neighboring homes, some with severed roofs; some, stripped of their siding which hung motionless off the exteriors like flaccid limbs in the breezeless air; others, violated by uprooted trees that set down in the middle of living rooms; and still others, reduced to a pile of rubble. While only yards away stood homes, severely shaken but still intact, as if a rampaging giant had cherry-picked a reckless path of destruction through the neighborhood.

Rising plumes of black smoke from ruptured oil tanks contributed to the already murky sky. The unmistakable smell of propane gas choked her lungs on the first whiff. Neighbors' meekly staggered out into the grayness to join the few who already clustered on front lawns. Distraught survivors, they wept over the missing among them who apparently never made it out from homes, now completely demolished.

Jennifer turned to survey their own home. Except for the blown-out glass in the windows, the missing roof shingles and a surface layer of filthy muck, it looked remarkably solid. Especially considering the thorough beating it sustained. Her VW Beetle, which had been parked in the driveway, now rested cater-corner on the front lawn and looked none-the-worse-for-wear. She and Rachel then walked toward the cracked and sod littered street in front of their house. There, Justin stood along with two other neighbors.

They were about to join them when suddenly, a titanic blast ripped through their mournful lull. Frayed nerves were stunned with yet another worry as heads whipped in unison toward the general direction of it. Before they could get a fix on the exact location, they were rocked again by a similar blast only a head's turn away from the first. That's when the rocks began to fall; first one by one, and then several at a time, varying in size and either flaming or smoldering hot when they hit the ground. The salvo of impacts resounded with ponderous *THUNKs* that sent them all screaming for cover. At the same time, a random wave of loose fire, ignited by the flames, and fed by the leaked propane gas came rushing their way, and only seconds short of engulfing them.

Jennifer, Justin, and Rachel dashed back toward the house, stumbling over unexpected rocks while their arms shielded their heads from the malevolent rain. Throughout, countless more rocks slammed into its pitched roof, rolled off and down onto the front doorstep. Once inside, Justin pushed the door shut behind him and then fell back against it in an exhausted heap. The gut-wrenching sounds of the house being pummeled were heard as a deafening roar.

Terrified, Jennifer and Rachel both ran for the nearest corner. They turned, pressed their backs to the wall, and cringed in fear beneath the tablecloth as though it were a protective cloak. And there, stared horror-struck at the fiery rocks whizzing past the front window.

Chapter 8

A burst of glowing embers, thrown out from the consuming flames along a row of rooftops, got caught up by the winds. Then rose and fell like a swarm of fireflies. There they flickered against the dimly lit expanse where plumes of black smoke now formed hellish clouds for the new sky.

Dust was everywhere, falling to the ground as a barely visible mist of tiny particles that coated every solid surface with a layer of gray powder. The fire's glow spread out to the surrounding space, charging the airborne dust with an eerie luminescence like finely ground glass. Further down the row, the fire's rage waned into wispy flames that crawled up, down and around the charred and smoldering remains of what was once a community of adjoined town homes.

Trent glanced down at his watch in a newly adopted habit. One that as of this afternoon, he performed with the unconscious regularity of someone in search of a distraction. A gift from Nora on their tenth wedding anniversary, its golden glisten was dulled by the same coat of grit and dust that layered him from head to feet. He recalled his eagerness on the day she gave it to him; and the little-girl smile on her face as she happily waited for him to unwrap it. Though he owned a more expensive watch, this one was by far his favorite. Mostly, he was pleased that it was still keeping time under such jarring conditions. In the absence of normalcy, it provided a comforting connection to things warmly remembered.

Unable to see it clearly, he raised the dial high enough to catch the fire's glare, and then dropped his hand with a disgruntled slap to his thigh. He was approaching two hours into his journey home and was growing increasingly frustrated by the relatively short gains made. Along the way, the small party of a few dozen that he originally set out with had swelled to, by his estimation, over one-hundred. The prevailing conditions, harsh and unforgiving, were a formidable challenge. It forced even the most intrepid of loners to rethink the old, there's-safety-in-numbers, adage.

A motley collection of survivors, they lumbered en masse through the devastated streets of a blighted village that, after the onslaught, more resembled a blitzed war zone. The fires, breathing on both sides of them raged uncontained, belching out flames like a hungry furnace as the trekkers carefully scaled the treacherous roadway. Under the scant light, their faces bore the anguish of the preceding hours, erasing their varied ethnicities into a single monochrome shade of engraved disbelief and commonality.

Many were hobbled by twisted or broken limbs, blows to the head, and deep wounds that seemed to bleed incessantly. Most others limped along in a state of bewilderment, uncertain of where to turn or what to do next. And having lost everything, were desperate for even the slightest show of governance to lead them. Their ranks grew larger, still, with newly homeless. Despondent, and carrying with them a few salvaged possessions, they joined the exodus north, irrespective of where it led, or who was doing the leading.

In all, they created a formless pack whose members, those able-bodied among them, walked a respectable distance from one another; conserving their words until the tableau of ruin became less shocking. Trent, likewise, exchanged few words with his fellow travelers. He chose instead to fix his thoughts squarely on the goal of just getting home and avoiding altogether, any errant speculation about what scene may await him when he got there.

Their way was made especially difficult by the abandoned vehicles that obstructed their path. Still, there were fewer than that encountered on the interstate where they started out from. A veritable river of junked automobiles, it made what would have been the quickest route north, virtually impassable. Hence, the decision was made to find the most favorable route in lieu of the shortest distance.

At first, all course changes were decided by unanimous vote. But as the party's numbers increased, so did the level of disagreements among them. Soon, every move was debated and argued. A few came to realize that a natural disaster was no place to start employing democratic principles.

A brazen power grab ensued among twelve headstrong survivors. Each thought they knew better than the other on how to best lead the party. Trent, who was out in front at the start, decided it best to leave them to their egos and gradually fell back to join the others. He was content to just follow behind, as long as they continued in the right direction and didn't take too many rest breaks.

The local streets may have been less obstacle-choked, but between the broken water mains flooding entire stretches of roadway with torrents of rushing water; the snapped power lines dangling around them and spitting sparks out the open end like roman candles; the strong smell of gasoline, and the occasional panic-inducing aftershocks, it made the choice to leave the congested interstate seem incredibly ill-fated. Trent lifted his watch arm, took his other hand and lightly brushed his fingers over the crystal to loosen dust from its face. He then dropped a squinty-eyed glance down at it, and noted the minutes that passed since he last checked.

"Is there someplace you have to be?" a sullen voice asked, coming from not far behind him.

Trent, certain the words were directed at him, turned briefly to see who in the crowd was asking. His attention was drawn to a stringy-haired, elderly gentleman whose sad comb-over had clearly seen better days, and who through the muck-dried strands that fell over his eyes, gazed hauntingly at him. Clad in pajamas and a pair of house slippers, his face bore the cuts and bruises of a fresh ordeal. He also seemed to take two steps for Trent's every one; apparently in an effort to avoid the fate of his feebler contemporaries who, unable to keep up, had fallen back and out of sight.

Trent simply ignored the old man, cutting his eyes away from him and back to the road as if the query had missed its mark. He was comfortable in his rationale of being too tired, too restless, and far too hungry to care what anyone thought of him; least of all, a crusty old man who was clearly too senile to recognize a full-blown disaster when he saw one.

Only a few hours earlier he would have indulged the tactless intrusion with a benign quip of his own. Now he showed little consideration for civility. It did not matter that he had not spoken a single word in hours. He resented the inappropriate levity of the question, and the presumption that he should even have answered it. The tragic vistas partially illuminating their present path should have overwrought his sensibilities, by now.

"Pardon me, mister. I was only joking," the same voice once again said from behind him. "I didn't mean anything by it. It's just that I've been walking behind you now for...well, it feels like an hour. I must've seen you check your watch at least six or seven times. And...umm, it just looks peculiar from where I'm standing, that's all. Really, I didn't mean anything by it."

Trent heard every word, but kept his attention fixed forward, maintaining his pace without the slightest acknowledgement that anything was being said to him.

"You're probably wondering how anyone could find humor on a day like this," the old man continued. "I assure you...I'm not crazy. My wife, she'd often accuse me of thinking out loud. She'd give me a nudge whenever I'd said something I shouldn't have. After she'd gotten over the embarrassment, we'd both have a good laugh. Sometimes I think she knew me better than I knew myself. If she were here, she'd have given me a good nudge before I'd gotten a chance to say what I said to you. She was quite a woman. She would've been seventy-eight this year."

The old man rambled incessantly on, reminiscing through the weathered pages of his life's journal as though someone cared. And with the sort of detail that would have been better shared with a close friend. Trent did not want the weight of yet another emotion, but found himself yielding, nonetheless, to the wistful strains of longing poured out in the man's voice. Only half listening, his thoughts immediately went to Nora, their twenty-eight years together, their family, and then the icy way they said goodbye that morning.

Where might she be? he wondered tentatively, not wanting to explore the question too deeply. *Is she trapped somewhere? Or maybe she's trying to get home...same as me.* Her imagined plight was all it took to awaken his civility, certain that wherever she was, she could only benefit from small acts of kindness, similar to the sort he currently tried to shunt aside. It compelled him to slow his pace a bit, just enough to allow the old man to draw a little closer.

"How long were you and your wife married?" Trent asked, glancing over his shoulder as a signal to the old man that he found an audience.

"Next month would've made fifty-two years," he said with a boost in his voice, apparently delighted that he was no longer talking to himself. "She would've been seventy-eight this year. Our birthdays were only a week apart. I was four years younger than her. I used to kid her about that a lot. 'You're too old for me. I'm gonna leave you for a younger woman,' I'd say. She would just laugh and threaten she'd leave me before I left her." He paused and sighed. "I would've never guessed her words would come true. Now I'm all alone."

"You're not really alone. You must have family somewhere," Trent said.

"We had a daughter. She and her family lived in San Francisco...but they all died during that cataclysm a couple of years ago. Since then, it's been just the two of us. I had to leave her, though. I had to...I had to."

By now, Trent had slowed his pace considerably, as did the old man until they both walked a moderate speed, only this time side-by-side. He had to admit he enjoyed listening to him, if only to fill the time, and was intrigued by his last statement, especially given what was already revealed. "Did I hear you say you had to leave her?"

"Yes. She wanted me to."

"I don't understand. I thought she passed away."

"Yes...she did. And I had to leave her. I guess I should explain. You see, she was diagnosed with cancer five years ago. The doctors, they thought they got it all, but it came back last year. By the time they discovered it, it had already spread too far. There wasn't anything they could do except make her comfortable. That meant filling her full of pain medication. I'd been taking care of her ever since. She'd been sick for weeks...her entire body was hurting. She spent the last few months in bed hooked up to an IV. I can't tell you how painful it was for me to see her wasting away like she did. So anyway, this morning, just like every other morning, I'd lay there beside her. We'd watch the television together for a while until she fell off to sleep. That's when we heard the explosion. The television screen...it just went blank. When I heard the battery backup on her IV pump switch on, that's when I knew the power was out. Right outside our window, I heard all these car alarms sounding all at once. I didn't know what to think. Then all of a sudden, the house started to shake something awful. It must've shaken me out of bed, 'cause the next thing I knew, I was on the floor. So I just laid there for a second or two. That's when I looked up and saw the ceiling come crashing down on my sweet Estelle."

The old man's recounting built up to a warbling crack that settled into his voice like a dryness he couldn't clear. His eyes became misty with the likely visual of it as he raised an opened hand and wiped it down his bruised and dusty face. "That was the last thing I saw," he continued. "And then I must've passed out. When I came to, I was covered in all kinds of stuff. After I freed myself, I started clearing away as much as I could off of my Estelle. I checked for a pulse, but I already knew she was dead. So I just laid down next to her, grabbed her by the hand, and stared up at the sky. I was prepared to die right there beside her when all of a sudden, rocks started dropping through the hole in the ceiling. The room caught on fire, but I stayed with her, anyway. And that's when I heard her tell me to go. Yeah...she told me to go. She was dead...but I heard her voice say, '*go*'...just as clearly as I hear my own. So I kissed her, said goodbye and rushed out of there, minutes before the whole house went up in flames. She didn't want me to die like that...not that way. I could think of a couple of ways I'd like to leave this earth, but being burned alive isn't one of them. She knew that."

The old man then looked up, and for a moment, watched reverently as the smoky clouds swept overhead. He began to nod affirmatively and his mouth started to twist into a negligible smirk that seemed to cut through his recurrent despair.

"I can't begin to imagine what it must've been like for you...losing your wife that way. You seem to be holding up okay, though. I can't say that I'd be in the same emotional state if it were me," Trent said.

"That's only because I know she's not suffering anymore. She's up there," the old man said, pointing a finger toward the sky. "Probably looking down on me right now, and wondering why I don't shut up and leave you alone."

And then, as if heeding some ghostly instruction, the old man turned oddly quiet. He walked blithely, like a liberated man at peace with himself and whatever absolution he believed was given him through full disclosure. Trent, curious to see just how much time had passed, wanted to look at his watch, but did not care to invite another comment and discourse—at least not yet.

He didn't realize just how much he needed that break from the surrounding madness until it was forced on him. Even though they were quiet the rest of the way, he did appreciate the old man's company. He chose to stay by his side, even if it meant walking a little slower than he cared to. Whatever the number of minutes used up by chit-chat, he knew he would need more of the same if he hoped to make it home with his sanity intact.

At the moment, the overriding thought on Trent's mind was his hunger. He had not eaten anything since breakfast that morning and wasn't sure how much longer he could go without food or water. The few visible storefronts they passed had already been looted clean of anything edible or even useful. Soon, what started out as a murmur of irritability among the horde had escalated into a vociferous wave of grumbling; of empty stomachs and short tempers, the combination of which, threatened to breakdown what little order existed. Trent knew he was walking among a powder keg. But with no other options open to him, he stayed the course and hoped they could find some type of food before a spark of anger ignited them.

His throat was so parched that it often hurt to swallow. He forced a dry harrumph to clear it of the tiny dust particles that had found their way up his nostrils, or were brought into his mouth whenever he unconsciously licked his lips. What he would not have given right then for a tall, cool glass of water and a place to sit.

Trent needed a distraction, but felt himself too weak to engage in any other activity except walking. He no longer did so at the begrudging pace to the old man's, but in short, conservative steps that set the new pace for a number of others to follow. That placed them somewhere in the middle of an ever-growing pack of like-survivors whose numbers were now close to two-hundred.

He motioned to check his wristwatch, but hesitated, uncertain that he wanted to know just how little time had elapsed. Still, he raised his arm, anyway, straining to catch the last remnant of light that remained from the receding fires. He then looked up and saw a rustle of movement in the body of people directly in front of him. Their backs were all moving away from him in an advancing move forward, joined by what sounded like a strange commotion brewing further up ahead. The commotion seemed to be growing louder by the second. Then suddenly, as if propelled by a surge of stored-aggression, the crowd rushed forward in a veritable stampede that incited those behind them to do the same. Trent grabbed the old man by the arm and started running.

"What's happening? What are we running for?" the old man asked, wearily pushing the words out of his mouth and stumbling over unseen debris as he was pulled along.

"They must've seen something up ahead," Trent said. "Maybe it's help...the Red Cross, or the National Guard."

"Or maybe it's water...and food," the old man said with a hopeful rise in his voice. His tone contradicted the mild jostling he took from a belligerent tide of curiosity seekers who thought him too slow.

"Could be...but if so, at the rate you and I are going, it'll all be gone by the time we get there."

"Then you've got to go on ahead. You need water."

"Well, that's assuming there *is* water...but what about you?"

"Don't worry about me. I'll be fine. I'll catch up to you. These legs may be old, but they still have a little get-up'n-go left in them."

"I'll save a bottle of water for you," Trent said, slowly backing away while at the same time, conflicted between his eagerness to run for it and his reluctance to leave him.

"Oh, and a sandwich, too...if they have any," the old man shouted.

"Sure thing!" And with that, Trent dashed off, adrenaline fueled, to join the flow of bodies. Exactly what they were rushing toward—he didn't know. It was fast approaching night. Even though, according to his watch, it was just about late afternoon and should have still been very bright out for a summer day in July. He tried to run at first, but couldn't get his already sore legs to move much faster than a jog.

Meanwhile, standing between him and the source of the pandemonium was an endless course of twisted, flipped over and fallen obstacles which he had to negotiate around. And without the fire's light to aid him, it proved difficult amidst the rush of others, all aiming for the same goal.

After several minutes of dodging, and jostling, he was finally able to catch a faint outline of a lone structure up ahead. Encouraged, he pushed his way through until he reached the front of what appeared to be a 7-11 style convenience store. Its glass had been shattered from end to end, and its interior, repeatedly violated by hordes of people moving in and out like bees around a hive. Trent followed suit, stepping through the gaping window frame, all the while hoping he wouldn't trip over something or someone and be cut to ribbons under a stampede of feet.

Once inside, a flickering glow from a cart loaded up with magazines and set on fire provided what little light there was to see. It revealed a state of absolute bedlam where grown men and women pushed and elbowed each other in a desperate grab for anything they deemed theirs to take. Others, meanwhile, spent their time on hands and knees foraging the floor for whatever the free-for-all had knocked off the store shelves. Still others, in their frenzy, rushed past him greedily toting more snack foods, beverages and candy than they could easily carry out.

Trent knew he had to move quickly or else there would be nothing left for him and the old man. In a spur-of-the-moment choice between thirst and hunger, his thirst won out and drove him to the rear of the store. There he hoped to find the non-working coolers, and with any luck, a bottle of something to drink. When he got there, though, all he found was a mess of spilled milk, splattered eggs and a few smashed bottles of beer.

There was not a single drink to be had, and the clock was fast ticking on whatever chance there was of him finding anything to eat. He immediately dropped to the shadowy floor and started sweeping his hands through the litter, hoping by chance they'd happen upon something, anything he could either eat or use for later. Everyplace he set his hand was nearly crushed by a random foot from other passersby.

Most of what he touched was garbage, but occasionally his hand would brush something of significance. He quickly grabbed it up, shoved it into his pocket without any idea of what it was, and continued indigently groping the immediate surround.

Soon, two other people dropped down within inches of him and began a search of their own. Trent glanced up at them, and then back down at their six hands, all communally darting from side to side. *What must this look like*, he wondered.

That's when he pictured himself on his hands and knees competing for scraps in an all-or-nothing contest he likened to a game of Hungry, Hungry Hippos. The humbled image of himself was a bit more than his self-respect could take. He rose to his feet and looked for the quickest way out, satisfied that whatever was down there, he was able to get to it before his corrivals did.

Once outside, Trent hurried to an isolated spot well away from the center of activity. Along the way, he was surprised to discover a number of bodies—dead or barely alive, he could not be certain—lying throughout street. Some were being dragged off and unceremoniously left on the side of the road. He didn't know quite what to make of the ghastly task. Only that at present, he was too responsibly numb to be shocked by anything; and too preoccupied by hunger and dehydration to muster any real compassion for them.

He reached into his pockets and curiously pulled out the items he had taken. Though the sky was pitch black, several mounds of debris had been formed and set ablaze, creating an array of bonfires for light. In one hand he held two packs of Starburst candies, one five-pack of single-edged razor blades; and in the other hand, one set of shoelaces, and a pack of Juicy Fruit Chewing Gum.

Not exactly the-pick-of-the-litter, but it's better than nothing, he reasoned before pushing them back into his pocket. He then turned, got his bearings, and set out to search for the old man.

The fires that were set inside the convenience store had grown out of control. The flames began a hungry ascent up to meet the ceiling; each separate blaze, fanning out like an errant spill to form a single, unquenchable inferno.

Trent walked past the hot flames of the nearest bonfires and studied the amber shaded faces congregating around them. He thought he might see the old man, but there was no sign of him. He then turned his head in a slow, deliberate pan and pointedly squinted through the haze of smoke and cinders for him.

The expansive area was now teeming with newly arrived survivors. Their countenances were marked by trial as they meandered through the congestion, likely in search of family, friends, or simply a familiar face. His mind and body weary, Trent decided to search for a suitable place to rest for the night. He promised himself he would search for the old man at daybreak—whatever that might look like.

The rain of dust was continual. Falling like otherworldly snow, it would waft upward above the bonfires as glowing cinders, before dropping back to earth to join the accumulating soot and ash. For many, the countless abandoned cars grid-locking the street provided the perfect shelter from the contaminants. They were also a sufficient barrier against the escalating tumult that carried on just beyond their windows. Trent walked for a bit hoping to spot an empty car seat to occupy. But each vehicle he approached was either loaded up, or its frightened occupants, unwilling to make room for him. He walked further, all the while covering his nose from the assaulting stench of feces drifting over from the shadowy underbrush along the roadside. It was a putrid reminder of what only this morning had been a deeply private act, now gone horribly public.

His sphincter clenched at the likelihood of performing a bowel movement at the foot of some tree in the woods; made all the more offensive in the absence of toilet paper and a spritz of hand sanitizer. Though clear of the underbrush, the fetid scent still lingered around his nostrils. It joined with the musk, and the assorted odors already in the air, to settle onto the back of his throat like a bad taste. At that moment, a sickly frown took hold of his face as he began choking back a combination of dry mouth and the sudden onset of queasiness. Seconds later, he was bent over and heaving up an acidy soup of the only meal he had all day.

Afterwards, Trent stood up relieved, but now even emptier than he started out. And, with a taste in his mouth much like week old oatmeal and sour milk. Right then, he remembered the pack of Juicy Fruit Chewing Gum he had found and immediately shoved his hand into his pocket. He hoped its flavor would reverse the taste and quell his stomach of any recurring bout of upset.

He was about to pop a stick of it into his mouth when he noticed, through the breaks in the crowd, a quiet stirring among a densely packed collection of survivors. He had no idea what was getting them so excited. In no time at all, word of it rippled through the crowd in a pass-it-along fashion until it finally reached him.

"Did you hear the news, mister?" a man asked, walking through the masses as though he were the town crier.

Trent's eyes opened wide with anticipation. "Not yet," he said, chewing his gum feverishly. "What's happening? And I sure hope it's good news."

"Yeah…great news. Word has it that the National Guard set up a relief station about a mile from here. They say there's food, water…maybe even cots to sleep on. Most of us are gonna move out tonight rather than wait till morning. It's better to go now. If you wait, there might not be anything left." With that said, the man moved onto the next person.

The news, if it was not a cruel joke, was hopeful at best. Some men had already begun constructing crude torches; then draining gas tanks and oil pans and soaking the cloth-wrapped ends in them. Trent had just about chewed the last bit of flavor out of his gum and was now more than ready to leave. But that meant having to abandon the old man. Not a difficult choice in the scheme of things, he reasoned; choosing his family over the fate of some elderly gentleman that he just met about two hours ago—and, given the present state of confusion—is likely never to see again.

At peace with his decision, he weaved his way through groups of survivors who stood huddled together, seemingly gripped by indecision. He hurriedly joined the larger segment, already on the move and torches raised high in a jubilant march toward their presumed salvation. Trent followed along, walking livelier than he had in hours, and hoping with every step that disappointment wasn't waiting at the end of their trek.

Chapter 9

Nora sat trembling on the subway platform floor, nervously waiting for the next round of rocks to pound the surface. She feared this time another barrage might bring the tunnel ceiling crashing down on their heads. Luckily, the last twenty minutes had been relatively quiet. Enough so, that a few had noticeably dropped their shoulders and breathed an overdue sigh of momentary rest. While others either stretched out on the wet floor or slumped over where they sat; their eyes closed in an adrenaline-crash induced sleep they could no longer fight against.

However, those still alert sat vacant of composure and edgy with expectancy, unwilling to declare the rock shower over just yet. But even through their respite, the sounds of tragedy could be heard seeping down through the subway grates as a blare of police sirens, untold alarms and anguished screams that roamed the crammed platform like a rabid animal.

Between her fears that the rocks would start falling, the questionable safety of the subway tunnel, and worrying over the whereabouts and wellbeing of her family, Nora could feel her sanity approaching critical mass. If something promising didn't happen soon, she fully expected to lose it right there on the platform in front of everyone. No different than a handful of others who, unable to contain their emotions, simply let loose with an expulsive outburst of sobbing.

She glanced over at her two neighbors sitting on each side of her, curious to see if they, too, were as tightly wound as she was. To her right sat a gray-haired gentleman, legs crossed in front of him, one foot over the other, his stained and ripped business suit bearing all the earmarks of a near escape. His starched white collar opened above a loosened necktie while a look of total fatigue accompanied a head-down, deadpanned gaze at his hands. The gold face of a Patek Philippe watch peaked out from beneath his shirt cuff.

Nora was certain of the make having briefly entertained purchasing the extravagant timepiece as an anniversary gift for Trent. Or better still, as a salve she could apply on the sensitive abrasions afflicting their marriage. But with a price tag of $30,000+, she reasoned it made little sense to spend so much on something so small. Instead, she settled on a lesser make, at a fraction the cost and had engraved on the underside a promise of everlasting love for another ten years.

Sadly, it was two months later that she discovered he had an affair with a colleague during an overnight business trip. Though he swore it only happened once, she equated one act of infidelity for every business trip he had ever gone on. At the time, she wanted nothing more than to leave him single, broken and penniless. Now, fourteen years later, all she could think about was how much she needed him.

The recollection of his watch brought their wedding day to mind, the pomp and ceremony, their vows; all coming back in a flood of mixed emotions, made especially heartfelt after her second glance over at the gray-haired gentleman. After thoroughly studying him, she concluded that he must have had some influence among the Wall Street hotshots. To see him, humbled by abjection and staring down at his hands as he somberly stroked his wedding band, all but negated whatever lofty heights he had reached up to that point.

Just to her right sat a young woman of apparent Mexican heritage who, judging from her dress, lived her life at the opposite end of the pecking order where an honest day's work often meant long hours for minimal wages. There, she wept softly, and in inconspicuous shrugs that purposely drew little attention her way. Stealthiness was made easier by her diminutive stature which, like camouflage, allowed her to exist almost unnoticed.

Her hands were clasped together, likely to lessen their trembling, which was obvious whenever she would use one to wipe away a tear. Whatever her concerns, she wore them like a second skin, same as the others sitting nearby whose body language Nora took the time to study. It exposed among them an equitable state to that of the gray-haired gentleman. His wristwatch alone was likely three times more than what the young Mexican woman earned in a single year.

Nora then looked down at herself and the high-fashion skirt she wore which was hiked immodestly above the knees. Her brown legs, though riddled with pantyhose runs, were held together and folded in front of her as close as the taut fabric of her skirt would allow. Its matching jacket had lost its buttons somewhere between the office place and the subway platform. A silk white blouse spilled sloppily out from her waistband. It was a pricey ensemble. One which she loved to put on, and surreptitiously model throughout the day's activities as though every instance were a strut down a Paris runway.

Right then she realized just how frivolous her preoccupation with fashion was, and how little it mattered to anyone but her. Or, how little anything mattered at this point—her possessions, her clients, making partner; even that Patek Philippe watch on her neighbor's wrist and whatever his occupation that afforded it. None of it mattered. Both of them were now just as needy and newly destitute as the poor Mexican woman who, just hours earlier, they would have passed on the street without so much as a glance.

Nora thought back to earlier and how dismissive she was with Trent as he drove her into work this morning. She wanted to start the day over again; back to before she left the house, to at least say goodbye to the kids. Her regrets began to mount when, in the middle of her mea culpa, she caught the sounds of a conversation brewing close by.

The words, "home," and, "upstate New York," leaped out from their discussion and grabbed hold of her like two old friends. She immediately stood up, ignoring the wet seat of her summer skirt, and the opaque outline it surely revealed, and made her way over to where they sat. There, she took a seat next to them without saying a word.

"Yeah, but you saw the streets. They're all broken up. There's no way you're gonna get a cab, or a bus to anywhere. We've been sitting here for about half'n hour and not one train has gone by. I'm telling you, we're gonna have to walk," Preston, a Principal for a New York City public high school, said. "My family's in central New Jersey. All I need to do is get over the bridge, and off this island. Once I get on the other side, I'm sure I can get a ride home from there."

"Are you sure? We have no idea what's going on up there," one of the others said. "For all we know, we may even be at war, and if so, down here is the safest place to be. Y'know, back during World War II, the Londoners used the subways as a shelter from German air raids. They'd spend the entire night down there."

"What about food, though?" one woman asked.

"Yeah, and how would we go to the bathroom," another woman added.

"Hey...I don't know. All I know is if there *is* any fighting going on up there, they don't need a bunch of civilians getting in the way."

"I can't say that I feel completely safe down here. If we are at war, what's stopping whoever from marching down here and taking us prisoner...or even shooting us all dead," Laura, a 50-ish and unmarried administrative assistant, asked.

"You all keep saying war, war! War with, *who*? Or maybe I should ask with, *what*. Those didn't look like any bombs that I've ever seen.

They didn't even explode. They were just rocks. Where'd they come from? Can you tell me *who*, or *what* would use rocks in a war?"

"I know. It doesn't make any sense. That's why I can't stay down here," Dale, an investment banker, said impatiently. "It's like there's a total news blackout. My phone doesn't work. I'm getting no service. I need to find out what's going on."

"It's not just your phone. None of our phones are working. And where are the police...the firemen? Shouldn't they be down here directing us?"

"Forget about waiting for them. They're probably up top cleaning up all the mess. That's why we need to take care of ourselves. We can't wait for anybody," Sonia, an attractive Latina, said. "I have to get home to my mom and dad. They're old and they need me. I'm all they've got."

"Does anybody live near Ellisville," Nora asked.

"Where's that?"

"It's in Orange County, between Washingtonville and Newburgh."

"Newburgh, that's where I live," Sonia said excitedly. "You people can stay here if you want, but I'm going. Do you want to come with me?" she asked Nora.

The question came suddenly and it caught Nora unprepared as she looked into Sonia's face to gauge her seriousness, and then in the few seconds that followed, tried to extrapolate the facts as she knew them. The lawyer in her flipped though her mental checklist of PROS and CONS as though the case of leaving verses staying was on trial, and one of them was fighting for its life. Just the thought of venturing back outside sent a palpable fear through her that made staying seem the pragmatic choice. But soon, the weight of her family began to tip the scales, taking her fear and replacing it with an indomitable need to see them. "Yes," she said. "I'll go with you. My family's at home waiting for me...my children...my husband. I just hope what's ever happened here, didn't touch them."

"If you're heading in that direction, then I'm going with you. I live one county down from you in Rockland," Dale said. "It's better if we travel together, anyway. There's no telling what sort of kooks are on the loose out there...what with the police occupied, n'all. Who else wants to come with us?"

"I will," Laura said. "But I live even farther out. My home's in Poughkeepsie, up in Dutchess County. My commute has always been hard. But after twenty-two years, you sort of get used to it. Right after 9-11 what normally would've taken me two-and-a-half hours to get home, took eight hours. I sure hope it doesn't take that long this time."

"Okay...that's makes four. Anybody else coming?"

"I live up that way, too. I was gonna go it alone, but I'll go with you all," Miguel, an accountant for PricewaterhouseCoopers, said.

"Well then, let's go," Preston said, then standing to his feet.

A man sitting nearby with his back to them turned his head, "Wait...I'm coming, too. I've got some business up that way," he said, apparently having heard everything. He then stood and joined them as they proceeded toward the exit. Several dozen along the platform had apparently reached a similar conclusion and ventured out ahead of them. Many others, seeing the brisk exodus, prepared to leave as well. Of the hundreds who had taken shelter in the subway, roughly half chose to stay, apparently for safety's sake and no doubt believing help was soon to arrive.

Nora and her party followed the others through the turnstiles. As they went, their feet splashed through a great pool of ankle deep water. Created by a continuous flow that ran down the steps like a spillway, it came between them and the exit to the street. They ascended the steps, escorted by trepidation and dire curiosity. The sky was hued an unnatural gray and clouded over with threat. Nora could see the caps of buildings rising into view over the heads in front of her. As she neared street level, her heart began to race with anxiety over the shocking conditions that undoubtedly awaited them.

At that moment, a sudden, unmistakable rumble froze everyone in their steps; coming on like an angry growl that roared from the pit of their bellies. The ground, seconds later, began to tremble underfoot until it abruptly dropped out from beneath them. Nora, only five steps from breaking the surface, was tossed backward, but managed to stay on her feet as everything around her shook wildly. Unable to keep her balance any longer, or move forward, she dropped to the steps and braced herself for what she believed would be an inevitable stampede coming up from behind her. Instead, what she heard were frantic screams amplified by the walled subway cavern; upending her sensibilities with a horror unlike anything her mind could imagine.

That's when she looked behind her and saw the water level rapidly rising at several feet per second. And the hysterical rush of those trailing along the steps, desperate to escape before they were swallowed up by the deluge. All of them were slapping, grabbing and clawing with clumsy ferocity at anything in front of them, which included Nora. That she couldn't swim, and would undoubtedly drown, was not as frightening as the thought of staring down death's attempt for a second time.

The jarring tremors finally ceased, but the water behind her continued to rise. Nora, fearing there was little time to stand to her feet, began crawling up the slippery steps on hands and knees. More often than not, they would slide out from under her as if on an icy hill.

Suddenly, a flailing hand reached up from the flood and grabbed her by the ankle. Nora screamed the instant she felt its hold on her, followed by immediate panic as it tightened around with an unrelenting grip. She tried to pull herself up, struggling amid the harrowing cries. But every attempt at gaining ground was thwarted by the sheer weight of desperate hordes, fighting and clinging for dear life onto anything, and the unknown hand still firmly retaining its hold on her ankle.

Panic quickly turned into anger and a survival instinct of her own. She began to kick furiously with her free leg; stabbing at the arm with the long heel of her pump in an effort to extricate herself. Meanwhile, the water continued to rise, eventually submerging the determined arm and those unfortunate souls trapped behind it. The arm's hand, though, still hadn't let go. Nora could now feel the chilly water inching up her leg and the weight of death trying to pull her down beneath it.

Determined not to go under, Nora gritted her teeth for one last wrestle with the Grim Reaper when she suddenly felt an arm wrap around her waist. The same person reached down and pried loose the rigid hand from her ankle, then lifted her out the water with the help of Sonia who stood anxiously watching at street level.

By now, the water pressure had equalized and began to recede almost as quickly as it rose. It revealed a tangled and contorted mass of bodies collected in the shallow depths at the base of the stair.

"Oh my God, lady, are you alright?" Sonia asked, holding her steady by the arm.

Nora took hungry breaths as she stood off balance, her drenched hair sending the water down her face and into her mouth. "I think so. Was it you who saved me?"

"No. It wasn't me. It was him," Sonia said, pointing to the other side of Nora. "He ran down there and pulled you out."

Nora turned to face her rescuer. She recognized him as one of the members of their traveling party; the last person to join them. He was holding her other arm in a strong, supportive grip and stared attentively into her face while she collected herself.

"You had a pretty close call there, Miss. Are you sure you're alright?" he asked.

"Yes. I believe so," Nora said, her hands trembling from the ordeal. "Thank you for saving me. I tried to get free, but that...person...he wouldn't let go of me."

"Yes, I know. Self-preservation can be a son-of-a-gun. But you're okay now."

Nora looked down the subway entrance, then turned away horrified. "Yes, but those people down there. They all drowned. They're dead. What happened? Where did all that water come from?"

"Well...I'm only guessing, mind you...but since this subway tunnel takes a run under the East River into Brooklyn, I believe the first quake probably weakened the tunnel walls...and that last tremor, I guess, must've finished it off. We were lucky we left when we did."

"Yeah, very lucky...especially for me! I wouldn't have made it had it not been for you. Thank you, again."

"Not a problem. Are we ready to go?"

Nora looked over to see the rest of her party standing off to the side and staring aghast at all the devastation that surrounded them. She stepped off to join them, but stumbled, and then realized upon looking down that she only had one shoe. "I must've lost my other shoe down there."

"Don't worry. We can fix that," her rescuer said, and right away began scanning the immediate area. He released Nora's arm and walked over to the gutter where, among other things, a woman about Nora's size laid face down in debris; her skull clearly crushed. He knelt down, pulled off her sneakers, and then brought them over to Nora. "Here. I think these ought'a fit."

His kind act, though audaciously necessary, smacked of desecration in her mind. She accepted them with uneasiness, concerned over how many more ethical compromises she would have to make before this day was over. "Thank you...again," she said, kicking off her one shoe and slipping the new pair—dust covered, scuffed, and still hauntingly warm—onto her feet.

"You're quite welcome, Miss...uhhh..."

"Nora."

"Miss Nora," he said in earnest.

"No. Just Nora. And your name?"

"Taylor," he said.

"Are we done yet? Can we leave now?" Dale yelled over to them, seemingly unmoved by her near-death-experience. He stood alongside the others who, like himself, appeared eager to leave. "Y'know, the Federal Reserve Bank is only two blocks from here. This place is gonna be crawling with troops in no time. They need to protect all that gold bullion in there before there's a breach...and with all these people still running around down here, some innocent person's libel to get shot. Trust me...the feds don't play when it comes to their money. Therefore, I suggest we get going."

One look around and he got no arguments from anyone. The sights and sounds were as if someone had snatched them out of reality and dropped them onto the set of a horror movie. A cloudy haze of dust and smoke floated between everything. It colored the surroundings in a veil of gray that cast an eerie halo around the few light sources remaining. The tall office buildings that had towered proud and majestic over lower Manhattan now stood battered and disfigured. Their once gleaming facades now stood pock marked in shattered plates of glass, gaping for nearly their full length, and exposing their insides like week old road-kill.

Automobiles burned ferociously in the streets, sending up embers that ignited fields of debris. A great expanse of glass, papers, CD's, and every manner of litter stretched as far as the eye could see. Most shocking among the debris were the untold bodies, randomly spread and lying motionless while a procession of dazed and ashen-faced survivors maneuvered around them out of respect for the dead.

The strident wail of an air-raid siren sounded in the distance, and was quickly replaced by the rapid *whap, whap, whap* of police and National Guard choppers. Their pilots, hampered by poor visibility, approached dangerously low over the building rooftops. Unable to find anyplace safe to set down, they swept their flood lamps over the ground in a blinding blitz, and then hovered high over the street as dozens of heavily armed National Guardsmen fast-roped their way down to the surface.

Nearly every street was vehicle choked and impassable by anything short of a Bigfoot monster truck. Firefighters laden in heavy gear, and forced to leave their trucks behind, valiantly spread out on foot to attack the countless blazes before a full-scale conflagration erupted.

Meanwhile, search and rescue teams combed through the rubble alongside too few paramedics, and even fewer doctors who rushed out from the neighboring hospitals. The police, undermanned and ill-equipped, looked on like helpless cadets as scores of looters pillaged retail establishments with impunity. Most were seen walking away with items that would do them little good in a crisis.

With no explanation yet on the exact cause of the disaster, rumors and speculation ran rampant among the survivors.

Nora and her party walked north through the chaos along with a multitude of others heading in the same direction. She wished there was some way she could contact home, just to let everyone know that she was alright and doing her very best to get to them. But Dale's repeated checks of his phone confirmed communications were still out. Even if they did manage to get a cell tower functioning, she would need to borrow a cell phone. Her own phone and all her identification was sitting in her satchel, inside her desk drawer back in what was left of her office. She hated being empty handed and felt naked without a bag of some kind over her shoulder.

They approached a well-known clothing store where looters were busily trafficking in and out with their spoils. Taylor, who happened to be walking in front of the others, stopped just short of the stores' decimated entrance.

"Give me a few minutes. I'm going inside there to see what's what," he said.

"You mean you're going in there to steal something," Sonia said boldly.

"I'm not stealing. I'm surviving. Look around, lady—"

"Sonia. My name is Sonia."

"Okay then, Sonia. Look around. This entire area looks like a small nuke just went off in the center of it. In fact, it wouldn't surprise me if the whole city looks like this. I'm thinking we might have a long trek ahead of us. So I'm going in there to look for whatever I might need for later...supplies, maybe some food. If you're smart, you'll do the same."

Nora, though not thrilled with the idea of looting, couldn't deny the logic in Taylor's argument. She had already scaled down her expectations on how long it would take to get home; adjusting it from what she thought might take several hours to now taking possibly a day and a half. If so, then he was right to suggest they take a few provisions for the journey, and judging by the silence coming from the others, there seemed to be unanimous agreement. They decided to meet back outside in fifteen minutes. Taylor was the first to enter, followed by Nora, and then the others.

Once inside the dimly lit store, they were met with unintentional pushes and shoves from the looters rushing past them, and the shocking sight of bodies lying seemingly trampled on the floor. Bodies that after a closer look, turned out to be only smartly dressed mannequins that had fallen over. The looters ran hell-bent through the aisled racks of clothing; hastily grabbing up garments by the armful and then rushing for the exit. Nora, Sonia and Laura decided to stay together while the men went off to search individually. The lights would flicker off and on, raising fears that the current brownout would become a full-fledged blackout.

Nora knew exactly what she wanted. With little time to waste, she momentarily left Sonia and Laura and rushed for one of the racks that still had a few clothes hanging from it. She found herself standing in the men's section, but it clearly didn't matter to her as she searched through the assorted items and pulled out a large pair of blue denim trousers. Using the faint lighting as cover, she discreetly slipped the pants on underneath her skirt. She then unzipped the skirt, raised it up over her head and casually tossed it aside.

Finally free of that restricting garment, she began searching for any type of belt to keep her new, oversized pants from falling down. She found one hanging from a nearby accessories rack. Although its waist was twice the size of hers, she looped it through the jeans and, ignoring the buckle, tied it securely at the front.

By the time Nora got outside, Sonia and Laura were already out there waiting. Both had discarded their impractical high heels inside, in favor of sneakers. Preston and Miguel waited alongside them, but neither had found anything useful inside and stood there empty-handed. Dale showed up minutes later, also without anything to show for his efforts. That left Taylor as the only one of them still inside. While waiting for him, they used the time to properly introduce themselves and lament over their predicament.

It was several minutes later and Taylor still hadn't come out. Preston and Miguel were about to go back inside to look for him when they saw him finally exiting out the front door. He appeared to be limping and seemed out of breath as he came toward them.

"Are you alright? What took you so long? I looked around for you before I left, but when I didn't see you, I figured you were outside. Where were you?" Dale asked quizzically. "And did you find anything?"

"Whoa, so many questions. I'm okay...really. I was going through the back office hoping to find a flashlight or something, but it had already been trashed. On the way out, I tripped over something and banged my shin. I can walk it off, though. It's nothing serious."

Sonia appeared to study him closely as if dissecting his explanation. "Did it hit you in the face, too?" she asked suspiciously.

"What do mean?"

"I mean, you have a little mouse just under your right eye."

Taylor reached up and felt the space underneath his right eye and winced upon touching it. "Ouch! That's strange," he said, poking it disbelievingly. "I can't explain that. I guess I must've hit it somehow."

He then turned and looked down the street toward the direction they were to head in. "We should be on our way."

Taylor took the lead as they started out, at which point Miguel leaned over to Sonia. "Who appointed him leader?" he asked quietly in Spanish.

"I was wondering the same thing," she said.

Chapter 10

Once it was clear that the rock shower was over, Justin was back outside surveying the damage to their home, and the surrounding neighborhood. Blackened, golf ball sized rocks polka-dotted the landscape, covering the street and lawns like fallen leaves in autumn. Cars sat rock-pummeled to uselessness in driveways, while scattered fires raged wild; freely consuming homes and property only houses away from their own. The larger rocks wrought the most destruction, taking homes, already quake damaged and barely standing upright, and making them utterly unlivable.

Jennifer and Rachel had changed out of their swimsuits and came out to assist Justin. Together, they walked the entire perimeter of their home, carefully checking for danger signs such as smoldering fires in the lawn shrubs, and whether the roof was sagging. These were consequential details which they normally would not have given a second thought to. But now, after witnessing one neighbors flame ravaged house fall in on itself, seemed acutely obvious.

By all appearances, theirs and a few other homes nearby had escaped serious damage. Besides the ugly depressions marring the exterior, the two rock-holes in the roof, the one outside wall that was stripped down to its plywood sheathing, and the front windows now devoid of glass, the house was otherwise still habitable.

By now, the entire neighborhood's residents had gathered in the street; grieving in small, doleful groups, then moving from one to another as they tried to figure out what to do next. Among them were Ezra and Edna Weinstein who lived in the house right next door to theirs. Longtime residents in the community, Ezra had just recently sold his furniture business and had, before today, been comfortably settling into retirement. Sadly, their home did not fare well during the storm. It had fallen victim to a basketball-sized rock that crashed through the roof, upstairs bath, and dining room before coming to rest on the concrete slab floor of their basement.

Edna, wearing only a bathrobe and slippers, was distraught. Her eyes caught Jennifer's, and once locked on, drew them mutually toward one another like mother to child. Jennifer welled up with emotion at the sight of Edna so tearful on approach, and with arms affectionately opening in readiness to receive her young friend. It was the one thing she needed right then more than anything. As contact came nearer, she held back her own tears until the instant they touched, permitting a sob to burst forth at the exact moment of embrace. They held each other tight and cried until there was nothing left.

"Your mom and dad...they're not here?" Edna asked, stepping back to study the face of her longtime neighbor.

"No. They left early this morning. Dad drove Mom into work, and...well, I haven't heard from either of them. I did speak to Dad briefly on his cell phone, but that was before all of this happened. I didn't even say bye to him," Jennifer said, her eyes glistening with remembrance over her boorish behavior when she last spoke to him. "What if they're dead, Mrs. Weinstein...what if I never see them again? What am I going to do?" Her hands began to tremble with the likelihood, nearly tripping the flimsy wires that held her imagination in check.

"Keep it together, dear. We don't know that they were even affected by this. They might be trying to contact home right now, but aren't able to get through because the phone lines are down. Just wait. I'm sure they're okay."

"Does anybody know what happened?"

"No. Nobody knows. And with nothing working, we can't get any news. Some of the neighbors are planning to go into town to the high school...that is if it's still standing. That seems like the most logical place to go after a disaster like this...especially with so many families now homeless." Edna turned and looked painfully over at her house. "Ezra and I are going into town, too. Our home...it isn't safe to stay there." By now, Justin and Rachel had walked up and were standing alongside Jennifer. "You all should come with us. Fortunately, the Range Rover was in the garage and didn't get damaged. We're going back inside, just to collect a few things."

"We're ready to leave now," Justin said, subjectively speaking for them.

Jennifer looked over at Justin, unsure of how to respond to his presumptuous statement. She then turned and looked at their home; its superstructure not as sturdy, but still standing all the same. The thought of abandoning it as though it were an old car that had outlived its usefulness was an upsetting proposition. She felt it shouldn't be arrived at as casually as Justin implied, nor did she feel capable of even making such a decision. *It would be so much simpler if Mom and Dad were here,* she thought between lamenting. *That way, they'd be the ones to shoulder the decision, good or bad. And me and the others could simply follow along as always—in total disagreement if need be—but free of any responsibility.* "We're not sure what we're going to do right now, Mrs. Weinstein. We'll need to talk about it first."

"I understand. Your house isn't as bad off as ours, but it doesn't look like your car will be going anywhere," Mrs. Weinstein said after a glance over at Jennifer's thoroughly totaled Volkswagen. "Well, darling...make your decision quickly, 'cause Ezra and me aren't going to be here long. As soon as we gather up all our papers and grab some photos, we're leaving. If you do decide to come, meet us over by the garage in a few minutes, okay?" She then went back over to join her husband who was busy consoling a neighbor whose wife had been critically injured, and only minutes ago had died in his arms.

"We'll be there," Justin shouted, after which he turned and headed for home.

Rachel and Jennifer turned and followed behind him. "Jen, are we really going with them?"

"I'm not sure yet. Let's wait until we get inside."

Justin had already run up to his bedroom and came back down minutes later carrying a backpack, undoubtedly full of essentials he wanted to bring with him. Jennifer and Rachel were waiting at the foot of the stairs.

"What are you guys doing? Why aren't you getting ready to leave?" he asked.

"We need to talk. You can't decide for us what we're going to do," Rachel said.

"Don't tell me you two are thinking about staying. Maybe you haven't noticed, but our home is messed up. We got no electricity, and no windows. What could we possibly do in here...sit and stare at each other until it gets dark?"

"I'm not suggesting we stay, necessarily. We need to think about Mom and Dad. They're out there...probably trying their best to get to us. I'm thinking the least we could do is be here when they get home."

Justin, seemingly conflicted by the mention of his parents, shrugged his shoulders and then, cocking his head in annoyance, began an animated pace where he stood without saying a word. "Well," he said seconds later, "maybe somebody could tell them where we are. We could even leave a note on the front door saying we're at the high school. When they get there, either they'll see us, or we'll see them."

"And what if when we get to the school, it's not there anymore...the quake and the storm flattened it...then what? Where do we go then? And how are Mom and Dad going to find us? They'll be worried to death. We can't do that to them. In fact, the more I think about it, the more I'm convinced we're better off just staying put. I don't want us to miss them when they walk through that door."

"Me neither," Rachel added. "That makes it two against one."

"Hey, I don't recall anyone saying we were taking a vote. You guys can stay here. I'm going with Ezra and Edna."

"Come on...you don't really mean that. You wouldn't actually leave your two sisters here...all alone...after everything that's happened today. Y'know Dad would flip if he knew what you were about to do."

"Dad's not here right now, but if he were, I know he'd agree with me," Justin said angrily.

"But that's the point. Dad's *not* here and neither is Mom. If they were, then we would all leave here together. We go now...we don't know where we'll end up. You remember the news reports of how things were right after the cataclysm. Families were separated for weeks. People were searching high and low trying to locate a spouse, a parent...a brother or sister. It must've been awful. I don't want that to happen to us. We shouldn't go anywhere...not without Mom and Dad."

"There's one thing you haven't considered."

"What's that?" Jennifer asked.

Justin paused. "What if, well...they're—"

"Stop it, Justin," Rachel interrupted. "Don't even say it. They're coming home. Jennifer and I are staying. So if you wanna leave so bad...then leave. But if you do, you're a coward."

Jennifer said nothing as she waited for his usual, antagonizing comeback. She was also glad that Rachel kept silent since they both were well aware of Justin's tempestuous headiness when it came to her. He never could handle being abased by little sis, who this time managed to summarily slam his ego with a coup de grace closing critique. One that Jennifer knew could either infuriate him to obstinacy, or shame him into surrender.

He glared at both of them for a moment, his brow furrowed in likely contemplation of the grief he would get from his father if he did come home and find him not there, dutifully protecting his sisters. He then cut his eyes away in a slow, contemptuous roll as he turned his back to them and headed back up to his bedroom, peevishly dragging his backpack behind him. "I'm telling you, this is a mistake," he said, his figure fading into the dimness upstairs.

Jennifer and Rachel waited until he was gone, then looked at each other with apparent relief at the outcome. "Hooray," Rachel whispered softly under her breath and wearing a dry smirk. "Let's hear it for small victories, huh?"

"I wouldn't go cheering just yet. He's liable to leave anyway after he thinks about it long enough."

"I know, but at least we have him here for a little while. 'Cause honestly...I might've been right behind him if he did leave...no offense. 'Cause I ain't even trying to be alone in here with you. You ain't hardly any protection," she said, cutting her eyes away in a benign gesture, characteristic of her somewhat pampered status among the family.

"Yeah...okay, princess. Don't start getting cocky, now. Otherwise, you just might need Justin to protect you from me," Jennifer quipped. That said, they both seemed to relax in the moment; holding onto a fleeting reflection of the past before the surrounding fabric of devastation returned to steal it away.

***

Rachel walked into the living room and stood at the front window, her figure silhouetted in the frame where glass and exquisite draperies had been only hours earlier. There, she quietly looked out as she watched her neighbors along the cul-de-sac appreciatively pack themselves into the few vehicles available. Crying tears of sadness, they prepared to leave everything they had in the world behind. Mr. and Mrs. Weinstein had just pulled onto the street from their driveway and looked over to see her standing at the window. Ezra slowed the Range Rover in front of their house while Edna, sitting on the passenger side, arm gestured for her and the others to hurry along.

Rachel, however, simply raised her arm, waving it in wide left-to-right sweeps that unmistakably replied, "No," followed by shorter waves that signified to them a heartfelt goodbye. They returned her wave, and pulled off down the cul-de-sac, stopping a little ways ahead only to pick up another neighboring family before driving away. The few neighbors that had chosen to stay gradually dispersed, one after another until before long, the street in front of their home was completely deserted.

That only left the bleak, gray sky and the even darker billows, rising up from the remnants of their community like columns of angry twisters to focus one's gaze on. Rachel obliged its call and looked out over the landscape, taking in its ubiquitous transformation in one heartbreaking pan from end to end. That's when the sweeping silence suddenly settled in her ear, and with it came the harsh realization that they were now alone. She turned away from the window and headed for the noises coming from the kitchen where Jennifer was.

"Well, it looks like it's just us now," Rachel said as she entered, and there saw her big sister searching through a draw.

"Did everybody leave?" Jennifer asked without looking up.

"No, not everybody. A few stayed behind, but nobody on our street. What are you looking for?"

"I found a flashlight, but it needs batteries. I'm not sure what size, though. We're also gonna need some candles and matches."

"Well, if anybody has batteries, it's Justin. It wouldn't surprise me if everything in his room ran on double-A batteries...including him. And if I know him, he's probably got matches in there, too...and you know what I mean."

"Yeah...well, in any case, can you ask him if he's got anything up there we can use...or if he can think of anything, to come down and help us out. While you're doing that, I'm gonna see how much food we've got. Oh, by the way...do you know where Dad keeps that emergency radio he got for whenever there's a power failure?"

"If you mean the one that you just crank the handle, and doesn't need batteries, it's probably in his office. I'll go look for it after I get Justin."

✳✳✳

Jennifer gave up her search for batteries and walked over to the pantry that was their safe haven during the windstorm. She reached for the light switch out of habit again. Then catching her error the instant she flipped it, stood in the doorway staring curiously into the space as if she were seeing it for the first time. All she could make out in the dark was an assortment of canned goods and boxed dried goods that, *by themselves probably wouldn't make a fitting meal*, she thought. *But together, just might sustain us until Mom and Dad get home.*

On that hopeful thought, she grabbed two items from one of the shelves and carried them out into the slightly better light. Then repeated the chore until soon, the entire contents of the pantry crowded the island counter of their kitchen like the collective donations of a goodwill give-away. Next, she went over to the refrigerator. There, she hoped to find something left over from the restaurant leftovers Trent routinely brought home for their dinner.

Once opened, she found nothing except what she deemed to be a bunch of useless ingredients that combined together, wouldn't amount to anything. She did find inside the door a full half-gallon carton of milk which, judging from its coolness, would likely spoil if not drank within a couple of hours. Right above that were seven 12-ounce bottles of water. Looking at them, she immediately feared

Justin might help himself to a bottle whenever he wanted. So she took three and hid them under a cabinet—just in case.

Guardedly pleased with herself and her novice's effort at crisis management, Jennifer stepped back to assess the stockpiles likely unsavoriness when held up against their usual diet of burgers and pizza. Nevertheless, she was confident that they would only have to suffer through do-it-yourself food for no more than two days—three days at the most. In the meantime, she began sorting through the choices, picking up and putting down cans as if she were shopping for tonight's dinner.

Justin, back from his self-imposed exile, entered the kitchen carrying several batteries of varying sizes. He then carelessly dropped them onto the island between him and Jennifer. "Rachel said you needed batteries," he said as he watched two of them roll off the counter and onto the floor somewhere next to her.

"Do any of those fit that flashlight behind you?" she asked bluntly before picking up the two that fell and setting them down beside the others.

Justin turned, grabbed the flashlight, and unscrewed the cap. "You think you got enough food there?" he asked, gesturing toward the array of canned goods as he dropped three size-D batteries into the empty cylinder.

"Yeah, there's enough for a few days."

"Well, I think you're forgetting something."

Jennifer looked at him with a puzzled expression. "What are you talking about?"

"How exactly do you plan on getting those cans open?" Justin asked.

"With a can opener...how else?"

"As far as I know, the only can opener we have is an electric one."

Right then, whatever tempered satisfaction Jennifer felt from her accomplishment, was completely erased by Justin's melodramatic and seemingly delight filled newsflash. He switched on the flashlight and directed its beam onto several objects in the room, and then annoyingly into Jennifer's face. The introduction of more light in her face than she had seen in hours caused her to flinch as though she were being assaulted. Her adverse expression gradually changed into one of waning confidence and the awakening acceptance that—in spite of her exaggerated hopefulness—nothing was guaranteed.

Chapter 11

The survivors followed behind each other, their steps weighted by body aches and voracious hunger that combined to make the mile they had already traveled feel like twice that. Several of the torches that were carried among them had burned out, creating scattered pockets of virtual darkness. Only the far off glow of a few raised and sputtering flames provided the modest light they needed to carry them forward.

Trent was working on his second stick of gum, trying to ignore the absence of flavor in it as well as the sandy grit on his lips that somehow found its way into the morsel. He could feel it grinding disagreeably between his teeth whenever he tightened his jaw. The dryness in his mouth only added to the discomfort, consequently sucking nearly every bit of moisture out of the gum until it chewed like a balled-up wad of cardboard, and tasted even worse.

He walked sluggishly through the ravaged village street where a throng of like travelers followed in loose procession, guided by the backs of others who lumbered a few paces ahead. And who themselves did likewise in a blind march that relied solely on trust, and the presumed navigational skills of whoever was upfront. Trent tried to get his directional bearings under the scant light, closely surveying the remaining landmarks and tree lines. He hoped on a whim that it might jog a memory of an infrequent route he may have taken some time ago. But he could not recall ever driving home this way. And even if he had taken it at one time, anything familiar was now burnt to a cinder or totally unrecognizable.

After a while, the images along the roadsides all began to blend into each other like a seamless montage of identical murals, until he could not tell one street from the next. It thus made it impossible to know exactly where he was, or even what town he was in. Every so often, thoughts of his family would replace the escorting monotony; routinely plaguing him with concern that gradually ratcheted up his imagination until it swelled unchecked with dire scenarios.

The pungent air was possessed with the weight of dissolution; of incinerated wood, vegetation, plastic, metal and every manner of thing and flesh. It all incorporated into a toxic rain that painted every surface, and triggered scattered fits of dry coughing throughout the trekking survivors. Several had already donned makeshift masks pulled up tight over their noses to ease respiration. Consequently, every inhale was translated as a smudgy, wet spot on the cloth directly over their mouths.

Trent, short on available fabric for such a thing, had yet to fashion one for himself. But expected he might have to soon enough if the dust didn't stop falling. So far, he'd been ignoring the intense gripe in his stomach which had been building since after losing his breakfast some hours ago. Since that time, his mind kept jumping back to the Starburst candies in his pocket. But now, in spite of his hunger, thought it better to save them for such a time when the pangs were nearer to being unbearable rather than just tolerable.

There was scattered coughing all around him. But one woman in particular, walking just to his right, was coughing with such ferocity, that Trent could not help but turn and look at her, just to see for himself that she wasn't choking to death. Another woman alongside was attending to her. "Is she alright?" Trent asked.

"She seems to be," said the woman. "I think she's just sensitive to all the dust in the air. Fortunately, I'm a smoker. My lungs are used to taking in crap. How are you managing?"

Trent gave his throat a quick clear. "Not too bad, I suppose. I just hope it doesn't get any worse than this. I don't think my mouth could take much more. It's never felt this dry before. If there's no water up ahead, I'm not sure what we're going to do." Meanwhile, the woman being attended to continued to cough, as did several others around them in a seeming concert of raucous throat clearing. Her own cough sounded much like a course harrumph in search of attention.

That's when Trent reached into his pocket, pulled out a stick of gum and tore it in half. "Here, take this, it should help some," he said, then discreetly placing the half into the coughing woman's hand. "You're welcome to the other half if you'd like," he said to the other woman. She gladly accepted it.

Within seconds both women were chewing with the sort of enthusiasm generally reserved for a choice cut of meat. The action soon produced a meager amount of saliva that appeared to ease the one woman's hard coughing a bit.

"Thank you," she said between vigorous chews. "I don't think I've ever coughed that much in my entire life. This whole situation is just terrible. It's like a bad dream or something. Can you believe any of this?"

"I know. I wish it were just a dream, but then if it were, I'd have to be in some type of coma that I can't wake up from. And strangely enough, I would take that, over any of this. All I want to do right now is get to my family."

"And where's your family?"

"They're up in Ellisville...at least my kids are. My wife is in New York City. I haven't heard from her since I dropped her off this morning. Given everything that's happened today, I don't even know if New York City is still on the map."

"Well...I say now, more than ever, is a time for positive thinking. I make it a habit to recite affirmations daily, even though I have to admit, they never prepared me for anything like this. Still, they were all part of my daily therapy for fostering a positive mental attitude...y'know, like a coping mechanism." She paused as if expecting Trent and the other women to chime in with a similar view. Neither of them said a word. "Are either of you familiar with the 'Law of Attraction'?"

"No," Trent said, then looking to the other woman whose furrowed expression and subtle shoulder spasms preceded another cough in lieu of an answer.

"Well anyway, it says that our thoughts have an energy that attracts whatever it is we're thinking. You want to be reunited with your wife and children. Just ask the universe for it, visualize it happening, and be ready to receive it."

"What do you mean by, 'ask the universe'?"

"I mean the cosmos...the stars and planets. I know it sounds strange to some, but it works for me. You should give it a try."

Since it was fairly black out, there was no need for Trent to mask the incredulity he felt at the mere notion of such a thing. He had spent much of his life being a hard-line skeptic, avoiding anything even remotely associated with religion. For him, to now start ascribing his successes, failures, and every mundane occurrence in between to either a guiding object, a deity, or some vague celestial reference was tantamount to losing his mind. "I'll think about it," he said in a temperate tone, unwilling to expend the energy to argue his lifelong position with her. "I have to say, though, that it doesn't seem like the cosmos has been too kind to us as of late."

"Well, I've already pictured myself sitting at home with my husband and us polishing off a bottle of cabernet while we wait for this whole thing to pass. And I'm sure he's there doing likewise. I can't wait to see him."

"How far do you have to go?" Trent asked.

"Monroe Township...that's not too far from you, is it?"

"Yeah...It's about twenty or so miles before Ellisville. I've got a close friend and his family who live in Monroe. I sure hope they're alright."

"By the way, my name is Janet. And that's Constance."

"Hello, and thanks again for the gum," Constance said between chews that seemed to savor the tangy flavors still bursting from the morsel. "My throat feels a lot better. Well...maybe not a lot better...but at least I'm not coughing like a ten-pack-a-day smoker...no offense, Janet."

"None taken. I'd smoke a cigarette right now if my lighter hadn't died. And I'll have you know I'm down from four packs a day, to two packs a day, thank you very much."

"Good for you. I really mean that. Except now I'm not entirely certain what the worst fate is...death from lung cancer, or death from starvation, or some other unknown thing just waiting out there to kill us all. It's hard to conjure up anything positive with so much misery surrounding us, but I'm gonna try. I just hope 'the cosmos' is listening."

"Oh, don't you worry. She's listening," Janet said.

"If you say so," Constance replied with a hint of sarcasm. "Anyway, what's your name, mister?"

"Trent...and there's no need to thank me. I'm just glad I could help. In fact, I think we all might end up having to help each other at some point. Otherwise, we might not make it to our destinations. Do you live in Monroe, also?"

"No, but I'm heading in the same direction. I live in Elmwood Lake with my folks, or I should say they live with me. They lost their home last year, and I had to take them in. Fortunately, I've got the space, so it's not so bad. In fact, it's kind of great. The house gets cleaned, there's always dinner waiting for me when I get home, and they stay out of my way. I was almost wishing their house had been foreclosed sooner. Of course I don't really mean that."

"Of course, you don't," Trent said. "Are the two of you friends, or sisters or something?"

"Oh no, we never met each other before today. But I guess you could say we're becoming fast friends," Janet said, glancing over at Constance for confirmation.

"That's right. We women have to stick together out here. Take now, for instance. It's pitch black out here...we're walking down this wooded road alongside complete strangers, and I've not seen one policeman since before the explosion. If it wasn't for Janet, here, I'd be feeling very vulnerable right now." Her words were not comforting to Trent who immediately thought of Nora and whatever ordeal she might be facing right now.

"You need to stop thinking like you're a victim in-waiting. Think protection, ask for it and believe it...and we'll get through this."

"Janet, I appreciate what you're saying, but we're not on the same page with that...not yet, at least. I respect it, though. I just don't understand it."

"Fair enough," Janet said.

"What you said earlier, Trent...about people having to help each other if they're going to make it home, or wherever they're headed. That's so true. And after you said that, I was wondering. Since the three of us are heading in the same direction, we should stay together...form an alliance like in that reality TV show. We can kind of watch each other's back. What do you think?"

"I think that's a good suggestion. And I have to say, it also helps the time to pass quickly. No sense being alone if you don't have to. Let's hope that if there is a relief station up ahead, that they'll provide some type of transportation to get us home. Or else, we could be walking for several days."

Just as he had finished saying that, a commotion was stirring further up ahead; unseen, but felt by the three of them. They stood silent for a moment as did everyone else nearby, hoping to piece together the varied bits of muttering heard while they waited for the inevitable wave of information to reach them. It came suddenly, not in words but in irresistible sensations that triggered an instinctive need to run. For what and, from what, wasn't clear. Still, there was no denying the impulses they felt surging through their limbs.

The darkness made it impossible to see more than three feet ahead. Nevertheless, they immediately abandoned the road they were taking, made an abrupt change of direction, and began heading for the dense woods to their left. They entered in, hundreds of them at once; barely able to see, and relying mostly on the sounds each other made as they stumbled over the uneven terrain of rocks, and maneuvered through the tall trees. The trunks of some were still hot, and radiated with a vestigial amber glow, whereas others had rippling rings of fire still clinging to them.

Constance and Janet held hands through the maze so as not to lose each other, while Trent followed close behind so as not to lose them. He happened to look up for a moment and noticed, through the trees, a hazy glow emanating in the distance. Not the orange type of glow that had become so familiar, and that announced another fire somewhere, but a white glow like the type produced by a flood lamp. That same glow revealed a clearing up ahead that incidentally showed the way out of the woods. Upon seeing it, they all made a frantic dash in the direction of the glow until they eventually flooded out from the tree line like a horde of fans exiting a sports arena.

They continued running toward the glow along what only several hours ago had been a quaint residential street of single-family homes, now decimated and totally deserted. The source of the light they chased was still out of sight; obscured, but rising above the backdrop of silhouetted rooftops and peering through the naked trees limbs like a shimmering beacon of hope. They approached a corner and were about to make their turn down the adjoining street when they were startled by the fast approaching roar and oncoming headlights of a military Humvee. It tore through the fractured intersection right past them and on down the road without even stopping.

For all of them, it was the first sighting of help of any kind since the drama began. And presented the first reassuring sign that their government was still intact and busily attempting to reestablish some semblance of order. The sight of the Humvee, and the prospect of food, water, and rest was all it took to energize them. They started en masse after the vehicle, running after it like a mob of kids chasing down an ice cream truck. The fleet-footed among them were at the front of the pack, a few dozen strong and remained in hot pursuit. They followed the red taillights of the Humvee as it disappeared around the next turn.

By the time they reached the intersection, their curiosity was at a fever pitch; culminating into a near chaotic scene when the first few of them rounded the corner. Finally, there it was—a huge, brightly lit field which was the town's local park, hastily transformed into a National Guard relief station. It was roughly a block away from them and spanned the end of the street like a brilliant, jewel studded oasis.

They ran toward it on a second wind, some clapping and cheering as they went. While others walked with brisk anticipation and their lips faintly stretched into an eager smile of belated relief. Their inspired cheering was soon interrupted by the unmistakable sound of a helicopter approaching fast from behind them. Like a whirling dervish its blades whipped the air and everything in its gale as it flew right over their heads on a direct route toward the camp.

With help now within their sights, the weight of anxieties that had plagued them began to yield slightly to the exhaustion, hunger and varied injuries that raked their bodies. It compelled those who ran, to slow down and join the rest who walked.

Trent spat out the tasteless wad of gum he chewed and attempted a tender-throated swallow as though he were readying his palate for something more savory. He then shouldered his way past two people whose pace had slowed to an irksome crawl. All the while he stayed transfixed on the camps glow, rising in front of him and nearly filling his field of view until its aura appeared to dominate the sky. *What a glorious sight,* he thought to himself while envisioning the cool bottle of water that he was sure would greet them all upon entering. That would no doubt be followed by some type of sandwich of which he unabashedly planned to take two of.

As they gradually stepped out from the darkness and drew closer to the station, its light began to cloak them like a warm blanket. The brightness revealed their frazzled features to one another, and for some, as a shocking first time face-to-face with those who walked alongside them. A soldier standing near the command center spotted their ghostly approach in the distance and immediately trained his flashlight on them.

"Maybe now we'll finally get some answers. Someone there should be able to tell us what happened," Trent said to Janet and Constance who were walking next to him.

"As much as I'd like to know what actually happened, there's a part of me that doesn't want to. Whatever they tell us, it's probably not going to be the whole story. I'm sure it's going to be much worse," Constance said.

"I know things look pretty bad now, but remember, the cataclysm was bad, too...really bad. But we survived it. What makes you think it'll be different this time?"

"I don't know. Just a feeling, I guess."

"Well, I'm just glad we made it this far. I guess we can thank our lucky stars for that...huh, Janet?"

"Luck had nothing to do with it," she replied, instantly pointing her finger toward the sky while her face displayed a look that said, *I told you so.*

A white Costco table stood opened in the center of the floor, generously reflecting the harsh glow from the fluorescent lantern that sat atop it. Its light created a cast of shadows against the tent walls of the dozen or so officers and soldiers who gathered around. There, they listened with rapt attention as their commander received a briefing from his 42nd Infantry Division superiors.

Colonel Heath Jefferies of the Army National Guard, 27th Infantry Brigade, sat in a folding chair at the front of the table, his helmet off and resting next to the lantern. His face bore the sun-baked creases of a combat veteran and his eyes, the no-nonsense glare of a man in charge as he stared with intimidating seriousness at nothing in particular. He leaned forward resting his elbows against the table; one hand jotting down tactical information onto a pocket-sized notepad; the other, holding the corded microphone of his multiband team radio out in front of him; the press-to-talk button, released while he waited for an opening to speak.

His opportunity came on hearing the last word spoken to him. He acknowledged his marching orders with a compliant, "Yes, sir," and clipped the microphone back onto his gear. "Well, gentleman," he said, closing his notepad, then leaning back in the chair to address his men, "you all heard the General. We've got quite a mess on our hands. With so many battalions' still unaccounted for, or deployed elsewhere, rescue and recovery for this sector is going to be totally up to us…at least until the 10th Mountain Division gets here with supplies and extra hands. I don't need to remind you that Fort Drum is about three-hundred miles upstate from here. With the 42nd CAB already stretched thin from MEDEVAC and search and rescue missions into New York City, 10th Mountain may not get any air transport to us for some time. Having said that, let's keep our wits about us. I know what you all heard was pretty unsettling, but it's our job to maintain order and civility here. Do your grieving in private…not in front of the civilians. These people are scared enough. And they're hungry and tired. Plus we've got a lot of injured out there. Help out the local authorities where you can…don't bully them. We don't need to be throwing our weight around. Is that understood?"

Right then there was a pause where there should have been the typical knee-jerk, unanimous assent normally given a superior officer. This was one time where Heath didn't expect the gung-ho resound of, "yes, sir" to bounce off the canvas. In fact, given the startling revelations they were privy to, he almost expected to see tears welling up in a few of them. Especially from two of his officers who, between them, were only three years removed from the military academy, as well as those officers and enlisted personnel with wives and husbands back home.

Fortunately for them, their greenness and heartache were tempered by Heath's over twenty years of military service; his having seen combat in two Middle East conflicts of which he unflinchingly volunteered for multiple tours; and two failed marriages that only contributed to his, at times, insufferable demeanor. Their affirmative response was a few ticks late, but it came, nonetheless.

"Yes, sir," they said.

"Good. You all know what you need to do. Let's take care of business. You're dismissed."

Heath stood to his feet, grabbed his helmet, and waited for his men to file out from the tent. After which he donned his helmet, expelled a breath of inescapable duty, and then briskly walked out behind them. He was not looking forward to his next task.

Chapter 12

The flame from a candle softly flickered on the kitchen island amidst a clutter of canned and dry goods left over from Jennifer's earlier food hunt. There, a jar of peanut butter, opened at the top and with a butter knife sticking out of it, sat nearby. And next to an empty box of Ritz Crackers that had fallen over on its side. Faint rays of light covered the walls, and everything within reach of it, in fluctuating shades of brown that stopped short of the doorways where blackness resided. In the next room, Justin stood in front of the fireplace, stoking the flame with whatever he could find lying around the house.

"No...stop, Justin! You can't throw that in there," Rachel, sitting across from him, yelled out. She interrupted Justin just seconds before he could toss one of Trent's prized collections of Senegalese wooden masks into the fire.

"Why shouldn't I? Just about everything in here is trashed, and we need to keep this fire going. Besides, I can't stand these things. They're creepy."

"Yeah...but they're Dad's. And he's not going to like you using them for firewood."

"Well, Dad's not here...we are, thanks to you and Jennifer. So unless you plan on going outside tonight and looking for wood, I'm gonna use this," Justin said brusquely as he proceeded to toss one after another into the fire.

"Stop him, Jen," Rachel pitifully begged, and looking on as though she were watching a small piece of her dad going up in flames along with the masks.

"No...just leave him alone. I'm not up to dealing with him right now," Jennifer said, standing with her back to them over by the window. There, she stared disquietingly out into the pitch darkness of their backyard. "You and me...we'll go out tomorrow and look for some firewood.

"But Dad loves those things. We can't just sit here and let them burn."

"We can, and we will. It's not important. They're only wood.

Dad will understand."

"No...you don't understand. If we destroy it, it's almost as if we're saying—"

"Don't worry. Dad is coming home...and so is Mom. Be brave, okay? And just between you and me...those masks *are* a little creepy." Jennifer's intended humor fell deafly before Rachel who, overwrought with fear and worry, had been subtly rocking in place for the past hour. Every so often she would look disbelievingly around the room as if confirming yet again the blackness and isolation just beyond the walls. And then efficaciously close her eyes and begin humming a calming melody to chase away the monsters that haunted her imagination.

Jennifer walked over and sat next to Rachel. She wanted to put her arm around her and let the embrace assuage the trembles that had become so tormenting. But again hesitated, uncertain how her attempt at sibling affection would be received. That's when Rachel gently lowered her head onto her big sister's shoulder and started to weep.

Jennifer's head instinctively tilted to meet it. And though she tried not to cry with her, she could not ignore the visceral emotion building up in her belly, like a dreadful forewarning of unimaginable things to come. The crackle of the fire only added to the surreal prescience of the moment; its bright orange glow creating a rhythmical storm of undulating light that gave unwanted breadth to her worry. She reached for Rachel's hand and began patting it gently with her own. The contact was warm and soothing—a simple touch to reassure and quicken a weakening spirit—a touch that Jennifer was as much in need of as Rachel.

"I'm so scared, Jen...more than I've ever been in my life. This house...it's like a big, open cave. We have no protection, here...none. No glass in the windows. We barely have a door. Somebody could be out there watching us...waiting to hurt us. I really wish Mom and Dad were here."

"You have to relax, Rachel. You're imagining things that aren't so. Nobody's going to hurt us. You need to trust me. We'll be fine."

"I know it made sense for us to stay. We had to wait for them to come home. I'm just not sure that I have enough courage to wait it out."

Jennifer took a disheartening look around the room. The glassless windows—dark and devoid of life—stared back at her like black velvet in gilded picture frames. Meanwhile, the ambient sounds coming through it; the shrill howl of dogs in the distance, and the sadness mixed with rage laden in their cries; the unnerving noises of crickets and the like; chirping, squealing and creaking as if they were only inches away. And lastly, the vivid flame in the fireplace, no doubt raging as bright as a beacon along their deserted stretch of cul-de-sac to draw unwanted attention their way. It was all Jennifer could do not to get swept up in Rachel's hysteria. Nevertheless, she was beginning to wonder if Justin wasn't right, and that maybe they should have left there when they had the chance.

"Have you been able to pick up anything on the radio yet?" Rachel asked.

"No I haven't. I'll keep trying, though. The darn thing is so cheap. Dad couldn't have paid more than ten dollars for it. Either that or he won it in a raffle. It has power. I just can't find a signal. All I get is static, but then that's how it is up here in the boondocks. Unless you have a good antenna, it's hard to get any kind of signal." Jennifer knew the interference was likely more than the result of a poor antenna, but from something that was affecting the radio stations themselves. For now, she was content to leave the cover-excuse as is and not stir up Rachel who no doubt had already conjured up a plethora of dire scenarios to dwell on.

As they sat there together, Jennifer posed as a pillar of strength while a belated stillness came over Rachel. Her nervous rocking stopped and the tension in her neck relaxed, allowing her head and eyelids to grow heavy with the welcomed onset of sleep. Jennifer was relieved to see her at peace for the moment. She was about to slip out from under her and go see what Justin was up to when she was suddenly startled close to screaming by three firm knocks at their front door.

Awakened by the knocks, Rachel let out a yelp sounding gasp and in a nanosecond was sitting straight up in her chair. Justin bolted out from the kitchen and stood in the doorway. He held a half empty bottle of water in his hand and appeared both nervous and excited at the same time.

Three more knocks followed, this time heavier and more demanding than before. They looked at each other with wondering. *Could it really be Mom and Dad?* That's when Rachel jumped up and ran to the foyer; a ready smile about to burst across her face.

"Wait, Rachel," Jennifer insisted in a strained whisper and with Justin right on her heels. "Find out who it is. Don't—" But before she could finish her sentence, Rachel pulled open the door. She fully expected to see her mom and dad standing in front of her. But instead, a disappointed sigh fell from her lips upon seeing the strapping figure of Rafer Reynolds filling up the doorway, flashlight in hand.

A varsity football standout, and friend of Jennifer's since high school, Rafer was never able to fully win her affection, so instead, settled for her friendship which she freely offered in return for the same. Still, there was always a gray area in their relationship where his attentiveness seemed more than just casually accepted by her.

"Man, what are you doing here?" Justin asked with anger filling his disappointment.

"I walked over here just to see what the neighborhood looked like. Then I saw the firelight coming from your house," Rafer said as he stepped inside and then shut the door behind him. "What are you guys doing here? Why didn't you leave? Practically the whole neighborhood is deserted."

"We're waiting for Mom and Dad. We haven't heard from them since this morning," Jennifer said. "How about you...how are you doing? How's your mom?"

"I'm okay. No cuts or bruises. I can't say the same for the house...but it's still standing. I don't know for how long, though. I told my mom it might not be sturdy. But I can't get her to leave. 'Too many memories,' she said. You know how she can be. She wants to stay, so that means I have to stay, too."

"Always the good son," Jennifer said facetiously.

"Yep...the good son...that's me," Rafer replied with a lighthearted roll of his eyes and a hint of sarcasm in his voice. It was an inside reference that only the two of them privately shared. And, though he seemed to accept it with the innocence intended, he at times appeared to be growing weary of its use, as if it somehow implied him to be too soft-hearted. Or maybe the suggestion that he was incapable of saying no to his mother, which actually wasn't far from the truth. Still, he clearly resented any comparison to that of a mama's boy.

Jennifer bestowed him with the apt nickname about three-and-a-half years ago right after the disappearances. That's when, as he tells the story, both his parents were driving back home after a full day of shopping. His dad was behind the wheel and his mother was simply relaxing in the seat next to him. They were only minutes from home when his mother jumped suddenly upon noticing out her passenger side window, a car about to veer into theirs.

The passing seconds seemed to slow to a full minute as she sat frozen in her seat, and caught somewhere between panic and a shout while staring aghast at the impending collision; all the while bracing herself for what she was certain would be a nasty crash. She was about to scream out to her husband when she heard the high-pitched squeal of tires skidding across pavement, and then a loud crash directly in front of them. She turned in the direction of it, only to see that the car in front of them had come to a dead stop while the car she sat in was barreling toward it at highway speed.

The next thing she knew, a kaleidoscope of iridescent colors had filled the moment's blackness before she opened her eyes and caught the airbag deflating in her lap. She instantly turned for her husband, but to her shock, he wasn't there. His airbag had deployed and was deflating between the steering wheel and the car seat. The clothes he had worn mysteriously lay in a pile, like tossed laundry on the floor near the gas pedal.

She started screaming out his name and frantically looking in every direction that the cramped confines would allow her to move. And all the while, she was too pumped-up on adrenaline to feel the warm flow of blood from a lower extremity wound, and the immense weight of the dashboard that had severely crushed both her legs. She passed out soon after.

When she regained consciousness, Rafer was there to break the news to her about his dad—that there was no sign of him—that he seemed to have somehow vanished. That the doctors were only able to save one of her legs was paled by the devastating discovery that she was now a widow of sorts. With no proof of death, she was unable to collect on his life insurance policy. And with nobody else to tend to her, the responsibility for her day-to-day care fell squarely on Rafer's broad shoulders. He dropped out of college his freshman year, forfeiting his scholarship and dreams of football stardom, all for the sake of his mother. Just like a good son.

"Have you heard anything about what happened?"

"Nope...nothing. And we don't own a single radio that doesn't plug into the wall. My car was totaled during the storm, so I've got no radio there, either."

"We've been using my dad's hand crank radio. It works well enough. We just can't get a signal."

"What does it look like out there?" Rachel asked, fearfully curious.

"Dark and pretty scary. There are still some fires burning. They're just about out, though. And I saw a lot of people on the main road heading into town. Some of them are hurt really bad...broken bones, burns and cuts. I just hope there's a doctor there that can take care of them. If not, the nearest hospital is at least fifteen miles away. They'd never make it."

"Are you hungry...can we offer you anything?"

"Yeah...we got peanut butter and warm milk. But we're out of crackers. We had those for dinner," Justin said bluntly.

"No thanks. I had a can of soup earlier. I'm good."

"How much food do you have?" Jennifer asked.

"Some, but not a lot. It's water that we really need. We've got about two gallons left...that's all."

"We're not doing much better ourselves. I'm not certain what we'll do if we run out of water? Hopefully the power will be back on before that happens."

"I have an idea," Rafer said. "Well, separately we don't have much, but together we'd have a lot more. I think we should share our resources...water, food, candles. Plus, you have a radio. We don't have one. It makes sense."

"You're right. It does make sense. You and your mom can come and stay with us."

"I was thinking you guys might want to come over and stay at our house. Since I'm already here, I can help carry some of your things over. It's only about a twenty-minute walk."

"We would if we didn't have to wait for our parents. I can't have them come home and find nobody here."

"Oh...okay. I understand. You have to stay...of course," Rafer said concededly. "It would be kind of difficult to get my mother over here, anyway...even if I could get her to leave. Also, the streets between there and here are pretty messed up. Her wheelchair would never make it through. I'd end up having to carry her most of the way."

There wasn't much to say after that. It left them quiet for a moment and looking somberly at one another while the gravity of their situation sank deep; until all they could hear was the silence of the foyer against the crackle of wood burning in the fireplace, and the inner voices in their heads upholding the fears which even rational thinking could not abate.

Exacerbating their dismay was the absence of a feasible solution for their water problem. Its mere mention was like a stimulant, triggering unbearable attacks of thirst where there hadn't been any before. As they lamented the day's events, the sound of a distant explosion was suddenly heard through the windows; entering the space like a far off clap of thunder to shake them out from despair's grip.

"That might have been a propane tank explosion," Rafer said. "A neighbor of mine down the street...he had a small outdoor tank next to his house. It cracked in the quake and was leaking propane. After that, the rock storm must've ignited it. The whole thing blew. It took out three houses. I'm told the owner was inside at the time. Three of his neighbors were killed. Always keep your nose open for propane. If you smell it in the air, don't hang around. Get as far away as possible." His cautionary tale, though helpful, only brought more anxiety into the room as silence ensued and they commenced to flaring their nostrils like hounds sniffing for blood.

"I'd better get home now. I'm sure that explosion has got my mom all rattled," Rafer said as he reached for the door handle. "You guys be careful. I'll stop by again when I can." With that, he pulled open the door, switched on his flashlight, and stepped out into the night. Jennifer closed the door behind him and locked it straight away.

***

Rafer stood on the front stoop for a moment, apprehensive as he scanned a beam of light through the blackness that lay ahead of him. And then, mentally projecting himself onto his college gridiron, took another moment to summon up some courage before setting out for home. He was about to rush across their front lawn when he heard the door unlock behind him and felt the edge of it swing open. He looked back to see Jennifer poking her head out between the narrow space.

"Rafer...wait," she said.

"What is it?" he asked, turning and then heading toward her as she stepped out onto the stoop to meet him. They stood a respectable distance apart, the flashlight glowing up between them and illuminating their faces in unflattering shadows while the sentiments that linked them waited for the awkwardness to pass.

"Promise me you'll be careful. There's got to be a lot of hidden dangers out there. I can't imagine what your mother would do if something were to happen to you."

Normally Rafer wouldn't have questioned her concern, accepting it at face value like any good friend would have done. But the tenor of her words somehow sounded different; more tender and heartfelt, like the goodbye between two people who were bound by more than just their friendship. Whether she was afraid for his safety, or simply afraid for theirs with his leaving, there was no denying the sense that something about their dynamic had changed. He believed her coming out to look for him, said as much. But still, he had to be sure. Now that an opportunity presented itself, he couldn't let it pass without testing out his hunch. "And what about you?" he asked.

"What do you mean?"

"I mean...if something happened to me. What would you do?"

Jennifer looked up at him, perplexed, yet fully aware of what he was driving at while the question dangled uncomfortably in front of her. Then glancing down, "Well, I wouldn't like it for one thing," she said with a demure tilt of her head before looking back up at him. "We've known each other a long time. You're one of my closest friends. I wouldn't want to see anything happen to you."

"Are you saying you'd miss me?" Rafer asked as he looked into her eyes.

"Of course, I'd miss you. Now get out of here. And be careful."

A discernable grin curled the corner of Rafer's mouth as he started backing away from Jennifer. Like two parting ships out in the open sea, his gaze held onto hers until he could no longer distinguish it. He then turned and slowly departed; his figure swallowed up by the darkness, leaving only the spot from his flashlight to detect him by.

Jennifer stood and watched the erratically moving spot guide him along a featureless path, no doubt marked with numerous risks on which she cared not to dwell. The moment it disappeared, she turned and went back inside the house and into the family room. There, Justin stood in front of the fireplace indiscriminately tossing anything that would ignite into the blaze. Sitting not far from him and fiddling with the radio was Rachel, her posture shaped by a mood of impatience as each gentle nudge she gave the dial returned only static.

I don't understand why we can't pick up a single station, Jennifer thought while listening to the noise. *Either we're doing something wrong, or that radio just doesn't work.*

For a fleeting moment she visualized the devastation just outside their window possibly prevailing well beyond the boundaries she had imagined; to the extent of the power being out across the entire eastern seaboard. Its likelihood was more than the fragile threads of her optimism could withstand. Instead, she took a seat on the sofa's edge right across from them and there, focused her hearing on the sounds coming out of the radio. She hoped a concentrated effort might detect a faint word, a garbled sentence, or a lone note of music; anything to stem the interminable suspense that companioned their wait. But after a full minute, and one complete revolution of the tuning dial, not a single comprehensible sound was heard.

Rachel cursed the radio's monotone static signature before switching it off in disgust. She then stood up and started for the kitchen. But hesitated at the entrance; apparently too afraid to step inside the dimly lit space, and its eerily dark corners where the light from the one lone candle could not reach around. Frustrated, she came back into the room and took a seat; visibly annoyed, and no doubt troubled by the monsters she perceived in the dark that could turn her away from her own kitchen.

The radio's failure to work once again brought their plight to the forefront. Its reminder snatched the sturdiness out of Jennifer's limbs causing her to slouch into a dispirited recline against the sofa's back; her head cocked up and resting flush against the well-padded top as she stared blankly ahead. Behind her eyes were fear, vulnerability, and misery—everything but sleep—and a sullen resignation that this night might prove to be the longest of her life.

Chapter 13

T rent was steps away from entering the relief station and, much to his chagrin, found himself bathed in more light than he had seen since the start of his day that morning. He glanced around at the other survivors walking alongside him, and then down at himself and wondered if he looked as wretched to them as they did to him. Even though he knew there was good reason for their shabby appearance, it didn't help being caught underneath the glare of the lights; the lot of them trudging bravely forward with such a decrepit mien that, to the soldiers on watch, they must have resembled the approaching zombies from "The Walking Dead."

The thought of it, though somewhat humorous, did make him just a wee bit self-conscious. Enough so that he surreptitiously threw back his shoulders and evened out his stride. One of the soldiers en route pointed the way to the food rations tent. The nearness of it generated a flurry of excitement that drove them all hobbling in the direction of it like some wandering clan of dehydrated, half-starved Gypsies.

Along the cross street directly in front of the facility, Humvee's were being used to push the last of the abandoned cars off to the side, leaving a clear road for their much larger Medium Tactical Vehicles to maneuver through. The outpost itself consisted of several dozen tents arranged in a uniformed grid and established in what was determined as the largest and flattest, open area of the park—the town's little league baseball grounds. Its three concentric diamonds formed a single, massive outfield; expansive enough to accommodate the non-stop flood of survivors from the neighboring towns and villages who came there seeking refuge.

The entire facility was encircled by one dozen towable generators with mast secured floodlights raised high above everything. The resonant and unceasing drone of their diesel engines could easily be heard beneath the chatter of tens-of-hundreds of beleaguered voices begging for assistance.

Throughout their walk, Trent remained directly behind Constance and Janet, keeping himself within a few feet of them so as not to lose them the same way he lost the old man. Though after a while, he couldn't help but notice that for all of his watching of their backs, neither one of them, after the first sighting of the Humvee, even looked back to see if he was still with them.

It was Constance's suggestion that they travel together. Trent only agreed because he thought it to be beneficially expedient if they looked out for each other. But now, with the first leg of their journey behind them, he started to wonder if they hadn't decided to forsake him and the fledgling alliance formed, for the relative comfort and security found at the relief station. If so, he thought they should have at least let him know, rather than have him following behind them like some sort of ignorant lap dog.

Up until he'd met the old man, he hadn't thought much about the need for traveling companions. But since then, he had come to appreciate it as a necessary means by which to pass the time. And best of all, as a welcome diversion from the worry that consumed him regarding the fate of his family.

He thought Janet and Constance would be the ones to fill that role. But their perceived snub of him, and his possibly having to face what could be a long journey home, was troubling. He didn't want to travel alone. His pride, though, would not allow him to ask either of them if the plans had changed.

Instead, he started to break off from them, convinced that they reneged on their arrangement. At that moment, Janet suddenly looked behind her. Seeing him falling back, she reached around, grabbed his arm and pulled him up alongside the two of them. It was a benevolent gesture, just when he needed one, and a reassuring sign that at least for the time being—they were a team. He only hoped that somewhere, Nora and the children were as fortunate in their encounters with other survivors.

Chapter 14

The night sky above Manhattan was a startling, bleak void; absent of the perceivable depth that typified its grandeur. The famous skyline had been transformed into a seamless canvas of black; silhouetted against an orange glow like a sleeping city in the midst of an inferno. The headlights of abandoned vehicles created a misty fog of brightness that rose up to meet it, while at street level, a logjam of cars, buses and trucks blocked every road and intersection. The resultant effect was trails of red and white lights that stretched almost the entire length and width of the island. For the countless thousands who navigated the insidious maze of obstacles, they provided a lighted path through the devastation, if not a clear way out as yet.

Every so often a Coast Guard HH-60 Jayhawk would do a fly-by; their spotlights beaming down across the expansive exodus of screaming, bewildered, and injured survivors. Many of whom frenetically waved their arms in a desperate plea to be airlifted out of there. Innumerable fires, those that had not already burned themselves out, continued to rage out of control, causing vehicle fuel tanks in reach of the flames to ignite in ground shaking explosions.

National Guardsmen waded through the bedlam under a declaration of martial law, their wrists cocked on their resting M-4 Carbines and fingers poised on triggers. They were, if necessary, ready to shoot-on-sight looters, or anyone exhibiting the slightest sign of disorderliness. Whenever asked, not one of them knew for sure what had caused such destruction, or the extent of it beyond what their eyes could see.

Dust and ash continued to rain from the sky onto Nora and her party who found walking through the now blighted canyons of lower Manhattan, a slow and laborious ordeal. Block after narrow block was fraught with hazards. Still, they managed to cover almost four miles; half the distance they would have reached if this had been yesterday under a powder blue sky.

After much debate and some fierce insistence on Taylor's part, it was decided that Broadway would be the most sensible uptown route to take to the George Washington Bridge. Dale argued that the West Side Highway, which ran along the bank of the Hudson River, and on the very edge of the island would've been faster, more direct, and had an on-ramp that would give them much easier access to the bridge. Even though Dale was right on all counts, Taylor won out purely on the strength of his conviction and his seeming savvy in matters of urban survival.

He was especially adamant about their needing to stay along the safer confines of the city streets. Unlike the West side Highway which in the dead of night was too close to the river's edge for comfort, Broadway cut an angular path straight though Manhattan from end to end, dissecting the borough like an airport runway. It was there, among the burned out edifices where several hundred body-bags lay in standing water like fish washed ashore, and added to the rising death toll. And it was here in the ruins, as Taylor pointed out, where the strongest show of search and rescue efforts appeared to be devoted.

And to his reasoning, wherever there are search and rescue teams, there would have to be some sort of aid station, or crews of relief workers somewhere nearby handing out food and water. By now, they were all admittedly hungry and parched. And though it made sense at the time to follow Taylor, after several hours of walking, they had yet to come across anything that even remotely resembled an organized relief effort.

With almost forty blocks now behind them, they were coming up to 14th Street and Union Square where a small park sat nestled along the crossroads next to Greenwich Village. Normally a venue for street vendors, it now held court to a slew of malcontent survivors whose patience seemed to be reaching its boiling point. It was there that they also noticed a white glow rising up from the center of the commotion, its purpose obscured by the raucous uprising surrounding it. But still cutting into the darkness where the outside row of cars headlights were not bright enough to fill. Taylor, curious to see what lied at the center of it, crossed the street to investigate. Nora and the others followed grudgingly behind him.

They stopped short of following him into the simmering crowd and from there, watched as he proceeded to indelicately squeeze his way through whatever breaks in the throng his shoulder could introduce. He inched and nudged his way through until his back was swallowed up completely.

Nora looked on quizzically as a ripple of pushing and shoving seemed to emanate from the center of the crowd. It escalated quickly, like a spring wound too tight and only seconds from snapping, which it did eventually in a sudden, expletive laced scuffle. She held her breath and hoped that Taylor was not somehow caught in the middle of it—or more bothersome—was not the cause of it.

Nora always thought herself to be a good judge of character. Her prosecutorial lineage almost predisposed her to it. She had never met a client, colleague, or otherwise whom she could not sum up within the first few minutes of meeting them. Taylor, though, seemed to be the exception. He did not fit neatly into any of the archetypes she had held onto and used to assess her acquaintances by.

His enigmatic personality prevented her from getting an accurate read on him. One moment he seemed like the perfect gentleman, stalwart and a veritable picture of calm in the face of overwhelming odds. And the next minute, a brooding, self-opinionated loner who would just as soon make the trip solo, than be bothered with the likes of them. It was either a cunningly deliberate ploy to keep people guessing about him, or a behavioral quirk that needed just the right catastrophe to show off its upside.

All the same, he seemed to have taken a liking to her. Never once did he assail her with the petulant side that he at times displayed to the others. Even his suggestions, shrewd and reasonable though they were, usually came out sounding more like instructions, much to the annoyance of the others. But having already earned most of their trust, there was little disagreement among them regarding his leadership.

Sonia, on the other hand, did not mind expressing her displeasure at his penchant for bossiness. Every comment by him, no matter how innocuous, was generally followed by a not so subtle blow of exasperation, or a caustic statement of contradiction made into the air, but never at him directly. He, in turn, would answer the air back in defense of himself, and without so much as a glance over in acknowledgement of her.

Where Sonia was a tendentious critic who was careful not to push the envelope with him, Dale, the investment banker, was much less so. His condescending personality had become a thorn in everyone's side, Taylor's in particular. Dale would routinely take him to task on every decision, setting off a heated exchange between them. From the very start of their walk, Dale was finding one reason or another to complain about something. Not surprisingly, he was not well regarded among the rest of the group.

Whatever animosity was brewing between the two of them clearly was not going to end well. Nora only hoped that it would not come to a head right in front of her. Taylor may not have been an Eagle Scout, but he was getting her closer to home. Because of that, she wanted to believe that somewhere beneath the layers of gruffness there existed a misunderstood man of virtue. She then went on to hope that he wouldn't prove her wrong.

Before long, the scuffle occurring in front of them quickly escalated into a full-fledged mêlée. Elbows and fists began flying with reckless intent, regardless of which sex they came in contact with. Nora moved back to avoid getting caught up in the fracas. That's when several gunshots rang out, crisp and rapid, and sounding much like the explosive backfire from an old jalopy. Their echo was still bouncing off the surrounding buildings as the mob immediately fell silent and steady with attention.

"The next bullet is gonna hit the first person who moves," a National Guardsman in full combat gear yelled out as he strode up from behind the pack. He was flanked by four other soldiers, their heads cocked against raised M-1's which they held trained on their choice of random targets standing before them. "You've all got five minutes to clear this area. I don't care where you go, just don't hang around here. It's best to keep moving. If you can...try to make it up to Central Park. I'm told they've set up a refugee camp there."

"What about food? We're all hungry and thirsty," someone shouted from within the horde.

"I'm sure they'll have food and water. They should also have medical attention there if you need it."

With his answer came a flood of more vociferous questions, all at once and sounding like an angry town hall meeting. He managed to grab one from out of the babble.

"Do you have any word on what happened? Did we have an earthquake?" someone asked.

"I don't know. But if there's anyone that does know, I'm sure they'll be up at the camp. That's where you need to go. Okay, everyone...I want you all to disperse...right now." His voice, though still possessed with the sternness of authority, now contained a smidgen less threat than before as he watched the gathering disband. Nora and her party stood far enough back that they could not be confused with those in the mob. Nevertheless, they knew they had to move from there as instructed.

"Let's get out of here before one of those knuckleheads over there shoots us in the back," Dale said anxiously.

Laura walked slowly behind him, her head turning back repeatedly to peer into the dispersing mob. "What about Taylor? Are we just going to leave him?" she asked.

"Hell yeah, why not? We don't need him. Who doesn't know how to get to Central Park from here?"

"That's not the point. We should stay together."

"Frankly, I'm not gonna miss him," Sonia said, walking off to catch up to Dale.

"C'mon, guys. You have to admit...the man was right. He said all along that we should stay on Broadway. And sure enough, Broadway takes us right to Central Park...to food and water. I say we should wait for him."

"Well, you can wait here if you want, but me and Sonia are going on ahead. Isn't that right, Sonia?" Dale asked confidently.

***

Not bothering to answer, Sonia walked up alongside him and together they started up Broadway. They had not gotten more than three steps when a light skirmish suddenly erupted only feet away from them. Two men, apparently still riled over the earlier fracas decided to continue their brawl. Startled, both Sonia and Dale stopped in their tracks and looked on. Those nearby, intervened, likely trying to settle things before the soldiers caught sight of it and started firing their weapons.

Sonia, wanting to stay clear of the conflict, started to walk a wide path around them. She fully expected to see Dale right behind her, but when she turned to look for him, he wasn't there.

After a few seconds of searching, she spotted him standing nervously in the doorway of a nearby building, his back to the wall and looking out onto the scene. It was at that moment, seeing him cowering in the doorway like a frightened Chihuahua, that Sonia started to have second thoughts about their traveling together.

The streets of New York City, even under the most controlled conditions, can still be a perilous place for a single woman. She believed herself to be uniquely qualified to know this fact better than anyone. From the moment Sonia was old enough to wear high heels, she had been accosted by male admirers more times than she cared to recall. The exquisite features of her face, together with her comely proportions more often than not turned a simple after-work walk to the subway station into a daring escape from New York. And now, with the streets about as safe as an unguarded prison yard, she knew the odds of her being assaulted would have to be off the charts.

As the crowd started to thin, she stretched her neck out and determinedly peered around them to see if Nora and the others were still waiting where she had left them. Though difficult to make out at first under the scant light, she did glimpse their familiar attire, standing together a short ways down the block, and in seeming vigil at the side of a building. Apparently, they were still trying to locate Taylor.

She truly detested Taylor's demeanor. But, rejoining them did mean she would at least have a degree of protection that presumably would be absent in Dale's company. The scuffle didn't last long and was quickly taken in hand without any shots being fired. That's when Dale found his courage and walked over to where Sonia was standing.

"Wow, that was close...huh?" he said with wide-eyed indignity. "These people out here are crazy. They're ready to kill each other over the slightest thing. From here on, we'd better stay close."

"*We're*...not going to do anything. You're on your own," Sonia said. "I'm going back to join the others. I'll feel a lot safer traveling with them." She then turned to leave.

"Wait a minute. What's that supposed to mean."

She turned back to him and with a slight smirk, looked him incredulously in the face. His eyes reeked of cowardice and shame as he looked with a hint of confirmation into hers. "I think you already know the answer to that," Sonia said. She then turned away and walked off, leaving him standing there in the crowd.

***

Roughly twenty minutes had passed since they had last seen Taylor. They were growing restless in their wait and increasingly irritated by their presumed obligation to have to do so. There were still a good number of people milling about in front of them; their features draped in a near uniformed shade of dust that made one from another practically indistinguishable from a distance.

Laura happened to spot Sonia weaving through them and mirrored her approach as she came toward her.

"What happened...I thought you were leaving with Dale," she asked.

"I always suspected Dale was full of it. Now I know for sure. He's a wimp. Definitely not the person you want to get caught in a dark alley with. I'm staying with you guys."

Preston stood not far from them, his arms folded across his chest and looking out toward the avenue as his feet moved an antsy step in place from side to side. "I'm done with this. I think it's time we moved on," he said firmly. "We did the decent thing...we waited. That's more than a lot of people would've done. But clearly he's either badly hurt, and we can't see him...or he's left without us. I don't know about you all, but I'm thinking it's the latter."

Nora, still feeling a degree of faithfulness, wasn't convinced and was quick to defend him. "That doesn't make sense. Why would he come this far with us, just to leave us?" she said, perplexed by his rush to judgment. "He could've done that anytime he wanted...and without using this commotion as a ruse to sneak away."

Just as she said that, an indistinct figure emerged from out the crowd and started toward her. She caught its approach from the corner of her eye and immediately turned to face it. They were all looking toward it, now; surprised as a puffy faced and bruised Taylor started coming into view. He walked right up to Nora.

"What happened to you? We've been waiting here for it seems like almost half'n hour," she said.

"Yeah, ummm...I'm sorry about that. But you saw what happened. They started fighting. I tried to get out, but I couldn't. And I just got caught up in it. That's all," Taylor said matter-of-factly.

"Well, what was the fight about? Who started it?" Sonia asked in a rare moment of confrontation.

Taylor didn't look at her, choosing to direct his answers at Nora. "Oh, you know...pushing...shoving. Sooner or later someone's gonna throw a punch. It was wild in there, but I made sure I gave as good as I got."

"What were they fighting over?"

"I'm thinking a military helicopter must've flown in and dropped off some provisions. Some volunteers were distributing them when, I guess, they ran out. Things must've got out of control from there. In all the ruckus somebody must've dropped this." He reached into his pocket, pulled out a hard, air-tight sealed, palm sized square of foil and held it up in front of Nora. The front of it read, "EMERGENCY FOOD RATION BAR – 400 CALORIES." "I don't know what's in it. Hopefully, it doesn't taste like sawdust."

"At least you've got something to eat. The rest of us need food, too," Preston said angrily. "By now, we could've been so many blocks closer to Central Park. But instead, we were wasting time standing here waiting while you ran off to play ultimate fighter. I still don't understand what took you so long. They broke that fight up almost twenty minutes ago."

Taylor looked around at their faces, all full of contention and poised with rightful curiosity. Behind him, the crowd had dispersed and appeared to be heading north toward Central Park. He shoved the ration bar back into his pocket, stepped back from Nora, raised his hands and began brushing the accumulated dust off his shirt. "This dust is irritating, isn't it? It just won't stop," he said as his hands then moved up to his head and began vigorously sweeping his hair. "I'd like to know where it's all coming from. But really...I like looking for things...y'know...stuff we can use. I was in that store right over there." He pointed to a thoroughly looted retail establishment just up the street from where they were standing. "But I couldn't find anything useful. I didn't realize how long I was in there." Once he finished cleaning himself up, he directed a half-hearted smile at them. "Thanks for waiting for me. I'm sure a couple of you must've wanted to leave."

On hearing that, Sonia turned away in a huff, cutting her eyes from him in the process as she walked off a short distance and stood next to what was left of a newspaper stand.

"You realize this makes the second time today we've had to wait for you. The next time we may not be so forgiving," Laura said.

"Understood," Taylor replied.

"Hey, haven't we wasted enough time here. Let's go...c'mon," Preston insisted, then stood and waited for someone to make the first move. Taylor stepped off without hesitation and assumed a lead position that they all, for the most part, had grown acceptingly comfortable with.

They entered into the northern flow of survivors and coalesced into an itinerant band of wayfaring strangers all heading up Broadway toward Central Park. Laura walked wearily alongside Preston. Nora, Sonia, and Miguel walked only steps behind them and alongside each other. Meanwhile, a few yards in back of them and bringing up the rear walked Dale who, without any comment or invitation, had quietly rejoined the group.

Chapter 15

onklin Road was a quiet, secluded street nestled within the country-esque woodlands of Bingham, New York. Rolling hills created a breathtaking ascent up its modest incline; rising along a winding path that neatly snaked through the affluent subdivision of Windermere Estates. There, stately homes, set on half-acre lots offered a passing motorist a brief glimpse into the conspicuous lifestyles of the other half. Each home was 6000-square-feet on average, and veneered with exquisite stone, wood or stuccowork that bespoke the status of their inhabitants. A German made automobile, or some other pricey exotic, left their expensive marks on stone-paved driveways made especially for them.

One house in particular, possessed of similar trappings, stood proudly overlooking the gabled rooftops of homes further down the hill. In the driveway sat a shiny red Porsche 911 Carrera, polished to a mirror finish and waiting outside one of the doors to a three-car garage. From there, a flagstone walkway led to a solid oak double-door front entrance, ornately etched and crowned by a great arched window. Behind its glass, a grand foyer welcomed, and was accented by a sweeping staircase that hugged the contour of the wall like custom window dressing. The room to the right of it was without any furnishings, as was the room to the left and the gourmet kitchen.

In fact, every room in the house contained not a single piece of furniture, with the exception of one.

Inside the largest of the five bedrooms on the second level, a lone queen-sized mattress lay in the middle of the floor. A mess of bedding covered the top of it while all around, empty beer bottles, soda cans and Chinese take-out cartons stood like toy soldiers on sentry duty. Sitting in a chair directly across from it all was Dale.

Clad only in a pair of boxers and a T-shirt, he sat eagerly forward in front of a collapsible table and facing three computer monitors. One monitor displayed several stock charts, all of which appeared to be fixed in a precipitous plunge. Another monitor displayed a quote tracker containing stock symbols and their current bids in real-time. Within the stock charts, each dollar amount showed as a red loss with not a single green gain to be seen. The last monitor was tuned to CNN.

He watched with keen interest as all the charts graphs continue to drop and their corresponding bids plummet to record lows. A giddy smile seized his face as he split his attention between the two monitors and a breaking news event unfolding on the third.

We will be continuing with our coverage of this breaking news story throughout the day. In case you're just joining us, approximately thirty minutes ago...at 6:32 AM, Pacific Standard Time...a major earthquake measuring 12.7, the largest ever recorded, struck in the pacific northwest. Its epicenter was located fifty miles off the coast of Vancouver, British Columbia somewhere along the Cascadia fault. It's believed to have triggered California's San Andreas Fault...as thirteen minutes later...a second major quake measuring 10.9 struck the city of Santa Ana, setting off multiple quakes of 10-plus magnitudes along the entire fault line. The quakes, which occurred only minutes apart from each other, began cascading south along the fault, ending in San Bernardino...a distance of almost 500 miles, and only sixty miles from Los Angeles. Reports are pouring in from our local affiliate stations describing scenes of suffering and destruction on an unprecedented scale. There have already been several aftershocks, many causing buildings that were once thought to be earthquake proof to topple over like toy structures. Tsunami warnings have been issued for the entire Pacific Rim, forcing a massive evacuation effort effecting forty-two coastal and island nations. The western half of the United States is currently on high alert in preparation for any volcanic activity that may arise as a result of this catastrophic disaster. California is the most populous state in the country, with almost thirty-seven-million residents calling it home. Many are wondering if this is in fact "the big one" that seismologists have been warning us about for years. Conservative estimates speculate that the number of deaths may well reach into the millions.

While the rest of the world no doubt staggered in mournful observance over the horrific events of this day; Dale appeared not at all surprised. In fact—he expected it months ago. Twelve months earlier, mired in a swamp of bad investments, low-performing stock trades, and excessive gambling woes, he was only weeks away from losing everything.

He confided in a close colleague from South America who, in the midst of a current bear market, was having remarkable success picking stocks. He asked him what his secret was. His friend then referred him to an acquaintance living in the Peruvian Amazon whom he credited with much of his success.

He instructed Dale to get to Manu Province in the jungles of Madre de Dios, Peru. From there, he's to find his way to the district of Huaypetue located in the heart of the Amazon and ask for a curanderos named Cayo; that he alone would be able to unlock the secrets. And all for a small fee, which would likely amount to nothing more than pocket change for Dale. When asked what curanderos meant, his friend replied, "shaman."

Dale could think of a dozen things he would rather be doing other than jetting off to Peru at the crack of dawn. But he was desperate, and willing to try anything if it meant a change in his fortunes. *If nothing else, at least the time away from the desk might do me some good,* he thought as he sat in his cramped economy class seat awaiting takeoff.

Twenty-four hours later he was touching down onto the tarmac of Cuzco Airport. It was surprisingly warm and temperate, not hot like he would have expected for a country so close to the equator. After checking into his hotel room, and enlisting the services of a translator for the day, he arrived at a small village in Huaypetue where he was told Cayo could be found.

He was directed through a labyrinth of rainforest flora into a clearing where stood a ramshackle structure of weathered wood. It was covered by a grass roof that no doubt repelled the seasonal rains better than any tarp. And there, sitting prominently out front under its canopy was a gentle-looking man of small stature. Judging from the getup he wore, and the solitude he enjoyed, it was a safe bet that this was Cayo, the shaman.

As Dale approached, it was as though Cayo were expecting him. His face, smooth and brown, showed no hint of surprise, while on his head was a fauna of colorful feathers that conjured images of the Indian medicine man in Hollywood westerns. An elaborate collection of assorted shells and sundry items hung from around his neck, down his torso.

The translator proceeded to communicate Dale's request leading to a baffling exchange in their native language, Quechua. When relayed through his translator that "he shouldn't expect something for nothing," Dale reached into his pocket, pulled out a fifty-dollar bill, and handed it to the shaman. He accepted it with a quick snatch and immediately tucked it into his shirt pocket like someone who had more than a passing familiarity with President Grant's portrait. He then rose to his feet, his necklace of shells rattling with every move he made. He uttered a few more words in Quechua, then turned and went inside the hut.

"Come," he said loudly, and with confident mastery of his simple monosyllabic English. Dale followed him inside, glancing back at his translator who seemed to ignore him, and knew better to stay outside. Upon entering, he immediately felt an eerie sensation; a brush against his shirt as if someone, or something, had stepped between the two of them. There were no windows, yet he could feel a gentle breeze blowing from inside. He looked up expecting to see a ceiling fan, but there wasn't one. The only light in the room came in through the open door behind him. On the walls he could faintly see the outlines of masks and other paraphernalia that the shaman had at his disposal.

"Sit," the old man said, pointing to a spot on the floor next to a wall, and having likely exhausted the limits of his English. Dale looked down at the spot which appeared to have the telltale wear of others who had come before him. He did as he was instructed, though; nervously wondering in the semi-dark quarters what sort of ritual was about to take place here that required this level of secrecy.

The shaman then stepped back outside, leaving Dale there to further ponder what inescapable mess he might be getting himself into. Sitting there alone, he looked around at the walls of the hut and strained to make out the mysterious objects hanging from them. He was tempted to get up and examine them more closely; maybe even steal one as a souvenir before the shaman returned, but was discouraged from doing so by an undeniable sense that he was not really alone in there.

A cool chill suddenly invaded the space where he sat, lasting all of a few seconds, but long enough to raise gooseflesh and his fright meter, significantly. At that moment, his first instinct was to get up and get the heck out of there. But he resisted the urge, emboldened by an insatiable need for wealth that, for him, was more powerful than his fear of the unknown.

Stop it. Now is not the time to be having second thoughts. In for a penny...in for a pound, he reasoned as the thought of his declining net worth sustained his resolve to see it through.

When Cayo finally returned, almost an hour had passed. He was carrying a cup in his hand which he held out for Dale to take. "You drink," he said, pushing it at him with an insistent voice.

"What is it?" Dale asked.

Cayo kept pushing the cup toward his face. "Drink, drink...ayahuasca. You drink."

"What's ayahuasca?" Dale looked at the cup, then at Cayo, then back at the cup again with a sigh of resignation before reluctantly reaching up to take it. Unable to clearly make out its color or consistency, he held it up to his nose and sniffed. The smell was overpowering; pungent and reeking like regurgitated leaves. Having already come this far, he was not about to turn tail and run. Dale raised the cup to his mouth, took a deep breath in audacious preparation, and drank the warm concoction in one fell gulp. The taste was sweeter than he had anticipated, but still quite nasty going down.

"You sit," Cayo said before turning to leave. As he left, he pulled a door shut behind him, subjecting Dale to total darkness. His face was still a grimace from the lingering taste that at least acted as a distraction from the darkness and isolation of the moment. He hoped that he wouldn't suddenly become ill and interrupt the ritual with an unseemly bathroom break right there on the floor. Fortunately, there were no immediate adverse effects from the strange brew—leaving him to wonder—*now what*? There was no telling how much time had passed, but "*now what*" was about to show itself as he rested his back against the wall and closed his eyes.

Within minutes of his dropping his head back, a sense of wellbeing began to slowly envelope him; as if the weight of concerns that had brought him there were suddenly lifted off of his shoulders. He luxuriated in the sensations curative effects, hoping to stretch it out for as long as he could. Before long, intoxicating waves of tranquility were soothing him like pleasant sunshine against his face. His physical self may have been in a dark hut in the middle of the jungle, but his spirit felt as though he had left that part of him behind and was now one with the universe.

As he basked in the newness of transcendentalism, flashes of light suddenly appeared on the blank screen behind his eyelids; dozens at a time growing bolder and more intense the longer he continued to gaze upon them. They then exploded in ultra-vivid shades of saturated hues that perfectly complimented the other sensations exciting him. This was no typical high, he thought lucidly, but more an aberration of joy that would rewrite everything he thought he knew about the states of euphoria.

For the next few minutes, Dale was in the throes of a mind-bending light show like nothing he had ever experienced. If he could, he would be happy to spend the rest of his life consumed by the light; even as the scene started to transition, and he began to see images within the color bursts.

They were of people and faces unfamiliar to him; of twisted bodies, raging fires, and cities laid waste. And with them came the voices; bouncing off the walls to surround him with awful screams and unimaginable agony. Yet he felt safe in his cocoon of ecstasy; far removed from the scenes of havoc that were being presented to him. The images continued to bombard him, one after another as he watched in a dream, or actuality—he could no longer tell the difference.

***

His South America trip now a year behind him, Dale sat squarely in front of his three monitors, transfixed on the spiraling downward bids. He was calculating the odds of probability for the opportune moment to place his buy order.

Weeks after his return home from Peru, he was still no closer to solving his debt crisis. Everything about his life was just as he had left it—in a dismal state, and on the verge of financial ruin.

In the Amazon jungle he had undergone a consciousness altering experience. And even though he found it enlightening and life affirming, he wasn't sure what to do with it. He would later come to learn that the psychotropic effects of ayahuasca were different for every participant—that no vision is the same—and what works for one, may not work for another. So he kept his to himself until he could make sense of it all.

For him, that revelation came one afternoon while following the stock ticker. Among the myriad symbols that scrolled in caption on the screen, one in particular leapt out at him. He recalled seeing it in his vision, clear as day; that, along with palm trees, mountain ranges, and cars—thousands of cars all completely totaled in a massive pileup. That's when he made the connection and instantly fell back in his seat upon speculating the odds. It was a long shot—a fool's bet, at most; fraught with complications, and enormously risky—but at this point, he had nothing to lose, and possibly the world to gain.

Short selling involves the sale of stocks that the trader doesn't own, but has borrowed, to be paid for at a later date. When the stocks are sold, the proceeds are credited to the trader's account. If the stock price drops, the trader, upon his buying them back, will have hit the jackpot. If the price rises, the trader will be forced to buy them back at a huge loss, and with money he never had to begin with.

Eight months ago, Dale quietly began short selling California based, investor-owned utilities; gas and electric; phone company; cable television, and transportation—those companies whose stock prices he believed would be most impacted by a catastrophic event. The cars, palm trees and mountain ranges from memory pointed to only one logical location. Dale was betting the farm that he had seen an earthquake in his vision, and that it was bound to strike California in the coming months.

As Dale continued to watch the stocks plummet, he was already wealthy beyond his wildest dreams. The untold suffering, the devastation, the countless dead, and the economic impact on the nation were of no importance to him. Whatever compassion he had, he traded it all away with one click of his mouse.

Chapter 16

A stagnant mist seemed to sit in the air that hung over the command center. Every so often, someone could be seen fanning their hands out in front of them to escape the powdery haze; or sliding them in a repeated sweep across their bodies to clear away in futility another persistent layer of dust. Its residue lay an inch thick atop the tents that dotted the grounds and served as temporary shelters for those fortunate enough to find space in them.

Signs were staked into the ground along different paths throughout, pointing the way to essential services and provisions. The largest tent, and bearing the Red Cross symbol, was the field hospital. Inside, a complete trauma unit tended to the overflow of critically injured. While outside, the less-so, waited on line for their turn to be triaged, and then directed to yet another line before their wounds could be properly treated.

In fact, for every vital service, there was an articulated line for it snaking through the command center; a line for emergency medical; a line for the latrines; a line for blankets; and a line for emergency food rations which was by far the longest. A one to two hour wait resulted in a set of three 400-calorie mini meal bars, and two, kid's lunch sized, 8.45-oz., non-resealable cartons of purified water for each person.

A vitamin packed square of chewy sustenance, the meal bar was not hot, or particularly tasty. But it did meet the government's new standards for ABSOLUTE MINIMUM DAILY NUTRITIONAL REQUIREMENTS deemed adequate to ensure survival for an average-sized adult.

During the first cataclysm, rations hording was rampant and, in some places, had become a cottage industry. Unscrupulous suppliers would setup tents in devastated areas, and through a practice of sale or barter, control the distribution of necessary goods to the needy. To deter that type of widespread abuse in future crises, the Federal Emergency Management Association was given a mandate to devise a new method for rations distribution that would be straightforward and equitable.

The government's abolishment of monetary notes solved the problem of underground profiteering. But the equal distribution of rations, especially during a breakdown of social order, proved more challenging. Their solution was to use personal identification as a means of tracking and dispensing goods to the people.

In order to receive their daily allotment of rations, a person was required to possess either a private banking card, a government-issued I.D., or a VERIF-i microchip implant in their right hand. The possessor's card, or hand, is passed under a scanner and their activity is instantly recorded and sent along the network. In the absence of either one of these forms of I.D., a meal ticket would then be issued and would have to be renewed daily before rations could be given.

Trent, Constance and Janet were among the several hundreds who stood on the rations line waiting to receive their allotment of food for the day. There, they had been for almost half'n-hour as the line stepped along, through and around the camp at a sluggish pace. For them to have walked for many miles, and now be reduced to standing for an indefinite time, was tantamount to a slow, excruciating form of torture.

They were mostly silent in their wait, keeping their words to a minimum since doing so usually led to an attack of dry mouth. Any complaints that arose were met with a harsh rebuke by the armed soldiers whose standing orders were to keep the peace. Trent had given up the routine of checking his watch hours ago. It only reminded him of the precious minutes spent away from his family, and made him long to be with them even more.

***

Fifty yards away from there, at another location within the command center, Colonel Jeffries stood wearing a light coat of fallen dust while he carefully reviewed his notes. Directly behind him, a public address system had been erected and was undergoing a sound check.

Few things made him nervous; among them, urban warfare, and speaking before large groups of civilians. Any anxiety he experienced, as a rule, was always kept just below the surface. This time was no different. In every instance, his men counted on him to be fearless, even when they themselves were struggling with fear. But the news which he was about to address to the camp, and to rank and file not privy to the dispatch, could create more anxiety than it might resolve. He knew he would have to speak plainly and not mince his words, or over edit himself for simplicity sake. The circumstances called for it. Besides, the people had a right to know. *Better to deal with it now,* he reasoned.

An amplified pop was heard just above his head, followed by acoustical feedback that gradually faded with a slight adjustment of the gain knob on the amplifier's control panel. An army Specialist unhooked the microphone from the amp, gave it another sound check and then handed it over to Heath.

"Ladies and Gentlemen, can I have your attention, please." The activity that dominated the camp suddenly ceased as his authoritative voice came through the loudspeaker. He waited until it was all quiet. "My name is Colonel Heath Jefferies of the Army National Guard, 27th

Infantry Brigade. I'm also the commander of this base. I'm sure you all have a lot of questions. Up until now, we've all been in the dark regarding what's happened. Information is just now coming in. I'm going to ask that you allow me to explain to you exactly what I know. I promise you full disclosure. I will not hold back anything. And hopefully that will answer some, if not all of your questions."

Heath paused for a short breath, mindful of their stillness as he flipped open the pages of his pocket notepad. "At precisely ten-forty-seven this morning, an asteroid of undetermined size somehow escaped detection by our space surveillance systems, entered our atmosphere, and struck somewhere off the coast of New Jersey."

A collective gasp of shock rose up from the grounds, followed by an eruption of chatter that swept the entire base. "Please...please everyone. I know it's hard to imagine such a thing happening. I had a hard time accepting it myself, but I assure you...it did happen. There's more...so please allow me to finish. We're still receiving telemetry, so we haven't as yet pinpointed the impact's epicenter. What we do know for certain is that it struck the continental shelf, and *not* deep-water ocean. Also, as I understand it, the angle of approach was such that the full force of the impact was felt across four states. That's also the reason why we were spared significant tsunami damage. Most of the wave's force was directed away from us and out into the Atlantic. Unfortunately, New Jersey has suffered catastrophic damage and has been designated as ground zero. The other affected states in the blast radius were Pennsylvania, Maryland, Delaware, and New York. According to data received from the USGS's seismic stations in the affected areas, New York City experienced a magnitude 8.2 earthquake...Philadelphia, a magnitude 7.4 earthquake...and Washington, D.C., a magnitude 8.1 earthquake."

Heath paused for a moment and then cleared his throat. "It is my unfortunate duty to report to you that...President Schaefer is dead. He was onboard Air Force One when it was fatally struck by falling debris. There were no survivors. The Vice President was in the senate chamber at the time of the earthquake and was critically injured. He's been airlifted to an undisclosed location. Due to his present incapacity, he is medically unfit to lead the country and for that reason, cannot be sworn in as acting president. In the proceeding hours directly after the impact, nobody else in the presidential line of succession had come forward or been located. The fear is that some, or all of them, were either killed in the blast and subsequent quake...or severely injured somewhere. That would automatically disqualify anyone of them from assuming the presidency. What that means is, for the first time in this nation's history, several hours went by where there was no person leading the country. We were without a President. And since apparently, there are no provisions in place for what to do in the event that the entire line of succession is incapacitated...approximately two hours ago, the surviving members of congress, after first ratifying a declaration of Martial Law in the affected regions...and then, after consulting with legal experts on constitutional law...convened and concluded that the only recourse, due to the extraordinary nature of events, would be to hold a special election. As you know, President Schaefer was the incumbent in the upcoming election. His challenger, Senator Bartlett as it turns out, was not in the United States at the time of the impact. He was with a delegation visiting Federation of States President Jović in Brussels."

Unease stalled Heath's tongue for a moment, causing him to pause for a second time as the weight of his words ponderously settled into fact. He briefly looked around at his audience standing in silence under the smoky white glare of floodlights; their faces marked by a spate of dismay, and then imagined their bated breaths hanging on his every statement. His pause only allowed them a moment to breathe and reflect, before his next notated jolt snatched the air from them once again.

"At precisely twenty-three-hundred-fifty-two hours, Senator Bartlett was contacted by Congressman Delroy of Massachusetts and offered the presidency. He accepted."

The intervening silence that had gripped the base went off like a hand grenade as the survivors collectively grappled with the unprecedented news. Some stood in place and wept in despair, while others either simply stared ahead, dumbstruck, or looked in disbelief at one another. The sum total of information had clearly shaken them, almost as much as, if not even more than, the actual earthquake itself.

"That's all I've been given for now. I'll notify you all the minute more information is released. Thank you." Heath handed the microphone over to the army Specialist, turned and headed back to the command tent accompanied by his aides.

***

Trent stood speechless on the rations line, which had not moved for several minutes while the news went forth. And even after the colonel was clearly done, those waiting still needed a moment to collect themselves before their hunger took hold again.

His arms and legs grew restless with trembling. His hands longed for something to do; anything to arrest the panic that was starting to overtake him. He had always been his family's rock, their hero and protector. But now, in the wake of what was just revealed, his increasing sense of helplessness seemed more than he could bear.

How badly was the damage to New York City, he wondered through his thirst. *Are the buildings still standing? Was it flooded? Nora can't swim. She would've drowned. What if she's...dead?* The questions plagued him as he securely locked his fingers together, brought his clasped hands up and rested them atop his head in a posture of worry. Right then, all he wanted to do was break down and weep like a teenager. But somewhere down in his soul, a small voice whispered to him an inkling of hope.

No...she can't be...she's not. She's trying to get home...just like me. She's got to be, he thought, defiantly refusing to accept the alternative. *Where is she right now? What must she be going through? And what are the kids doing?* "I've got to get home," Trent muttered under his breath, his determination now more resolute than ever.

Janet and Constance were equally as distraught and had been sharing their worry with a couple standing in front of them on the line. Trent interrupted them just as the line resumed moving. "Excuse me, Janet...Constance. How would you two feel about traveling in a smaller group?"

"I don't know. I never really thought about it," Janet said. "How much smaller are we talking here?"

"Smaller as in the three of us...now before you say anything, Constance, hear me out. I know you might feel safer traveling in a large group, but the truth is, after hearing what we just heard, we have no idea how long it might take us to get home. We could be adding days to our journey. And frankly, I need to get home. Also, I don't think numbers guarantee safety. It's easier to turn up lost in a crowd than it is in a trio. How badly do you guys want to get home?"

"I think he's right, Constance. If we look out for each other, we'll be fine. Besides, the stars told me we would."

"Oh, yeah...that's reassuring," Constance said sarcastically. "Well, I'm certainly not going to let the two of you leave me here. I just hope you're not thinking about doing this tonight."

"No. We'll get our rations, rest up tonight and leave early in the morning," Trent said.

"Can we come with you?" the woman standing in front of them asked, speaking for her and the man she was with. "We're all pretty much going in the same direction. My name is Loretta, and this is my boyfriend, Ben."

"Hi. Um...yeah, we're just trying to get home to our dog," he said, giving a one-handed self-massage to the back of his neck while his other arm rested affectionately around Loretta's waist.

"It's a Shih Tzu. He's only two years old. He must be scared to death through all of this. I know he's looking for us...wondering why we're not home yet. Please, can we come with you? Three is good, but five is better."

"Sure...you can come. But we can't get any larger than this. Otherwise, we'll be right back where we started," Trent said.

The lines pace had picked up only slightly, and they still had no idea how much closer they were to getting fed. They had already seen the type of rations they could expect. It was a far cry from what their growling stomachs envisioned. But at this point, they were ready to accept anything as long as it was edible.

Trent hoped whatever it was, that it would be enough to sustain them. Especially since there was no telling how few and far between the next meal would be. Just then, another pang wrenched his stomach, sending a grimace across his face. Wanting to take his mind off the sensation, he looked ahead to tomorrow and tried to imagine a bright spot. Instead, what his mind saw was a dreary landscape, and the resultant aftermath of what it believed the next morning might possibly look like.

Chapter 17

Nora's feet felt like they had swollen to twice their normal size. She and the others had covered some forty-six additional blocks through what had become an endless reel of misery and destruction; past the blacked-out shopping hub of Herald Square where a stretch of vandalized storefronts stood looted and spookily deserted in the dismal night; and on into Times Square where iconic displays were dimmed of their brilliance and resoundingly pummeled like the face of an old, vacant house; finally ending up in Central Park where an impressive ring of floodlights encircled a veritable tent city numbering in the tens of hundreds.

There, countless survivors wandered throughout in a seeming daze, while all around them, armed soldiers tended to the crisis in their midst. Humvees traversed the scorched acreage outside of the camp where the park grounds, under the blackness of night, more resembled a hostile jungle than the urban oasis it once was. Some carried injured civilians on stretchers for drop off at any one of the two medical tents on the base. Others transported dozens of plasti-cuffed felons to the rows of chain-linked cages that served as temporary jails, set well away from the general population. Just over a ridge, a CH-47 heavy-lift helicopter sat on a field several yards away from the base, its rotors spinning at a pre-takeoff speed as soldiers unloaded boxes of fresh supplies from its cargo area.

At the other end of the base, Nora sat on a dirt patch at the foot of a large tree, her legs crossed loosely in front of her as she leaned forward and worked a massage into the balls and arches of her bare feet. Taylor, sitting nearby, had warned her to guard her sneakers since they were now considered a hot commodity on the street. Alongside Nora sat Sonia, her knees touching and bent sharply in front of her while her head rested in a drowsy tilt against the trunk of the tree.

With the first leg of their journey behind them, and after waiting on one of the several rations lines for more than two hours, they were all sufficiently nourished and thoroughly spent of energy. They were also grieving over the news just shared over the base's PA system of the asteroid impact. It was especially nerve racking for Preston whose sole motivation was to get home to his wife and son in central New Jersey. But now that the entire state had been declared as ground zero, and presumably much worse off than New York City, he could only wonder over the fate of his family.

Tears ran down Nora's cheeks as she rubbed her swollen ankles and tried to ignore the horrific images of Trent and her children possibly dead or dying. Its likelihood almost made her want to give up and let depression take her, right there where she sat. But she knew she had to soldier on—if only just to prove the naysaying voice wrong.

She looked over at Sonia sitting next to her and staring sleepily up at the night sky. She, too, had been crying and only now settled into melancholy while traces of emotion cast a rosy hue across her cheeks and nose. "Are you okay, Sonia?"

"I don't know how I feel. I'm scared...I'm worried...I'm tired, and everything hurts. Girl, I'm a'mess," she said with a light chuckle. "I don't know if things can get much worse than this. But I'm not dead yet...so I guess that means I'm okay. How about yourself...how are you holding up?"

"You just described exactly how I'm feeling. Maybe more scared than anything else. Why is all this happening? First the cataclysm and now this. Is the world coming to an end?"

"I don't know about the end of the world, but I do think God is real upset with us right now. This could all be happening as part of his judgment on us sinners."

"You really believe there's someone up there causing all this to happen...really?" Preston, who was listening in, asked facetiously. "And let me guess. He's an old man with a long white beard who sits on a throne and obviously has some type of gripe against us. So instead of fixing the problem like you'd expect an all-powerful, omniscient God to do, he instead, starts picking up rocks and hurling them at us. Oh yeah, that makes plenty of sense. If that's your idea of God, then it's no wonder I don't believe in him."

"I'm not telling you what to believe in. I'm just saying what I think it could be. And I wasn't even talking to you. I was talking to Nora. You should mind your own business."

"It just irks me when people propagate a myth like its fact, then dogmatically build religions around them without any hard evidence that what they believe in even exists."

"It's called faith."

"Well, I call it foolishness. If you knew anything about science, you'd know that events like this happen once every few thousand years. This is nothing new. We were practically expecting it. We just thought we'd have some warning." Preston said, then stood to his feet and started to walk off. "I got'a take a leak. If I'm not back in ten minutes—"

"Then we'll assume you're dead and go on with our lives," Sonia said loudly, then watched him disappear around a tent corner. "Hmmp...intellectuals. They're so busy intellectualizing that they can't see what's right there in front of them. That's how people like him are. They're very defensive about things they don't understand."

"No offence, but I kind of agree with Preston."

"No sweat, honey, you're entitled. At least you're not a snob about it like *that* fool. He was practically calling me stupid. He probably thinks I don't know what dogmatically means, too. That's why he threw it in there. But I know what it means. I may not have graduated college, but I read a lot."

"What line of work are you in, if you don't mind my asking."

"I'm a dancer."

"Oh...you mean like Broadway?"

"No, not exactly."

Nora picked up on Sonia's hesitation and began searching for a different subject to raise.

"I'm an exotic dancer," Sonia replied seconds later. "Preston ought'a get a chuckle out of that if he knew, huh. Score one for another stereotype. That's okay, though. I'm not ashamed of it...at least not most of the time."

"I'm a little confused. Did I hear you say you believed in God, or did I misunderstand?"

"You're wondering how I can believe in God and take my clothes off for a living. I know it sounds like a contradiction, but believe it or not, I grew up in the church. Iglesia de Cristo on Southern Boulevard in the Bronx. Every Sunday, Wednesday and Thursday, me and my mother...my father, he was always working. But the two of us, we'd be there almost all the time, it seemed. My mother, she never grew tired of it...but I did. As I got older, she started telling me what to do, what not to do. I said 'that's it, I'm done with this.' I left home as soon as I graduated high school. I went to college for a year, but it didn't work out."

"What made you start dancing?"

"It was my boyfriend's idea. We're not together anymore. But at the time, he said it would be an easy way to make some extra money...except there was nothing easy about it. The first time I did it, I was so scared. It took so many drinks before I could get up the nerve to get out there. I'm surprised I wasn't falling down drunk. Now, I can't go out there without having at least one drink first."

"So why do you do it? 'Cause from what I'm hearing, it doesn't sound like you're completely okay with it."

"That's complicated. The first time may have been scary, but I'd be lying if I said it wasn't exhilarating...having all that control, and the attention. And then there's the money. Some nights my take home is...well, let's just say it's real good. My parents, they have no idea what I do. They think I work the night shift at a hospital. A part of me keeps saying I should stop once and for all and get a real job. But what am I gonna do...I can't do anything else. I feel like I'm trapped. God must be so fed up with me." Sonia paused briefly as if regretting the box of memories she had opened. "But enough about me. What kind of work do you do?" she asked.

"I'm an attorney," Nora said with a hint of embarrassment.

"How do you like it?"

"How do I like what?"

"How do you like being an attorney?"

Nora opened her mouth to answer, but nothing came out as her mind went momentarily blank with the question. She rolled it around a few times and tried to come up with an answer that would sum up her true feelings in five words or less. But what came to mind was not quite what she had expected. After years of telling herself she loved her job, what should have been an instantaneous response, wasn't quite so automatic; and somewhere between this morning and sitting there on the hard, dirty ground in Central Park, her priorities had changed.

"You know, you're the first person who's ever asked me that question. My father never asked me. He was an attorney and a partner at his law firm. I grew up surrounded by lawyers. I knew what jurisprudence meant long before I got my first training bra. It was just a given that I'd become a lawyer, too. And I would've done anything to please my father. I was always trying to get his attention...trying to make him proud of me. My mother couldn't wait to boast to everyone about her daughter, the future attorney...and all the awards I won...my scholarship. In all that time, nobody ever asked me if I really enjoyed it."

"Well, do you enjoy it?"

"I honestly don't know anymore. Right now, I just want to see my family again. I only hope my husband made it home before the impact. I hope they're all alive and safe...including your mother and father."

"Thank you. Y'know, for me this would be the perfect time to pray...only I haven't done it in so long I wouldn't even know how to begin. God would probably be like, '*Who's that*? Oh...it's you,' then look away from me in disgust."

"Well, that doesn't sound like a God that I'd want to know. Any God that could do all of this deserves to have a huge revolt on his hands."

"You don't understand. God may have done it. But he didn't cause it. We did that...I did...not Him."

"What about forgiveness? Isn't God supposed to be forgiving?"

Sonia expelled a deep sigh and leaned her head against the tree. "I don't know. I'm still working on that. I haven't quite earned His forgiveness yet...not until I make some changes. We all need to make changes. My mother used to say, 'You can only go to the well so many times before it runs dry.' I'm afraid I may have dried my well out."

Nora could sense Sonia's melancholy returning and respectfully gave her the silence she needed to grieve. Though she could not identify with Sonia's career choice, or the depths to which she felt remorseful, she could relate to her feelings of emptiness; to the seeming futility of her existence that negated the true person living inside her. She thought about what Sonia said...that we all need to make changes...and then thought about her own life. Everything about it had become so regimented, so predictable, like the hands of a clock that kept time in years rather than hours. *And to what end,* she wondered. *Afterwards, then what?*

She never felt the hole until now; a small but undeniable void right in the center of her being. Whatever filled it before had lost its importance. Her thoughts turned melancholy with exaggerated scenes of her life and all that was missing in it, including her family. She wept quietly upon seeing their faces. Then closed her eyes and tried to join Sonia and the others in getting a night's rest before morning.

Just across the way from her, sitting alone at the foot of a tree was Taylor. His legs were stretched out in front of him and his hands, clasped together and resting across his waist. He was wide awake—and unbeknown to Nora—had been secretly staring at her from the moment she sat down. In fact, his eyes were still on her; watching intently as she soon succumbed to a need for sleep. And even then, he still hadn't averted his curious fixation on her.

DAY TWO

Chapter 18

Morning's arrival over the cul-de-sac was like a cruel thief for Jennifer. Its murky light had stolen the charm from their once beautiful neighborhood; replacing it with a panorama of ugliness, and set it against a bleak horizon that sadly mirrored yesterday's.

She and Rachel were out collecting firewood to set aside for that evening. The fact that she knew nothing about wood and how to go about gathering it, only complicated matters. Still, whatever she could produce was better than the alternative of watching Justin incinerate more of their parent's belongings. At times he seemed almost delighted to be throwing certain items into the fire. It was an odd reaction, and maybe even worthy of a few sessions of psychotherapy, Jennifer thought. But that was a matter for another time. For now he was occupying himself inside the house. And most likely raiding the food reserves which Jennifer, more than once, had to ask him to eat sparingly.

She had never seen the street in front of their house so deserted, or heard it so quiet. There was rarely even a bird seen that had not been forced to the ground from the weight of dust on its wings, or that wasn't lying dead in the street among the rest of the debris. A charred and wind stripped cluster of trees stood petrified in the background where little more than dead air separated each timber. Against this stark setting, the inherent sounds of desolation enveloped Jennifer and Rachel like a dilapidated dome of misery. The combination of images created a surreal vista of a winter's gloom that looked harshly out of season given the tepid summer climate.

Piece by piece Jennifer and Rachel brought the wood they found— mainly twigs and broken branches—back to the house and dropped them onto a pile near the front door.

Jennifer stood back to inspect their haul. "I don't think this is enough. All we have here is a bunch of sticks. They're too light. They'll burn too quickly. What we really need are logs," she said before turning and heading back out across the lawn. "Are you coming?"

Rachel, who had flung her meager collection onto the pile, was not thrilled about the amount of physical labor involved. Between loads, she would repeatedly check her hands and arms for any wood splinters, cuts and scrapes, and then with a huff, proceed to air her grievances as if it could somehow make a difference. "Why doesn't Justin get his lazy butt out here and help us?" she asked angrily. "He's always looking for something to set fire to. You'd think he'd be the first one out here. Why's he being such a jerk?"

"I don't know. Sometimes I think he doesn't have a crisis meter like the rest of us. Either that or he's still angry about us staying behind and not leaving with the others."

"Well he should get over it. We have to work together. It shouldn't be just you and me doing everything."

Jennifer walked over to an area of the lawn that they hadn't covered yet.

"Hey, doesn't Daddy have an ax, or something like it in the garage?" Rachel asked as she followed her, sweeping her foot through the debris while she walked.

"I doubt it. In all my life I've never seen Daddy chop anything except an onion. I'm not sure, but I think we always had our firewood delivered. All I know is, every winter we always had logs for the fireplace. Come to think of it...we also had food, clothes, money and just about anything else we needed."

"I know...it just makes you think. We never really had to worry about much of anything, did we?"

"No, we didn't. And now I'm starting to realize just how much we took Mom and Dad for granted," Jennifer said, picking up pieces of wood and tucking them under her arm as she spoke. "We were all pretty selfish. It was always about us...what we wanted, and what we had to have. We want this...we want that. And they usually gave in, which in hindsight may not have been the best thing to do. But I know they only did it because they loved us."

Rachel stood close by, gently sweeping the debris back and forth with her foot, and seemingly in no mood to assist Jennifer. "I have a lot of regrets. Two days ago I was mad at both of them and said some awful things...things that I can't take back," she said, standing over Jennifer who knelt down to sort through the debris. "Y'know we haven't really spoken since. I keep thinking about the argument and how angry I was. They didn't deserve me yelling at them the way I did. They're not here, now...and I can't help but wonder if I'll ever have a chance to tell them I'm sorry. What if they don't come home? What do we do? It's been a long time since I said to either one of them that I loved them. That's what I'm feeling now...and it hurts."

Jennifer felt the same hurt, tightening around her conscience like a truss. She was often guilty of similar tirades towards her mom and dad; leveling petulant commentary that no child should direct at their parents. But such was the nature of their upbringing where an inch given, leads to a foot taken, and so on. Now, after not having seen her parents in over twenty-four hours, she would give anything for a chance to atone and to say to both of them—I love you. They carried their wood scraps back to the pile and then turned around to look for more. "What was the argument about, anyway?" Jennifer asked as they headed out.

"It was about Rodney. They didn't want me seeing him anymore."

"Isn't he a senior now?"

Rachel stopped and looked at Jennifer. "Yeah, he is. So what?" she answered brusquely.

"So...they probably didn't want to see their freshman daughter dating a senior," Jennifer said as she bent down to pick up a few scraps of wood she'd spotted. "If he's anything like his older brother was when I was in high school, I think they had good reason to be concerned."

"Look, I know you've been gone for a while, so let me catch you up on things. First, I'm not a freshman anymore. I'm a sophomore this year. Second, I'm not doing anything different from what you did when you were in high school. I can remember you doing a lot of sneaking around behind Mom and Dad's backs. So don't judge me."

Jennifer stopped gathering wood and stood up to face Rachel. "I'm not judging you. And you're right...I was a wild child. And maybe I didn't set the best example for you. But I'm older now, and I can see where that type of behavior can lead. I'll bet Rodney's no different than his older brother. They're the type that likes to keep score. Every girl they're with ends up as a notch on their belts...and that's all. You don't want that to happen. 'Cause after a while, you stop respecting yourself. And then others stop respecting you as well. You're still so young. I don't want you to end up as just another notch on Rodney's belt."

"You don't have to worry about me. I'll be fine. I'm not stupid, y'know."

"I don't think you understand. You need to listen to me. How do you think I know so much about Rodney's older brother?"

Rachel, appeared puzzled by Jennifer's insistence and looked into her face. There, she must have noticed a visible change come over it; and then looking into her eyes and the depth of concern that seemed to reach down into a painfully private place.

"Did you and him—"

"Yes," Jennifer said ashamedly. "I was exactly your age when he started paying attention to me. And why wouldn't he? I was always sticking my chest out like a love-starved fool whenever he was around...just trying to get him to notice me. Anyway, I thought he was cute, and he seemed nice. He was older...he dressed good and had his own car. When he started talking to me, all I could think about was how lucky I was to be seen with him, and how jealous all the other girls would be when they found out that I was his girlfriend."

As Jennifer recalled her high school crush, she spat her words out with a palpable loathing that held Rachel's attention. "After he got what he wanted, I became nothing more than a nuisance to him...and he was on to the next girl. Things only got worse after that."

"What do you mean, 'got worse'? Did he do something to you?"

"No. It had nothing to do with him...it was me. I changed after that."

"Changed how?"

Jennifer didn't care to elaborate, preferring instead to hint at all the things that could go wrong. "Can you answer me this? I know this is a personal question, but...are you still a virgin?"

"That's none of your business."

"I know, and I'm sorry...but you don't understand how important it is that you wait. Otherwise, you'll lose yourself."

"I don't know what you mean by that. You're not explaining anything."

"Just tell me you're still a virgin."

"Okay, yes...I still am."

"Are you telling me the truth?"

"Yes! Now leave me alone. I thought we were talking about Mom and Dad. How did we get on this topic anyway?"

Jennifer gave her a probing look. And although she detected some hesitancy to make eye contact, she thought it best not to push the issue. "C'mon, we'd better get back inside before Justin eats up what little food we have," she said, then turning toward the house, and with the few sticks of wood she collected under her arm.

***

As Jennifer headed over to the woodpile, Rachel walked slowly behind her. The constant dust fall had coated her hair and clothes in an ashy gray color that ironically matched her mood. She hadn't thought much about Rodney. Not since after the storm destroyed everything and put the kibosh on her pool party. Sadly, he was everything Jennifer had so astutely described—cute, older and attentive. And it sickened her to think that she could be so easily manipulated by him. She was especially angry at herself for allowing this boy, whom she may have liked, but still thought of as irritating, drive a wedge between her and her parents.

She meditated on her sister's warning as they approached the front door; confounded that it took a catastrophe like this one to bring Rodney's motives into question. Meanwhile, the words, "you'll lose yourself...you'll lose yourself," kept repeating over and over in her mind; its meaning shrouded in some humiliating event that, she reasoned, must've been too personal for Jennifer to reveal. Either way, it hit its mark—dare she confess the whole truth—as she wondered there in the sterile surroundings whether it may have been too late for her.

Chapter 19

The afternoon sky over Manhattan was the color of slate; dark, threatening, and pocked with black smoke clouds that hung like balloons high above the tension still smoldering at street level. A stream of survivors—some well rested, and others not so— flowed north and south along city streets, passing each other in a dispirited posture of shock and bewilderment.

After an early morning departure from the base at Central Park, Nora and her party were approaching 90th Street and the 117th block of their trek up Broadway. Taylor still helmed their progress and, since having gained a measure of their confidence, began to wield his earned clout with next to no opposition. He decided it best they forgo picking up their day's allotment of rations that morning at the base. He reasoned it would save them at least two hours that would otherwise be spent waiting on line. Instead, he favored an early start. That way, they could get ahead of the late risers outside of the base, and all the foot traffic he expected would congest the streets by the afternoon.

Dale, as usual, thought Taylor's strategy was flawed from the start. Before they left, he tried to persuade the others into agreeing with him and claiming their day's rations. But since they still had some leftover from the day before, it was not a matter of urgency as of yet. Taylor's argument once again proved more compelling. And with the next military base said to be established at Morningside Park on 110th Street, the earlier they got started, the sooner they would arrive there.

In the meantime, they nibbled on their 400-calorie bars en route. At the same time, taking care to eat discreetly so as not to rile the growing number of aggressive survivors who found forcibly taking others food, much easier than having to wait for it themselves.

This was especially true as they made their way further up Broadway, and noticed the thinning military and police presence, which strangely—or not so—wasn't the case upon their passing through the financial, cultural, and more affluent areas of Manhattan. Either way, the absence of armed patrols for several blocks created a situation rife for thuggery as they entered the more street-gang infested parts of town. A gallery of imaginative, but indecipherable graffiti marked several walls; their visage crying out like muraled warnings in pictograph.

By the time they reached Morningside Park on 110th Street it was already late afternoon. Having finished off their allotment of water some hours ago, and with only a few bites remaining of their ration bars, they fully expected to have their meal and thirst anxiety eased the minute they got to the park. But with evening's approach, they saw no floodlit halo in the sky to guide them to a waiting military base as before.

Instead, they were greeted by a chaotic scene of proliferating outrage on the very edge; of mostly brown and beige skinned survivors ranging from hostile to timid in character who, beneath a thickening coat of gray dust, were sadly entering their second night waiting for help to arrive.

A vociferous clamor of discontent echoed through the neighboring streets where eighty-year-old apartment buildings teetered on quake weakened foundations; condemnable structures that some residents still bravely called home. And gathered just outside of them were a multitude of survivors, all appearing tired, hungry and in desperate need of direction. And yet, they seemed none too surprised by the lack of aid to their community. Whatever the reason for the delay, it exacted a toll of disregard that rubbed away at their patience until only a raw nerve was left.

Intermittent pops of gunfire could be heard down the dark, alley-like streets that adjoined the intersections. While overhead, Black Hawk helicopters made repeated passes as they scanned a spotlight of warning onto the crowd, hoping to quell their seeming intent to riot. Apparently, keeping troops in the air was safer than setting them on the ground where a heavily armed unit might be easily ambushed by an incensed and equally armed band of gang members.

Abandoned car headlights were still the only form of evening light available. Taylor, from the moment he reached the park and discovered there was no base established, was bent on finding a way out. He wanted to get clear of the turmoil before heightened frustrations began to look for a scapegoat. Dust was flying off his pant legs as he rapidly cut through the headlight beams on a course away from the perceived threat.

Dale, Preston and Laura, wary of the same fate, followed only inches behind him; their eyes darting in a nervous quiver that looked at nothing, but saw everything. Directly behind them were Nora, Sonia and Miguel, themselves burdened by an equal weight of concerns, but for a different set of reasons. They hurried along, wearing a mask of stoic indifference that hopefully wouldn't lend itself to notice.

They followed Taylor's lead through a weaving maze of agitated bodies, many of which pleaded to the passing helicopter to land and help them. While some just shouted up epithets daring it to land.

Through it all, Nora and the others had no idea where they were headed, or what direction Taylor was taking them in. Only that as they walked further, the crowd surrounding them began to thin. Until soon, they were standing on the corner of 115th Street. And among a lot fewer people who seemingly were content to leave their anger on simmer rather than allow it boil over.

Dale turned and took a moment to appreciate what he considered to be a near escape; taking in all the sights and sounds that he was afraid to study while mired in the thick of it. "Okay, now what?" he said, turning back to face them. "There's no base here, and we're down to crumbs, and no water. I knew we should've gotten our rations this morning. Oh...and did I forget to mention, we were almost killed back there?"

"What are you talking about? I didn't see any such thing," Nora said, frowning as she looked at him.

"I'm saying I remember the L.A. riots. I had family in Santa Monica at the time. They saw it up close. It's situations like this one where the innocent get targeted. Okay, I'll say it. Where the whites get targeted, alright?"

"I was walking behind you the entire time," Sonia said, "and I didn't see anybody trying to kill you. Anyway, who cares if you're white...we can't even see what color you are. We're all the same color right now...stink'n gray, so stop acting like a victim. If anything, those folks back there are the victims. We already got our rations. Most of them are still waiting for theirs."

Dale looked away in annoyance and then turned back. "Alright, whatever. I was still right, though...I mean about the rations. Now we've got nothing. What are we supposed to do tomorrow? We don't even know where the next base is located," he said.

"I don't care about tomorrow. It's tonight I'm worried about. I'm tired. I can't walk any farther. And I've got to pee." Laura said, then examining their faces to see whether any of them shared her exhaustion. After which, she looked around the immediate area for a safe place to go relieve herself while they pondered what to do next.

Answering nature's call had been an ongoing challenge for the women. They would go in pairs with one always looking out while the other ducked into a corner with whatever cloth or loose paper they could find to finish the job with. It was about as unsanitary a dilemma as they could ever imagine being caught in. But with a roll of toilet paper impossible to come by, there was little else they could do.

Nora accompanied Laura over to a deserted spot behind a tree and there, waited for her to finish. All the while she dreaded a new worst-case scenario, and what she herself might be reduced to doing if she couldn't locate any Tampons two weeks from now.

They both went to rejoin the others, though they could barely distinguish them within the faint light that draped the corner. Meanwhile, in all this time, Taylor still hadn't said much. Not even in defense of his decision. With the exception of Sonia, and sometimes Dale, the rest of them did not seem particularly bothered by it. They had already pegged him as a bit of an enigma. This allowed him the freedom to be aloof whenever the mood struck.

At the moment, he was busily applying a two-handed, finger massage to his temples in an apparent attempt to thwart a migraine headache, just as Laura showed up. "Can you at least walk two more blocks so we can get back onto Broadway?" he asked her.

"And then what?" Laura responded.

"Then we'll look for someplace to rest for the night."

"And what if we don't find anything right away? We could be walking all night. No...definitely not. I'm not up to it."

"We *could* just leave without you," Dale said, followed by a harsh rebuke from some of them.

"This is a reasonably quiet block. Why can't we just stay here for the night," Nora added on the heels of Dale's ludicrous suggestion. "We're not the only ones trying to get uptown, y'know. Those other people we see walking along with us are probably squatting in some of the same buildings we're passing. We can rest in one of these lobbies and then leave in the morning."

Miguel yawned just as Nora finished, setting off a yawn-chain among those standing closest to him. "That sounds good to me. We should probably rest," he said. "I do wish we had some water, though. I'm really thirsty...but there isn't much we can do about that tonight."

Once both sides drew their line in the sand, they immediately looked to Taylor to render a final decision. But for the first time since they started out on foot together, he made no attempt to force his position on them. Judging from his sluggish posture and hung over demeanor, he was likely just as tired as the other side was. But couldn't bring himself to admit it. "We'll stay on this block. One of these building has got to have a few people still in them. Let's go," he said in a forceful tone that gave the impression of it being completely his idea.

They started down the narrow street; maneuvering around battered cars and past roaming survivors who, like themselves, seemed unsure of where to spend the night. The buildings all resembled hallowed out sets from a studio backlot; lifeless, fractured and stripped of the character that so honestly defined this neighborhood.

Nora followed behind, wincing with every step as her calf muscles contracted in protest to her continued walking. She wanted to sit more than anything, and hoped that somewhere among the ruins, a commune of benevolent locals might be kind enough to offer refuge to six weary travelers.

Chapter 20

The taste of dust had become a tormenting nuisance for Trent. The light blanket he was given back at the base was to impractical to be used for anything other than sleep. Earlier he had fashioned a cloth mask for himself to keep the particulates from invading his airways. But with the air already compromised by dust, a cloth covering his nose and mouth for long stretches made every breath feel as though he were suffering from asthma. The walk alone was difficult enough. To then, in addition to that, have to struggle with breathing was like having an elastic band tied to his waist, and the other end anchored into the ground. He decided to wear it for only a few minutes at a time, if that much.

After having departed the base early that morning, he and his party were on their eighth hour of walking. With no map to follow, and no visible sun during the day to guide them, they relied on each other's sense of direction. For much of the day, they ambled along obstacle ridden roads that they believed would take them part of the way upstate. Crowding the roads were other survivors; all trekking in divergent paths toward their own objectives, while inadvertently making the way home a tedious and drawn out journey for them.

They had no idea how much distance they covered. Only that, at the pace they were walking, it had to be a fraction of what they could have accomplished on an unobstructed road. Factor in the physical demands of fatigue, thirst, hunger, and the emotional malaise of knowing that their lives might never be the same again, and you have what amounts to maybe six miles walked at the end of the day, on average.

At the moment, they were taking a break in the driveway of a home that had apparently taken heavy damage in the rock storm and was left abandoned by its owner. The sky, though not pitch black, was deceivingly dark, speeding evening's onset when the actual hour said differently. Before leaving the base that morning, they made it a point to pick up the day's rations allotment which if eaten conservatively, could last for two days at the most.

Trent had just taken a bite out of one of his ration bars, carefully rewrapped the foil around it, and slid it back into his pocket. He still had one whole bar left and a carton of water. And if needed, two small packs of Starbursts which he promised himself only to eat in the event that starvation seemed imminent. Conserving his water, though, was another problem altogether.

Whatever government think-tank was behind the decision to use child sized, non-resealable cartons for dispensing water rations, had clearly not held one focus group. The infuriating little box provoked the ire of every survivor who was forced to suck down their entire carton when they would have preferred to save some of that water for later.

"Would I love to strangle the guy who came up with this cockamamie box for storing water in. You can't close the darn thing, and you certainly can't put it in your pocket after it's been opened. You just end up with wet pants. This is stupid...am I right?" Ben said after a sip of his water, and then looking around for agreement.

"You won't get any argument from me. As far as strangling someone, I think you'll have to get on line. Whoever that genius was, he's got a lot of people angry with him," Trent said.

Constance sat with her back against the garage wall; her face poking through the opening of her blanket which she wore draped over her head and shoulders like a burnoose. "Does anybody have any idea what town we're in?" she asked.

"I don't know. Nothing looks familiar anymore. I believe we're still parallel to Highway-87 about a half a mile or so from here. As long as that's heading north, we'll be okay," Ben said. "I'm just sorry there were no military bases along our route. It seems like we may end up having to spend the night in someplace that's not so nice."

"What about some of these abandoned houses along the road? Why can't we use them for shelter?" Constance asked.

"From what I've seen, the ones that are still standing have people staying in them," Trent, offering an answer, said. "And the ones that are empty look like they're barely standing. I wouldn't want to be inside one of those barely standing homes when the roof collapses...which we've all seen happen. Any type of wood frame house is too risky. We passed a lot of buildings on the way here. Those usually have steel frames which would make them a lot safer. If we keep walking, we're sure to see another supermarket, a strip mall, school building or something. We can stay in one of them for the night."

"This is crazy. There's got to be an easier way to travel than this," Loretta blurted. "We should not have had to make it all this way on foot. Why can't they clear the roads and put buses on them so people can get home? And what about the railroads...are the trains out of service, too? I thought after the cataclysm, they were supposed to have a system in place for when things like this happen. If we have to walk all the way home, it's going to take us days. What about Coco?" she asked looking distressingly over at Ben. "He won't survive without us...he won't, Ben." She then placed her head on his shoulder and started to weep.

"You have to understand. Coco is more than just a dog to us. He's like our very own child," Ben said, with his arm placed consolingly around Loretta. "We lost our son three-and-a-half years ago. He disappeared...like the others. Abducted I guess...I don't know. He was taking a nap that afternoon. When Loretta went into his room to check on him...he was gone. Everything else was just as she left it...but *he* was gone. He was only two years old. Then we found out that we couldn't have any more children...and that we couldn't even adopt because all the other children had been...taken, also. It was hard on both of us after that...especially Loretta. When we brought Coco home, it was as though somebody turned the lights back on. Things started to change for us almost immediately. He gave us our joy back. He gave us someone to care for again...besides each other, I mean. That's why we have to get home."

"And you will. We all will," Janet said, sitting next to Loretta. "My niece and nephew, they were taken that day, also. They were seven and nine. Somehow it doesn't make sense that they would go after all the children. And the babies...why the babies?"

"Just who exactly is this 'they,' anyway?" Constance, sounding mildly annoyed, asked. "Y'know, there's still a lot of debate out there regarding what really happened. We never did get a definitive answer on who all was behind these abductions."

"Sure, we did," Ben said. "It was the aliens. Who else could it have been? I can't think of anything that could make over two billion people disappear in an instant other than something outside of this world. Didn't you see their space ships? It was all over the news."

"Yes, I saw the spaceships, and call me a skeptic, but...why didn't they land? What do they need with two billion plus humans? Why didn't they take you, me or any one of us? Why'd they leave us here? It's all very peculiar. Almost as if they knew something in advance and decided to take only a select few people."

"Y'know, what you're saying," Janet said, "sounds almost biblical. I know of a few people who think God was somehow behind it."

"Yeah, I remember what some were saying right after the abductions. That's all foolishness if you ask me. I never saw God...but

I sure as heck saw those space ships. Oh...and another thing. Why would they make a percentage of the population sterile? They take our children...then prevent some from having more children. Like I said, it's all very peculiar."

Janet leaned forward and looked over to Constance. "Okay, skeptic. So tell us what you think is going on."

"I think the aliens had a co-conspirator."

"And who would that be?"

"The governments of the world...I think they were behind it somehow, and we're working with the aliens. Some type of deal was made. Take lives to spare lives, I guess. Exactly why, I don't know."

"This may sound crazy," Ben said in a tone that expressed some reluctance to share with them, "but, just before the UFO sightings...a good friend of ours told us this terrifying story about being visited by alien creatures at night while in bed. He said he would wake up and see them standing over him, and then they would disappear. It was chilling the way he described it. And he said it happened more than once, too. Now this is somebody that I've known for over twelve years. I've always considered him one of the smartest people I know. We met in college. The guy holds a Masters in eastern philosophy. He's traveled all over the world. Him and his husband are co-owners of the New Age Bookstore down in Soho. He's reputable...well respected. If he says that's what happened, then I believe him. He's as credible as they come."

"Y'know what I think? I think it's time we started broadening our concept of what, or who, our gods are," Janet said. "I consider myself a very spiritual person...mind, body and spirit...that's my mantra. And I'm familiar with your friend's bookstore. I've been in there several times. He's a walking encyclopedia on new age spirituality. I may never be as knowledgeable as he is on the subject, but there are some things that just make sense to me. Unless you're an atheist, I believe we've had this narrow view of gods...like they have to be this way, or they have to look a certain way. What if all the worlds' religions are wrong and the gods' of our ancestors aren't as we imagined them?" Janet paused. "What if they're an advanced civilization of highly evolved, flesh and blood beings? They may even be responsible for seeding this planet with life. If our scientists can create life in a test tube, then why couldn't the aliens have created life and brought it here. Ever since we walked on all fours, we've been looking up at the stars. And all this time they've been looking down at us...mostly in secret...but not anymore."

"Are you saying you believe the aliens...are gods?" Ben asked in a judgmental sounding tone.

"I'm saying it's possible. Hey...any civilization that can make over two billion people vanish right out of their clothes, and sterilize some of the rest of us, as far as I'm concerned, are gods, ipso facto."

"Y'know, what she's saying isn't that implausible. Who says gods can't be little green men, anyway? I've seen more evidence from them up there than I've ever seen from those Christians and their God," Loretta said.

"Wait a minute. If there are so many gods out there...or at least what people perceive to be God...then why single out the Christians?" Trent asked.

Loretta turned to him. "I don't profess to know much about religions, and I don't like labels. But I suppose if you had to put a label on me and Ben, you can probably call us both agnostics. There's no one thing we believe in over another thing. We just sort of live our lives and try to do right by people and hope that it comes back to us. In that regard, I guess you can say we do believe in something. But my experience with Christians is I find them to be very close-minded and rigid about what they believe, and how you're supposed to behave, and what to do, and what not to do. They think theirs is the only way...that everybody else is wrong, and they're right. Now how can that be? For instance, Ben is Jewish...he's not orthodox, and he doesn't attend synagogue at all. What about him? I always thought the Jewish people were chosen by God? Are they wrong, too?"

"I blame the Christian church," Constance said, not hiding her indignation. "They're very arrogant...always forcing their God on everyone. That's why there's so much anger directed at them. I don't need anyone telling me how to live. And I certainly don't need anyone judging me or making me feel guilty about my choices. It's my life."

Trent sat beneath the gathering nightfall and reticently listened as they bandied their notions off one another. He could easily have made a case for his own irreligiousness, he thought. But there was already enough God bashing and theorizing among them that his humble opinion would only further the debate and delay their rest.

The disappearances were still a sensitive subject for everyone. In the company of others, it had become almost a taboo topic. There was not a person living that hadn't lost at least one family member, dear friend, neighbor or co-worker on that day. In an instant, lives were torn apart. And for weeks after that the world, for the first time, wept together as one family. They were connected by a single, extraordinary event that in its profundity, prompted warring nations to set down their weapons for a day, forced airports around the globe to cancel all flights, and sent scores of people flocking in droves to their local houses of worship. There they gathered, often in the absence of clergy, and communally cried for the missing, for the suffering, and for their own futures which at the moment looked uncertain.

Trent could only imagine the heartache Ben and Loretta experienced over their lost child. Why his own wife and children were spared, and others taken, would jar his intellect. Especially during those moments when he was free to ponder the why's and how's, and what were the intangibles that set those individuals apart from his family. The most nagging question was—where were they taken?

There was a time, before the rash of sightings and the disappearances, when talk of alien gods would have been dismissed by the mainstream as ludicrous. Now, such errant speculation had become credible in the minds of many. It made the likelihood of a race of supreme beings seem more than probable. For most people, seeing was believing. On the strength of this, there was no doubting what they saw.

As for Trent, Janet's assumption that they all might be the illegitimate offspring of extraterrestrials was, at the very least, an intriguing idea. And only slightly less absurd than the belief that humankind descended from apes. That was one article of faith that his good common sense could never quite accept.

Trent's theoretical mind—spoon fed on years of science fiction and fantasy—began to envision the diversity of strange worlds and cultures that possibly inhabited the universe; their bizarre customs, dress and language; whether they were human in appearance, or a grotesque assemblage of limbs, organs and hairy parts as the evolutionists would have people believe. Maybe the abductions were a prelude of sorts prior to their making first contact. Maybe even followed by Earth's induction into an intergalactic league of planets like on Star Trek.

But with every fanciful scenario his imagination conceived, his rational mind found reasons to reject. It discovered a loose thread in the timeline, leaving him to ask—*If space aliens did father the human race, and seeded the earth with their DNA—then who seeded their planet, and the planet before theirs*? The more he pulled on the thread, the more his fanciful scenarios began to unravel, until only one inescapable question remained—who supplied the original seed which all sentient life sprang from?

For the moment, Trent found himself wrestling with the eternal conundrum; mooring it to his intellect and dragging it through the facts as he knew them. He quickly realized, after a minute or two of staring at a blank slate in his head, that he lacked both the capacity, and the emotional stamina to tackle such a mind-bending, philosophical question in one sitting. There were far more pressing matters that deserved his full attention; the approaching darkness being one of them as he looked up and saw the receding gray transitioning into black.

"We have to leave now. Otherwise, we risk not finding any place to stay tonight," he said.

With that, they all stood and started out down the road together; joining the other survivors' who no doubt, also hoped that luck would find them a suitable place to bed down for the night.

DAY THREE

Chapter 21

The halls and corridors of the Grove Street Elementary School were awash in quarter-light, creating a somnolent collection of dimly lit passageways. There, the barely visible daylight filtered in through the classroom doorways to reveal the faint visage of sleeping survivors in the hundreds; all tightly packed and laying across the floor like prehistoric cave dwellers.

Dust covered, tattered, and reeking with the stench of two days, they slept in a jumble with scarcely any space between them; families, strangers, friends and foes alike, congregating under one roof in a seeming slumber while they waited for the fullness of daylight to arrive.

Though mostly subdued in their wait, a smattering of lament could be heard in the midst of them; standing out as delicate whimpers that crept throughout the room to prick the hearts of those still awake and aching in collective despair.

Just down the hall, the school's gymnasium resembled a warehouse of human wreckage. With too few kerosene lamps sitting atop the last bleacher row, there the sick, the sleeping, and the distressed lay every which way across the sprawling hardwood floor.

A town police officer, with the help of two volunteers from the local Red Cross chapter, walked gingerly, flashlights in hand, through the lying bodies. One of them carried a hand written short list of missing persons who were still being searched for by their families. He read off the names as he went, but so far, was hearing no replies.

Trent lay on his side, a blanket covering his upper half and a hefty corner of it bunched into a makeshift pillow under his head. His eyes were closed, but he was fully awake, and freely indulging in the morning's calm while his thoughts fled away to visions of home; to Nora and the kids; to his life and the way things were before the asteroid impact. In his mind it was all still a perfect picture; their faces, so close; every little subtly; the shade of their skin; the curl of their lips when they smiled; from birthmarks to blemishes and everything in between appeared as vivid to him as if they were standing only feet away.

It had been a long time since he recalled their features in such detail. In doing so, he tried not to read too much into his memories. Even as their images became more defined, and even troubled him slightly, like the reflection of things that would never be seen again. Though bittersweet in its recollection, after two days of depressing scenery, there was too much to enjoy in the fleeting moments that his mind spent with them.

He thought back to their recent holidays together; to last year's Thanksgiving Day dinner which routinely took place at his restaurant, and the sumptuous meal that his wait staff brought out for them. The atmosphere may have been lacking in homespun charm, but it *was* festive as they dove into their meal, and without so much as one blessing of thanks beforehand.

Their ignorance declared that the significance of the day—its reason for being—was totally lost on him and his family. It also didn't seem to matter that Trent was spending much of his time tending to the needs of his other patrons that night. Nevertheless, they would make the most of the evening which as in years past, became nothing more than a celebration of epicurean excess. And marked yet another infrequent occasion where they could sit together at the same table and enjoy each other's company.

Much like Thanksgiving, the Christmas seasons inspired more of the same sort of apathy towards its origin. The result was a celebration where the only spirit present in their household was one of conspicuous consumption. The holiday had become so completely watered down over the years; its customs and traditions hijacked by secularized carols and nondescript imagery to the point of irrelevance, that not one of them, if asked, could say with any certainty what their reason for even celebrating it was.

It now all seemed, in hindsight, to be so disrespectful, and maybe even sacrilegious if he pondered its supposed religious implications. He and his family were celebrating with indifference what some still considered two of the most hallowed days on the calendar. It smacked sickeningly of hubris, with an added after-sting of insensitivity.

He always prided himself on being respectful of others beliefs, whether he agreed with them or not. But now, with deaths menace looming just beyond the school walls, it was those same beliefs that caused him to question his own mortality, and to once again revisit the eternal conundrum.

Where did all life spring from? Oddly, the question nagged him like an inevitable consequence; testing every problem-solving algorithm his thought-laden mind could muster.

Trent was about to spin another theory when his thoughts were interrupted by the sound of a woman's shocked gasp. It came from directly behind him. Startled, he sat up to a degree along with several others who had heard the same gasp, and immediately turned in the direction of it. By now, a glimmer of diffused daylight was starting to break through the skylights above the gym; bathing everything beneath it in a twilight shade.

There, he saw Janet sitting up, her blanket draped over her shoulders, and her handbag, which she always kept close to her, resting open on her thigh. One hand held the bag still while the other hand, buried up to her forearm, anxiously moved its contents around in quick motions indicating something was amiss.

"Janet! What happened...are you alright?" Trent asked.

"Someone's been in my bag," she said angrily. "I had it underneath the blanket with me last night. When I woke up, it was outside the blanket and half off my shoulder. My rations are gone, and so is my wallet with my I.D.," she continued, and then looking around in a show of disdain for the culprit whom she no doubt hoped was within earshot. "What am I supposed to do now? I have nothing to eat or drink, and I can't get anything more without my I.D."

Constance, Ben and Loretta, upon hearing all the commotion, sat up also and came to Janet's aide. "Don't worry. After we leave here, we're sure to come across a military base at some point today," Ben said as he wiped the sleep from his eyes. "I can't see them denying anyone rations if their I.D. was stolen. That would just be cruel."

"I don't understand how you couldn't feel anything. Didn't you have your bag over your shoulder?" Constance asked.

"Yes, I did. I always keep it over my shoulder. I was really exhausted after all that walking we did yesterday. I guess I must've been in a deeper sleep than usual. The rations *maybe* I could understand, but they could've at least left my wallet. What good is that to them, anyway?"

"They'll either use your I.D. to get extra rations for themselves, or trade it for something they need. Whatever cash you had on your card is pretty much useless to anyone," Ben said. "What bothers me is that we're only three days into this crisis and people are already starting to turn on one another. If things don't get any better, soon...what's it going to be like after a week?" His query was less a question than it was a warning, and it occupied the space between them like a foregone conclusion.

They said nothing in that brief span, likely contemplating how much worse things might get. That's when Janet broke their silence. "Well, I just hope whoever it was, chokes on what they took. It's a despicable thing to steal someone's food...especially at a time like this."

"Its times like this when the stealing begins," Constance added after checking her own bag. And then satisfied that nothing was missing, clutched it tight between her bent arm and body.

Trent stared up at the skylight. "It seems like there's enough light outside. Now that we're all up, we might as well leave," he said, then stiffly rising to his feet. Fortunately, he could still feel the weight of his pockets' contents pressing him below his waist; creating awkward, but reassuring bulges that confirmed they had not been picked empty in his sleep. He went over and helped Constance to her feet, and then Janet whose hand bag, securely sandwiched between her arm and body, made for an off-balance rise as he pulled her forward. Ben and Loretta, their blankets draped loosely across their shoulders, were holding each other's hand and already standing in wait for them. Ben then stared out across the packed gym as if he were surveying it for the quickest way out.

Prepared to leave, they headed out across the gym floor towards the exit, stepping along a jagged survivor-strewn path, and—after last night's robbery—looking into a slew of faces with jaundiced suspicion. Up until now, there had always been a modicum of mutual deference accorded between survivors whom undoubtedly identified with each other's plight. Their anxieties, heartaches and wounds had inextricably bound them in fraternal kinship. And where, in spite of their difficulties, occasional acts of kindness could still be displayed toward the least of them. But that was early on.

At present, overt gestures of caution had seized their behavior, effusing selfish concern through their ranks with pandemic swiftness. Where a blanket, food, or water was a visible source of envy for some, the rest had been smitten by an attitude of leeriness directed at anyone who dared to get too close. It stalked Trent's party as they pushed through the doors of the school and out onto the street;

stepping over the dozens who, unable to find room inside, camped out beneath the awning at the entrance landing.

"Before we start out, I think it would be a good idea if we gave Janet a portion of our rations," Trent said. "Since she doesn't have any...if we each gave her a piece, it would be enough to hold her until we reach the next military base."

Janet stood graciously silent. Meanwhile, among the others there was a peculiar moment of hesitation where they seemed to be deliberating in silence.

Constance, no doubt feeling the pressure, gave her co-sympathizers a quick glance, and then looked at Trent. "You say that like you know exactly where the next base is located," she said.

"I don't know where the next base is any more than you do. I just think if we're supposed to be looking after one another, that it should include nourishment as well, don't you think?"

"Yes, you're right...but. We all started out with the same amount. That doesn't mean we all eat the same amount. I've been nibbling on my ration from the moment I got it. If anyone of us prefers not to nibble, and takes bigger bites, that means they've consumed more than the person who nibbles."

"What are you trying to say, Constance? You think just because I'm a little bigger than you, that I need to eat more?"

"No! I'm not saying that at all. You misunderstood."

"I think what she's saying is...from here on...we need to safeguard our belongings. Ben and me don't mind sharing our rations...this time," Loretta said, then pulling out her remaining ration and breaking off a small piece, as did Ben. Trent broke off a chunk from his. Constance, in an effort not to appear petty, broke a sizeable chunk off of hers and gave it to Janet along with an apology.

The scene ahead of them, even at that early hour, was much the same as it had been for the past two days; bleakly gray, and overrun by a diaspora of haggard survivors in search of a safe haven. Trent and his party entered into the menagerie—blending in with steadfast optimism that the day's end would see them that much closer to home.

Chapter 22

The bell outside Preston's office sounded with the sudden blare of an alarm clock. Its ring lasted all of ten seconds, but considering its proximity to him, seemed indefinite to his ears. He sat behind his desk and there, kept his attention stayed on the opened file folder directly in front of him. All the while, he barely reacted to the buildup of adolescent commotion going on right outside his closed office door.

Since his appointment to Principal of John Jay High School on Manhattan's lower east side, the demands of the position had not gotten any easier. There was always a near crisis to avert, a budget to try to get below, or some race-related incident that needed to be extinguished. Still, he enjoyed the responsibilities that came with the office, and in particular, the marginal latitude it offered him outside of the office. Policing the halls of the school and lightly engaging with the student body was his preferred pastime. He did so with relish, taking each encounter with the kids as an opportunity to pass on to them life lessons.

In the past two years he had watched in horror as the global cataclysm reshaped the continental topography of the planet; felt the underpinnings of the nation's emergency response agencies struggle to keep pace against an unprecedented wave of disasters; saw the ensuing geo-political furor reach a fever pitch; and learned, to his shock, that an eighth of his student body, a sixth of his faculty, two Education Council members for his district, including the Community Superintendent all vanished without a trace during the disappearances. The sheer sum of tragedies had left him shaken and dumbfounded.

In the immediate aftermath, the resultant anxiety drove those who remained, to shut themselves in their homes, consequently transforming a once thriving New York metropolis into a veritable ghost town. So devastating was the effect on society, that had it not been for the post cataclysm migration of survivors, and their infusion of labor and talent into the nation's eastern half, the United States might not have recovered.

Preston, along with his wife and son, were among those inhabitants who had hunkered down in their Somerville, New Jersey home. After weeks of living like recluses, the resumption of school was a welcomed sign to everyone that the city was slowly returning to normal again.

It was late morning, and to his dismay, there was enough paperwork on his desk to keep him from his hall patrol for much of the day. Foremost on his to-do list was determining the appropriate disciplinary action against a teacher who, having reached his breaking point with a particularly disruptive student, slapped the child across the face during class. That the student was black, and the teacher white, only added to the drama. Immediately thereafter, the atmosphere was charged with racially divisive indignation, setting off vituperative demands for the teacher's arrest once word of the incident hit the streets.

Complicating Preston's decision was his relationship with the teacher. They had been friends for a number of years, going back to their days as starry-eyed science teachers fresh out of graduate school. It was only after repeated concessions on Preston's part that the boy's mother agreed not to press charges against his friend, who by this time, had already been placed on paid administrative leave.

Since termination was out of the question, the only dilemma facing Preston now was deciding whether to suspend him for a time, or have him transferred to another school district where he could continue teaching without any backlash. Either way, he would be required to attend anger management classes, but at least he would still be employed.

Preston reached for his computer mouse and clicked it, instantly bringing his monitor to life. He guided the pointer to his Favorites list, dropped it down, and opened the New York City Department of Education webpage. From there, he clicked on the Principal's Portal link and started reviewing the policy regarding teacher misconduct. He was finger scrolling through several pages of a PDF file when he suddenly heard a knock at the door just seconds before the school bell rang signaling the start of the next period. A blurred figure stood in the door's opaque glass window. "Come in," he said in a distracted tone as his eyes poured over the paragraph headings zipping past on the screen.

He still hadn't looked up; even as the door opened, sending in a blast of chatter that gradually began to fade with students hurrying off to their next classes. Only when it closed shut did he turn away from the monitor and there saw standing at the entrance a fetching young schoolgirl of about sixteen; trendily dressed and cradling a textbook in her arm.

"Good morning, Laurie," Preston said with surprise, and then glancing down at the time displayed in the corner of his monitor. "Or maybe I should be saying good afternoon. I didn't realize how long I'd been sitting here. Shouldn't you be at lunch, now?"

"Yes...but I wanted to talk to you first. There's a problem," she said as she approached his desk and took a seat in one of the two chairs facing it.

Preston went back to his topic search, all the while being careful not to appear unconcerned before her. "What sort of problem are we talking about? Is it one of your teachers...a problem at home?"

"No, nothing like that."

"Okay." He paused for a moment to give more of his attention to the screen, and the heading, "Disciplinary Actions" as it scrolled up. "Is it a boy problem?"

"No, of course not. How could you think that?"

Preston darted a glance over at her, quickly surmising her upset before resuming his scan of the information in front of him "Sorry. I was just asking...that's all. Well, if not that, then what is it?"

"I think I'm...pregnant."

Upon hearing that, Preston immediately stopped what he was doing and turned toward Laurie, this time with rapt attention. "You think you're pregnant? How do you know?"

"Because I'm two months late...because I'm throwing up at least twice a day, that's how. I'm sick all the time. I don't even want to go to lunch, that's how bad it is."

"And, why are you coming to me with this?"

"Because it's your baby."

"No...that's impossible. I'm sterile. I have been since the disappearances. It's got to be somebody else's baby."

"No, it's not. How could you even think that? I've never been with anyone else except you...you know that. I guess you're not as sterile as you thought, 'cause this *is* your baby." Laurie's eyes began to well up. "What am I going to do, Mr. Fields? I can't have a baby," she said in a desperate sounding plea, exacerbated by her tears.

The volume of her pleas caused Preston to jump up from his seat like it was on fire. He hurried to the other side of his desk and sat in the chair next to her. "Okay...shh!" he said, his voice consoling, but insistent. He then quickly looked over his shoulder at the office door's window to see if any of his administrative staff were within sight. Satisfied with their privacy, he assumed an appropriate posture with

Laurie—one that would not lead to any rumors in the event of someone walking past and catching a glimpse of them. "Look, let's not get hysterical, here. You need to be strong now, okay? If you say it's mine, then I believe you. Give me time to figure something out, okay?"

"What is there to figure out, Mr. Fields? I don't want it. I don't want this baby."

"I know. And I'll make a few phone calls today. We might be able to take care of it sometime next week. I'll call you the minute I have something arranged."

Laurie, her head down and textbook in her lap, wrung her hands anxiously while he spoke. She wore a sickly expression as if she were seconds away from being ill.

"Umm...you haven't told anyone about us, have you...maybe a girlfriend who you swore to secrecy, or someone like that?"

"No...no one."

"Good girl. Now dry your eyes. You can't go out there looking like that," Preston said, at which point he got up, walked to the other side of the desk, and sat down in his chair. He opened a draw, pulled out a late-pass sheet and signed it in quick, cursive strokes while Laurie cleaned the tears from her face. "Here, take this," he said, handing it to her. "Go to Study Hall if you're not up to lunch. I'll talk to you soon."

He watched Laurie as she rose from the chair and headed for the door. Before opening it, she looked back at him; her face pained as though she were bearing the weight of the world. Preston gave her a reassuring nod to see her on her way. She opened the door and left, pulling it shut behind her.

He fell back in his chair, smacked his hand onto his head and dragged it over his hair from front to back in a disbelieving sweep, accompanied by a heavy sigh. His affair with Laurie lasted only a brief while. She was a transfer student from out of state; the product of a broken home where she lived alone with her mother. She also walked with a slight limp, the result of a playground injury she suffered as a child. Consequently, it was difficult for her to make friends. Especially among the image conscience cliques whose job it was to determine the caste of kids they believed were physically inferior.

Preston was the only person outside of her teachers who actually talked to her, at first in casual greetings, enough to make her feel visible. And then over time, light small talk and compliments which lessened her insecurities and made her feel attractive. Their eventual trysts took place after school; well outside of the city limits in seedy, rent-by-the-hour motels where nobody asks any questions.

After several weeks, and fearful of being found out, Preston abruptly ended their relationship. And now, even on the heels of Laurie's dilemma, and his having to find a quick solution, it still was not registering with him that his actions were reprehensible. Nor was there sufficient regard for his wife of sixteen years and their teenage son.

For the moment, all he could think about was the possibility of his being charged with having committed a federal felony—transporting a minor across state lines for sex, and the all but certain conviction that would follow if Laurie were ever to talk. The potential of that alone made the question of the baby's paternity irrelevant.

As he sat there lamenting his predicament, he cursed his dumb luck for getting intimate with someone who was not among Earth's newly sterile.

Chapter 23

The battered streets of Manhattan Island were a trackless, zigzag of upended obstacles that tested the resolve of all who spent the day winding through them. The approaching evening made navigating the dense environs even more treacherous as sharp edges of glass, and jagged metal shards threatened to prick the skin with infection at every turn. After spending the night holed up in an empty storefront, Nora and her party had covered several dozen blocks and were now only a few away from the George Washington Bridge.

Broadway continued to be their yellow brick road, of sorts; turning them into reluctant tourists on an exhaustive walking tour of the west side of Manhattan. From the Financial District, on through Tribeca, and then into Soho, Greenwich Village, then on through Times Square, past Hell's Kitchen and currently into Washington Heights where the threat of being mugged had them looking around every corner.

So far, after having walked a full day, they had not come across a single military base or rations drop point en route. What little rations they had leftover from yesterday were finished off hours ago. And to make matters worse, the desperate hordes who meandered among the ruins were busily roaming the boulevard in unabashed anarchy; their guile strengthened by selfishness as they, in some instances, snatched and grabbed, and even assaulted those less bold than themselves.

Bodies still lay in the street, tens of hundreds of them; bloated and decaying alongside the sprawl of refuse that had spilled out from violated storefronts. There, it mixed with the remains of the dead to escort the living in the putrid stench left from their departure. Every so often, semiautomatic rounds of gunfire could be heard over the wail of distraught residents. Its nearness, seeming too irresponsible to be mistaken for friendly fire, resonated off the building surfaces to sound like a Fourth of July party was just around the next corner. Some residents, either as a deterrent or solely to intimidate, openly carried their weapons for all to see; and did so with an audacious swagger that was surely a disincentive for a few would-be thieves. Meanwhile, rumor had it that survivors were being picked off by sniper fire from the rooftops—no doubt someone's twisted idea of fun.

Laura held onto Preston's arm, locking it in her own as though it were a lifeline out from the pit of quicksand the city had become. There was much to be frightened of, not the least of which were the strangers who wandered an aimless course round about, many of whom had eyed them in passing with seemingly malicious intentions. With most of the car headlights gone black after three days of continuous operation, the primary source of illumination came from tons of debris that had been set ablaze and left to burn in the streets. Varying in size, the largest of them roared with unbridled fury, sending up a spray of glowing embers like the spew from an active volcano. Excited residents gathered close and continuously fed its flames as if caught up in a pagan celebration to a wicker man.

Then there were the groans of the dying; the shouts and the moans hitting her ear like a steady barrage of agony—all indicative of a neighborhood in the throes of turmoil. The rare sound of hungry infants crying in the background, or the sight of one lying limp and lifeless in the arms of its grieving mother, only added to the emotional cascade buffeting her senses.

She spent her entire adult life working and playing in Manhattan, and never once had she laid eyes on this part of the island. It was as alien to her as a stroll through some remote Tibetan village in central Asia. Then, just as it had all evening, another random shot suddenly rang out, sending a fright-filled twitch up her back that almost knocked Preston off balance.

"Why can't they do something about this...where's the National Guard...the Police? We need protection," she said nervously, her chatter acting as a self-induced form of distraction.

"It's almost dark. They're not stupid enough to come into this neighborhood at night," Preston said.

"Then we must all have a combined I.Q. of sixty, 'cause here we are, right in the thick of it...just like sitting ducks," Dale said, followed by a quick glance over his shoulder. "If I have to die tonight, I'd at least like to have one last meal. Oh...but that's right...I can't, because someone decided we shouldn't waste time picking up rations before leaving the base yesterday. Isn't that right, Taylor?"

The others kept quiet, either too weak from hunger, or too distracted in their own peril to comment. The ill effects of a bad decision weighed unfavorably on their faces, while their silence all but confirmed Dale's caustic critique. "Well, Taylor...what have you got to say for yourself?" Dale asked insistently.

"We have to keep moving while we still have some light," Taylor said, pushing forward with prideful disregard. "As long as those fires are burning, we're alright. It's when they burn out that we may have some problems. This isn't the sort of place where you want to get caught in the dark."

"If you all had listened to me, we might not have had to worry about getting caught up here...*and* we would've gotten our rations. I don't mind saying I told you so. Next time, you need to listen to me."

"Well, can't we stop now? It's practically dark, and I don't see why we can't pick up from here in the morning. We've got all this light," Laura said.

"Because, I don't see any place safe for us to stop, that's why," Taylor said.

"What about all these empty stores we're passing...why can't we go inside one of them?"

"Trust me...you don't want to go inside any of them. There are some bad things going on in some of those stores."

"How do you know that?"

"I just do. We need to keep moving...just a little further. I know this neighborhood. There's a school about two blocks from here. If it's not too badly damaged, we can bed down there for the night."

"And will there be food and water there?" Dale asked.

Up until now, Nora hadn't said anything. She preferred they walk in silence, mistakenly believing that it somehow rendered them all invisible to the neighborhood thugs. Miguel and Sonia presumably shared her thinking since they too had been quiet for much of the way. The others, though, judging from their careless banter, did not seem as respectful of the threats in their vicinity. They continued to throw caution to the wind; Dale criticizing Taylor as if he had every right to; Laura bemoaning her anxieties with rhetorical questions which she likely knew had no answers.

Nora, apprehensive as she was, walked with her arms folded across her front in a protective clutch. She hoped her self-embrace might quell the incessant trembling that was surging through her like a steady current. There was so much happening—so many atrocities—that they began to take on the primitive aspect of a nightmare.

To her right were the gutted, windowless storefronts where inside, a palpitating orange reflection flirted with the black shadows. And where there was no activity except for those awful things which she imagined were happening in the back, out of sight, as Taylor so reticently warned. To her left, an eclectic mix of temperaments rampaged like untamed creatures loosed from a lifetime of compulsory restraint. She kept her eyes focused front, trying not to look into either the black void, or into the face of anyone nearby who had the potential to harm her. Meanwhile, the faces that she did rely on, those of Trent and the children to help her through, for the moment, no longer worked; short-circuited by a sensory overload of nerve-racking images.

She stepped frugally along a littered path, her feet rarely settling on a clean surface as the haunting scenery moved past. Hunger seized her for the past several hours, feeling much like a beast in her belly trying to punch its way out. Spasms tugged along her ribcage, creating a discernable slouch in her posture that made walking any further, a test of endurance. She was in misery, and three days into her journey home, became depressed by the reality that it had only just begun.

The sky was almost black, leaving only the orange glow from randomly spaced bonfires, and the brown incandescence from a paltry succession of headlights to lead them on. Meanwhile, Dale continued to badger Taylor regarding his ineptitude at leading thus far. "Well, Taylor. I'm waiting. Is there going to be any food and water where we're going, or what?"

"Shut up and walk," Taylor barked at him without glancing back.

"C'mon. You're the man with all the answers. How come you don't have one for us this time?" As he waited for an answer, the others kept silent; seemingly content to let Dale's rant run its course as though his venting were cathartically expelling their own frustrations. "Admit it. You have no idea what you're doing, or how to get us safely out of here, do you?" he continued. "You know what I think? I think you're a phony...a big fraud on some kind of power trip," Dale said, then looking around with condemnation at the others, "and you've all got yourselves to blame. He's fooled you into following him," he said, pointing a finger at Taylor. "And now he wants to lead us over the edge of a cliff. This has gone far enough." Right then, as they neared the corner of West 145th Street, Dale stopped walking and stood his ground. Never one to shy away from self-expression or controversy, he was in rare form, and was not backing down this time. His hunger fueled tirade caused the others to stop and look on. "I say we make a change in leadership...now, before he gets us all killed."

Taylor, unflappable for the most part, now turned to face him. His patience wearing thin, he was seemingly in wait for the customary show of support from the others. But this time, for the first time since his leading them, they refrained from taking sides.

"Who here agrees with me? Who thinks it's time for a leadership change?"

Nora looked on poignantly while the power grab unfolded in front of her. She thought Taylor had done an admirable job thus far, and didn't deserve the revolt that was rising up against him. And after all, he did save her life. If there were a litmus-test for worthiness, surely that would have to count for something.

But that was three days ago. Right now, she was hungry, and he was responsible for sacrificing what would have been their day's meal, on the altar of expediency for the sake of time management. It was counterintuitive to good sense, she thought; even if he had no way of predicting their rations predicament. In spite of her misgivings, this was one time where she could not bring herself to rally to his defense.

Dale, no doubt sensing victory, directed a snide smirk over at Taylor. "I think your time is up," he said.

"Shut up," Taylor demanded, then slowly began approaching him.

"No. I think you need to pay attention to what's happening here. By their silence, the people are speaking—"

"I said to shut up!"

"Okay...maybe you're not understanding me. I'll make it easier for you. We're all hungry. We want food. And we think you're a little crazy."

Suddenly, a fist came arcing up from Taylor's hip and connected flush with Dale's jaw, knocking him off balance. As he fell back, Taylor rushed forward, grabbed him by the collar and ran him, back first, hard against a brick storefront wall. With Dale's pleas for him to stop, falling deaf in his ear, he began striking him with open-handed slaps across the face; one after another in short, powerful blows that were oddly untypical given the spontaneity of the assault.

The others, after getting over their initial shock, rushed over to separate them.

"Taylor, stop! What are you doing?" Nora shouted from a few feet away.

"What's it look like I'm doing? I'm beating the crap out of this fool, that's what."

"Well, you've made your point. Now stop."

"Hey...c'mon, guy...it's over now. Let the man go," Preston said as he and Miguel attempted to pull them apart.

Taylor was still raining slaps onto Dale when he felt the pull from behind, and seemed bent on getting a few more licks in, regardless of the distance growing between him and his target. Finally, he released Dale's collar and stumbled back. He applied a thumb massage to the palm of his striking hand as he backed away, then turned and walked a few feet off to collect himself.

"You have to admit...he did have it coming," Preston said quietly to Laura.

"Maybe so, but that still doesn't make it right."

Now extricated from his assailant, Dale leaned back against the wall, his eyes vacantly searching for focus as he tried to clear the cobwebs clouding his perception. His legs soon weakened, causing him to slide down the wall onto his rear. And then, with his knees pointing straight up, he raised both hands and brought them to his face. He then lowered his head into them and began bawling in boisterous sobs that for a grown man, was uncomfortable to watch.

Nora looked on, conflicted over what the proper response to his weeping should be. The others stood over him with likewise ambivalence. Sonia was the first to walk away. She headed toward a nearby parked car; its windows busted out, and its dust covered sheet metal pummeled to unrecognizability, and there, took a seat atop its hood. Nora took the moment to walk over to Taylor. "You didn't have to do that to him," she said.

"C'mon...you can't tell me I'm the only one that wanted to slap that pompous, windbag. All I did...was do you all a favor."

"But we're supposed to be protecting each other from the things outside of our circle...not from each other. We can't go physically attacking one another whenever there's a disagreement."

"I told him to shut up...I did. And you all heard me. But he wouldn't. He was warned. His mouth got him into something his butt couldn't get him out of," Taylor said. "He had to know what was coming next. What did he think...I was just going to stand there and let him call me crazy? Nobody talks to me like that."

"Well, he did provoke you, there's no denying that. And unless he decides to go the rest of the way alone, I'm pretty sure he'll think twice before trying to challenge you again. We just need to remember who we're dealing with here. I know Dale's type. I've seen it before. He's insecure and overcompensates for it by being a loudmouth. There's not much you can do with people like him except ignore them."

"Well, that might work for you, but I can think of a few other ways of handling it."

Just as Taylor said that, the familiar sound of helicopter blades could be heard directly overhead. But unlike the far off noise of those that routinely flew high above them, and kept on going, on a direct approach to Central Park, these blades sounded closer than usual, and were growing louder by the second.

Nora and Taylor both looked up at the same time; wary of the new development that had succeeded in bringing the neighborhood commotion to a standstill and now drew all attention toward the sky. Within seconds, a low flying Army National Guard helicopter burst out from over the rooftops, and then another after that. Their brilliant high beams were directed down onto the gathering mob, ostensibly seducing them like fish bait on a hook. They flew straight across their field of view, disappearing over the rooftops on their way toward the Hudson River.

It was an unusual sight, the sudden appearance of working technology in a neighborhood that had just recently been thrust back to the Stone Age. As Nora tried to process the event, suddenly and without explanation, every able-bodied person outside of her traveling party it seemed, turned and ran in the direction of the aircrafts. She looked over at Taylor. "What's going on? Why are they going after those helicopters?"

"I'm not sure," Taylor said as he watched them run. "I think they're heading for Riverbank Park. It's only one block over from here. If I'm right, they might be heading there expecting a rations drop off. There's no way to know for sure. Just in case, we should make our way over there." By now, Preston and the others had already reached the same conclusion and were preparing to leave with them— except for Dale. He hadn't budged from his pitiful reclusion; his legs, bent at the knee and held together in his clasped arms while his head hung disrepute between them.

"Dale...c'mon, it's time to leave," Preston yelled.

Miguel momentarily left the others and rushed over to where Dale was sitting. "The National Guard may be handing out rations at the park. We need to hurry up and get over there before they run out. Get up!" he insisted, then reaching down and grabbing him by the arm to help him to his feet.

Dale rose without much resistance. Once on his feet, he kept his head at a slight angle to hide his swollen left cheek and bruised eye from the others in the group. Together they joined the procession down 145th Street. Up ahead, they could see the lights of the helicopters descending against the empty sky. Their pace picked up upon sighting them, and soon, they were competing in a beleaguered footrace with other abject survivors, all hoping for their turn at the dinner table.

Chapter 24

Trent and his party had gotten off the bustling main road of the unknown town they were currently passing through. The crowds had grown increasingly hostile, forcing them, for safety's sake, to abandon the more direct route home, for the quieter side streets and back roads. So quiet, in fact, that when they spoke, their words trailed off in a haunting echo.

On one side of the street, a wooded tract of tall but charred timbers stretched far along a winding, debris scattered road. Opposite them, a bedroom community of modest two-story and ranch style homes stood. Many of them were either burned to the ground, or so damaged that they were hopelessly unlivable. But a few were still intact, albeit just barely.

Those same homes were fiercely guarded by their occupants; some of whom stood sentry on front porches and brandishing loaded weapons, while others simply shoved the muzzle of a shotgun out the port of a boarded-up window if anyone so much as approached their front door.

Though the hour wasn't late, the darkening sky said otherwise. And with night soon approaching, they resigned themselves to sleeping outdoors for the night. They began searching along the wooded tract for any tree that still retained enough of its leaves for them to campout beneath. The street was fairly deserted allowing them to search without the competitive jockeying that plagued them earlier. After finding a suitable spot, they each claimed their individual patch of earth for the night, and then cooperatively began clearing away the debris that covered the site.

Suddenly, in the middle of their cleaning, cries of, *"Help! Please. Is anybody out there...somebody? Please help me!"* cut through the seeming tranquility and struck their ears like a harsh siren. The voice was unmistakably female.

"Where did that come from?" Ben asked immediately afterwards, then turned and looked every which way for it.

"It sounded like it came from one of those houses down the street," Janet said. "She might be hurt or something. Maybe we should help her."

"Help her! Help her how?" Constance asked. I think there are quite enough dangers out here for us, as it is. We don't need to be looking for any new ones. It might be nothing more than some crazy old woman, anyway. I can't imagine we'd be the first ones to hear her. Somebody before us had to have heard her...tried to help...then realized she was crazy."

"You don't know that. What if you're wrong? What if it were you?"

"If it were, then believe me, I would've found some way to slit my wrists by now. 'Cause I'd rather die than be trapped somewhere for days...unable to move. I say it makes no sense for us to intentionally put ourselves in harm's way. We can't risk it."

As Constance went on protesting, Trent could not deny the salient points she had made, even if they were blatantly self-serving. It would be unwise for them to get caught up in a situation that they might not be able to get free of. In the ensuing minutes, the quiets return made it easier to explain the cries away as an aberration, or some teenage prank. Nevertheless, uneasiness beset his conscience as they each gradually went back to clearing away the campsite.

Seconds later, *"Help somebody...please! Anybody!"*

They almost expected the stirring plea, and once it returned, it snatched their attention with the very first utterance. Her voice was filled with exhaustion and encumbered by a softening resignation to whatever circumstance she had found herself in.

Trent stopped what he was doing and turned towards its point of origin while its echo dissipated into the atmosphere. He couldn't shake the words out of his head. And although he clearly knew it wasn't Nora's voice, his conscience was telling him that it could have been. He looked back at the others. "I think we should go and check it out. It's only right. And besides, we couldn't stay here and listen to that all night, and then not do anything. That would just be inhuman."

Constance glanced up at the sky. "It'll be dark soon. Remember, none of us has any matches. How do you expect to see anything?" she asked.

Trent looked at his watch. "We still have about forty minutes of light left. We should be back before nightfall."

"Then we had better hurry," Ben said as he tossed aside his makeshift broom and then grabbed Loretta by the hand.

Constance's expression was full of disagreement, but being clearly outnumbered, she no doubt saw no point in trying to discourage their effort. They began walking toward where they believed the cry for help originated from. Besides them, there were now no other people on the street. The isolation was unsettling, like entering into a maleficent vacuum where nothing could escape.

As they approached the house in question; its two-story face, partially obscured behind a veil of shrubs, and flanked on both sides by abandoned homes, they could hear pitiful whimpering coming from somewhere inside. The windows on the main floor were boarded up, and those upstairs were dark except for one room where a candle light flickered behind a chiffon curtain.

They stopped at the foot of a flagstone walkway leading to the entrance and there, listened carefully for any other sounds.

After hearing no other voices mixed in with her sobbing, Trent, still affected over Nora's wellbeing, was the first to venture out onto the walkway. Upon reaching the front door, he leaned his ear in close, just to confirm, and then looked back. He fully expected to see Ben right behind him. To his surprise, Ben was still standing at the foot of the walkway.

Shielded by the quiet, their tongues were inhibited with apprehension as Trent gestured for him to come along. Ben immediately looked at Loretta, and then back at Trent before giving him a regretful shrug of his shoulders as if to say, *she doesn't want me to go.*

Trent didn't like that he was now left to investigate this mystery by himself. He couldn't imagine that he was the only one who cared enough to try and help this poor woman. But then, he couldn't quite fault Loretta for not wanting to let go of her boyfriend. He was certain Nora would have done the same thing had it been him—or so he hoped. Aware that it was all up to him now, he turned face forward, and after a moment's pause, knocked firmly on the front door.

The screams from inside were almost instantaneous, setting off a bloodcurdling chill that coursed through him like ice water.

"I'm here to help. Are you able to open the door," Trent yelled from the other side.

"I can't...I can't. Please hurry. He'll be back soon," the woman shouted. There was panic in her voice, then fading into trailing groans of urgency. Trent, feeling the pressure of the moment confounding his good sense, took a nervous gulp and pushed hard on the door. When it wouldn't budge, he raised his leg and began pounding it with his foot like he'd seen in the movies. After four thrusts, the door's frame started to give, eventually breaking away from its post on his last push.

Waiting before him was a curtain of absolute blackness looking to engulf him the minute he dared to step inside.

"Is that you? Are you down there? I'm upstairs. Hurry...please. He'll be back any minute."

Having already committed himself, Trent knew there was no turning back. He proceeded to enter into the void. Each step he would start to make had an unknown finish, so was taken with caution until firmly planted. He reached his arms out in front of him and blindly groped the space ahead hoping to avoid whatever furniture might be there to trip him up. The scant light from the open doorway at his back was completely devoured by the voluminous black vista facing him.

"It's too dark. I can't find the staircase. Say something so I can follow your voice."

"I'm in a room upstairs. You've got to get up here now...what's wrong with you? Help me, please. Don't you leave me here."

"I'm not. Just keep talking."

As he continued to feel his way deeper into the house, his sense of direction was honing in on the sound of her voice. Once he filtered out the hollow dissonance within the shuttered main floor, he could hear her voice gradually pulling him toward her like words on a leash around his neck. He turned left with the sound of them and continued further until he felt the newel of a banister touch his right hand. His heart raced beneath his chest; enough so, that he feared cardiac arrest if he didn't find her soon. Its every beat was transferred to his limbs, creating a tremulous throb that stole all the fluidity from his movements with each step he climbed.

Once he reached the landing, her pleas directed him straight ahead to the end of a hall. There, he noticed a slip of light peeking out from underneath a closed door. He went up to the door, turned the knob, and was surprised to find it unlocked. Then bracing himself for whatever scene lay on the other side, he opened the door slowly. The light spilled out and then washed over his face as he guardedly peered inside.

The room was small, austere at first sight, and only sparingly furnished. A candle flickered alone on a bureau across from a sheetless, full sized bed where a naked woman lay face up. She was bound at both wrists to a brass headboard and left prone in one position; arms up straight over her head, legs closed tight—apparently by choice—and knees pointing up to the ceiling. A bandana which most likely was used to gag her, had been worked loose and fell limp around her neck.

"Come here and untie me...quick! Hurry!" she demanded. "He might be on his way back."

"Who might be on his way back? How did this happen to you?"

"Just hurry up...will you?"

"I'm going as fast as I can. He's got several knots in here." Trent's hands shook as he fumbled to untie her. Through it all, he found time to feel a bit insulted by the ungrateful tone she used with him. But then, not knowing what came before, it was easy to put two and two together and conclude that something awful must have happened, here. If anyone deserved a pass for behaving like a shrew, it was her, he reasoned.

Once Trent loosed the final knot, she yanked her arms free. Then shielding her chest with one arm, she awkwardly brought her legs around to a sitting position on the edge of the bed.

"My clothes are in that corner over there," she said, gesturing a head point to the other side of the room.

Trent went over, grabbed her clothes—a pair of flat shoes, denim jeans, and a T-shirt—from off the floor and handed them to her, then politely turned away so she could dress herself. Before he could even grasp that a naked woman was dressing behind him, she was up and heading out the room door.

"C'mon, we have to leave, now," she said just before disappearing into the hallway.

Trent rushed out right behind her. "Do you know where you're going?" he asked.

"No. How do we get out of here?"

"Just take my arm. I'll get us out." Trent led her down the staircase to the main floor where, in his rush to get out, he nervously crashed into more furniture than he had on the way in. He spotted what looked like a faint shade of light up ahead which he knew could only be coming from the open front doorway. They both ran for it, and within seconds, burst through into the open air.

The others likely watched in amazement as the two suddenly came rushing out of the house. The unknown woman released Trent's arm the second her foot touched the flagstone walkway. She then took off running toward the woods like someone was chasing after her.

"Don't just stand there. Run!" she said as she rushed past them.

"Trent, what's going on? What was she doing in there?" Loretta asked.

"I don't know for sure, but whatever happened in there, has got her really spooked," Trent said, backing away from the house as he spoke. "The only thing I'm certain of is that the man who owns this house is dangerous. We need to leave here...now, before he gets back."

With that, they all moved quickly off the property and ran behind the unknown woman who, by now, was halfway across the street. They followed her into the woods opposite the house. Since her rescue had taken longer than expected, the sky was only minutes away from total darkness. They were barely able to make her out as she ran deep into the woods, stopped well clear of the street, and hid behind the trunk of a scorched oak. Trent and the others, confused as they were, continued to follow her lead and stayed out of sight behind the trees.

"Can somebody please tell me what's going on?" Janet asked.

"Shhh...keep your voice down. Words travel like the wind out here. I don't want him to hear us," the woman whispered while peering out from behind the tree.

"Who's *him* and why should we be afraid?"

"I'm talking about the creep that's been holding me captive in there. He's got a gun." She then paused for a moment to look around the immediate area. "How many days has it been since the asteroid?"

"Almost three days, now," Ben said.

"Really? Wow...a day and a half. That's how long I was in there. He kept me drugged. I didn't know the time or anything."

"Did he abduct you?"

"No...it wasn't like that. I went with him. Wait...I think I see him coming. Everyone be quiet."

The white spot of a flashlight could be seen bouncing a path against a dark background; its beam penetrating the evening like a detached object in search of something. The scene all around it was devoid of all other signs of life except for them. They stayed hidden from view and kept absolutely still.

From there, they watched the light skim along the broken street pavement and turn onto the walkway leading to the house. To no one's surprise, it abruptly stopped at the front door. It spent almost no time studying the damage done to it before disappearing into the house. Trent kept his eye on the little square of light that was the upstairs window and started counting the seconds it would take for the man to reach the room. On his eight-count, he saw the white spot of the flashlight streak past the window's curtain, and then fluctuate the room's light as if it were searching in and under every possible hiding place. Soon after that, the room went completely dark.

The rescued woman, upon seeing the light go out, and no doubt feeling safer now in the company of others, breathed a relieving exhale, then immediately dropped to a seated position at the base of the tree. In fact, with her captor no longer posing a threat to any of them, they were all finally able to relax.

Trent took a seat at the base of his tree and leaned back against its broad trunk. He could feel the adrenaline in his system gradually leveling off, and the fatigue brought on by his evenings exploits creeping in behind it. The pitch blackness meant there would be no leaving there that night.

He took his blanket and was about to tent it over himself when his eye caught a flash of light breaking through the trees. He peered out quickly from behind his tree and saw that the light came from the street directly in front of the house he had broken into. Whoever this man was, he was clearly ticked off over the loss of his hostage, and judging from the way he searched the area, seemed intent on reclaiming her.

Trent watched for several petrifying seconds as the shaft of light sliced into the dark; its radiance partially revealing to him the others hiding in frozen silence within the shadow of their trees. It then cut a darting line in and out, reflecting off every dead surface as it went from one spot to another. Finally, after a tense few minutes of holding his breath, the invading beam of light was gone. Soon after that, he heard what sounded like a door slam shut. As far as he could tell, the man had gone back inside his house, and hopefully, given up trying to locate his runaway. Nevertheless, they all kept silent and didn't move a muscle for several minutes after, just in case he returned for a second attempt.

"That was close," Ben whispered. "Are you sure he had a gun?"

"Of course I am. I was staring down the barrel of it every few hours."

"What's your name?" Loretta asked.

"Gina."

One by one, and under the cover of total darkness, they introduced themselves to her. The varied spacing of their voices created a dizzying effect of stereophonic whispers that seemed to emanate from nothingness.

"You said you voluntarily went with that guy. What's your connection to him?" Trent asked.

"There is no connection. I'd never met him before a day and a half ago. I had just come down from Boston about a month ago. A friend of mine was letting me stay with her for a while. Then the rock storm happened. Her home was destroyed. I was inside at the time. She was at work. I waited in front of that house for hours, but she never came home. I still don't know where she is...or whether she's even alive. By that day's end, the military were handing rations out in the park...but they don't last long. The next day, people were hungry and thirsty all over again. That's when this guy walks up to me and asks if I have someplace to stay...and I didn't...but I wasn't going to tell him that. Anyway, he says that him and his wife have extra food and water at their place, and that they've taken in a few of their neighbors whose homes were lost. All I had were the clothes on my back. I figured, what's the harm...so I went with him. On the way there he offered me some type of cookie, or something, that he had with him...said it was packed full of nutrients. I was hungry, so I ate a few. He must have put some roofies in them, or something...because minutes later I felt myself getting drunk. After a while he could have led me anywhere and I wouldn't have resisted."

"What did he do to you in there?"

"I'd rather not talk about it. Say, do any of you happen to have some food, maybe? All he gave me was bread and water this morning. Literally...bread and water...that's it. I'm really hungry right now."

Gina's question was met with awkward silence, giving way to several seconds where not one of them seemed the least bit willing to part with their bit of rations. Since they were all familiar with hunger, their reaction lacked the empathy one might expect toward a fellow survivor.

Trent, who had been down this road before, had allowed himself to vacillate in indecisions grip ever so briefly. That she needed food should not have presented an ethical dilemma to any of them. But yet, there they were—coyly unresponsive, and with seemingly no inclination to want to share with her. His own selfish interests notwithstanding, he could no more refuse her request for food than he could ignore her earlier cries for help; not when he could so clearly envision Nora in some dire strait of her own, and unable to find a compassionate soul to reach out to.

He reached into his pocket, pulled out the last, third-of-a-square piece of ration bar he had left, broke it in half, and held it out to Gina. "Here...you can take this."

"Who's that?"

"It's me...Trent...the guy who rescued you? Hold out your hand." Trent reached his hand toward her voice. Gina did likewise, feeling the space in front of her until her hand finally came in contact with his. Her fingers brushed across his ever so slightly before accepting; and done in such a way that it left Trent room to interpret. It was a touch that seemed to convey more than two words might do justice; simple and to the point. It said, thank you—for everything.

DAY FOUR

Chapter 25

Dawn's light arrived like a thin, gray veil over the small, deserted town nestled just thirty miles north of New York City. Its idyllic rural character had been stripped away by the impacts aftermath, forcing its residents to flee to the shelter of the nearest tent city. Formally quaint homes, now sat wrecked and empty along country roads where the only sounds heard came from the rustle of small animals hiding in the underbrush.

Along one of those roads, a scrawny Boston Terrier, going on his fourth day without food, stood on trembling legs in front of a small mound of rubble. There, he sniffed indiscriminately through the pile hunting for a scent that might lead to something edible. He would bury his nose in one of the crannies; and then finding nothing, withdraw it and move on to another. Throughout his search, he whined continuously; and in a pathetic, modulating pitch as pitiable sounding as an infant's cry. Every so often he would step back and there, pawed valiantly on the spot where his nose led him, only to turn away with not even a crumb.

He continued to trace a random sniff pattern over the area when he suddenly raised his head high and sprang his ears up like two antennas. Standing on three legs, and with his front paw curled beneath him in readiness, he struck a rock solid pose. There was a new sound among the old ones and it instantly caught his ear. It was far off, and although faint, there was something familiar in it; something inviting. Not like the voice of his absent master, but of the only other sound capable of perking him up—the call of another dog. He leapt off of the mound and began a steady trot toward the direction where it seemed to come from.

Within minutes the sound turned into distinct howls that grew louder and more enticing the closer he got to it. He zeroed in on it like radar and now followed it with the ease of a bloodhound. It led him for about a mile, finally placing him on a rock-strewn dirt road somewhere on the outskirts of town. Directly up ahead of him sat an isolated farmhouse. Pummeled during the storm, it leaned precariously to one side and seemed on the verge of collapse. By now, the constant howling had stopped. It was replaced by the sounds of multiple dogs barking and fiercely growling over some unseen struggle taking place inside the farmhouse. Hunger driven, he proceeded to sheepishly venture toward the sounds.

He made his way onto the farmhouse's covered porch, stopped, and peered through the open entrance where the door had been torn from its hinges. Enticed by the sounds of canines presumably roughhousing, he entered with a cautious mien. From all appearances, the main level was deserted. All the activity seemed to be occurring upstairs on the second level. He stopped in front of the staircase and listened for a moment to the boisterous commotion taking place, up there. He then began a slow ascent up, ears flattened back in a worry reflex that failed to silence the beckon tempting his instincts. Once he reached the top, the amplified sounds were even more fascinating. And they were all coming from a room at the very end of the hall.

He started toward it when suddenly, a black Labrador Retriever stepped out from the room and into the hallway. He flinched upon seeing the somewhat menacing looking Lab squaring off only a few feet away from him. They briefly stared at each other, sniffing out whatever menace might exist between them. Then, apparently satisfied to find none, the Lab turned and reentered the room. Its behavior read like an open invitation to the Terrier. He proceeded to creep down the hall accompanied by a raucous medley of dog noises. He stopped upon reaching the doorway and quietly stuck his head inside room.

Crimson red paw prints tracked a mess all over its oak floor. From there, his attention was drawn straight to one corner of the room. That's where a pack of feral dogs, about twelve in number, and standing in a broad stain of dried blood, gnawed on what was left of a dead woman's body. They would take turns, lunging at it with ferocious bites, then a frenzied pull that dragged the body slightly until a chunk of meat tore free. Across from them, another body lay on the floor in gruesome detail. With no face to speak of, much of its flesh had been eaten away almost clear to the bone leaving its features ravaged and genderless. The Terrier, still poised in the doorway, was reluctant to step into this bloodbath. Never in its comfortable life had he seen anything so horrific; and yet—so intensely stimulating; even as the overpowering scent of blood triggered a primal urge to go inside and join the pack. Watching them, he could feel their innate comradeship for one another; their compulsion to act as a single-minded collective in all matters related to survival.

Of the roughly eighteen dogs present, the largest, and no doubt the top-dog in the room, was a black-haired Rottweiler. He sat off to one side, likely having already gotten his full, and looked on with his lieutenants while those weakest among the pack got to pick over what was left. Between their command-structure that insured order, the safety found in their numbers, and the cooperative sharing of food between them, the hungry Terrier could find little reason to turn away. Whatever guerrilla tactics they used to stay alive, he found himself quickly becoming akin to and decided—to join them.

As he approached the grotesque body, there was only a slight show of resistance from the others feeding on it. And once he got his first of taste of human flesh, his old life from then on became but a distant memory.

Chapter 26

Rachel squatted in a secluded patch of shrubs behind her house. And there, holding a roll of toilet paper in one hand, tried to maintain her composure so that her overloaded bladder could empty completely. The countless unseen critters scurrying and flitting about in the brush around her made for an unnerving experience. Every sound she heard caused her to jump and clench, or prompted a voluntary reflex to dash, in mid-flow, back to the safety of her home.

The morning light did little to alleviate her stress. One look up revealed a wake of vultures soaring in graceful circles before swooping down to peck at the many carcasses, both animal and human, that lay rotting out in the open. After finishing, she tidied herself up and ran back inside, keeping a close eye on those vultures overhead as she did so.

***

Jennifer was sitting over by the living room window with the portable shortwave radio in her lap. She had been trying to find a receivable station now for three days, but was having no luck. Every turn of the dial produced the same monotone, static signature with not a trace of signal in it. After so many attempts, she decided that the problem might not be with the broadcasting stations, but with the antenna itself.

Armed with a screwdriver and plenty of idle time, she embarked on a crash course in electronics. She removed the back cover of the radio, and from there, proceeded to examine the internal circuitry until something—*anything*—jumped out at her as having to do with the antenna. As she stared blankly at the exposed circuit board, every transistor, diode, and capacitor seemed to holler back at her a warning of, "Don't even think about it."

In spite of their intimidating configuration, she zeroed in on a sliver of wire just beneath the header that appeared to connect the board to the antenna. There was nothing remarkable about it, but she gave it a jiggle, anyway, only because it seemed like the thing to do. Satisfied that she had done a little something, Jennifer turned the radio face front, and switched on the power.

Right away, the difference jumped out at her; crackling with a sound that offered the first encouraging development for them since their ordeal began. She smiled a hopeful grin and immediately turned up the volume.

Rachel, upon hearing the difference, came running in from the kitchen. "Did you get it to work? It sounds different," she said.

"We'll know soon enough," Jennifer said as she slowly began rotating the tuning knob, ignorant to the number of short-wave modulation settings available to her. The crackles leapt out the speaker. Filled with pops and clicks, and oscillating wavelengths in need of a frequency, they seized her with suspense for what might come after.

Suddenly, a word, two words, and then a full sentence; faint and static charged, but still distinguishable as it caught their ears.

"Justin...come quick! Jen fixed the radio," Rachel shouted excitedly as the hum of electrified sound replaced the silence on its visit through their home. Jennifer extended the antenna and began twisting it on its axis to improve the reception. Then ever so delicately, she rotated the knob in minute increments that she hoped would fine tune some of the static out from the speaker's voice. Finally, a voice other than the three of theirs was now speaking to them. And though not crystal clear, it was at least intelligible, just as Justin came rushing in to listen.

In other news today, we're still waiting for the start of the scheduled news conference from President Bartlett. This will be his first official address since he was sworn in two days ago as the nation's new Commander in Chief. The conference is to take place at Langley Air Force Base in Virginia. President Bartlett, then Senator Bartlett, was in Europe at the time of the impact when he was informed by phone of his election by congress to succeed the late President Schaefer. His acceptance marks the first time in this nation's history that such an extraordinary measure was taken. In his first official act as president, he declared a federal state of emergency with respect to national security. The FEMA regional offices in New York and Philadelphia that would normally respond to disaster events in those areas were severely damaged after the impact. In the interim, the Chicago and Boston FEMA offices have had their duties reassigned, and due to logistical challenges, are just now establishing joint field offices in the devastated regions...those being areas in and around New Jersey, New York, Pennsylvania, Delaware and Maryland. We're told President Bartlett will not be taking any questions at the conference, but that he will outline a national response plan. Although hampering any such plans will be the extensive damage inflicted on Washington D.C., and the destabilization of those government agencies that determine protocol during disasters of this magnitude. It's hoped that the President's close ties with Federation of States President Jović might help to expedite foreign aid, which so far has been slow in coming. This is station WGN 720 broadcasting from Chicago. For those of you just tuning in outside of Chicago, the nation is presently recovering from an unspeakable natural disaster. Four days ago, an asteroid tore through the Earth's atmosphere and slammed into the Atlantic Ocean approximately half a mile off the coast of New Jersey. The size of the asteroid, by some estimates, was between two and four miles across, which on impact, we're told, unleashed a destructive force equivalent to ten million megatons of TNT. The dense ash cloud blanketing much of the east coast makes satellite imagery impossible. The only reconnaissance we have, so far, is by way of military fly-over, and the images they've released of the area are almost beyond description. Most of the state of New Jersey has been transformed into a wasteland...its surface features and man-made structures, practically obliterated. Not since the cataclysm has so much devastation been seen over this large an area. New York City, Philadelphia, and Washington, D.C. have also suffered catastrophic damage. Their infrastructures are in ruins, and power is still out along two-thirds of the eastern seaboard. It may be several months before we know just how many people perished in this disaster. For now, the number of dead is incalculable. Many are wondering how an asteroid the size of a small island was able to escape detection by NASA's early warning systems. Or, how it was able to approach our planet, even though it should've been the brightest star in the sky for several weeks, but yet, still somehow go unnoticed by everyone until the exact moment of impact. It's a baffling mystery that some are speculating was orchestrated by extraterrestrials.

Jennifer, Justin and Rachel remained still throughout the news report and quietly listened as it drew for them in their minds, what their eyes couldn't see. And with each startling revelation, shock gave way to horror, and horror to grief, leaving only anguish to mark their expressions. The broadcast went on to seed already crimsoned eyes with tears that started to fall upon hearing the condition of New York City.

"What do we do now?" Rachel asked as she wiped the tears from her face. "This wasn't just an earthquake. This is much worse than I could even imagine. New York City might be destroyed. Mom and Dad...they're out there somewhere. How are they supposed to get home?"

"I don't know, but I have to believe they're doing everything in their power to reach us. I only hope that they weren't separated...that they were together before the asteroid hit. If not, Dad may have gone back to look for Mom, first, if he was near enough to the city," Jennifer said.

"But why would he do that...it doesn't make sense," Rachel said. "There are too many people. Where would he begin to look? He'd have to assume that Mom would try to find her way home, right?"

"You're right. That's the only thing either one of them could do. Separately or together, they're going to try to get home the best way they can."

Justin sat on the steps of their staircase, his head down and listening with tears in his eyes while his sisters clung to a slender hope of their parents finding them. "I hate to be the bearer of bad news, here. Nobody wants Mom and Dad to come home more than me. But the fact of the matter is...they may not," he said.

"Stop talking like that! Why can't you think more positively?" Rachel said angrily.

"Thinking positively won't change anything. You both heard what the man said. New York City is completely broken...nothing is working. And just think. If the asteroid could do this much damage up here...can you imagine what it must look like down in the city."

"You're talking like they're dead, or something. Why couldn't they have survived? Even after the cataclysm there were survivors. Not everybody gets killed. Maybe they were injured and are being treated somewhere."

"That's right...maybe they are. And if so, how are they going to reach us? They can't drive...they can't take a bus...they can't hail a cab, and I don't expect to see a helicopter landing on our front lawn to drop them off, either."

"Justin, I don't understand why you're talking like this. Don't you love Mom and Dad...don't you want them to come home?"

"Of course I do. But you're crazy if you think things are still the same as they were. Everything's different now. It's all changed. We need to face the real possibility that Mom and Dad may not have survived...and that it may be just the three of us from here on."

"So what are you suggesting we do?"

"The same thing that I've been suggesting all along...that we leave this house and go find shelter somewhere in town where there's food and water. Mom and Dad would want us to be smart, here...and not do anything that would put us in danger. Staying here puts us in danger."

Jennifer had a retort on her lips, but kept it to herself. Justin might act like a fool most times, but even in his bluntness, he could be quite convincing when he wants to be. She had to admit that her tendency for self-delusion might be clouding her better judgment, especially now that the facts are known to them. Her heart wanted to stay put and wait for her mom and dad. But with no news of their whereabouts, or their fates, they might be waiting there for them indefinitely. The nights there were growing more frightening, leaving their imaginations to conjure up the worst possible outcomes.

Meanwhile, Rachel was growing antsy as the pause widened between them, and the only voice heard was that of the crackly newscaster's on the radio. "Jen...you're not seriously considering what he wants, are you? I'm telling you...they're alive. They're not hurt...they're on their way home. I know it. If we leave here, it would be a big mistake. 'Cause number one...this is our home. We can't just walk away from it like that. And number two...if we did leave here, I'd never let you hear the end of it. You've never listened to anything he had to say before. Don't start listening to him now."

Jennifer fell back in her seat and brought both hands behind her neck. They kneaded away at the tightness constricting her from the shoulders up while closed eyes tried to quell the struggle going on behind them. "It hurts me to say this, Justin...but everything you said was right. Even so...we have to stay. It wouldn't feel right leaving. I do think we should have a plan...just in case we have to leave here for some reason, like if we run out of food, or something. Is that a fair compromise?"

"I could live with that," Rachel said, looking relieved.

Justin got up from the steps and started for the foyer. "You guys are crazy. You know that, right? I'm telling you...this whole plan of yours is gonna backfire on you," he said, walking past them.

He turned a corner and headed toward the front door. "Where are you going?" Rachel asked.

"I have to pee. Is that okay with you?" he shouted and abruptly left.

Jennifer got up, grabbed the radio, and went into the kitchen. The voice in the box faded in and out in between the move. She set it down on the counter and moved it around hoping that the change of locale might reduce some of the background noise. There was no difference, so she left it alone and turned to face the center island. There, they kept their entire food supply laid out like groceries at a checkout register.

"Well, what do you think?" Rachel asked as she stood in the kitchen entrance, her shoulders frozen in a shrug, and fingers buried in her front pockets in a restive pose.

"I think if we ate like birds, we might have enough food to last us another five days. Water is another story. I don't think we have enough for more than two days."

"We don't have to drink every day. As for me...I only need a sip. Don't worry. We can stretch it. But what do we do when we run out?"

"I don't know."

"Maybe we could go by Rafer's house. He might have some extra water he could spare."

"If I know Rafer, he'd give it to us whether he could spare it or not. No, we can't do that. They need their water."

"Well, maybe you can't, but I wouldn't have a problem with it," Rachel said as she flashed a mocking expression at what must've sounded to her like self-righteous moralizing. That's when it occurred to her. "Hey, I just remembered something. What about the wine cellar?"

It was an area separate from the basement, but in a room all its own, and accessible only through a removable panel in the wall just below the stairs. The previous owner of the house was a world traveler and wine connoisseur. He had the modest-sized room expressly built for storing his collection of vintages—and judging from the elaborate measures taken to hide the cellar's entrance—was also very protective of. After purchasing the home, Trent made good use of the space which he playfully referred to as "the hole," storing extra bottles of his restaurant's wine selections there. Other than him, there was no reason for anyone else to venture down into its unwelcoming confines.

Jennifer wondered about the soundness of their drinking wine in place of water. Still, she had to admit, it was better than suffering from thirst. Rachel had already started for the staircase. "Wait a minute. I'm not sure about this," Jennifer said, rushing to catch up to her.

Rachel reached the rise of the staircase and immediately began feeling along the seams of the wainscoted accent wall for the secret passage. She pushed on each square in search of the loose panel that, as memory served, would open out into a special entrance. "What's there to be unsure about? You said yourself...we've only got two days of water left."

"This isn't exactly water we're talking about."

"I know that, but what choice have we got. And anyway…didn't I hear something about wine being good for you?"

"Yes…maybe…as long as it's not your primary source of fluid intake. This is alcohol…not juice. If we're going to do this, we have to be smart about it. There's no sense in our waiting days for Mom and Dad to get home, only to have them find us falling down drunk, or passed out somewhere when they get here. We have to limit it to only a few sips a day, and only *after* the water runs out, okay?"

"Okay, okay. Hopefully, that's all it'll take for me to get my buzz on. Where is this stupid opening, anyway…did Dad seal it up or something?" Rachel asked in frustration.

"Not as far as I know. Here, let me try," Jennifer said, then moving in to replace Rachel. She slid her finger along the seam as she remembered it from when they were younger and their using the space inside as a hiding place. Now, years later, it was difficult to recall the exact location, or the unusual technique they had used to open it up. After several attempts, "There…I think I found it," she said.

Jennifer took both hands and pushed on the panel with even pressure, followed by a slight push up to disengage the catch on the opposite side. Suddenly, a double-section of panel parted at the seam. She pulled it open to reveal a narrow, six-foot high doorway and the dungeon-like passage that led down below the main floor. They both stuck their heads in and looked down into the pit.

"Wow…this is just as spooky as I remember it," Rachel commented. "At least before, we were able to switch a light on. Now it's just plain dark."

"Can you go into the kitchen and bring me that flashlight on the counter?"

When Rachel returned, Jennifer grabbed the flashlight and aimed its beam onto the unfinished wood stairs leading down to the cellar floor. She stepped through the opening and onto the landing and then looked out at Rachel. "Are you coming?"

"Do I have to? There could be mice down there."

"Hey, this was your idea," Jennifer said, pointing the flashlight at her. "If you don't come with me, we're not gonna do this."

"Oh, alright," Rachel said, then warily stepping in behind her. The strong smell of wine was the first thing that struck them, that and the coolness coming off the exposed concrete blocks that walled the cellar. After going down a few steps, Jennifer got a sense that something was wrong. The overpowering scent of fruity alcohol seemed out of place from what she'd remembered since last visiting the hole. She aimed the flashlight at the floor and was surprised to see a reflection bounce off and up onto the facing wall.

"That's strange," she said, moving the light across the floor as they descended. "Did Dad put tiles on the floor?"

"I'm not sure...he might have."

"Oh no. I think I know what happened," Jennifer said as the real problem started to become more evident the closer they got to the bottom. Her suspicions were confirmed the moment her foot splashed down on the cellar floor. Apparently, "the hole" hadn't escaped the earthquake's fury and ended up having its precious contents tossed around like cans of soda. The wooden rack used to store the wine had tipped over, sending all of the bottles crashing to the concrete slab floor. Not one was spared. From there, the spillage spread outward in a complete mess that pooled in spots, and dried in others.

A small, translucent window; its glass oddly still intact, was alone at the top of one of the walls. There, it provided a stark picture of the color that existed on the other side. Its face shone dimly like a back-lit picture, yet did not introduce a trace of discernable light to the room. Whatever illusions Jennifer and Rachel had of dulling their wait with a little alcohol, were—for better or worse—dashed with the discovery. They turned and headed back up the stairs; dejected, and no doubt mired by an increasing fear of their nagging thirst.

Chapter 27

179th Street in the Washington Heights section of Manhattan had the distinction of running parallel to I-95; the preeminent corridor leading in and out of New York City. It was also the point of entry into New Jersey for tens of thousands of vehicles that would cross over its connecting gateway—the George Washington Bridge.

Nora and her party walked along the I-95 conduit amidst countless other survivors, and an endless stretch of abandoned vehicles that clogged the roadway leading to the bridge. They had set out early that morning from Riverbank Park where they'd spent most of the night waiting on line for rations and getting little sleep. After a thirty-four block trek uptown, they were finally on the last leg of their journey to get off the island. And only a short walk away from what they no doubt knew would be the start of another.

They traveled along a causeway set beneath a series of broad overpasses that gave a tunnel-like appearance to the road. Up ahead were open sky, and the visible first tower of the bridge set against a backdrop of sullen gray. With escape from New York finally within their sights, they anxiously weaved through a maze of automotive ruins; stepped over pocked asphalt, and up onto uneven chunks of pavement; squeezed past frustrated pedestrians, rambunctious teenagers, and frighteningly close encounters; ignored the distressing pleas of mothers carrying hungry infants, the shantytown of cardboard boxes and makeshift tents clogging the roadside, and every other thing that stood in their way.

When they emerged from the underpass, the George Washington Bridge was seen in all its meticulously erected splendor; still standing strong, and with a sea of cars and trucks littering its eight-lanes in a singular, massive pileup. The traffic jam extended out onto the roadway, only to fall off sharply at the crest of the road's obscuring arc where hid the New Jersey end of the bridge.

As they drew closer, there was a buzz of idle chatter surrounding them; of rising complaints and agitation which they paid little attention to; and a retreat from the edge of stepping onto the span by some who likely had second thoughts about crossing. Others gathered at its foot in seeming confusion over what to do. Up until now, it was believed the bridge had withstood the brunt of the asteroid's effects. But it was not until Nora's party reached its pedestrian walkway that they understood the reason for the unhappy gathering.

From where they stood, the two towers of the bridge appeared structurally sound, showing no obvious lean or other impairment. The vertical cables that suspended the deck on both sides also seemed to be intact, had no visible gaps, and draped neatly over the main supporting cables.

What stopped people short of crossing was the condition of the walkway. The once sturdy path that set along the outer edge of the bridge, and was the route for joggers, bicyclists and the like had sustained significant damage. Slabs of its concrete footpath had fallen away, exposing in some sections, a lattice of cured-in rebar; and in others, gaping holes that saw straight down into the Hudson River. Huge sections of the railing that once stood between crossing pedestrians and the river below were now missing, or dangled off the edge of the remaining pieces of concrete walkway. What was left was a partial catwalk with barely a rail to grasp for stability, and where one false step could send a person plummeting to their death.

The surface roadway, after a closer look, had not fared much better. The vehicles were crowded sloppily atop the pavement and were resting on shaky ground; cracked, pitted, and as hazardous as the current walkway. Some cars had flipped over from the gale created by the impact, while still others went fully airborne and now hung trapped in the suspension cables like flies caught in a web.

A number of courageous souls, undeterred by its condition, had already accepted the bridges challenge and dared to cross over into New Jersey. They could be seen negotiating the twists and turns of the obstacle choked roadbed, or along the walkway before vanishing over the flat horizon of the bridge's arc. Their success or failure remained a mystery.

Nora looked out at the colossal structure in an awe induced gaze. Standing at the foot of the bridge, she began to feel phobias rising up within her that weren't there before, and a sense of defeat trying to steal her optimism. To have come this far and not be able to cross was a blow to her resolve. *What do we do now,* she wondered as she placed her hopes on standby and tried to come to terms with their failed plan.

"It looks like we came all the way up here for nothing," Laura said, dejectedly. "Do we have a plan-B that nobody told me about?"

"I think crossing this bridge was plan-A, B, C and D," Preston said.

"Seriously...what are we going to do? All the other bridges are on the other side of the island. That's a full day's walk from here."

"No way am I going to be doing any more walking today. It'll be dark out here in about three hours. We need to decide where we're going to rest for the night," Sonia insisted.

"We still have a problem, here. If this bridge is too risky to cross, what makes us believe the other bridges are any safer?" Miguel said.

"He's right. If the bridges and the rivers are impassable, then there have got to be designated locations where the military are airlifting people off the island," Preston said.

"Where are they, though?" Laura asked. "How are we supposed to know where to go if there's nobody to ask? Those soldiers last night...all they did was dispense rations...got in their helicopters, and flew off. They weren't thinking about taking anybody with them. If anything, they looked like they were going to shoot anyone who got too close."

While they discussed their plight, Taylor stood a few feet off from them and staring out at the bridge. He seemed more interested in watching the survivors scale the walkway than anything that was being said behind him. Nora wondered how much more disappointed he must feel than she and the others. Even though there was no way for him to know, still it had to be disheartening, she imagined; to feel as though he led them all on a wild goose chase.

Taylor was reclusive, yes; and short on explanations; and never quite connected with anyone else in the group—save for her. But he did lead them that far, and given the ordeal of the first few days, he could arguably be hailed as their hero. She felt it only right that he know how much his efforts were appreciated—not in so many words that might cause awkwardness for either of them, but in simple gestures of inclusion. Besides, she felt duly obligated to reach out to him; to show gratitude, in spite of the tension present between him and the others. *If I don't...who will*, she thought as she walked over to him.

"We were just saying how there's no way of knowing what condition the other bridges are in. And how there might be locations where the military are airlifting people off the island. What do you think?" Nora asked.

"I think Miguel was right...the other bridges probably don't look much better than this one. And if there's going to be any airlifting going on, I'll bet it's going to be further downtown. Either that...or they've done all the airlifting they're going to do. By now, the refugee camps have got to be seriously overcrowded. They may not want to take anymore survivors."

"So how are we supposed to get off this island? I need to get home."

"There's only one way that I can see. We need to cross this bridge."

Nora looked at him as if he were crazy. "You can't be serious."

"Sure I am. I've been watching people start across since we got here. And yeah, it's risky...but I've not seen anybody fall off yet."

"The fact that there's even a remote chance of falling off is all the disincentive I need. There's no way the others are going to agree to that."

"Not if it's coming from me alone. But coming from both of us...they just might."

"What makes you think I'm going to agree to it?"

"Because you're a smart woman. Because you know this is the only way we have of getting off this island. As it is, they think I take too many chances. But they'll listen to you. If you say it's okay...they might go for it."

"*I'm* not sure that I *want* to go for it."

"Look...you're going to have to make a decision. 'Cause I'm crossing this bridge with, or without you all."

With that, Nora turned her attention to the bridge and the courageous procession of survivors daring to cross the walkway. Whether it was Taylor's threat to leave them, or her own wish not to offend him, she surprisingly found herself weighing his ultimatum with all seriousness. Her consideration wasn't tempered by loss of life and limb as much as by an intense need to see her family—and apparently at any cost, she was discovering. Watching the walkway, she was relieved to not have seen any fatalities occurring thus far. She reasoned that crossing it might be a lot worse in her imagination than it was in reality.

If this is going to happen...better with Taylor than attempting it on my own, she thought to herself. "Okay...I'll do it."

"Good. We'd better let them know."

They both walked over to join the others. "Are we all set to go?" Nora asked poker-faced.

"Set to go where?" Sonia asked.

"Set to go across the bridge."

"Are you kidding? There's no way I'm crossing that thing," Sonia said.

"Taylor and I were talking about it...and it makes sense to go. Remember...the other bridges may be in the same condition, or worse. If so, there's no way off this island. There are people crossing it as we speak. What makes them so much more braver than us?"

"Well, I've been watching, too. And I see people getting bottlenecked before they get halfway up the roadway and having to turn back because they can't go any further. Plus, we don't know what it looks like on the other side of that hump. Those people who do make it over might be dropping into the river for all we know."

"We wouldn't take the roadway. We'd use the footpath," Taylor said earnestly, which caused even Nora to stop and give him a look.

"You have to be kidding. There's barely any railing left. What are we supposed to hold on to? And that footpath you're talking about? It's crumbling. We'll never make it over," Sonia said.

Nora turned to Taylor. "I have to agree with Sonia. Trying to cross that way is suicidal," she said.

"We're wasting time, here. Who's coming with us?" Taylor asked.

"I am," they heard unexpectedly, then turned and looked over at Dale. "I'll go with you," he said. "I don't know about the rest of you, but I didn't come all this way just to turn around and look for another way out. If this is the only way off this island...then so be it."

That Dale even agreed to do it at all was surprising considering that he had barely spoken a word since his confrontation with Taylor the evening before. His bold decision was like a challenge to the others. Apparently shamed by Dale's newfound bravery, they refrained from their objections and were no doubt pondering the alternatives, if any.

Preston stared out at the bridge for a moment, then looked over at Taylor. "I'll go with you," he said, then shaking his head in apparent disbelief over his decision. His wife and son were in New Jersey. Therefore, he had the most to gain in choosing to go. He'd been quiet for the most part; no doubt torn over his desire to get home and not wanting to kill himself in the process. As frightened as he may have been at the prospect of crossing, he clearly reasoned it was better to take a chance now, rather than wait for a miracle airlift by helicopter.

"Anybody else coming?" Taylor asked, looking directly at the last three remaining holdouts—Laura, Sonia, and Miguel. They, in turn, glanced at each other, then out at the source of their trepidation before eventually agreeing to join them.

They all started for the walkway together. As they made their way through the crowd, Nora tried to ignore the spasms of anxiety tossing her stomach. Up until now, the most risky thing she had ever done was, while vacationing in Aruba, climb aboard a jet-ski on Trent's dare, even though she couldn't swim. She wrapped her arms around him and held on for dear life; screaming, giggling, then screaming again with excitement as they whipped around the Atlantic. And all the while she was deathly afraid of falling into the deep water. The fear she was experiencing now was that, times two; only minus the exhilaration and idyllic Caribbean locale.

Her breathing was rapid, and coupled with the pounding in her chest, she feared might trigger an episode of lightheadedness at the worst possible time. Meanwhile, the sounds of commotion around her had meshed into a continuous tenor. She set her focus on it in hopes of muting an onset of whispering bugaboos.

In the midst of all the chaos, an orderly system had been established by those using the walkways flanking the two sides of the bridge. One side accommodated survivors' crossing over into New

Jersey. The other side, and clearly the busier of the two, was used by those entering into New York. Nora stopped along with the others just short of the southbound walkway for New Jersey. One look over the side of the bridge revealed down below a flotilla of cars and trucks, capsized boats, steeply listed ships and several bloated corpses floating like flotsam along the river surface.

Though already nervous to begin with, the sight of so much death among the wreckage was quickly redefining her understanding of fear. Just as she was about to reconsider her decision, Taylor stepped onto the walkway and started across. Nora was the next to go. After a moment's pause, she held her breath and stepped out onto the concrete footing. Much of the eight-foot wide walkway was still intact, thanks in large part to the steel rebar that ran the full length of it. But where it had failed, large chunks of concrete dropped away, leaving potholes of embedded crisscrossing rods in its path. A few yards up ahead, several feet of railing had fallen away.

Nora, hugging what railing there was on her right hand side, steadily pulled herself along inch by inch. She kept her eyes fixed on the back of Taylor's head, making sure to avoid the expanse just to her left. An accidental glance in that direction looked out onto the flowing river and the missing barrier between her and it. Sonia was a few steps behind her. Visibly trembling, she pulled herself hand over hand along the railing and whatever other stable thing she could grab a hold of. At random points, the uneven floor would dip and rise making their footing tantamount to walking along a layer of discarded brick blocks. It was especially difficult for Sonia. Her uncontrollable jitters compromised every step she took.

By now, fifteen minutes had passed, and they still hadn't reached the halfway point. The New Jersey horizon, dark and resembling an approaching storm, could be seen coming up over the bridge's crest. The borough of Fort Lee at the foot of the bridge was mostly obscured by the roadway. There was no telling what to expect once it came into full view. Judging from the seeming five-to-one ratio of those leaving

New Jersey, versus those entering, it was safe to assume the worst possible condition prevailed.

As they proceeded forward, Taylor suddenly stopped and called out to the others. "We may have a problem, here. There's no concrete at all on this part of the walkway...only reinforcing rods. There're good sized gaps between them. We'll have to step carefully. Otherwise, a foot's liable to go straight through...literally. There's no bottom on some of them. I can see straight down into the river. It's about twenty yards between here and solid concrete. Everybody watch your step."

At that moment, Nora couldn't tell an inch from a yard since it all felt and sounded like a country mile to her. She held onto whatever she could get her hands around. Then used it to steady herself as she prepared to follow behind Taylor. Looking past him, she could see the length of reinforcing rods stretching out before them. She moved closer to the end of the concrete and ever so carefully peered over the edge. There, she found herself staring down the mouth of, a no less than, ten-inch square gap; part of an array of similar sized gaps set above a tangled mesh of intersecting rods. A hesitant look in-between the spaces showed the distant tops of floating debris passing with frightening clarity directly beneath her.

Before the images could completely overwhelm her, Nora shut her eyes and struggled to turn back the fear that sought to paralyze her. When she opened her eyes again, Taylor had moved ahead several steps, widening the gap between them. Meanwhile, Preston, three places in back of her was frantically urging her to move on and stop holding up the line.

On hearing that, Nora gritted her teeth and stepped both feet down onto one of the steel rods. From there, she began to inch her way forward; almost sliding rather than picking up her feet, and both hands grabbing onto any available thing within reach as she went. The rod was narrow with raised threads along its length. Together, they tormented the soles of her feet and made the way across feel like walking a tightrope studded with nails. Guided by a protective sort of tunnel vision that focused on where she set her feet, at no point did she look through the bars at the river below. Taylor had already reached the other side and was standing there with his arm outstretched waiting to assist her.

When she spotted the concrete step just a few feet in front of her, she raised her head and prepared to reach for Taylor's hand. That's when she heard the scream from directly behind her, and the wail of agony that followed it. Nora knew right away it was Sonia. Forgetting her own fear for the moment, she turned her head slowly to see what had happened. There was Sonia, clutching the rail and grimacing in pain; one foot on a narrow rod and the other, lodged ankle deep inside one of the gaps of tangled rebar. She was frozen with fear and seemed incapable of going any further. Directly behind her was Laura who, although engaged in the throes of her own panic, placed her hand atop Sonia's.

Nora, with the rail still firmly in her grips, slid one hand over and placed it on top of Sonia's other hand. She then moved it down to her wrist, grabbed it tight and started pulling her forward. "C'mon, girl...we have to go. Please!"

"My ankle...I think it's broken."

"Well, whatever is wrong with it, you can't stay here. We've got to move. We're almost there."

"I can't. It hurts too much."

"Yes you can. Now c'mon, move. There're people behind you."

While Nora pulled, Laura pushed, and together they were able to force Sonia to lift her injured foot out of the hole. She continued on, hobbled by pain, and with Nora tugging on her arm as if she were holding life and death in her hands. Finally, after a few tense moments, they both made it onto the concrete platform. There, Sonia took a moment and reached for her calf, overcome by the pain below it as it surged up her leg.

"We have to keep moving," Taylor said, having already stepped off and looking back at them.

"Give her a minute. She's in pain," Nora said.

"We don't have a minute."

"Uh...excuse us. We hate to interrupt, but...the rest of us are still standing out here on this stupid ledge staring down death's door. We'd like to move off it now if that's okay with you," Preston said, peering out from behind Laura.

"C'mon, Sonia...we're almost there," Nora said, then looking out onto the rest of the walkway. "It doesn't look too bad from here on. Just hold on to me, okay? We'll figure out what to do about your ankle when we reach the other side."

With that, Sonia wrapped her arm around Nora's. Then grasping the rail with her other hand, she hobbled off; wincing and moaning on the slightest contact her foot made against the concrete. The end of the walkway was now well within sight.

Some twenty heart pounding minutes later, they had finally reached the end of the bridge and were triumphantly standing on Jersey soil. From there, they walked off to one side and collectively dropped to the ground; emotionally spent and weakened from the almost hour-long crossing.

Fort Lee, like every other town they had been through, was a nightmarish picture of devastation. Hundreds upon hundreds of smashed and abandoned vehicles came to a bottleneck at the toll crossing. Every other thing was a continuation of what they had left behind on the island; homelessness, bedlam, falling dust, and buildings, either collapsed, barely livable, or completely gutted by earlier fires. The only difference was in the number of survivors who, four days after the impact, were still fleeing New Jersey in droves. They did so, believing that a safe haven was waiting for them on the other side of the bridge. In time they would find out otherwise.

"Okay, we're here...now what?" Dale asked, adrenaline fueled, and likely feeling empowered after his conquering the mighty George Washington Bridge.

"There's not much more we can do today. It'll be dark soon," Miguel said with the usual economy of opinion they'd come to expect from him.

"He's right. There's isn't any place to go that can't wait until tomorrow," Preston said. "You guys should rest here for the night."

"What do you mean, 'you guys'?"

"I have to go. I need to see my wife and son. My house is a good fifty miles into New Jersey. Now that we're over the bridge, I'd like to get home to them as soon as possible. That's granted I still have a home to go to."

Laura looked at him with sympathetic eyes. They had grown close to each other in the last four days, sharing a purely cerebral connection that made conversation between them easy. He had become her friend. The thought of her traveling companion leaving so abruptly, and after all they had been through, was no doubt a bit upsetting. Still, it was one he had prepared her for well in advance. "Are you sure you don't want to wait until the morning?" Laura asked.

New Jersey's designation as ground zero was common knowledge, the evidence of which could be seen far in the distance. Preston looked around at the darkening sky and the devastated landscape. Combined, they began to torment him as if he were looking into the face of his own shame. "Yeah...I'm sure. From here on, whatever happens...happens. You all take care of yourselves. And good luck," he said, turning to each of them, and then lastly holding his gaze on Laura in a transparent recognition of something shared. With that, he stood to his feet and walked off; his back softly disappearing within the mutable flux of survivors as the five of them looked on.

Taylor closed his eyes and laid flat on the ground. Then clasping his hands across his chest, bent one leg at the knee, and began lazily rocking it back and forth. "You know his family is most likely dead, right?" he said to Nora who was sitting nearby, and who in spite of her hopefulness, was feeling much less so after his remark.

"Yeah...I know," she said.

Chapter 28

The beach at Playa Portomari sat nestled within a picturesque bay on the island of Curacao. The white sand and calming trade winds wrapped a seducing embrace around the tourists who lounged like kings and queens along its pristine cove. Sitting among them was Constance, her chaise set at a lazy recline and positioned only feet away from the gently lapping waves of the Caribbean Sea. She sat lounging back, her eyes closed and indulging rest beneath the shade of a beach umbrella.

On this picture-perfect day, her feet, facing out at the ocean, were feeling the heat from the sun as it inched overhead to steal its first bit of her shade. Meanwhile, her pale, tan resistant skin was coated in a pasty layer of SPF-60 that at first glance, gave her a less than flattering appearance.

In the past year she had successfully shed fifteen pounds off her frame. With newfound confidence, she decided for the first time in her adult life to wear a two-piece swimsuit. Her choice of beachwear attire was aided by the anonymity she enjoyed on the tiny island. She knew the odds of her bumping into a familiar face there would be practically zero.

At 46 years old, she had thrown in the towel on marriage and having children, and resigned herself to the life of a relative spinster.

Unfulfilling though it was, she could at least find solace in the fact that she was answerable to nobody but herself.

Still there were moments, mainly during the holiday season, where loneliness saw no advantages to being single. That's when she would embark on her yearly pilgrimage to some remote location in the tropics.

She briefly opened her eyes and stared out onto the sparkling turquoise waters. There, frolicking in the gentle waves like two teenagers on spring break were her mother and father. She would always bring them along on distant getaways. Their servile temperaments were the perfect complement to her overbearing and often obsessive need for being catered to. To their credit they were reasonably good company, always jovial, and never pried into her affairs.

They'd been vacationing together for five years. In that time, her parents never once asked how she was able to afford to fly them all first-class on an accountant's salary. Or, how they were able to stay at five-star hotels and dine at some of the finest restaurants on the islands. They likely didn't want to know.

When not vacationing, Constance managed the finances for a well-known coffee house chain in New York City. For nearly ten years she was in complete control of income tax filing, salaries, accounts payable and accounts receivable. So adept was she at accounting, that she earned the owner's absolute trust. He would never suspect that for five of those years, she had been falsifying entries in the company ledger. The deception was audacious and allowed her to write several checks to herself, as needed. The practice was simple, addictive, and a veritable a cash cow that so far, brought in an extra $75,000 in unearned income. She also lived in fear of one day being caught.

For now, though, the anxiety of being busted was a distant concern. Constance closed her eyes and allowed the warm trade winds to ease her back into a state of sublime relaxation. In six days, they would be on a plane heading back to the U.S.; back to sleepless nights spent wondering if tomorrow will be her day of reckoning.

Chapter 29

The family room fireplace raged with freshly collected wood. Its incandescent roar cast a vivid glow onto everything within its reach. There, Jennifer, Justin, and Rachel sat well apart from each other, and in seeming self-imposed isolation like three strangers in a waiting room. The portable radio, which was their lifeline to the outside world, sat in the next room on the kitchen counter where the strongest signal resided. Its volume was set at a tolerable level and could be heard throughout the house, providing a welcomed replacement for the other sounds so glaringly absent.

Night would be on them in less than an hour. Having already dined on cold soup, there was little else for them to do besides idle the time away and wait for evening's arrival. The voice of the newscaster, temperate and serious, had become the fourth person in the room. The asteroid impact was still the most widely covered news event since the disappearances, preempting all the world's other news. Though the reports had grown repetitive and even tedious by cataclysm standards, they could still elicit enough shock and awe to keep them fascinated through the wee hours.

They lounged in their respective places, engrossed in the broadcast and their own daydreams when suddenly, a loud knock was heard at their front door. They jumped forward in their seats and nervously looked across at each other. A second and third knock followed the first in quick succession.

"It's me...Rafer!" a voice called out.

On hearing that, Jennifer jumped up and ran to the front door. She undid its one lock and opened it to see him standing at the entrance, flashlight in one hand and a baseball bat in the other. Her increasing interest in his wellbeing had become a surprising development over the days since his last visit. She found her thoughts drifting to him at odd times, and with the sort of regularity not usually associated with a best friend. To see him framed there in the doorway, tall, handsome, and gallant evoked pleasant feelings that her smile could not adequately convey. "I'm glad to see you made it home okay," she said. "You did make it home okay...right?"

"I'm here, aren't I?" Rafer said smiling, then after a few awkward seconds, "Can I come in?"

"Oh...I'm sorry," Jennifer said, then stepping aside to let him enter. While closing the door behind him, she wanted to kick herself for gawking at him like a silly schoolgirl. That she would even have such a heartfelt, visceral reaction was discomfiting to exhibit in his presence. Whatever the reason, she didn't care to dwell on it—not now. Things were already complicated enough. "What's with the baseball bat?" she asked as she led him through the foyer and into the family room.

"It's just for protection. Yesterday, I saw a bear roaming the woods looking for food. I wanted to have something for him, just in case he saw me and got any crazy ideas about his place on the food chain. Hopefully, he's long gone from here."

"Please don't tell me there're bears out there," Rachel, who no doubt would've preferred to remain blissfully ignorant on the subject, said.

Rafer set down his bat and took a seat on the sofa. "I wouldn't worry about it...really. They're more afraid of you than you are of them. Just watch your back whenever you go outside, and keep a stick handy."

"Have you heard about the asteroid?" Jennifer asked before dropping down to a seat on the edge of the sofa.

"Yeah, I heard. I walked into town yesterday hoping to get some water to take back home. That's when I found out. I couldn't believe it...first the cataclysm, and now this. It's like one thing after another. I'm really starting to think all these things are happening for a reason."

"What sort of reason?" Rachel asked.

"I wish I knew. When I went into town yesterday, I saw things that you couldn't imagine. They turned the high school's gymnasium into a huge shelter. The military came by once...dropped off a few resources and haven't been back since. There're hundreds of people in there...friends and neighbors...and hundreds more outside. And only three doctors for all of them. And no more medicine from what I'm told. People are hurt and hungry. There's no food...no water. You walk by somebody who you think is sleeping...only to find out they're dead. They take the bodies and stack them out in the field away from everything. There are no bags for them, so they're just out there, uncovered...men, women, babies. It's awful...I've never seen anything like it...at least not up close. Believe me...what you see on TV can't prepare you for the real thing. I can't even begin to describe the smell. I heard someone say that one of the local contractors was going to try and get his excavator over there and dig a mass grave. I hope they get it over there soon. When things like this happen...especially so close together...I think we all need to start paying attention."

"Whatever you're trying to say...just say it, alright?" Justin, growing impatient with Rafer's hinting, said.

"Okay...here's what I think. Everything that's happening, and the disappearances might all be connected somehow...and I'm not talking about aliens, either."

"Then what are you talking about?"

"This may sound crazy to you, but I think it's all biblical."

"You're right...that is crazy," Justin said with a smirk.

"Don't laugh. Not too long ago people used to call anyone who believed in UFO's crazy, too. But we've all seen them. I don't know what they are, or where they came from...but they're out there. All I'm saying is...we need to look at everything that's happened in total, and not as separate incidents. When you add it all up, it's kind of weird. I'm going to share something with you that I've never told anyone. My dad...he didn't disappear while driving with my mom. I know that's what I've always told everyone. But it didn't happen that way. They were at home, sitting across the table from each other...just eating lunch and talking. To this day, my mom doesn't go into detail about it. All she would say was that he vanished right before her eyes...in an instant. They'd been married for twenty-three years, and as fast as you can blink, he was gone. It was too much for her to take. That same day she climbed into the car and drove for miles. She ended up driving head on into a tree. When I got the call at school, they told me she was in an accident and to hurry home. But when I got to the hospital, that's when I found out she was really trying to commit suicide. That's how she ended up losing her leg."

Stunned by the revelation, they sat quiet for a moment and allowed the truth to marinate the lie until all that remained were multiple reasons of little consequence to them.

"Don't take this the wrong way. I'm really sorry about your mom, n'everything, but I don't see how that translates into all of this being biblical," Jennifer said.

"My mother was never the same after that. I guess I wouldn't be either if I saw what she did. But I think what bothered her even more was something that my dad had been saying. Before I left for college, my mom and I both noticed something different about him. He was always worried about one thing or another, but he stopped worrying. He even gave up drinking. Then he started watching those TV preachers. After I left, my mom said he'd started going to church.

He'd invite her, but she wouldn't have anything to do with it. He'd called and reached out to me a few times at school, but I was too busy doing my own thing. It was during that time that my mom said he'd started having dreams and making crazy predictions about the future."

"What sort of predictions...what was he saying?"

"I wasn't there at the time, and my mom doesn't give any details. But from what I could piece together...I think he was warning her."

"So you're saying that everybody who believed in God, and went to church every Sunday, somehow were given advance warning...in a dream...really?" Justin said disbelievingly.

"No, it's not that simple. I've got other family members who've disappeared. We all do. I've also got a few who I know go to church all the time, but none of them disappeared. They're still very much here. And that's where it all gets very confusing."

"Do you really believe your father may have gotten some type of premonition from...God, or whomever?"

"Honestly...I'm not sure what to believe. But I'm open to the possibility."

Another break ensued where they seemed to reflect on Rafer's theory. Jennifer, who had always scoffed at most things spiritual, was especially intrigued by the notion of there being a biblical connection. She could not explain her sudden fascination. All she knew was that she wanted to know more.

"Oh...before I forget. I brought this for you guys," Rafer said as he reached under his shirt and pulled out a tarnished gray pistol. "It used to belong to my grandfather. He brought it back with him from Vietnam. I want you to take this."

Jennifer looked at it—and then him. "What do we need a gun for?" she asked.

"People aren't just sick and hungry back in town. A lot of them are angry. The police are overwhelmed. They're recruiting anyone who owns a gun and who they can trust to help maintain law and order...but it's not working. I'm seeing packs of rowdy fools roaming the streets, looking for trouble. They seem mostly from out of town...just passing through, I guess. Some of them are kids from the high school. And a few of them are friends of yours," he said, looking directly at Justin, who then cut his eyes away in a contemptuous roll. Rafer then turned to Jennifer, grabbed her hand, and placed the gun in it. "It's got a full magazine in it...seven rounds. It won't fire unless you release the safety," he said, briefly taking it from her for a quick visual. "Then you just aim and pull the trigger. I want you to take this...keep it handy...and use it if you have to." With that, he turned the gun butt side toward her and offered it to her. Jennifer looked at it for a moment.

"I'm not sure why you're hesitating. Have you looked around? We're sitting ducks, here. Take the darn thing. Otherwise, give it to me. I'm not afraid to use it," Justin said with his hand out and ready to receive it.

The second Jennifer saw what would've been the worst-case alternative in Justin; she immediately accepted the gun from Rafer. "When did you learn so much about guns?" she asked, still looking at it as though it were a living thing in her hand.

"I used to secretly play around with it when I was younger. I'm lucky I didn't blow my head off."

"If you came all the way over here to cheer us up...it didn't work," Rachel said.

"I'm sorry. I'm not trying to scare you, but it's important that you know what it really looks like out there. You're all still better off staying here than in town." Rafer stood to his feet. "I'd better leave now while there's still some light out. No sense wasting good battery juice. Remember what I said. And I'd also turn this radio down, some. You can hear it from all the way down the road. I'll stop back again in a few days."

As he started for the front door, Jennifer stood to her feet and followed behind him until they were both standing outside on the front stoop. From there on, he seemed in no hurry to leave. "For a second, there, you weren't really thinking about handing this gun over to Justin, were you?" she asked softly.

"No way. Your brother needs a hand gun like I need a hole in the head. No...I was just waiting for you to come to your senses," he said with an easy smile as he looked into her eyes, then holding it for a few precious seconds. "How are you holding up?"

"Let's see. I've got a brother who crisis strangely brings out the worst in...and who so far has been no help at all. There's my sister who at times is afraid of her own shadow, and whose hand I have to hold for almost everything except going to the bathroom. We've been surviving on one meal and spoonsful of water a day. I nailed some sheets up to the front windows, but really, we have no privacy at all. I haven't bathed, or showered in four days. My hair is a mess. And right now, I would give anything for a slice of pizza. But beyond that...I'm good."

"I'm glad to see you haven't lost your sense of humor."

Jennifer's wit was a welcomed break from what had become the norm for them these past few days. They both smiled with it, grateful for the relief it gave.

"Thank you for checking on us. I know it's not easy having to take care of your mom, and then coming all the way over here to see how we're doing. I just want you to know how much it means to me...knowing that you care enough to do that. You're a good man...and a good friend."

"Is that still all I am to you...just a good friend?"

Right then, Jennifer wanted to guard her affections. She feared there wasn't room in her heart for a third person to love, and to worry about. Only she could not deny what she was feeling any longer. She looked into his eyes. "No. you're more than just a friend to me," she said.

Rafer took her by the hand and pulled her towards him. "So all it took was an asteroid striking the earth...leveling New Jersey, and hurling us back to the Stone Age to accomplish what I'd been trying to do since tenth grade."

Jennifer leaned comfortably against his tall physique. "I guess it did. Let's just think of it as a sign from heaven," she said with a soft smile and sultry expression as she looked up at him.

"I thought you didn't believe in heaven," Rafer said.

Right then, Jennifer imagined his lips on hers; curious to know for certain if what she felt was genuine, or simply a byproduct of circumstances. "Are you gonna kiss me, or what?"

On hearing that, Rafer grabbed her at the waist and brought his lips down to meet hers. Within seconds of their touching, Jennifer relaxed in his arms; content now to know that what she felt was real.

DAY FIVE

Chapter 30

The rations line sliced its way through the military base like an out-of-control organism. For those on it, their faces told the story of suffering, while their body language punctuated the lethargy of hopelessness infecting them. Hunger and fatigue became the common thread that linked them into a seemingly endless chain.

This afternoon found Trent and his party standing among them, hunched over in the same road weary posture as the others. After having walked all of yesterday in search of a military installation, they were still maybe two hours away from their first receipt of rations in almost three days. With nothing new to speak of, they shared barely a word during their wait. As the line moved with a seeming disregard for urgency, the sound of an approaching helicopter was heard whipping the air overhead.

Within seconds, a UH-60 Black Hawk roared past in rapid descent toward an open field not far from where they were standing. There, it touched down to a whirlwind of risen dust. Its blades were still rotating when the fuselage door slid open. Out stepped Colonel Heath Jefferies, his head lowered and hand clutching the rim of his helmet as he trotted out from under the turning blades. He was accompanied by his adjutant, a Command Sergeant Major who carried his briefcase, and by three other enlisted men who served as his personal security detachment.

"That rations line isn't moving fast enough. Go see if you can straighten that out," he instructed one of his men.

Directly after the asteroid impact, Heath had been given a 100-mile purview of twelve disaster response base camps to command. This was his third stop today, and if he didn't know any better, he would swear they were only circling and returning back to the exact same base after each take off. The same dispiriting scenes greeted him at every stop. At the time of the west coast cataclysm, foreign aid was dispatched almost immediately; the first shipments arriving within hours of the initial quake. But such wasn't the case this time. So far, the international community has been slow to respond to this new natural disaster. The humanitarian aid that did arrive was not nearly enough to supplement America's already dwindling stockpiles. That alone didn't explain why there was still so many hungry among the survivors.

From day one, C-17's had been air dropping crates of care packages containing emergency rations, and such, over remote towns and villages. It should have been enough to sustain them until a temporary base camp was set up in their vicinity. Unfortunately, with nine other camps left to visit, investigating the reasons for the shortage would have to wait. For now, Heath's main focus was on reassuring the civilians that their government was on top of things.

In his almost thirty years of service to the military, Heath had seen the horrors of war and its often depraved indifference to collateral damage; as a young Second Lieutenant, the unintentional bombing of Iraqi civilians by U.S. forces during the Gulf War; the starvation of thousands of Somali refugees by local clan leaders during the U.S. operation in Mogadishu; and the targeted suicide bombings by al-Qaeda insurgents against innocent civilians during Operation Iraqi Freedom. The aftermath of each conflict was felt hardest among the non-combatants. But unlike those instances, these folks were no casualties of war. Not since the cataclysm had he seen so much death and devastation on U.S. soil.

With each passing day, the rations lines were getting longer; and the conditions, more severe for the thousands of survivors who were now looking to him as their savior. Meanwhile, he had nothing to offer them beyond maintaining the status quo, and passing on any new info that made its way down the pipeline. Consequently, it forced him to deal with his outrage in private, and the increasing sense of helplessness that clouded his sense of purpose. His frustration also kept him from openly criticizing his new Commander in Chief.

At the time of the disappearances, the United States armed forces suffered the greatest number of losses of any other military power in the world. They had lost over a quarter of their active and reserve personnel, reducing their manpower by a staggering figure of nearly eight-million. Once the most powerful fighting force in the world, their military was now significantly weakened and thus deemed an unreliable deterrent among the NATO allies. To make matters worse, the country seemed headed on a political course that could ultimately prove detrimental to its very existence.

Heath had never been a fan of new president, Bartlett and his globalization leanings. During his run for the oval office, he had campaigned on a platform of "collective sovereignty," the new catch phrase that had swept across Europe. He claimed it would restore the country's military and economic prominence; but at the cost of unifying with other nations to form a single sovereign power. And under the supreme rule of the Federation of States president, Baldo Jović.

Americans were split on globalization; especially after the cataclysm and its ensuing impact on the populace. At the time, Baldo Jović opponents decried his promises as tantamount to extortion— paid protection. But in an increasingly hostile world, many viewed it as a necessary sacrifice to ensure the continued safety of the nation. As a stopgap measure to prevent a breakdown of order, private militias were utilized. Their job was strictly to assist when called upon. But the government's increasing reliance on them resulted in militia leaders being accorded the same ranking as non-commissioned officers. The decision provoked resentment throughout the branches of the military. As for Heath, he considered it an act of lunacy; granting gun-toting civilians—some of whose extreme ideologies were already on the fringe—what amounted to a license to kill.

United States Northern Command, Invoking NSP Directive-51, and in direct violation of the Posse Comitatus Act, assigned the U.S. Army 3rd Infantry Division to secure with deadly force, vulnerable government buildings in the nation's battered capital. That left the patrol of towns and cities, in the hands of the National Guard and local militias. As the highest ranking field officer, Heath had absolute jurisdiction over all militias. Nevertheless, he knew from past experience that enforcing that authority on bands of undisciplined paramilitary units was a lot easier said than done. So far, he hadn't had any trouble with them, and hoped it might stay that way for the duration.

Wishful thinking aside, the combination of developments was causing him to wonder if he hadn't reached his limit; if he had gone as far in the military as his unwavering sense of patriotism would allow. Approaching thirty years of service to the Army, and only two years away from mandatory retirement he was a career officer; an ROTC graduate of the Citadel; loyal to his men and to his country. But the landscape as he knew it was starting to change, and he was bound by duty to change along with it—or so he kept telling himself.

***

After waiting on line for over two hours, Trent and the others were finally inside the rations tent. They approached a table where, on the other side, two armed soldiers stood. Their wrists were cocked and resting on M-16's to ensure an orderly procession while two others administered the allocation of rations. As Trent drew closer, he could hear them barking out instructions, and the murmur of complaints erupting from those closest who seemed surprised by the demand. It was only after he reached the table that he learned the actual reason for much of their discontent.

With the regions GSM network of cell towers still inoperative, the military had been utilizing their WIN-T network, via direct satellite, for all sending and receiving of information. Designed primarily for use in combat situations, its peacetime application proved just as invaluable; most notably after catastrophic events similar to this one—a breakdown of the communications infrastructure. With the aid of a portable generator and a satellite dish, it gave every soldier in the field access to the internet and the Department of Homeland Security database of registered U.S. residents.

"Pass your right hand beneath the scanner...everyone. You must pass your right hand beneath the scanner," said a slight-looking soldier who sat facing a rugged-laptop computer monitor. A can opener sized scanner was plugged into it and rested on the table between them.

"What's the purpose of this?" Trent asked.

"Pass your right hand beneath the scanner...everyone," the young soldier said in rote repetition, and seemingly oblivious to the barrage of questions asked of him.

"Why are we doing this? We never had to, before."

"Please pass your right hand beneath the scanner. Everyone must be scanned. These are direct orders from Washington."

"But why?"

"We have to take a census. It's just a headcount...nothing more. Let's move. You're holding up the line."

"But I'm not chipped. Does that mean I don't get any rations?"

"Do you have a state-issued I.D.?"

"Yes."

"Then pass it under the scanner and keep moving." Trent pulled his driver's license out from his wallet, turned it barcode side up, and held it under the scanner. Once the device beeped, it took less than a second for his identity to be confirmed. Another soldier handed him a day's worth of rations and told him to move on. Before exiting the tent, Trent looked back at Janet who was next in line, and wondered how she would fare against the attending soldiers' curt demeanors.

"My I.D. was stolen. I'm not chipped," she said in a pitiful tone that conveyed her thirst.

"Your name and social security number," the soldier asked.

After complying, Janet watched as he entered her information into the database and waited for verification. It appeared on screen in the form of her driver's license photo and other vital statistics. After confirming her identity, he initiated a print command, activating a small printer next to his laptop. It produced a narrow strip of perforated paper, which he immediately tore off.

"Hold out your right hand," he instructed. As Janet did that, he exposed a section of adhesive and secured the strip around her outstretched wrist. "This is your new I.D. Try not to lose it this time."

"I didn't lose anything. It was stolen. What happens if this one rips?"

"It's tear resistant. But it's not indestructible...so just make certain you don't lose it. You can't get rations without it. Who's next?" the soldier asked, making it abundantly clear that he was done with her.

Getting chipped had first gained popularity among the celebrity set. They embraced it as a high tech, and trendy alternative to carrying a cash card; the elimination of plastics, lessening their carbon footprints on the planet—so they claimed. As unsolicited advocates of the technology, they succeeded in glamorizing the invasive procedure until the expression, "getting chipped," had become part of the popular culture. Despite the millions of people who had elected to be chipped, there was a good percentage who still believed in their personal right to privacy.

Trent and his family were among those who were opposed to any type of implant, even though by all accounts it had made life easier for those who were. Of the six of them, only Constance was chipped. And after witnessing the hassle that the others experienced at the rations table, she did not mind extolling the benefits of her implant.

Even though nightfall was still a good three hours away, they decided to remain at the camp. There, they would bask in the abundance of electricity and port-a-potties, and then leave it all behind in the morning.

Chapter 31

The debris in the road was like a thorn in the side of Sonia. Her every other step was plagued by the combination of uneven terrain and the unceasing throb in her ankle. Since injuring it yesterday afternoon, she had been limping behind the others for much of the day; enduring the hurt as it radiated up her leg. It was concluded to be nothing more than a bad sprain, even though the pain she was experiencing seemed to be saying otherwise. Nora had been walking alongside her the entire time, all the while keeping a watchful eye on Taylor and the others. They were only a few yards ahead of them, but could easily be lost sight of in the dense traffic of survivors.

As expected, Fort Lee, New Jersey was a town trapped along the outer edges of annihilation; its inhabitants gripped by a virulent languor that seized their will like a strain of resignation. There was no fight left in them, only lethargy as they sought relief from the hurt and hunger that had been their bane for the last five days.

"Would you like to stop and rest? I could run up ahead and let the others know," Nora said.

"No thanks. They're already mad enough with me for slowing them down. I wouldn't want them to get fed up and leave us...then I'd have you mad at me, too."

"Don't worry...they're not going to leave. I wouldn't let that happen."

"I don't know. That Taylor is a pretty tough character. Once he decides to do something, there's no changing his mind," Sonia said.

"He's not so bad...just a little headstrong. I know he sometimes tries to act like he's superman, but he's not exempt from getting stressed out. Who wouldn't under these conditions? At least he's been right for the most part. He's gotten us this far."

"Yeah, maybe...but how do you explain him going headstrong on Dale's face the other night. He had that look in his eyes...like he wanted to kill him. And believe me...I'm no fan of Dale's. If anybody was overdue for a whupping, it was him. I never saw another man getting pimp slapped like that before. It almost made me feel sorry for him."

As they walked, Nora turned for a moment and looked at Sonia. "You...felt sorry for Dale?" she asked with surprise.

"I said almost. I was okay with it after a few seconds. I don't know why he has to act like such an idiot. He doesn't seem to want to get along with anybody."

"I think he's used to getting whatever he wants. When he doesn't...lashing out is how he deals with it. It's his way of throwing an adult-sized tantrum. It's all fairly harmless until somebody gets hurt."

"Since he's the one getting hurt, let's hope for his sake that he learned his lesson." Just as Sonia said that, they were startled to see up ahead what looked like another standoff between Dale and Taylor. By the time they caught up with them—

"You starting up with me again? Wasn't that last beating I gave you enough?" Taylor said as he aggressively headed toward Dale.

"I'm not afraid of you. And I have a right to speak my mind," Dale said, hastily inching back from Taylor's approach, just as Miguel jumped between them.

"What's going on, now?" Nora asked. "I thought we resolved all of this."

"All I'm saying is we should stay on the main road. That's our best chance of reaching a military base. He wants to take us along deserted back roads."

"Only because we'll make better time. Most of these people are trying to get to where we just came from. We've been walking against them all day. They're slowing us down," Taylor insisted.

"Maybe...but what about rations? I'm all out, and so is everybody else. The heck with speed. Right now we need food and water."

"I think Dale might be right. If we get off the main road, we lose our information network. As long as we stay where the people are, if there's a base up ahead, we're sure to hear about it."

"Have you looked into their faces?" Taylor said harshly. "We've been walking against them all day, and so far I haven't seen one person who looks even remotely nourished. That's because anything worth taking along this road has already been cleaned out. If we're going to find anything, it's going to be along the road less traveled...not on this one."

His point resonated with enough logic to elicit a momentary pause among all but one. "I say we take a vote," said Dale. "All those in favor of staying put, raise your hands." His was the first to go up. Laura's hand was next, and then Miguel's.

When it appeared as though that was it, "It looks like we've got a tie. I guess that means we're splitting up. Are you sure you want to do this?" Taylor asked, looking directly at Laura. She, in turn, looked at Nora as second thoughts appeared to stir.

"We really should stay together. Now's not the time for us to be splitting up," Nora said delicately. "Besides, Laura, you've got farther to go than all of us. And Dale's home is right in the next county. Then it'll just be you and Miguel. What Taylor said does make sense if you think about it. There's nothing left along this road."

Laura turned to Dale. "She's right. You'll be home in another day or two. Then it's down to just me and Miguel. I'm not comfortable with that...no offense Miguel."

"None taken...I decided I'm going with them, too. It's safer," he said, stepping over to join them.

Sonia, no doubt believing her handicap had made her a liability in Taylor's eyes, remained quiet throughout.

"I don't believe you people. Why do you allow him to manipulate you like that? Can't you think for yourselves?" Dale argued as they slowly began to walk off, leaving him standing there. "What if they're setting up a base right now, not more than an hour from here? What if they've even arranged transportation to take people home?" he shouted. Still, they kept walking. "Okay...just wait. When your mouths are so dry that you can't even make any saliva, and your stomachs start to swell from hunger...you'll wish you had listened to me."

Nora stopped for a moment and looked back at him. "Are you coming?" she asked loudly.

Dale kicked the debris at his feet; then yelled out a curse that in it its timbre seemed directed more at his own cowardice, than at them. "Yeah...I'm coming."

Chapter 32

A SATCOM mobile vehicle was stationed just outside a series of connecting TEMPER tents. There, its dish was directed up at a precise angle that allowed a signal to pierce through the dust-cloud cover between it and the geosynchronous orbiting MILSTAR satellite. Arranged like blocks in a grid, the tents combined to create a micro-complex of stations that served as the camp's command center. Inside one of the tents, Heath had just finished issuing last-minute instructions to the lieutenant colonel in charge. He was about to leave for his next camp inspection when a PFC SATCOM Operator burst in from a connecting tent.

"Pardon me, sir. I just received an urgent email from General Eubanks addressed to the camp commander," he said, then pausing for a moment, visibly uncertain as to which officer he should hand it to. Heath, in keeping with protocol, automatically reached for it. He didn't like having to pull rank; especially considering that he had far less to do with the day-to-day operations of the base than the lieutenant colonel. But it wasn't every day that an email is received from the Chairman of the Joint Chiefs.

To: All base commanders

By order of our Commander-in-Chief, President Thomas Bartlett, in an effort to better facilitate and monitor the distribution of rations, all disaster response base camps and military installations within the impact radius are hereby instructed to deny rations to any civilian, regardless of age, who does not possess a VERIF-i chip implant. Furthermore, all military personnel throughout the branches of the armed services, and by executive order, National Guard members in all fifty states, are hereby ordered to submit to mandatory VERIF-i chip implantation effective immediately. A refusal to obey by any service member, in accordance with Article-92 of the Uniform Code of Military Justice, and subject to executive order, will result in automatic confinement leading to a general court-martial. To expedite the directive, each base will be receiving a complete VERIF-i outfit containing 500,000 microchips, encoding hardware, installation disc, syringes and scanners within forty-eight hours of receipt of this email. All ration stations are to offer and administer, by request, a microchip implant to any civilian not in possession of one. Lastly, the president, in the interest of crowd control has authorized the use of deadly force to quell any acts of civil unrest that could arise with the announcement of the new rations guidelines.

Otis T. Eubanks
General, U.S. Army
Chairman
Of the Joint Chiefs of Staff

While waiting, the lieutenant colonel watched Heath's expression change from all business to one of concern. "What is it, sir?" he asked.

"What it is...is not good," replied Heath, who then handed the email over to him. "You'll need to triple the number of guards working the rations tent. Things are liable to get very heated over there once you make that announcement."

"Are they really expecting us to shoot tired civilians whose only crime is being hungry?"

"I guess they don't see it that way...in the interest of crowd control...remember," Heath said with a hint of sarcasm. "The minute one shot is fired...an already bad situation gets instantly worse. But then who am I to question my superiors. We just do as we're told. I don't know what they're eating in Washington tonight, but I'm sure it's not MRE rations. If things do get out of control, I think a few simple warning shots might suffice. Also, don't make that announcement until the morning. There's no sense in upsetting anyone tonight. Let them rest. I'll be visiting back here again in a day or two."

With that, Heath exited the tent and headed towards the waiting helicopter; its blades already spinning in a pre-liftoff rotation as he approached. He could not imagine what form of insanity had taken over in Washington. If imposing chipping every man and woman in the armed forces by threat of court-martial wasn't bad enough, they were about to use starvation tactics to pressure civilians who were not chipped, into getting implanted. It was fascist style coercion the likes of which he had only seen in the repressed regions of the world. And at the very least, a civil rights violation of the worst kind. Either the conditions in Washington were far worse than he realized and a skeleton crew was running the government, or some other agenda was afoot. Whatever the cause, this new president was clearly abusing his executive privilege by playing fast and loose with the rule of law.

Heath understood his job all too well. He was to restore order—even if it meant taking a life. He had heard the stories coming out of New York City and nearby towns; stories of prison inmates who, during the post-impact chaos, were able to escape and went on to conduct a mini terror spree; of social deviants living clandestinely among their neighbors and who saw in the bedlam a golden opportunity to run amok. Some were arrested by patrolling troops and neighborhood militias; some were killed; but most were sadly still on the loose. Nevertheless, there was a distinct difference between that use of force, and a standing order to shoot if necessary, innocent

American citizens. Just the thought of it stuck in Heath's craw as he boarded the helicopter for his next stopover.

***

Trent sat on a patch of dusty ground outside one of the tents; his back resting against a wall of duck cloth, and a blanket draped over his head so that only his face was exposed. The nights were growing cooler. Sitting only inches to his right was Gina, her face framed by a donated blanket that she used to cover the rest of her. Their hunger relieved for the moment, they relaxed not far from the others, and among a multitude of survivors who, like themselves, used their blankets for shelter against the persistent but diminishing dust. Flood lamps throughout the base temporarily turned night into day, shedding light on their communal discomfort; while beneath their blankets, judiciously conserved rations kept tempers from bubbling over like so much pent-up rage.

The background noise from a spinning helicopter rotor had dominated their hearing for the past several minutes. Its agitated whir built up to a crescendo just before its fuselage was seen ascending over the tent peaks and then flying off across the night sky. A collective relief seemed to follow its departure, and the welcomed return of quiet. Trent closed his eyes and used the opportunity to envision his family again. He searched through his memory and retrieved another image, back to a time when life was simpler; to when he and Nora were younger and romantic gestures came as naturally as breathing. He recalled their children, happily playing together and basking in the joys of prepubescent innocence. Trent purposefully focused on the memory until he felt for them a cathartic swell of sympathy that was both painful and pleasing at the same time.

Gina, sitting next to him, didn't seem able to find a restful posture and fidgeted beneath her blanket. She would expel her frustration in occasional sighs, then mumble something profane under her breath as if the words could somehow change her predicament. "How come you never got chipped?" she asked out of the blue, and seemingly without regard for whatever dreams Trent may have been entertaining.

"Excuse me?"

"You never got chipped. I was just wondering how come."

"I guess I didn't for the same reasons that a lot of people didn't. I don't think the government needs to know what I'm doing every second of the day."

"Why would they be that interested in you? Do you really think you're that important to them?"

"No...but I do think keeping an eye on folks for the sake of homeland security has gotten out of control. I lead a pretty simple life. There's no reason for me to be on anybody's radar. I was fine with it when it was all about watching the bad guys. Once that number started to grow, then it became about watching everyone. It's not enough that they take over a third of my earnings...now they want my privacy, too. That's where I draw the line."

"Just so I understand...by 'they', you do mean the government, right? Not the law."

"I'm not a fugitive if that's what you're thinking. And I'm not anti-government, either. It's about making a statement. I'm exercising my right to choose while I still can. And what about you...what's your reason for no chip?"

"I really don't have a good one. I never gave it a lot of thought. So far I've been getting by just fine without one. I guess it helps, though, when you have some stability in your life. I haven't had that for a while, and by the looks of things, I probably won't for some time."

"Don't you have any family?"

"None that I want to go back to. We're kind of like oil and water," Gina said.

"I understand."

"No you don't."

Trent kept quiet, believing his response might've insulted her.

"It's complicated, alright?" Gina went on to say. "What about your family? Do you...I mean...did you have children?"

"Yeah, I've got three, and no...they weren't taken. They're at home, but my wife was in New York when the asteroid struck."

"I'm sorry."

"No need to be sorry. She's trying to get back home...same as I am."

"Have you spoken to her?"

"No."

"New York had to have been hit pretty hard. How can you be certain she's still alive?"

Trent, for the first time coming face to face with the question, thought seriously for a moment. "I can't...but then that's all I have to hold on to...that and my children." He had spent the last five days convincing himself that they were very much alive and well. Yet, it took Gina only a few seconds to revive terrifying doubts in his mind. Before she could dash anymore of his optimism, "I'd like to get some sleep, now. Maybe you should, too," he said, then closed his eyes and tried to resume the daydream she had interrupted.

DAY SIX

Chapter 33

"Hey, wakeup...it's time to get going," Taylor said in a startling voice like the sound of morning reveille.

Nora jumped out of her half sleep and, in a protective reflex, pulled the blanket she was wrapped in tight around her. With wide eyes she looked around and accessed what if any threats were near, then seeing none, relaxed back against the tree trunk where she sat. Her movements alerted both Laura and Sonia who each awoke from their semi-slumber and, likewise, surveyed the immediate area. In the days following the impact they had grown accustomed to sleeping lightly—and with good reason.

Of all the post-impact dangers threatening their survival, none was more horrifying than the rumors of women being brutally raped and left for dead in the streets. Though they had not encountered any evidence of such, still, the mere thought of it haunted them like an ominous specter just waiting for opportunity. It kept them in a place of constant fear; cautiously looking over their shoulders during the day, and wondering, with the approach of evening, what might be lurking around every darkened corner. It compelled them, for safety sake, to sleep within a few feet of each other at night, and to never leave their backs exposed for too long.

As they rose to their feet in preparation to leave, Nora turned to see Taylor standing off to one side of their campsite, and with his back to them. The sight of his indomitable visage no doubt offered a small degree of comfort to the women. They deniably not only looked to him for leadership, but protection as well. He stood gazing through the trees at the deserted roadway they were about to take. Miguel was already up and pounding his blanket free of dust against the side of a tree.

"If you guys are ready, let's head out," Taylor said before stepping off.

"Wait a minute. Dale's not here," Nora said, looking around.

"Well, where is he?"

"He's probably somewhere relieving himself," Miguel said with a quick scan of the area. "Dale, hurry up. We're about to leave," he shouted, only to hear his own echoed voice in return.

"Dale, this isn't funny. If you're out there, you'd better say something...or we're going to leave without you," Sonia called out, her voice containing a hint of anxiety as its echo returned her trailing words. "He's not answering. I don't think he's out there."

Taylor walked over to a cluster of trees. "Dale! This is your last chance. Either come out now, or we're leaving without you," he yelled angrily.

Still, there was no answer.

"Something must've happened to him," Laura said.

Taylor started back for the roadway. "Or, he could've just decided to go on ahead. He's been itching to go his own way for a while, now," he said.

"Yeah, but I don't think he would've...it's not like him. He's not that brave. He wouldn't just disappear like that."

"Then where is he?"

"Maybe he fell and hit his head, or something. We should at least look around," Nora said.

"And if we find him, then what? Are you planning on carrying him the rest of the way? You do realize, just standing around talking about this, we're losing precious time. Now you want to waste more of it searching for him. If you ask me, I'm thinking he's gone back to the main road. He never did want to come this way if you recall," Taylor said.

"Maybe we should just leave," Sonia, favoring her injured ankle, said as she stood next to Nora. She was visibly shaken by Dale's disappearance, and given her dislike of him, was perhaps unsure which emotion to attach to his absence. In spite of that, her tone and body language suggested she wasn't too keen on venturing into the wilderness to search for him. "Taylor's right. We should assume he either turned back, or went on ahead without us. He would have been the first of us to reach home, anyway. I guess he didn't want to wait any longer. And if he were hurt, he would've called out for help. One of us would've heard him. We shouldn't waste anymore time here," she said.

Taylor then looked at Laura and Miguel. "What about you two?" he asked. They both reluctantly agreed with Sonia. "That settles it. Sorry, Nora. Dale made his bed." With that, they started for the roadway.

As they headed out, Nora turned and took a last look around the area in the slim hope that she might spot his return. In the short time that she had been traveling with Dale, she might've accused him of being a lot of things, but impulsive would not have been one of them. If anything, she saw hidden beneath his provocative personality a deliberate scoundrel whose motives were wholly self-serving. He may not have been well liked, but he was still one of them; and for him to leave without even saying goodbye, was puzzling.

Chapter 34

The sound of gunshots, like several balloons bursting one after another, interrupted Jennifer as she lay sleeping on the sofa. Startled, she sat straight up and immediately looked for Rachel who, on the other side of the room, was already sitting up and looking nervously across at her. They had heard it before; the infrequent gunshots sounding as distant pops in the days right after the impact. And even then, the faint echoes were always far-off enough that the likelihood of a stray bullet coming through their window was remote, or so they told themselves. But on this morning, the shots rang with surprising nearness. It sent Jennifer scurrying to the window, her adrenaline surging as she parted the bed sheet curtain and peered through the opening out onto the street in front of the house.

A palate of bleak shades stared back at her; motionless and silent like a traumatized witness to something horrific. The few small birds that early on would dart across the sky, stopped their chatter days ago, and had fallen to earth—dead. They dotted the landscape in feathered clumps that over time were pecked at by larger birds, or carried off by some other hungry predator.

She looked up, eager to see if there was a small break in the overcast and any trace of blue sky to place her hopes on. But there was no change. Much like a bloated rain cloud that refused to rain, it maintained a depressive veil over everything.

The radio, which they never switched off, was still tuned to the same station. The familiar voice of the morning newscaster spoke in earnest behind her as she watched at the window for anything unusual.

We've just received breaking news that President Bartlett, in a preemptive move brought on by the current catastrophe, and in order to better facilitate future disaster relief efforts, has enacted by proclamation a requirement that every American citizen must submit to mandatory chip implantation. Enforcement will begin immediately with a nationwide completion date set for December 25th. Those areas affected by the asteroid impact will receive priority during this initiative, which has been given the name, Project Cover Every American. To expedite swift implantation in the impact regions, rations are being denied to any survivor who refuses to get chipped. We're told that any resistance will be met with as yet undisclosed consequences. This action is a complete departure from the policies of the previous administration. The late President Schaefer, an opponent of forced chipping, had vetoed every bill that landed on his desk looking for passage. Even though at the time, a public opinion poll concluded that seventy-three percent of Americans were in favor of it. At present, the only other industrialized societies with government-enforced chip implantation are those countries within the IEU, and those within the newly formed Federation of States.

Rachel, still frozen in the same position she woke up in, sat staring at Jennifer's back. "What is it? Do you see anything?" she asked.

"No. Whoever was out there must've left. I don't hear anything."

"Maybe they're hiding behind a tree. What did you do with the gun Rafer gave you?"

"I hid it. I didn't want Justin getting his hands on it. And frankly, I'd prefer not to have my hands on it, either. It makes me uncomfortable," Jennifer said as she closed the curtain and walked away from the window.

"Well, you had better get over that, and quick. That gun is the only protection we have. If you're too afraid to use it, maybe you should give it over to Justin."

"I said it makes me uncomfortable. I didn't say I wouldn't use it if I had to. And would you really want to see Justin carrying a loaded gun?"

Rachel, no doubt realizing the folly in such a suggestion, answered with a shrug of her shoulders and a tacit look away.

"Speaking of Justin, where is he? I know he must've heard those gunshots, too."

"He must still be upstairs in his bedroom. I don't know why he chooses to stay up there rather than down here with us. If something were to happen to you and me, he wouldn't even know about it until he came down to eat."

"I think retreating upstairs is his way of showing us how much he disagrees with our decision to stay. By not coming down, he's pretty much saying don't look to him for any type of help."

"Really, he can act like such a baby sometimes. How much longer does he think he can ignore us? We've been stuck here for what...six days, now? I'm sure it's got to be getting pretty lonely up there."

"You already know how stubborn he can be. It wouldn't surprise me if—" Jennifer gasped suddenly as two more gunshots were heard outside their window. Sounding similar to the last, this time she was able to place the point of origin as somewhere in the vicinity of Wheeler Park—roughly a twenty-minute walk from their home, and close enough to send a chill through her. She turned to Rachel who lately it seemed was just a hairsbreadth away from an emotional meltdown. Just as she feared, terror had little sister in an unrelenting grip that seemed to be getting tighter by the second.

At that point, Jennifer ran into her father's office and, stepping over the debris, reached behind a dusty leather recliner and pulled out the pistol Rafer had given her. Holding it out in front of her like a soaked rag, she rushed back into the other room and headed straight for the window. There, she parted the curtain and once again peered out from behind it; her hand, now firmly wrapped around the gun's handle, and all the while hoping that whoever was out there, wouldn't curiously wander onto their street.

"Quick, go turn off the radio," she whispered to Rachel who, after collecting herself, jumped up from her makeshift bed. Jennifer leaned her ear into the window opening, and with heightened senses, listened through the dead silence for so much as the snap of a twig breaking. After a few heart-pounding seconds of intense listening, and hearing nothing again, she assumed the threat had passed. Relieved, she turned away from the window, heaved her chest and released a longwinded sigh of nervous exhaustion that caused her shoulders to slump upon exhale.

She started to return the gun back to its hiding place. That's when another sound suddenly caught her ear. It was faint but discernable, and with a haunting nearness that stood her still for a moment; conflicted by an instinct to flee, and a mind to stand and fight. The sound grew gradually louder and more distinct, like tin cans being dragged along pavement. She soon realized that it was emanating from the road just outside their window and that, whatever it was, was slowly making its way up their street.

With fleeing no longer an option, Jennifer headed back to the window. The weight of the gun still in her hand helped to minimize the tremble that had taken control of it. She carried it low against her hip; her arm rigid and straight as if fearful that any sudden move might cause it to discharge. She approached the window, the pastel colored sheet stretched across it hung flat and calm like a ship's sail in search of a breeze. It was all that stood between them and whatever mystery waited on the other side.

She listened to the noise growing louder and more distinct in front of her and wondered if it would not have been more prudent for her and Rachel to simply lay low, thereby allowing their house to blend in with all the other abandoned homes in the vicinity. Better that than risk being discovered, she reasoned. Except by now, her curiosity was fully aroused. Anything less than a full-on peek at the source would've been anticlimactic.

Up until now, she had done an adequate job of not allowing Rachel's nervousness to infect her. But with each *clank* heard outside the window, Rafer's warning rang like a bell in her head. It fueled her imagination to construct a graphic vision of ever worsening atrocities that she feared might be inflicted upon them if discovered. She tightened her grip around the gun, raised her other hand, and gingerly pulled the edge of the sheet away from the wall.

The creaky sounds continued out of sight, building in volume and seeming twice as loud within the desolation of the cul-de-sac. Through it all, Jennifer remained outwardly calm; even as the rapid breaths of Rachel expelled in tremulous pants that no doubt looked for the slightest panicked reaction from her on which to let loose a scream.

The mysterious sound was now closer than ever and only seconds away from coming into view. Jennifer leaned into the sheets narrow gap, angled her gaze toward the oncoming noise, and waited for its source to reveal itself.

In the cool dystopia that was late morning, she held her breath, and then gasped suddenly at the first sight of him. "It's Justin!" she said in a confused tone that overshadowed her relief.

He walked in leisurely strides, one arm extended behind him and pulling a rickety gardener's cart whose decrepit moving parts creaked with every roll of its wheels.

"Justin. What's he doing out there? I thought he was upstairs in his room," Rachel said, rushing to the window. Once there, she yanked the sheet fully open and saw him making his way toward them. "Justin! What are you doing out there, you idiot? Do you realize Jen almost popped a cap in your trifl'n butt? You scared us half to death."

"Good. Now maybe you'll come to your senses and we could leave this hellhole."

"Leave for where? You heard what Rafer said. Things aren't any better in town. If anything, they're worse. Can't you see we're better off staying right here?" Jennifer said as he turned up their driveway, still pulling the cart behind him.

"I thought you'd say that. That's why I decided to go shopping this morning."

Jennifer, on hearing that, quickly tucked the gun underneath the sofa cushion. She and Rachel then hurried to the front door and stepped outside to meet him. Eyeing the cart's unknown contents, she tempered her annoyance for the moment as a tingle of excitement not felt since she repaired the radio, aroused her inquiring mind.

Justin strode up to the front step like a man who had just robbed a leprechaun's treasure chest. In his audaciousness, Jennifer couldn't help but notice his newly acquired bling. He was wearing three watches on one wrist and four or five chains around his neck. "What exactly do you have in there...and is it anything we can *all* use?" she asked.

"Maybe...maybe not. I just went from house to house grabbing stuff. You'd be surprised at the sort of things people leave behind. You'll have to go through it yourself to see what you want. I already set my stuff aside. And don't bother looking for food...there wasn't any...at least none worth taking."

"How many houses did you check?" Rachel asked as she rummaged through the items, so far finding nothing more than useless junk.

"Only five. After I heard those gunshots, I knew it was time to head back. They sound like they're getting closer, though." He turned to Jennifer. "You still think staying here is a good idea?"

"If you've got any other suggestions that don't involve leaving, I'm all ears. Otherwise, stop being so difficult and start cooperating with us."

"Wait, didn't I hear something on the radio about the President forcing everyone to get chipped by the end of the year?" Rachel asked.

"Yeah...that's right. While you were out shopping, they made it mandatory that every American gets an implant...and they're starting with the survivors in the impact zones. That means us. They're not giving rations to anyone who isn't chipped."

"So what?" Justin said without the slightest reaction to the new developments.

"So...you know how Dad feels about chip implants. All I know is I don't want anybody forcing me to get chipped, and neither should you. For now, right here is the safest place for us. When Mom and Dad get back, they'll know what to do."

"And in the meantime, what do we do when we run out of food and water?" Justin asked pointedly.

Jennifer looked at him for a moment, her mouth paused to answer, then simply turned and went back inside the house. Rachel followed behind her, leaving Justin standing alone on the front step with his cart full of booty. "He's right, y'know. What are we supposed to do once our food and water runs out?" she whispered as she followed her toward the kitchen. Once there, they both stood in front of the center island and surveyed what was left of their food.

If they nibbled and sipped, Jennifer figured, they might have enough to last for five days at the most. And even that would be pushing it, she thought. With that, she raised both hands up to her face, then sighing deeply, brought them together in a clasp against her chin. "I don't know," she answered.

Chapter 35

Constance, from the moment she recognized the gutted pharmacy on the corner of Sutter and Vanderbilt, walked briskly for almost an hour. She knew it well. It was there where she would fill the prescriptions for her mother's blood pressure medication and her father's glaucoma drops.

The large plate-glass window that graced the front of it was now a gaping entrance. It showed off the darksome bowels where shelves had been stripped clean of goods. And the adjacent delicatessen; charred by fire and ravaged by looters, still had its familiar sign in place. Beyond that, there was little else recognizable about her neighborhood. Its small-town appearance had been reduced to the panorama of a blitzkrieg. Most of the residents, it seemed, had departed, turning the streets over to the feral dogs whose occasional howls cut like a whip through the dead air. The few signs of human life that remained were hunkered down in their homes, either unable or unwilling to leave.

Trent and the others kept pace a few steps behind Constance. They didn't want to intrude on her solemn rush to get home in light of the devastation she was seeing around her. Of no less importance to them was the prospect of maybe finding a meal where they were headed. For the past hour, all Constance could see in her mind were the faces of her parents; mother in the kitchen preparing the night's meal; father keeping busy by fixing something around the house that was barely broken to start. Only now did it occur to her that she might have been asking too much of them.

She was an only child, accustomed to hoarding their attention with precocious manners that never failed to elicit a chuckle from them. Her every achievement, no matter how small, was applauded—in essence, a praise-reward loop that she wholly embraced, and they likewise indulged.

While growing up, they would adorn her bedroom with a weekly supply of fresh lilacs, lilies and chrysanthemums; festoon it with elegant tapestry and garland; scent it with sweet smelling oils; and then during the night, tiptoe into her haloed chamber and marvel at their little angel as she slept peaceably. She was the joy of their life; the sole reason for their existence, it seemed.

Years later, upon her leaving for college, her vacated bedroom was pristinely maintained in wait for her return. In her absence, they would use it as a place of retreat and meditation on all things, Constance—until their obsession bordered on something closer to worship. Constance told herself that she loved her parent's selfless devotion to her. But there were times, mostly after the split from yet another boyfriend, that she often hated them.

Her house was just around the next corner. The street sign up ahead stood out aslant among the ruins like a desert directional marker. Constance, after spotting it, immediately sprung into a lumbering jog; her eyes tearing, and heart racing with anticipation as she pulled away from the others. On the way there, she prepped her sight to narrow onto the house the minute it came into view. As she approached the end of the block, her head leaned forward to catch the first glimpse of her home. What she saw, though, upon rounding the corner nearly caused her to stumble in horror. The home, for which she had endured inconceivable hardships to get back to, was gone.

From the start of their journey she wanted to believe that her place was among the few that had survived the storm with its skin intact. And that her elderly parents had made it through the onslaught unharmed. For days she envisioned the look of shock on their beleaguered faces the moment they heard the footsteps coming up the walk. They would swing the front door open, see her and rush out, teary-eyed and arms opened wide to receive her like a long-lost child.

More to her disappointment than surprise, her home fared no better than the countless hundreds she had seen along the way. It was all she could do to keep herself together as her feet rushed to meet up with the rubble that was home. With each step, the coughing prelude to an effusive sob was pushing at her throat.

By the time she reached the foot of her walkway, the cough had erupted into crying. Her head looked straight on at the horrible scene, convulsing in a weeping fit as she proceeded to forge through the charred debris. She stopped short of the concrete foundation and stared down into the belly of what had been her basement and the implosion of materials that lay at the bottom.

***

Trent walked up alongside Constance and stood looking mournfully at the mountain of blackened rubble. It spread out before him like a massive trash bin filled with deep trenches, sharp peaks and jagged edges. Reason enough to forbid any attempt by either of them at venturing out onto it. Its burnt smell, after days of inhaling as much, was barely noticeable to Trent's soot lined nostrils. At the moment, he was searching for something encouraging to say—something that would not be cancelled out by the reality facing her.

As the moment's anguish spilled out from her, he could feel every bit of it; as though he were stealing a glimpse of a scene that he shuddered to think might await him. The others, themselves standing in quiet observance over her despair, no doubt shared a similar gut reaction. Hope may have been the engine that brought them this far—but it offered no guarantees for a different outcome.

"They most likely made it out before the fire engulfed the place. There's got to be a refugee camp or military base nearby where all the survivors are staying. I'm sure that's where they are," he said in a scarcely convincing tone.

"No they're not," Constance, whose crying had now settled into a halting whimper, said.

"Isn't it better to believe they survived?"

"It *was* better...but it's over now. I've got nothing left. All that I have is buried in there...including my parents."

Trent turned and gave her a curious look. It was as if he wanted to see for himself the face of resignation, just in case it tried to creep up on him between there and his reaching home. "Why would you prefer to think the worst?"

"Because they would never leave this house unless they knew I was okay."

"The storm was sudden. It caught everyone by surprise. How would they know whether you survived or not without giving themselves a chance for you to contact them? It only makes sense that they would leave."

"Sure it does. But you don't know my parents." With that, Constance then turned to the others. "Goodbye, everyone. I'm going to stay here...collect what I can, and then search for the nearest camp. Who knows...maybe they did make it out okay and are out there somewhere." Just as she said that, the tears began to fall again. She paused briefly to wipe them away. "It's been quite an adventure traveling with you all. I will miss you. Be safe the rest of the way."

They all came towards her and each said their goodbyes—all except for Gina who stood off from them like an unwanted guest. Trent looked at his watch. It would not be dark for another three hours. With obviously no food to be had there, they wished Constance well, and resumed their journey north.

DAY SEVEN

Chapter 36

The dust rested heavy on the tree limbs that lined the path through the woods. Branches, already stressed from the trauma of a week ago, had cracked under the weight and now hung like the damage seen after an ice storm. Thankfully, the seemingly endless powder had finally ceased, giving way to more breathable air for the first time in almost a week. What remained lay close to three inches deep, blanketing every visible surface in a coat of gray ash.

Ben, hungry, and not in the best of moods, was walking through it as though his feet were encased in blocks of cement. His every step would kick up a cloud of dust that would slowly dissipate like the exhaust smoke from an old jalopy. At the same time, the small of his back was losing its battle at keeping him upright; culminating in a tortured lean forward that all but epitomized the severity of their present plight. He held Loretta, who looked as famished and fed-up as he did, firmly by the arm; feigning a strength for her that belied his own. Together they brought up the rear, mere steps behind Janet, Gina and Trent, who out in front, was exhibiting the same anguished posture.

It had been two days since their mouths had tasted anything short of the stomach acids that would occasionally belch up. The ache in their bellies had given them a new priority. Finding food and water was now more critical to them than reaching their respective homes. They had been walking nonstop since daybreak in the hope of locating a military installation before nightfall.

Though the dust rain had ended, the sun's light was still obscured by a gray canopy that seemed to hang in the upper atmosphere and refused to dissipate. And as usual, the approaching evening gave the descent of dark, new meaning. They were less than an hour away from pitch blackness and the certainty of entering a third day without so much as a bite of anything.

"Are you sure you've got none of that candy left?" Ben grouchily asked Trent.

"You asked me that yesterday and I told you, no. Why would today be any different? I'm not a vending machine. I can't just produce candy."

"He was just asking. You don't have to get defensive," Loretta said.

"Don't tell me not to get defensive. I know what he's trying to imply. He thinks I might be holding out on you all."

"Well...are you?" she asked.

"What? How can you stand there and ask me such a thing? All I've been doing since we started out was sharing what little bit there was with you guys, which I didn't even have to do. The both of you were right there when I divided up the last of it. Now, suddenly, you want to come down with amnesia. You're talking crazy."

"Then explain how is it that you've got so much more energy than the rest of us? We can barely keep up with you. Explain that," Ben asked.

"Speak for yourself. I'm keeping up just fine," Gina, standing next to Trent, inserted angrily.

"Hey, I can't help it if I'm more anxious to get home to my family than you are."

"So what are you saying...because all we have is a dog waiting at home, that somehow that doesn't count as having family?"

"You said that...not me." Trent replied, surprised that what lay between the lines of his subtle insinuation was so easily read by Ben—especially in his current debilitated state. Either way, he had no intention of taking back the comment. If anything, he wanted to take it up a notch. He was feeling particularly argumentative and made no apologies for it.

***

Meanwhile, Janet had backed away from the three of them and looked on nervously at their escalating back-and-forth. Trent's behavior seemed strangely out of character to her. In all of the days going back to their first meeting, she'd never seen him behave rudely or disrespectful towards anyone. To watch him now, so hotheaded and contentious was like watching a pot about to boil over.

"Who appointed you leader, anyway?" Ben asked. "Do you even know where you're going? Look where we are. We're out here in the woods...in the middle of nowhere."

"You leave him alone. He's taken the lead, 'cause it's obvious that you can't," Gina said.

"Shut your mouth. Don't say that about him," Loretta quickly demanded.

"Or what? What are you going to do?"

"Oh...and why am I not surprised that you'd be the one jumping to his defense? You realize he's the one that flew off the handle, not Ben. This whole thing is his fault."

"No it's not. It's your boyfriend's fault...him and his wild accusations."

"It was just a question," Ben shouted angrily.

"From where I'm standing, it looks like I'm not the only one here with a boyfriend."

On hearing that, "What are you trying to say?" Trent said, frowning as he looked squarely at Loretta.

Janet stood silent like an idle referee between the two spatting couples. Her ad hoc family was coming apart at the seams, and at the worst possible time—in the middle of nowhere, and with twenty or so minutes to go before it was totally black out. She winced with worry as the harsh words flew back and forth, all the while dreading what might become of her if things were to reach an irreconcilable conclusion.

Adding to her anxiety was Gina and her odd preoccupation with Trent. Though on the surface it didn't appear salacious, it did have the nuances of girlish infatuation. And of the type that only another woman would recognize; the attentiveness, the companioning that rarely placed her more than an arm's reach from his side. Their sudden alliance left Janet feeling like the proverbial fifth wheel on a double date. There were times, right after Constance's departure where she would catch Gina staring malignly at her as though her mere presence was a threat. As for Trent, it seemed he was either clueless to signs of affection, or simply too distracted with his own cares to concern himself with the psyche of this woman he had met only four days ago.

As their quarrel raged on, she did not want to add to the conflict by choosing a side; nevertheless, her loyalty was with Trent. That's when she looked up at the cosmos, albeit hidden behind a perpetual overcast, and proceeded to apply a "Law of Attraction" prayer, thoroughly believing that the stars would quell the conflict before all hell broke loose.

With her head tilted back and eyes half closed, she was in the middle of her ethereal request when she heard an unexpected sound between the breaks in their arguing. It was far off and emanating from somewhere in the woods directly behind her. It escaped the others who, in the heat of their bickering, were too worked up to hear anything outside of their own voices.

Janet did her best to tune them out. Then, holding onto the next word to her prayer, and keeping absolutely still as if the slightest move might cancel her ability to hear, she listened for the sound again.

Within seconds, a faint *pop* like gunfire was heard, and coming from the same direction as before.

Janet whipped her body around so that it faced the woods, at the same time, taking two steps backward toward the others. "Quiet, you guys...listen. No really...be quiet!" she said softly—and then loudly after getting no reaction. "I just heard something in the woods."

"Like what...an animal or something?"

"I don't know. Just listen."

They looked at her as if to assess her seriousness. And then, holding their positions, looked out past the tree line where a veil of blackness was just beginning to envelope the forest. There, they remained silent while their ears sought to penetrate the denseness.

After a few minutes, "I don't hear anything. Maybe you heard a bird falling out of the sky. They're all over the place. Too bad we can't eat them."

"It wasn't a bird."

"Well, what did it sound like?" Ben asked.

"It sounded like a gunshot."

"Are you sure?"

"No, not one hundred percent...but awfully close to it."

Loretta grabbed Ben's arm. "If she's right, and it was a gunshot...maybe we should get out of here," she said.

Ben looked at her. "What are you talking about, babe? It might only be a hunter. These are the woods, after all. And wherever there's a hunter...there's food—"

"Stop and think for a minute," Trent interrupted.

"What, now you're questioning my intelligence?"

"No, I'm not. Before the impact, I used to drive through these woods all the time. It should be teeming with deer. Has any of you seen one deer...'cause I sure haven't. Have you spotted any animals, at all...I mean besides the ones that aren't already dead?"

"What's your point?"

"What he's saying is...if that's a hunter out there, it's possible he might mistake us for prey," Gina said.

"That's a sobering thought...making it all this way just to get shot because some yokel mistook my messed up hair for a pair of antlers," Janet said, then turning to take a cautious look into the woods behind her.

"It's a real possibility."

"What if it's not a hunter? What if it's a soldier firing off his weapon? If so, that means there's a base nearby." Ben said, then turning to Janet. "Were you able to determine what direction it came from?"

"I think so." Janet pointed to the left of where they were heading.

"You're not really suggesting that we head toward it, are you?"

"I'm suggesting that we take a chance."

"That's your stomach talking," she said.

"Maybe so...but it's making sense. Anyway, it's getting dark. Hunters need light. You can't shoot what you can't see."

"Unless of course they're wearing night vision goggles," Trent said.

"How many people do you know who own night vision goggles?"

"None...but then I don't know any hunters, either. Let's just say it was a soldier. What reason would he have for firing off his weapon?"

"Who knows? Does it really matter?"

"So far she's the only one who's heard it," Gina said, referring to Janet. "How do we know she wasn't hearing things?"

"Um, excuse me...but I know what I heard."

"Well...all I know is, I already had a gun pointed at me once this week. No way do I want to experience that again."

"Okay. It's getting darker as we speak. We need to decide what we're going to do," Trent said. "I say we bed down right here, and whatever it was Janet heard, we search it out in the morning when there's light."

"Me, too," Gina promptly agreed.

"Why wait until morning. I'm already feeling stronger. There's still enough light out. We can cover about half-a-mile before dark. If you think we should go search it out in the morning...starting out now will get us that much closer."

Loretta, who'd been holding Ben's arm the entire time, turned to him. "Are you sure about this? Wouldn't it be better if we just waited until morning?" She said softly.

Ben brought his face closer to hers. "The only thing I'm sure about, sweetheart, is that we need to get to food and water before we die out here." His eyes were excited and glistened with a determination she hadn't seen from him in days. They were saying *trust me*, which apparently was all the assurance Loretta needed. With the battle lines drawn, all eyes then turned to Janet.

"I guess it's up to me now, huh." She said humbly. "While you all were talking, I was listening behind me hoping I'd hear that sound again, but it never happened. So I got to thinking. Just because we haven't seen any deer, doesn't mean they're not out here. I've had my share of encounters with them. They might not be the brightest when it comes to crossing a busy road, but they are smart enough to know how to avoid a predator. If it is a hunter out there...or even a soldier, he probably wouldn't take more than two shots to kill one. It's my guess he may have only maimed it with the first shot...then went in to kill it with the second. If that's what happened, there's probably going to be a lot of meat leftover." She then looked directly at Trent. "Any other time I would say, let's wait until morning. But if there's a chance at getting something to eat tonight...I'd like to take it."

Gina looked up at Trent. "That's okay, let them leave. We can go on without them," she said.

***

Meanwhile, Trent was listening for a hole in Janet's reasoning, but couldn't find one. In fact, his hunger-clouded judgment made her off-the-cuff deductions sound almost brilliant. *Why didn't I come up with that?* he thought. "No. That's not an option. We started out together, and we're going to stay together until we reach our destinations," he said to Gina.

He hoped that she might raise an objection, if only for the sake of the others listening. When she didn't, it likely served as confirmation for Loretta that her earlier allegation wasn't far off the mark. As for him, he was not so obsessed with getting home that he couldn't recognize the favoritism that he enjoyed with Gina. She had clearly taken a liking to him, almost to the exclusion of the others in their party.

But then, it was easy to understand why she might feel that way. He did, after all, rescue her from the clutches of a deranged captor; and then, in an act of generosity, shared the last of his rations with her when she was hungry. His were the sort of selfless gestures that became a common sight in the first few days following the impact.

In the aftermath, random acts of benevolence would rise up like an unexpected instinct to nudge even the most heartless of witnesses into action. The healthy would come to the aid of the injured, or those trapped beneath wreckage; responding with a knee-jerk reflex of valor in the face of unimaginable calamity. But now, seven days past the event, and in the mire of conditions where hearts have failed many, such gestures of compassion appeared almost foolish.

Fortunately for Gina, Trent was not the type to be governed by perceptions. That duty he left to his conscience. And thus far, it hadn't given him many insights about her other than her strong, seemingly pathological reliance on the goodwill of others. He assured himself that if she were feeling anything more than gratitude for him, it would have been through no fault of his. Always the perfect gentleman, he never intentionally sought her companionship, nor made any overt attempts to befriend her. If he was guilty of anything, it was of being overprotective of her. She had a way of making even the slightest request sound like a cry for help. He in turn would respond to her in the sort of fatherly tones that at times, reminded him of home.

At first, he would shy away from feeling anything even remotely paternal toward Gina. But looking after her was too easy, as if by instinct. Simply being near her inspired memories of the family he wished he could be with—the family he felt helpless to protect. At times, he could see his eldest daughter in her, if only in traces that bore no similarities except but as a wishful thought of her.

It took effort to keep his thoughts from drifting to them; especially in his current diminished state where a single image might lead to a deluge—and then bring on the sadness. Though, there had been times, usually just before sleep, where he would welcome its effects as a momentary indulgence, just to keep him company. It was a painful exercise. One that Gina's ward-like presence had an uncanny ability to interrupt. That he was having fewer of such episodes went largely unnoticed by him.

That she might be mistaking his good deeds for something more, was a matter left for another time. He was too busy looking at their circumstances through a narrow lens. And in it, all he could see was food and water. Right now, that was the only issue worth focusing on.

With dusk now almost on top of them, Ben turned and looked out at a specific area of the woods.

"Are you certain what you heard came from that direction?" he asked Janet.

"Yes...I'm positive."

"Then let's head out. We've got about ten minutes of light left before we're groping around in the dark."

Ben, decidedly taking the lead this time, grabbed Loretta's hand and was the first to enter the woods. Janet followed close behind them while Trent and Gina lagged several paces in back of her. Aside from a questionable claim of gunfire and the vague direction they set out on, there was little else to guide them. As they proceeded deeper into the forest, the only sounds heard were the snap and rustle of brush underfoot. Trees, beaten and scarred stood surrounding them like wounded soldiers on a battlefield. Their sturdy limbs quietly shrieked in a tangle of overhead branches that dimmed the remaining daylight to a shade just above dark. The terrain beneath their feet was dangerously uneven; made worse by hidden pitfalls that slowed their progress to a near crawl.

Ben was still out in front leading them, albeit with a visible agitation that kept all except Loretta at a distance. He did not seem comfortable in his new position and proceeded like a man who had bitten off more than he could chew. When he wasn't helping Loretta along, he rarely looked back to see how the others were managing.

Trent, as he assisted Gina and Janet through the minefield of obstacles, kept his opinions to himself. He was already on edge, and knew that one complaint, given Ben's recent volatility, would be like setting a match to tinder. He wasn't an advocate of their plan and did not like having to change course based on hypothetical assumptions. He preferred to go his own way, or at least to be in control again as he had been before Ben decided to assert himself.

They didn't think this thing through. They're allowing desperation to drive their decisions. There's no way that can be good, Trent thought just before nearly losing his footing on some unseen thing. Right then he wanted nothing more than to get his thought out in the open. But out of fairness to the group's morale, he decided not to. His only hope was that they would grow weary of the obstacles ahead and decide to turn back.

He went along with it for now; even as a spate of pettiness was getting the better of him. But for all of Trent's levelheaded arrogance at the outset, he could not deny the hunger gnawing away at his faculties; or the same inevitable plight of desperation, building up like so much rage to steal his rational thinking away from him as it did the others.

What if Janet was right? he began to wonder. *What if it really was gunshots she'd heard? And here we are chasing after them.*

Between his increasing sense of desperation, his gnawing pangs of hunger, and their roaming through the woods like a small herd of deer, they all seemed to combine to create a perfect storm of elements that could very well place them directly in the line of fire.

They were about fifteen minutes into their walk when Janet suddenly stopped. "Maybe my hearing is a little keener than the rest of yours, but does anybody else hear that?" she asked. "And please tell me yes so I'll know I'm not going crazy with the hunger."

The others kept their feet still, instantly creating an eerie silence that amplified everything within range.

"There it is. Can you hear it?" She asked again.

"Yes...I hear it," Loretta said, her expression altered by a bemused frown. "Am I mistaken or does that sound like...music?"

Trent, still not moving a muscle, had his ear turned as though he were a satellite dish, toward the unusual sound.

"I think it is, but how when there's no power...and why?"

"It could be coming from a military base. They could be playing music over the PA to help the civilians there to relax."

"Who cares?" Ben said. "All that means is that there's someone out there. And if they've got enough power for music, they've got food. What are we waiting for?"

On that note, there was no argument from any of them. They took their best guess as to its relative whereabouts and started heading toward it. Feeling renewed vigor, they forged onward in hopes of reaching it before nightfall. As they drew closer, and the music became more distinct, its melody jumped out at Trent. And he thought—

Why in the world would anyone be playing heavy metal music at a time like this?

Chapter 37

"Hey, Nora. Are you awake?"

The words were whispered in the dark, and were near enough to Nora that she opened her eyes upon recognizing Sonia's voice.

"Seeing as how I haven't truly slept in seven days...only catnap...yes I'm awake," she said, whispering back to the voice whose face she couldn't see in the darkness. They sat only inches apart, and with their backs against a tree as they usually did at day's end; blankets draped over their heads and securely wrapped around them for the long night ahead.

"Good. I need someone to talk to. I can't get to sleep either. And being hungry certainly isn't helping the situation."

"Neither is being cold. It's so chilly out her that this blanket is starting to feel more like a sheet. It must be below sixty degrees," Nora said.

"I've noticed it's gotten cooler, too. It feels like autumn out here. If only we had some matches...we'd be able to light a fire. This is ridiculous. I can't see anything. If anyone were to tell me that one day I'd be sitting out in the woods, in total darkness...unable to see my own hand in front of my face. I would've told them they were crazy."

"At least there's no more falling dust in the air. I thought it would never stop. Is Laura awake?"

"Laura," Sonia whispered around to the other side of the tree, and then waited for a response. On hearing nothing, "I don't think so. She was fast asleep before it was even totally dark out. She doesn't seem to have any trouble getting her shut-eye."

"Yeah, I know. I think she's figured out that you and I are way too nervous to get that comfortable out here. She knows we're light sleepers, so she takes full advantage of it by sleeping through the night. She knows that if anything threatening were to happen...one of us would wake her up."

"Well, I wouldn't be so sure of that if I were her. If she's listening back there, she'd better start sharing some of the guard duty, or she's liable to wake up and find us gone. Well, except maybe for me. I won't have gotten very far. Not with this bum ankle."

"Is it still bothering you?"

"Not too much right now. It mostly hurts when I put weight on it. I'm really starting to think it's broken."

"I doubt it. I'm sure it'd be hurting a lot more if it were. You just haven't been able to get it properly cared for. That's why it still hurts. As soon as we reach a military base, we'll get a doctor to look at it."

Sonia let out a sigh. "Let's both hope that we reach one by tomorrow. Otherwise, you may have to go on without me. It's swollen to at least twice the size. It doesn't even look like an ankle anymore. It's a *k'ankle*. Honestly, I don't know if I'll be able to walk another day on it."

"You're going to have to try. I can't speak for the others, but I don't intend to leave you here. And I'm not staying behind to keep you company, either. So it looks like you don't really have a choice. In the morning you're leaving with us."

"Taylor might think differently. I wouldn't want to become a burden to you all. I don't think he would take too kindly to that. In fact, he might even start smacking me around like he did Dale."

"He won't do any such thing," Nora said.

"I'm not so sure. I know you think he's misunderstood, and that since he did save your life, n'all...that he can't be but so bad. But you need to start taking a closer look at him."

"What are you talking about?"

Not certain of where Taylor was in proximity to them, Sonia leaned in close to Nora's ear and whispered. "Did you know that almost every morning at daybreak, or every night when he thinks we're all still asleep, he disappears for an hour or two?"

"No I didn't. How do you know this?"

"Because I sleep even lighter than you. I saw him with my own eyes. He thought I was sleeping. Believe me, I see a lot of creeps in my line of work, and I can spot them a mile away. Taylor fits the profile to a tee. I've never been comfortable around him."

"You're entitled to feel that way. And frankly, I'm not certain how I feel about him. I just want him to get me as close to home as possible."

"Well, while you're sorting out your feelings, think about this. I believe he had something to do with Dale's disappearance."

"Okay, now you're really stretching. Dale was a hothead...you know that. I wouldn't put it past him to just leave if he suddenly decided to."

"I know. That pretty much exonerates Taylor, if I can borrow one of your big legal words. Still, there's something about the way he left that just doesn't feel right."

Nora was familiar with the feeling, but didn't care to explore it further for fear of it becoming a distraction. "I can't think about Dale right now. I'm more concerned about you. I know Taylor can be a bit of a monarch when it comes to his leadership style. You let me deal with him. He won't give you any trouble. I'll be walking right alongside you."

"I appreciate your concern...really. But I know my limitations, and you don't look strong enough to carry me."

"It won't come to that. When it gets light out, maybe we can find something for you to use as a cane. It should help you to walk a bit easier."

"Thank you."

"You don't have to thank me."

"No...I do. I don't know that I would've made it this far without you. Let's face it. I'm not exactly the kind of girl someone like you would be planning to meet with for lunch. We live in two different worlds. Yet here we are...relating to each like we might've been best friends in another life. You treat me like an equal. I really appreciate that. You're a good person, Nora."

"It's nice of you to say that. Thank you. Only, I wish I could say I felt the same way about myself." Maybe because Sonia was another woman, or because sitting there in the pitch blackness had somehow created the illusion of anonymity; either way, it had the effect of lulling Nora into a place of confession. "I live with a lot of guilt," she said. "Guilt when it comes to my job...guilt over not seeing my children enough...guilt over not being a good enough wife to my husband. I should've been home with them. Instead, I'm here...sitting against a tree...too afraid to close my eyes...and passing through some backwater town that I don't even know the name of. And for what...for a career. I spend a third of my day commuting into the city. And to a job that I'm only now starting to realize may have cost me the most precious thing in the world...my family. I just wish it hadn't taken a catastrophe of this magnitude to cause me to see what I'd been missing."

"Girl, don't beat yourself up over having a career. It puts food on the table, right? You don't work...you don't eat," Sonia said.

"That's the irony. I don't even have to work. My husband's a chef. He's owns a restaurant. He's actually the one who puts the food on the table...not me."

"In that case, I take back everything I said. Exactly why aren't you at home enjoying the good life? Especially, as I understand it, you're not all that thrilled with your work anymore."

"It's like I was saying before. Being an attorney was almost predetermined for me. I set such high goals for myself...so did my parents. The only thing that would've trumped that was my becoming the first black, female Supreme Court justice."

"Do you mind if I play armchair shrink for a moment?"

"Sure, why not. You can't be much worse than the one I'm seeing now."

"Have you ever told this shrink how you feel about your career?"

"No. we mostly talk about my formative years...what it was like growing up...my parents...that sort of thing. It seems they're at the root of my problems...or so he tells me."

"The parents always get the blame," Sonia said. "It's too easy. They can't even defend themselves. I'm not saying it can't happen. A lot of parents have no idea just how much damage they're doing to their kids. But for every bad parent out there, I've got to believe there's a good parent that's done every right thing they know to do...and somehow they still end up with a messed-up kid."

"Okay, so if it's not my parents at the root of these issues, then who? Is it me?"

"Don't get me wrong. Some things are generational."

"You mean like a curse?"

"Yeah, that's right. Like a curse. What's troubling you may go all the back to your great, great grandmother. We'll never know. But that wouldn't make it her fault, either. Where I'm going with this has nothing to do with blame. 'Cause the fact of the matter is, if you're already feeling some guilt, then there should be no confusion regarding who's to blame. I'm more interested in the *why*."

As Nora sat there listening, "*the why*" spoken of was as baffling to her as it was curious to Sonia. She needed to hear another theory other than the one her therapist had come up with. Sonia was offering one, and she was open to hearing it.

"My parents were great to me," Sonia continued. "When I look back on the way they raised me, they may not have been perfect...but hindsight being twenty-twenty, they weren't far from it. They didn't spoil me, and they didn't deprive me of anything...at least not those things that they thought were good for me. Yet with all of that, I still ended up dancing on a stripper pole for a living."

"Yes, explain that to me. I knew from the moment you opened your mouth that you had a higher than average intelligence. Why would you choose such a degrading profession when you could be doing so much more?"

"Do you know there were nights between sets when I would ask myself that very same question. It was only a few months ago that I finally figured it out. I can appreciate my parents, now. But there was a time when I didn't like them very much. Remember when I told you that I grew up in the church."

Unsure of where Sonia was going with this, Nora braced herself for whatever truths it might uncover.

"Well, there was a lot of pressure on me to conform to what I saw at the time as a puritanical lifestyle," Sonia continued. "I was coming into my own as a teenager. My parents...the church...they both expected me to live by a strict code of conduct. Meanwhile, everybody I knew was having fun. I was prevented from socializing with any them. I hated that leash they had around my neck. It wasn't long before I found myself hating them as well. As soon as I turned eighteen, I fled...ran off to live with some boy that I was seeing behind their backs. And you know the rest of the story."

"So you rebelled. That's fairly classic behavior for a teenager. I've got three of my own in various stages of rebellion, right now. My oldest is twenty-two, but she still has a streak of teenager in her. The only difference between her and her siblings is that she can now rebel with impunity. I'm afraid I'm not seeing the connection."

"I was lashing out at my parents. I knew when I moved out that it might have serious consequences, but I did it anyway. I was angry with them, so I did things that I knew would upset them."

"You were just a kid at the time. I'm a grown woman. It's different. My parents were demanding, yes. Did they push me to succeed? Yes...but not anymore than I pushed myself. I've long since gotten over whatever bitterness I've held towards them."

"Then maybe you should be looking someplace else."

Nora started to recall the most hurtful things in her life. Trent's affair was at the top of the list. Neglecting her family was second. Right then, she wanted to change the subject, but thought it rude after having given Sonia permission to explore it. "Like I said earlier...I don't always feel like a good person. I have far too many regrets to be patting myself on the back," she said.

"That's okay. I believe regret is one of the first steps to having a pure heart. There are eight Bible scriptures that I remember reciting faithfully growing up. In fact, it was mandatory that I memorize them and several others. But one goes...blessed are the pure in heart...for they shall see God," Sonia said, followed by a muted chuckle. "I haven't uttered that in years. I'm surprised I still remember it."

"Is this the same God who you claim is raining His judgment down on a sinful world?" Nora said, recalling the comment.

"Yes...that God."

"Then explain to me how a God that's supposed to be so loving and merciful, can exact such unimaginable suffering on the guilty as well as the innocent. I'm not one of the bad guys. I'm one of the good guys that goes after them. I'm a good person. You said so yourself. And you don't even know me. I've spent the better part of my life helping people who can't help themselves...who've been hurt or injured. And have foolishly, even placed their needs ahead of my own family's needs. I've sacrificed too much of my life. I don't feel I deserve to be stuck here like this."

"Don't take this the wrong way, Nora...but you haven't sacrificed anything. The ultimate sacrifice was made two-thousand years ago. John 3:16...For God so loved the world that he gave his only begotten Son, that whosoever believeth in Him should not perish, but have everlasting life. His only requirement was that we love him back. Instead, we rejected him. Jesus gave his life so that we wouldn't have to suffer through these end times."

"You do realize your being here with me contradicts everything you've just said."

"No it doesn't. I knew God, once. My heart may even have been pure at one time...but not anymore. I've got too many skeletons in my closet...too many past sins that I need to atone for," Sonia said, then pausing to reflect. "I can still hear the tear-filled voices of my parents...pleading with me to turn away from this wicked lifestyle and come home...come to church with us. Little did they know the only thing their badgering did was make me dig my heels in more. Half of my life was spent bringing grief to them. God is not happy with me. For the misery I gave them, I'm prepared to serve my penance in hell."

Other than it being a place she envisioned as reserved only for the worst of the worst, Nora had no concept of hell. Just hearing Sonia's resignation on the matter sent a chill through her. *There are much worse choices in life than being a stripper*, she thought. Outside of that, she couldn't imagine what sort of unforgivable thing she must've done to justify such guilt; or why her obvious regret over it may have lacked the necessary purity of heart that she professed would lead one to see God. She also revealed what sounded like a fatalistic prognosis of humankind's demise. This could explain why she harbored such a bleak outlook when it came to her own forgiveness.

"So you believe the world is coming to an end?" Nora asked, hoping she hadn't insulted her.

"That's what I was taught."

"Well, what about your parents at home? That's where you're headed, isn't it? Aren't they going through the same thing as the rest of us?"

"No."

"And why not?"

"Because they're gone."

"I'm sorry. Maybe I misunderstood. I thought that's where you were heading. Are they passed away?"

"Not exactly," Sonia said.

The fact that she was so cryptic and didn't elaborate told Nora that the subject may have still been a sensitive one. But considering that they had shared so much already, it didn't seem right to her that she would purposely leave that part of the answer dangling. From the start of that evening, they managed to while away the time engaged in revealing discussion. But as the hour grew late, their whispers became slurred with the weight of exhaustion. Sleep was finally starting to seduce both of them. Nora could feel it nudging at her eyelids. She wanted closure to her question and decided to push Sonia for an answer.

"So what happened to them," she asked.

Sonia took the blanket she had draped over her and pulled it down just over her eyes. She then turned her back toward Nora and, using the tree to lean her shoulder against, brought her head to rest on its trunk.

"They vanished during the disappearances."

Chapter 38

The light up ahead shined like a night mirage, sending its glow outward to penetrate the woods where Trent and his party wended their way through. They could see activity through the breaks in the trees; blurred silhouettes darting across the harsh glare like ghostly apparitions beckoning them to come hither.

With the way now partially lit before them, they hurried toward it with excitement. The distant, nearly indistinguishable sound that first started them on their journey had gotten increasingly louder as they drew closer. It was now heard as a raucous, heavy metal barrage of thrashing guitar licks and excruciating lyrics.

Not exactly the best choice of music to grieve by, Trent thought with a frown that he hoped might lessen the impact to his senses. *Somebody ought'a shoot the DJ.*

He recognized the strident vocals and bruising riffs accosting them as belonging to the band, AC/DC. They and groups like them were a favorite among his college dorm friends. He, on the other hand, resisted becoming a fan of the music. Its gothic imagery and constant references to the netherworld, were all a bit too ghoulish for a young man spoon fed on rap, and rhythm and blues music.

His limited exposure to it, however, did give him an appreciation for the simple, yet complex chords that distinguished its sound; its counterculture shock value and almost trance inducing backbeat that a sub-group of listeners might even regard as something strangely more than music. Even now he found himself trying to push its invasive melody out of his head, fully aware that once embedded, it could be stuck in there for a good day or two. That aside, his anticipation of what lay just beyond the tree line acted like a shot of adrenaline to his road weary body. After almost an hour of trudging through rugged terrain, they were just about clear of the trees and seconds away from stepping out into the light.

Ben was the first one out, followed by Loretta and Janet, then Trent and Gina. Together, they stood at the edge of a sparsely lighted open field dominated by several military grade tents, and facing what appeared to be tens of hundreds of people; all milling about seemingly without a care. At a glance, their countenances bore the satisfied look of a full stomach.

As Trent looked around, he spotted a small group of survivors sitting on the ground just outside a nearby tent. Without excusing himself, he stepped away from the others and headed over to where they were. As he approached, he spotted among them a young man eagerly consuming a ration bar. Normally there would be nothing remotely mouthwatering about the vitamin fortified block of hydrogenated oils, corn syrup, and artificial flavorings. But on this night, the sight of one being eaten so fervently, looked more appetizing than anything his food obsessed mind could imagine. His gaze was still fixed on it when he walked up to them.

"Where can I find rations around here?" he asked loud enough to be heard over the blaring music in the background. He then waited several seconds while the group he addressed barely paid him any notice.

After rudely ignoring him for an inordinate spell, one of them, sighing as if he had just lost a coin flip, opened his mouth to respond. "Just head down there and make a left at the first tent," he said pointing. "You'll see the line. You can't miss it."

"Thanks," Trent said, perplexed over their seeming disinterest in helping him. Just before turning to leave, he darted a quick glance back at the young man he had spotted earlier eating the ration bar. Rheumy-eyed and lounging, he took small bites of it as if each one was a succulent piece of meat. In that instant, Trent wondered just how desperate things would have to become before he would ever resort to stealing food from another person.

From day one of the crisis he prided himself for maintaining his civility while so many around him were compromising theirs. Two days without food, though, was slowly whittling away at his perspective regarding such matters. The thought that he might stoop to such an action was unsettling. Especially now as he walked away, conscience-stricken over the undeniable sense of loathing he felt for the young man.

On the way back to rejoining the others, Trent did his level best to ignore the buildup of stomach acid crawling up his esophagus, and the muscle aches that felt as if he had just completed a seven-day marathon.

This day in particular seemed without end. The additional walking they did in order to reach the camp only contributed to its length. So much, that at this point all Trent wanted to do was eat, and then go find someplace to lie down. He pursed his lips and expelled a guttural groan at the thought of having to stand on another rations line so late in the day.

While he was gone, Gina had kept him firmly within her sights. She stepped forward to meet him as he came toward her. "What did they say?" she asked eagerly.

"He said there's a line for rations on the other side of that tent up ahead. If it's anything like the other lines we've encountered, we could be standing for another two hours."

"Did he say it was a long wait?"

"He didn't say, and I didn't ask. They weren't very friendly. I barely got that much info out of them. They were pretty much telling me to leave them alone. When someone finally did answer me...he didn't even bother to look at me."

"They could just be in shock, y'know...still trying to come to grips with everything that's happened. Remember how you found me? There's no telling what awful things may have happened to them before they got here. Maybe they're just traumatized," Gina said.

"Yeah, that could explain it. But excuse me if my heart isn't bleeding for them. These past seven days haven't exactly been a walk in the park for us, either. That asteroid that fell out of the sky...leveled most of New Jersey, and separated us from our families...it's taking its toll on us, as well. I think we've all been traumatized. It doesn't excuse his behavior."

"Are you two finished? Can we go now?" Ben asked, motioning forward to leave. He took Loretta by the hand and they both started off in the direction of the tent.

Janet watched them leave and then turned to Trent. "What are they doing? I thought the plan was for us to stay together."

"It still is. I think that's payback for my walking off the way I did. We'd better hurry. No sense in our standing any longer than we have to," Trent said, quite mindful of the tension still simmering between him and Ben. No doubt they could both plead guilty to stress related irritability as the primary catalyst for their spat. But with so many miles still ahead of them, he knew the two of them would have to settle their differences sooner rather than later if they expected to continue traveling together. Since he truly held no hard feelings toward Ben, he hoped to have an easier time of making peace once they both got some food and a few hours of rest behind them. Until then, he would have to contend with the snarky barbs that were hurled at him.

The three of them caught up to Ben and Loretta and together they all headed for the tent. Along the way, the sights and sounds of the camp were far departures from anything they would've expected to find. There were considerably fewer tents there than in the previous camps they had visited. The erected lighting, though adequate, lacked the intensity seen at other installations where a bright aura hovered like an immense bubble of daylight to envelope everything within it.

The usual Humvee's and Medium Tactical Vehicles that would commonly be found stationed along a camp's perimeter had yet to be seen here. Instead, a Ford Super Duty pickup truck, accessorized to the hilt and carrying two rifle toting men in combat uniform was parked opposite one of the tents. A portable generator, spewing out smoky fumes, belted out a monotonous drone from its rear bed as it powered a raised flood lamp positioned directly next to it. Between the generator noise and the jarring music, they barely heard the approach of the 4-wheel ATV coming up fast behind them. Gina jumped at the sight of it suddenly appearing out the corner of her eye and immediately grabbed Trent by the arm. They all watched as it drove past; its oversized wheels stirring up the dust on the ground and leaving a cloudy trail in its tracks. An armed soldier sat at the controls. He looked behind him with quick turns of his head, seemingly oblivious to the scurry of survivors all sidestepping out of his way like nervous cattle on a roundup. That's when another ATV, following just seconds after him, burst through the smoky haze, throwing up even more dust into the atmosphere before disappearing around a bend.

Trent stood still with the others and stared aghast at the havoc created by the two reckless drivers. *Something's not right here*, he thought.

As he looked around further, he spotted just up ahead, the source of the music that had been berating them for most of the evening. Parked off to the side of the road was a Chevy Silverado pickup; lights on, engine running, and tricked out with giant wheels that gave it a menacing look as if it had just escaped from a monster truck rally. Its tailgate was down, revealing a set of oversized subwoofers customized into the bed. Even from that distance, beneath the glare of the floodlight, he could see the white skin of the woofer cones pulsating with every low frequency beat it delivered.

There was still no change in the choice of music thrown out of it which, thanks to its excessive volume, vexed like a continual irritant in the ears. The survivors, most of whom seemed caught between complaint and capitulation, no doubt viewed the nuisance as an uneasy tradeoff for a meal and a night's rest.

Among them, some slept on the ground outside of tents already filled to capacity. Others sat nearby them, either in fleeting conversation or in the stoic torpor symptomatic of a person in the throes of shock. Still others walked with the same objective as Trent and his party.

While most of them carried only the shirts on their backs, a small number carried items that seemed out of place in the middle of a crisis. Trent's suspicion that something was amiss was further elevated when he caught sight of what appeared to be a father and son; both haggard, dust covered from head to foot, and carrying between them a large flat screen television.

With so many abandoned homes and businesses pervading the landscape, thievery had escalated into a crime of abundant opportunity. Jewelry and collectibles such as gold and silver coins topped the list of items most easily fenced. Home electronics, though useless for the time being, would regain their value once the power grid came back online. Items such as laptops, cell phones and small home appliances were easier to carry and made up the lion's share of goods that could be had on the black market. This would explain the numbers of survivors seen trolling the camp, merchandise in hand, hoping to make an equitable trade. Some of whom came away carrying considerably more than the standard allotment of rations.

Intermingled among the survivors were a small number of soldiers. They strolled along the immediate area toting AR-15's and looking fit and able-bodied in their army combat uniforms. Their healthy appearance was in stark contrast to the disheveled state that identified most everyone else. Yet even with that, Trent noticed they somehow lacked the usual spit and polish of the other military units they had encountered so far.

None of this is adding up, leading Trent to a precipitous conclusion. "These soldiers don't look like National Guard," he said quietly. "And they're definitely not Army."

"What else could they be?" Janet asked innocently.

"They're local militia," Ben said overhearing.

"What's a local militia?"

"It's a paramilitary force. Basically, a civilian run, volunteer army."

"Oh that's just great...an army run by civilians. Should I be worried about this?"

"That depends on who they've got in charge. Militia groups were fairly infamous during the cataclysm a few years ago. There's no telling what to expect from them. In times of crisis, they're supposed to be answerable to the government. The only problem is, during a crisis, the government has no easy way to monitor them. Unless there's someone from the military paying them regular visits, they could pretty much do whatever they want to do," Ben said.

As they walked along, Trent was busily assessing the situation. "Well, so far from what I've seen, everything looks pretty orderly...no fighting or stealing going on. And apparently more than enough rations to go around," he said as they approached the tent where they were to make their turn. "As long as we get our share of some, and find a comfortable spot to relax, there's no reason to believe we won't be safe here for one night."

Janet, having already ensconced herself securely within the group's center, walked a brisk pace, all the while keeping a sharp eye out for anything ominous. "You're forgetting one thing," she said, exhibiting the nervous jitters of someone wary of a surprise. "What about those gunshots I heard? We still don't know what that was all about. And now that I know this isn't an official military base, I have to wonder what reason could a person have for firing their weapon out here."

Trent, in fact, did forget the gunshots as their reason for being there. He approached the tent with an uneasy alertness and heightened suspicions that now saw the armed militia men more as a potential menace than peacekeepers.

Upon arriving at the tent, they rounded its corner and were instantly bathed in fresh rays of light; courtesy of a two flood lamps stationed at opposite ends of a bustling pedestrian thoroughfare. Placed wide apart like two all-seeing eyes, they illuminated every square inch of the corridor. There, a bustle of activity, not unlike a carnival midway, was in full swing. The unusual nature of it stopped Trent and his party dead in their tracks. They remained there for a moment, curiously gawking at the bizarre scene taking place in front of them.

Along the dusty strip of road, hundreds of survivors congregated in a brutal campaign of survival. They gathered in front of folding tables arranged end to end; cordoning them off from a parallel assemblage of identical tents, all standing in a line like row houses along a suburban street. Manning the tables were several militiamen who stood opposite them, barking repeated calls for order which few bothered to heed.

It was an eclectic gathering of survivors—oddly assembled—and at first made no sense; that is until Trent noticed among them a young woman standing at one of the tables. Hanging across her torso was a makeshift sling which judging from its fullness held an infant child. With clumsy arms, she took her right hand and carefully began working the wedding ring from off of the third finger of her left hand. Once the ring was removed, she set it down on the table, and with the same hand, wiped the onset of tears from her face. A militiaman standing across from her picked it up and began scrutinizing it with a pawnbroker's skepticism. A few seconds later he turned, reached beneath a tarp-covered stack, pulled out one-by-one a few indiscriminate rations and set them down on the table in front of her. She picked them up, stuffed them carefully inside her sling, and walked off.

Ben, who along with Loretta had just finished witnessing the same scene, turned to the others. "Did anyone else happen to see that woman over there just exchange her wedding ring for food?" he asked.

"It was so sad. She must've just lost her husband. Now it's just her and her baby. And the guy behind the table didn't show any sign of compassion. I can't imagine how anyone could be so heartless," Loretta said.

"If that's how we're expected to get our rations, here...by trading for them...then things have definitely taken a turn for the worse," Janet said as she watched others conduct similar transactions. Visibly infuriated, she then turned to Trent. "I thought you said there'd be a line for rations back here, 'cause I'm not seeing anything of the sort. Exactly where is this line, huh?"

"You say that as if I'd been here before and aren't seeing all this for the first time...same as you. I told you exactly what was told to me. As I said from the start...they weren't very helpful. All he said was there was a line for rations, and that we couldn't miss it. So let's just look for it, okay?"

"I'm sorry. I didn't mean that the way it sounded. I'm just feeling stressed...that's all."

"So am I," Trent said, throwing the weight of his resentment back at her. He then turned away and started walking into the crowd. Gina rushed to catch up to him leaving the others to follow behind them.

"At least now we know what to do to keep from starving to death. Start stealing," Gina joked as she walked alongside him. He gave her no response. "I guess that wasn't very funny, was it?"

"No, it wasn't. I'm sure most of these people here would prefer not to have to steal for their food. Or for that matter, feel pressured to trade away something they never in life thought they'd ever part with."

"Since we're on the topic, you don't think it was a joke about there being a line, do you?"

"I hope not. There's got to be a way for people just arriving to get food without having to resort to petty theft. If I had to guess, I'd say their little side business was intended for survivors looking for extra rations...that it wasn't meant for newcomers like us. But then that's only a guess. The one thing I know for certain is that I plan on keeping my wedding ring right where it is."

They continued to walk through the crowd, along the way passing open tents where a look inside one revealed a king's ransom of bartered merchandise. Meanwhile, just outside, armed militiamen stood watch at the doorway like sentries guarding the entrance to Fort Knox.

Only a few feet away from there stood another tent, its door left open and the folks around, all abuzz. Parked right outside of it were the two ATV's that earlier had nearly run them over. Between the ATV's and the tent stood a dozen or so militiamen, laughing and chatting with one another while inside, several more could be seen sitting and listening attentively to a robust-looking man standing front and center.

Apparently done addressing them, he proceeded to leave. Trent, still curious about the man, watched him as he exited the tent. Dressed in full army combat camouflage, he exuded an aura of ostensible clout that all but silenced the frivolity among the militiamen standing outside. A man of considerable stature, he walked with a determined stride toward one of the ATV's; his head faced forward and with not a trace of humility or even acknowledgement of the bitter hardships surrounding him.

In that instant, his cocksure mannerisms and bellicose demeanor shone through like a poorly concealed weapon. There was no doubt in Trent's mind that this was the man in charge. He climbed onto the ATV, and along with one of his men, rode off into the crowd.

"Maybe we should've stopped him and asked if this was the way to the rations line," Gina said.

"I doubt if his men would've let us get that close to him. Considering the black-market operation, he's running, it wouldn't surprise me if he has more enemies around here than friends."

Suddenly, "I think I see it," Ben said, peering intently through the crowd blocking his view. "That looks like a line."

Janet immediately perked up. "Where?" she insisted straining her neck to see over and through the bodies in front of her.

"It's about twenty yards up ahead. You see the guy wearing the red bandana...just past the flood lamp? That's where the line ends."

As soon as they spotted it, they all made a frantic dash for it hoping to secure a spot before anyone else could get ahead of them. Once there, they saw that the line disappeared around a corner, making it impossible to know just how long their wait would be. Ben walked on ahead to see what it looked like. He returned several minutes later with some sobering news.

Chapter 39

The night sounds interrupting Jennifer's sleep seemed to be getting louder with each day's end. She lay on the living room sofa, pensively covered beneath a bed spread that stopped just below her chin. And there, stared up at the ceiling, mesmerized by the flickering display painted onto it by the fireplace. Rachel lay across from her, stretched out as prostrate as King Tut's mummy in a cushy chair and ottoman—fast asleep. Justin was upstairs, no doubt doing the same in his bedroom.

In the intervening hours of Jennifer's solitude, her mind had entertained a hundred different thoughts, all random and weaved together by tenuous threads. Meanwhile, the insect life outside the glassless windows of her home provided a tedious serenade to her musing digressions. Their song was likely one of celebration since no longer threatened by pesticides, they were free to encroach on as much property as their tiny legs and wings could carry them. At night, Jennifer could clearly hear them flying into the sheet that hung from the living room window. Drawn by the firelight passing through it— quite possibly the only light seen for miles—they'd repeatedly bounce off of it with unnerving *thumps* as if in a collective effort to break through.

With nobody else to talk to that evening, Jennifer's only saving grace from going hysterical was the radio. It had been tuned to the same station for the past three days, repeating the news on a seeming loop to the point of monotony. After hearing for the umpteenth time, the evening newscaster expound on the governments' new mandatory chip implantation policy, Jennifer could take no more. She threw off her cover, rose from the sofa and headed over to the radio.

There's only so much news a person can take, she thought as she reached for the tuning dial and started searching for another station. The voice went dead the instant she turned it, followed by a mix of intermittent silence, then static for the first few seconds.

Somewhere in the middle of it, a male voice came through; smooth and deliberate, and minus the silky cadence of a public speaker. The signal was weak—it took up only a fraction of the band on the dial—but workable with a little finagling. Jennifer turned the knob back and forth a few millimeters, losing the station, regaining it, and losing it again before finally hitting it dead on. And even then, the reception was only fair. She was tempted to toy with it a little—just to see how much more she could squeeze out of it—but didn't at the risk of losing the signal altogether. Accepting that that was as good as it would get, she relaxed and welcomed the new voice into the room.

She could tell from his delivery that it was not another news report. And though she had no idea what he was talking about, it was still refreshing to have something else to listen to for a change. She picked him up from at the point of his last statement. His next few words jumped out at her.

Folks, the world as we knew it is over. The last page of human history is about to turn, and when it does...the book will be closed. We are living in the period of the Great Tribulation as prophesied in the Bible. A time of famine, war, untold death and suffering unlike anything the world has ever seen...or will ever see again.

The prophecies as described in the book of Revelation are happening right before our very eyes. The seven trumpet judgments are upon us, and the first and second trumps have already sounded.

Revelation eight, verses eight through nine reads...then the second angel's trump sounded and something like a great mountain burning with fire was thrown into the sea, and a third of the sea became blood, and a third of the living creatures in the sea died, and a third of the ships were destroyed.

Last week's asteroid impact wasn't some cosmic anomaly determined by the law of averages. It was a sign of God's righteous judgment...foretold two-thousand years ago by John the Apostle. And it's about to get worse...much worse. In fact, it will be more horrific than anything our minds can imagine.

The antichrist, Baldo Jović, that leopard beast, has already revealed himself with his unholy signs and wonders in the temple of Jerusalem. He has Europe under his total domination, and now with the death of President Schaefer, he's preparing to establish his evil mark in the Americas.

One by one, the governments of the world are bowing to him...giving up their sovereignty in order to join his accursed Federation of States with him as their leader. He'll then declare himself the supreme ruler of a new, one world government. And when that happens, the armies of every nation under his influence will converge on the tiny state of Israel. There the stage will be set for the final battle between good and evil—the battle of Armageddon. Most of us true believers won't live to see it. Because it's Satan's plan to kill us before that day comes.

Maybe you're still not convinced. Maybe you're thinking that the asteroid...the volcanoes...the giant hailstones...it was all just one big coincidence...that none of its proof that this age is nearing its end.

Well, guess what? That's exactly what Satan wants you to believe. And why would he do that? Because he's the great deceiver...the father of lies...and he's fooled us...he fooled me. He's the accuser...the man of sin...the ruler of demons...the son of perdition...and we bought in to all of his lies. He's the prince of the power of the air who disguises himself as an angel of light.

The wave of UFO sightings around the world was just one of his many deceptions. Satan, that serpent of old, has bamboozled us...sold us all a bill of goods. He appealed to our own sinful natures...my sinful nature. And I, like the rest of you who've been left behind, are paying a dear price.

For the sake of those tuning in for the first time, and who don't know my story...I shouldn't be here. I should be with my wife and my five-year-old daughter. But they're no longer here...they vanished. And no...they weren't abducted by aliens as the wicked one would have us believe. They were caught up in the heavens with the rest of Christ's church...raptured along with tens of millions of other believers around the world.

Where *they* are...the Great Tribulation can't touch them. That's where we should've been had we just listened. What's ironic is that I, of all people, should've known better. I pastored a church of over thirteen-hundred members. Thankfully, most of them were raptured, but a lot of them were not. I can't help feeling some responsibility for that. Secret sins are an awful thing. It blinds you...prevents you from calling out those people who you know in your heart have backslid'n. As a pastor, I looked the other way when I should've been confronting them. I wasn't able to address their condition, because to do so, would've meant having to come face-to-face with my own.

People, please...wake up...open your eyes, those of you out there listening to this broadcast. The time is now. Prepare for eternity before it's too late. Repeat after me...Father God, I've come to the end of myself, and now, I ask you to take over. I no longer believe that the life which I live is my own. I now know that it belongs to you. I believe in my heart and confess openly that you sent your son, Jesus Christ, to this world to die for my sins. I believe that He was crucified for me and my sins...that His blood was shed for me...and that He rose again for me so that I could have access to eternal life and access to you, my Father. I repent of my sins, and every thought and action that was less than who You called me to be. I accept this gift of salvation...I freely receive what You have freely given me. My life belongs to You...in Jesus' name. Amen.

If you've said that prayer out loud, and believed every word of it in your heart, you are now saved by grace. You needn't fret any longer over the horrors ahead. Because when death does come...you'll open your eyes again in paradise, and the first face you'll see will be our Lord and Savior's.

I must sign off now, saints. Please keep me in your prayers. I'm on the move again. I don't know how much longer I'll be able to evade capture by the militias. They're tracking my broadcasts. So far, God seems to be giving me favor enough so that I could continue to bring this word forth. Until you hear from me again, stay strong in the Lord and the power of his might. God bless you all.

With the close of his broadcast, the room became silent. There in the quiet, Jennifer sat still and earnestly reflected on the sermon she had just heard.

A part of her wanted to reject it outright; label it a bunch of nonsense as was her habit with anything having to do with religion. Only this time, she could not bring herself to do it. The haunting urgency in his voice would not allow her to. In fact, she could still hear it; appealing to her in the quiet of the moment; evoking frightening images that, had it not been for the nightmare she was living through right now, would be relegated to the absurd.

She recalled him blaming secret sin as the reason for his being left behind, and something about backsliding. Both expressions were as foreign to her as the context they were mentioned in. She never thought much about sin relative to her own behavior, and even less about its consequences.

In her mind, sin was more subjective than absolute, and riddled with too many gray areas to be relevant in today's world. As long as no laws are broken and nobody gets hurt, a person should be free to live life to the fullest. She spent the last four years away at college doing just that, and with only a few regrets—but increasingly more, now, in retrospect.

Her axiom on life, now shaken to its core, she found herself reexamining the meaning of it all. There was no denying the sermon had a profound effect on her; altering her perspective as if it had reached down into her soul and revived a part of it that was previously dead. She recalled Rafer's last visit and his layman's theory on the recent events as having a biblical basis. It was three days ago when he last stopped by to check on them. Jennifer missed seeing him and anxiously looked forward to his next visit; even more so, now that she felt able to shed some light on his dad's vanishing and its strange connection to the Great Tribulation.

The fact that he hadn't come by yet, was a bit troubling to her. His warning to them about gangs roaming the neighborhood would plague her mind routinely. Then there were the unexplained gunshots they had heard yesterday morning. There recollection sent a panic through Jennifer that seized her imagination with a single graphic picture; that of Rafer—assaulted in the early morning while on his way to see them, and lying hurt in the middle of some dusty road. Her eyes were already glistening as she tried to push the image out of her mind, and then cling to hope that he was okay.

I suppose now would be a good time to pray, she thought.

Chapter 40

After an hour-and-a-half of waiting on line, Trent and the others had finally reached the rations tent. Setup like a walk-through soup kitchen, the line entered through one end, and dispersed out the exit at the other end.

Inside, a row of tables separated them from four militiamen who were charged with keeping things moving. Two watched over the procession while the other two economically doled out rations as if their supply were running dangerously low. Earlier, Ben had walked up to the head of the line to see what was what. When he returned, he informed them of the less than adequate portions being handed out.

Given everything they had seen up to that point, it was no surprise that the camp would be skimping on rations. What better way to ensure a steady stream of merchandise for their illegal operation, than to keep the survivors hungry. That way, the pressure would be on them to scavenge the neighboring homes in search of anything tradable. It all but guaranteed they would return looking to exchange their loot for a little extra food.

Trent's turn at the table was coming up. The few survivors ahead of him were apparently chipped. One-by-one they each held out the back of their right hand and were scanned. Once their identities were confirmed, they were given a rations allotment and told to move along.

Janet, who all this time had been standing on line in front of Trent, was the first one up. She and Gina were the only two in their group wearing government issued wristbands in place of their lost ID's. Trent looked on as she passed her right hand below the scanner and waited to be confirmed.

A militiaman sitting directly across the table from her had yet to look up. His attention was fixed on the laptop screen in front of him. After a few seconds, "I'm not reading anything. Try again." he said, still staring at the screen.

Janet cleared some visible dust off the wristband's barcode. She was about to pass her hand below the scanner when he happened to glance up and spot the white strip around her wrist.

"Oh...no wonder. That wristband's no good here, lady."

"Why not...is it expired?" Janet asked.

"Yeah...sort of. They're not being used anymore."

"But this was put on at a National Guard base. They said never to take it off. If I did, I wouldn't be able to get rations."

"Well you can take it off, now. It's no good."

"Who says it's no good."

"President Bartlett."

"And you expect me to believe that?"

"I don't care whether you believe me or not," the militiaman said.

"So how am I supposed to get rations?"

"You have to get chipped. It's the tent right across from this one. There's no line. Just go right on in."

"And what if she doesn't want to get chipped?" Trent asked chiming in abruptly.

"Then you'll need to find something to trade. Let's move it. You're holding up the line."

"What about my driver's license? I suppose that's no good, either," Trent asked.

"That's right."

Janet looked sternly at the unsympathetic face sitting across from her. "I wonder what the President would say if he knew this camp was profiting off government supplied rations," she said in her most accusatory tone.

The militiaman who, up until now, had barely made eye contact with her, suddenly turned his full attention toward her. "What was that, lady? I don't think I heard you right," he said as he slowly began to stand to his feet. That's when Trent grabbed Janet by the arm and hastily started leading her toward the exit. Gina, Loretta and Ben followed behind them. "Did I hear you say something about us profiting? Cause if you did, then that sounds like a threat to disrupt the stability of this camp. Maybe you're trying to incite a revolt...is that what you're doing? Cause if so, that's an act of insurrection. New York is under martial law. And as a duly sworn member of the local militia and defender of this great nation, I'm authorized to shoot insurrectionists."

Just before reaching the exit, Ben turned and faced the riled militiaman. "Really, she didn't mean to imply anything, fella's. She's just tired and hungry...that's all. I'm sure we'll all feel better in the morning. You guys are doing a fine job here," he said, backing away graciously until he was standing safely outside the tent with the others. "That was close. I guess now we know the reason for those gunshots we heard. They're shooting anyone who they think might make trouble for them."

"Can they do that? Can they actually kill someone just for speaking up?"

"Sure, they can. Who's going to stop them? This place is starting to feel more like a concentration camp than a place of refuge."

"So what are we going to do, now? How do we get rations?"

"I don't understand," Gina said as she looked at each of them. "Let's just go get chipped and come back. What's the big deal?"

"The big deal is I don't want anybody planting a tracking device in me like I'm somebody's pet. If I'd wanted that, I would've done it a long time ago. This isn't right, what they're doing. They can't force people to get chipped," Janet said vehemently.

"I don't think they're giving us much choice. It's either that, or go look for empty houses to burglarize."

While they were discussing the issue, Trent was thoughtfully weighing his options. He was not in favor of chipping, and had already made his opposition to it quite clear to the others. Still, there was more at stake here than just his sentiments on the matter. He was growing weaker by the hour. Hunger and thirst were depleting him of the will to stay true to his convictions.

A sense of dread suddenly came over him. He thought he had known hunger before, but this was something different. It was pernicious, and bent on compromising seemingly every one of his bodily functions. Trent knew that if he didn't find nourishment soon, it could all end very badly for him. With life and death now hanging in the balance, the thought of getting a chip implant seemed a lot less invasive than the same said for an autopsy.

Burglary was not an option, but he wasn't prepared to rule it out— at least not yet. As he contemplated the risk to himself, the faces of Nora, Jennifer, Rachel, and Justin appeared in his mind. They then crystallized into a single portrait, before suddenly fragmenting like shattered glass. Trent knew at that moment what he needed to do. If he ever hoped to see his family again, his immediate survival would have to take precedence over principle.

"Look, I don't know about the rest of you. But I'm going to go get chipped and come back for my rations," Gina said as the others looked at her. "I'm hungry, okay?"

Ben slowly began to nod his head. "We're going with Gina," he said, speaking for himself and Loretta. "We don't feel that strongly about it. Plus, things being the way they are right now, it might not be such a bad idea to have it done. It helps when you can be easily identified. From what I understand, it's painless. Our dog Coco had it done...takes only a few seconds."

Meanwhile, Janet stared afar off with a sickly look on her face. Ben's decision had clearly backed her into a corner. She said nothing as if searching for one last objection before surrendering. She then turned and faced Trent. "I'll do it if you do it."

Taking a deep breath, Trent dropped his head, then raised it again and looked her in the eyes. "I'm going with them. We won't make it very far if we don't eat. It's a matter of survival. But just for the record...I'm against it."

"Then let's go," Ben said.

They started for the implant tent which was stationed right across from where they were standing.

"At least we won't have to stand on a line. Better to get it over and done with quickly," Janet said.

As they neared the tent, they were suddenly approached by a gray-haired woman pushing a weathered looking grocery store cart. A look inside revealed a few clothes, a blanket, framed photos and assorted items; apparently all she had left in the world, and nothing of any real value.

She stopped in front of them and smiling, "Can I help you folks?" she asked, invitingly. Her expression was surprising. They had not seen a genuine smile since before the impact. At first, they stared at her in bewilderment, followed by a degree of suspicion.

"No thanks," Trent said. They walked around the woman and her cart blocking them and resumed heading for the tent.

"You don't want to do that."

On hearing that, Janet stopped and looked back at her. "And why not?" she asked.

"Just come with me. It'll be good. You'll see."

They all looked at each other and purely out of curiosity, agreed to follow the woman. She led them to a sparsely trafficked area between two tents and where the light was less intrusive.

"Okay, lady...we're here. What's this all about?" Ben asked.

"Now, now...I'm here to help."

"Help us how?"

Smiling, the woman reached into her cart and carefully moved some of the clothing aside, exposing the blanket buried underneath them. She then pulled the fold of the blanket back to reveal a secret stash of over a dozen ration bars and small cartons of water. "Here...I want you to take this," she said as she grabbed two of each and handed them out to Trent and the others. Her kind gesture caught them completely by surprise. Once over the initial shock, they immediately broke open the cartons of water and drank as quickly as their parched throats could tolerate. One-by-one they tore the foil wrapper off their ration bars and took hearty bites, savoring every chew as if it were their last.

"Eat slowly, now. You don't want to throw up."

Only after they satisfied their stomachs did the thought of saying thank you occur to any of them. They conserved what was left of the rations for later.

Trent took the remainder of his and shoved them in his pockets. "How'd you manage to get your hands on all of that?" he asked.

"My son helps out in the rations tent. He secretly gives me what he can. I take it and give them out to people who look like they most need it," she said.

"But everyone here is hungry. Why us?"

"I have to be careful. There are people around here that wouldn't hesitate to hurt me and take it all if they knew what I was doing," she said as she quickly covered up her cache of provisions. "I chose you all because you looked honest. Was I mistaken? You wouldn't try to hurt me...would you?"

"No. nobody here would do that. We're very grateful. Thank you again," Ben said.

"Why do you do it, though? These militiamen would kill both you and your son if they found out," Janet said as she watched the woman arrange the layers of items in the cart.

"I do it for my reward."

"What reward is that?"

"My reward in heaven," the woman said. She then turned to leave. "I'd better be on my way."

"Wait...before you leave. Is there anything we can do for you?" Trent asked.

A broad smile stretched across the woman's face. "Whatever you could do for me, you could do for someone else. Just pay it forward. That's all I ask. You all be careful," she said as she walked off pushing the cart in front of her. She stepped out from between the two tents and into the light. There, she disappeared in the crowd.

"What now?" Janet asked.

"I guess we stay here until morning. This spot right here is as good a place as any," Ben said, taking a seat on the ground. Loretta joined him. Soon they were all sitting in the shadow of the tent.

Except for the music still blaring incessantly, it was more peaceful there than any other part of the camp they had seen. Relaxed for once, they laid their heads down in quiet repose; this time without the distraction of dire thirst and hunger that had plagued them.

Trent, lying beneath his blanket, had already drifted off. The others, by now, were asleep as well—that is except for Gina who was lying only a few feet away from him and tossing restlessly beneath her own blanket. Unable to sleep, she sat up and ever so discreetly, closed the space between her and Trent. Then taking her blanket, she covered them both with it and quietly laid down in a gentle descent so as not to stir him.